REUNITED WITH

The

CROWN

REUNITED WITH THE CROWN © 2024 by Harlequin Books S.A.

The publisher acknowledges the copyright holders of the individual works as follows:
ONE MORE NIGHT WITH HER DESERT PRINCE...
© 2014 by Jennifer Taylor   First Published 2014
Philippine Copyright 2014   Second Australian Paperback Edition 2024
Australian Copyright 2014   ISBN 978 1 038 90006 7
New Zealand Copyright 2014

SEDUCING HIS PRINCESS
© 2014 by Olivia Gates   First Published 2014
Philippine Copyright 2014   Third Australian Paperback Edition 2024
Australian Copyright 2014   ISBN 978 1 038 90006 7
New Zealand Copyright 2014

Katherine Garbera is acknowledged as the author of this work
CARRYING A KING'S CHILD
© 2015 by Harlequin Books S.A.   First Published 2015
Philippine Copyright 2015   Third Australian Paperback Edition 2024
Australian Copyright 2015   ISBN 978 1 038 90006 7
New Zealand Copyright 2015

® and ™ (apart from those relating to FSC®) are trademarks of Harlequin Enterprises
(Australia) Pty Limited or its corporate affiliates. Trademarks indicated with ® are
registered in Australia, New Zealand and in other countries.
Contact admin_legal@Harlequin.ca for details.

MIX
Paper | Supporting
responsible forestry
FSC® C001695
www.fsc.org

Published by
Harlequin Mills & Boon
An imprint of Harlequin Enterprises (Australia) Pty Limited
(ABN 47 001 180 918), a subsidiary of HarperCollins
Publishers Australia Pty Limited
(ABN 36 009 913 517)
Level 19, 201 Elizabeth Street
SYDNEY NSW 2000 AUSTRALIA

Printed and bound in Australia by McPherson's Printing Group

REUNITED WITH

The

CROWN

**JENNIFER
TAYLOR**

**OLIVIA
GATES**

**KATHERINE
GARBERA**

MILLS & BOON

CONTENTS

One More Night With Her Desert Prince...

Jennifer Taylor

MILLS & BOON

Dear Reader,

The desert has fascinated me for a very long time. In fact, spending time in the desert comes in at number two on my personal bucket list! As I'm not sure yet when I shall be able to get there, writing this book was the next best thing—and I have to admit, hand on heart, that I loved every single minute of it.

Bringing Sam and Khalid back together was always going to be an emotional experience. They parted on such bad terms, and each has been left badly scarred by the experience. There are so many reasons why they can't be together, and yet they both realise from the moment they meet again that the old feelings haven't disappeared as they believed. There is still something there, something that draws them to one other, and it makes no difference whatsoever that they each know the relationship is doomed, that it can never work when they come from such vastly different backgrounds.

Helping Sam and Khalid overcome their problems was a real pleasure. They are such lovely characters—brave, strong, determined and, yes, stubborn, too! I always fall a little in love with my heroes, and Khalid is definitely a hero to fall in love with. As for Sam—well, she is a woman who knows her own mind, a woman who has had to fight for what she wants from life, and I admire her gutsy attitude. I hope you will agree that Sam and Khalid get the ending they so deserve.

Do visit my blog and tell me what you think of this book, jennifertaylorauthor.wordpress.com.

I have a stack of wonderful photographs of the desert to show you. And who knows? I might even get the chance to take some myself!

Love to you all,

Jennifer

DEDICATION

For all the Medical series authors,
with thanks for your kindness and support.

We are definitely going to have that party
at the Ritz when my numbers come up!

Praise for
Jennifer Taylor:

"A superbly written tale of hope, redemption and
forgiveness, *The Son that Changed His Life* is a
first-class contemporary romance that plumbs deep into
the heart of the human spirit and touches the soul."
—*Cataromance.com*

"Powerful, compassionate and poignant,
The Son that Changed His Life is a brilliant read
from an outstanding writer who always delivers!"
—*Cataromance.com*

CHAPTER ONE

'No! I'm sorry, Peter, but I'm simply not prepared to take Samantha Warren along on this trip. You'll have to find someone else.'

Prince Khalid, youngest son of the ruler of the Kingdom of Azad, glared at his old friend, Peter Thompson. He took a deep breath, struggling to moderate his tone when he saw the surprise on Peter's face. His response *had* been over the top but he couldn't help that. It might be six years since he had seen Sam Warren but the memory of their last meeting was as clear as though it had happened only the previous day.

'How about Liv?' he suggested, refusing to dwell on the thought. He had done what he'd had to do and there was no point regretting it. He couldn't have taken Sam to his bed, not when he had known that it could never lead anywhere. It would have gone against everything he believed in, made a mockery of the moral code he lived by. Sam had deserved so much more than a night in his arms.

'Liv's gone back home to Stockholm.'

Peter shrugged, his thin face still mirroring surprise at the strength of Khalid's outburst. Although they had been friends since Cambridge, Khalid realised that Peter had no idea what had happened between him and Sam. He had never told Peter and neither had Sam, it seemed.

It was a small sop to his feelings to discover that nobody knew what had happened that night. He still felt guilty about it, still felt that he should never have allowed things to reach that point. The problem was he had wanted to spend as much time as possible with Sam, to enjoy her company with all that it had entailed. If truth be told, he had never known a woman he had wanted as much as he had wanted Samantha Warren.

It was unsettling to admit it. Khalid forced his mind back to their current problem. 'Phone Liv and see if she's willing to change her plans.'

'I doubt she'll do that. Apparently, her mother's ill and she's gone home to look after her,' Peter explained.

'I see.'

Khalid bit down on the oath that threatened to escape as he crossed to the window. It was the middle of May and the trees in Green Park were awash with fresh new leaves. He had flown to London straight from Azad and the contrast between the barrenness of the desert he had left behind and the lushness of the view from the hotel suite seemed to overwhelm his senses. His mind was suddenly swamped by images he'd thought he had put behind him ages ago: Sam's face smiling up at him; the way her dove-grey eyes had darkened as he had bent to kiss her...

He turned away from the view, unable to cope with thoughts like that. They needed to resolve this problem and they needed to do so soon otherwise they could forget about this venture. It had been his idea to take a team of medics into the desert. Although the Kingdom of Azad had made huge advances in the past few years and now boasted a comprehensive healthcare system that supported the needs of most of its citizens, the nomadic tribes still had little access to any proper medical facilities. TB and other such diseases were rife amongst the desert tribes-

men, whilst infant mortality rates were higher than anywhere else in the world. They urgently needed help, which
was why Khalid had set up this project. The thought of
how much effort and planning had gone into it focused his
mind as nothing else could have done.

'There must be someone else. Come on, Peter—think!'

'I've done nothing but wrack my brain ever since Abby
phoned and said she couldn't go,' Peter told him. 'However,
the fact is that there *isn't* anyone else. Or, at least, nobody
experienced enough. We need a top-notch female obstetrician and there are very few willing to take a couple of
months off from their careers to go with us.'

'So, basically, what you're saying is that it's Sam or
nobody,' Khalid said darkly, trying to control the sudden
tightening in his chest. He took a deep breath, realising
that he was beaten. If Sam didn't go along then they would
have to call off the trip and it would be madness to do that,
unforgivable to allow people to suffer because *he* couldn't
handle the thought of working with her. He shrugged, his
handsome face betraying little of what he was feeling.
Maybe he did feel raw inside but nobody would guess that;
he'd make sure they didn't.

'All right. If it's got to be Sam then I'll have to accept
it. Give her a call and tell her to meet us here tomorrow
morning at eight a.m. prompt.'

'There's no need to do that. I'm already here.'

Khalid spun round when he recognised the cool clear
voice issuing from the doorway. Just for a moment his vision blurred as the blood pounded through his veins before it suddenly cleared. He took rapid stock of the petite
blonde-haired woman standing in the doorway and felt
his heart sink as he was hit by a raft of emotions he had
hoped never to experience again. It might be six years

since he had last seen Samantha Warren but she still had the power to affect him, it seemed.

SAM FIXED A smile to her lips as Peter came hurrying over to her. He kissed her on both cheeks and she responded but she was merely going through the motions. Her attention was focused on the tall dark-haired man standing by the window, not that she was surprised. From the moment she had first seen Khalid, sitting with Peter in the hospital's crowded canteen when they had all been doing their rotations, he had commanded her attention.

She and Peter had become good friends by then and she hadn't hesitated when he had invited her to sit with them. He had introduced her, explaining that he and Khalid had been at Cambridge together studying medicine and it was a stroke of luck that they had both ended up working at St Gabriel's in Central London. Sam had listened to what Peter was saying but she had been aware that he could have been speaking double Dutch for all she had cared. Her attention had seemed to be wholly captured by the man sitting beside her, and it had stayed that way throughout the time she had known Khalid. When Khalid had been around, she had found it impossible to think about anything except him.

Now her eyes ran over him with lightning speed, almost as though she was afraid that if she allowed them to linger she would never be able to drag them away. He looked little changed from what she could tell, his jet-black hair as crisp as ever, his olive skin gleaming with good health. Her eyes skimmed down the powerful length of his body, taking stock of the hard, flat muscles in his chest, the trimness of his waist, the narrowness of his hips.

He was dressed as always in clothes that bore all the hallmarks of his wealth and status yet it wasn't the clothing that made him appear so imposing: it was Khalid himself. He possessed a natural arrogance and assurance that came from his position. As the younger son of one of the richest men in the world, Khalid had no reason to doubt himself. He knew who he was, appreciated his own worth, and didn't apologise for it either. No wonder he had rejected her that night.

The thought made her flinch and she looked away, afraid that Khalid would notice. She had thought long and hard after Peter had phoned and asked her if she would go with them. Although her initial reaction had been to refuse, Peter had been so persuasive that she had found herself agreeing to think about it. She had spent the whole week doing so, in fact. She knew that in other circumstances she would have leapt at the chance to be part of this venture. It would be good experience for her, a definite plus point to put on her CV when she applied for a consultant's post, as she was hoping to do very shortly. However, the fact that Khalid would be going too put a very different slant on things.

How did she feel about working with him after what had happened between them? *Would* she be able to work with him? As the days had passed and she'd still not made up her mind, she had realised that the only way she could do so was by seeing him. If she could see Khalid and speak to him without it causing a problem then she would go along. That was why she had travelled down from Manchester that morning. Peter had told her that Khalid was staying at the Ritz so she had decided to see for herself if they would be able to get along. If they could, fine, and if they couldn't…? Well!

'How about some tea? Or coffee perhaps?' Peter bustled around, opening cupboards to find the kettle. Sam could tell that he was nervous and couldn't help feeling sorry for him. Peter was a natural peacemaker. He hated discord and wanted everyone to be happy. However, in this instance it simply wasn't possible.

'Phone room service and tell them to bring up a tray.'

Sam looked up when Khalid spoke, feeling a little knot of resentment twist her guts. Did he have to speak to Peter that way, treat him like a lackey? It was on the tip of her tongue to say something but she managed to hold back. If she did agree to go along then there must be no emotions involved, neither anger nor anything else. She had to treat Khalid as he had treated her that night, coldly, distantly, *dismissively.*

'Ah, right. Yes. Good idea.' Peter picked up the phone, frowning when he failed to get a dial tone. 'Hmm, that's odd. It doesn't seem to be working. I'll just pop downstairs and ask Reception to sort something out.'

He hurried out of the room before Sam could say anything, not that it was her place to tell him to stay. It was Khalid's suite, his decision what to do. Walking over to the sofa, she sat down and crossed her legs neatly at the ankles, glad that she had opted to wear something stylish. Maybe her clothes weren't made by a top couturier like Khalid's were, but the black cashmere suit and pale grey silk blouse she'd chosen to wear with it were good quality, as were all her clothes these days. Nobody looking at her would guess that she came from such a humble background.

'So, you decided to come and see me?' Khalid dropped into a chair, stretching out his legs under the ornate glass and brass coffee table.

'That's right.' Sam deliberately moved her feet out of the way, making it clear that she wanted to avoid any contact with him. She had thought about how she intended to go about this on the train and had decided that the only way was to be honest. No way was she going to prevaricate, to lie; she would come straight out and tell him how she felt. She gave a little shrug, feeling a spurt of pleasure run through her when she saw his eyes darken in annoyance. Obviously, Khalid didn't appreciate her taking avoiding action. Good!

'There's no point me agreeing to go along if we can't work together, Khalid. It would be a waste of both our time.'

'I agree.' He steepled his fingers and regarded her steadily over the top. 'If we have personal issues to contend with, we won't be able to give our full attention to our patients. That is something I wish to avoid.'

'So do I.' Sam smiled politely although inside she was seething. *Personal issues*, he called them. Maybe she wasn't as experienced as him, but leading someone on, *almost* sleeping with them before rejecting them in the cruellest way possible, seemed rather more than mere personal issues to her.

'What happened between us that night is in the past and I hope that you have put it behind you as I have done.' He shrugged. 'If you haven't then I would appreciate it if you'd say so. Hopefully, we can talk it all through and put what happened into perspective.'

Oh, he must be desperate. Desperate to retain her services as a medic if not to possess her body. Sam's smile became even more brittle. 'There's no need to talk anything through, I assure you. What happened that night is history, Khalid. It doesn't have any bearing whatsoever on my life these days.'

'Good. In that case, I can't see that we shall have a problem working together.' He stood up and held out his hand. 'Welcome aboard, Sam. It's good to have you with us.'

Sam stood up, feeling her breath catch as she placed her hand in his. His fingers felt so cool as they closed around hers, cool and strong and so achingly familiar that she had to fight the urge to drag her hand away. She took a deep breath, forcing down the momentary panic. She wasn't in love with Khalid anymore, if, indeed, she had ever been in love with him. She had thought about it a lot over the years, examined her feelings, gone over them time and time again, and gradually realised the truth.

She had been dazzled by him—by his charm, by his sophistication, by his good looks—but love? No. It hadn't been love. It couldn't have been. Maybe she would have slept with him that night but that didn't mean it would have been out of love. Men and women slept together all the time and for all sorts of reasons too. Desire, loneliness, physical need—they were all grounds for intimacy. But love was rare, love was special, love was what everyone sought and very few found. Including her.

She hadn't been in love with Khalid and he hadn't been in love with her, so why was her heart racing, aching? Why did she feel so churned up inside? Why did she suddenly not believe all the reasoned arguments she had put together because she was standing here holding Khalid's hand?

As her eyes rose to his face, Sam realised with a sick feeling in her stomach that she had no idea. What she did know was that holding Khalid's hand, touching him and having him touch her, made her feel all sorts of things she had never wanted to feel again.

CHAPTER TWO

Sam closed her eyes, shutting out the view from the plane's window. They had been flying across the desert for over an hour now and her eyes were aching from the sight of the sunlight bouncing off the undulating waves of sand. She hadn't realised just how vast the desert was, how many miles of it there would be. Although Khalid had explained when they had stopped to refuel at Zadra, the capital of Azad, that they would need to fly to their base at the summer palace, it hadn't prepared her for its enormity. Just for a second she was filled with doubts. What if she couldn't cope in such a hostile environment? What if she ended up being a liability rather than a help? It wouldn't make her feel better to know that once again Khalid must regret getting involved with her.

'Cup of tea?'

Sam jumped when someone dropped down onto the seat beside her. Opening her eyes, she summoned a smile for the pleasant-faced woman holding a cup of tea out to her. It was pointless getting hung up on ideas like that. What had happened between her and Khalid in the past had no bearing on the present. She was six years older, six years wiser, six years more *experienced* and she wouldn't allow Khalid to make her doubt herself. She didn't need to prove her worth to him or to anyone else.

'Thanks.'

Sam took the cup and placed it carefully on the table, not wanting to spill tea on the butter-soft leather seat. They were using one of Khalid's father's fleet of private jets and the luxury had been rather overwhelming at first. She had only flown on scheduled aircraft before and hadn't been prepared for the opulence of real leather upholstery and genuine wooden panelling in the cabin. There was even marble in the bathrooms, smooth and cool to the touch, a world removed from the plastic and stainless steel she was more used to. If Khalid had wanted to highlight the differences in their backgrounds then he couldn't have found a better way than by inviting her to travel on this plane.

'Nothing like a cuppa to give you a boost.' The woman—Jessica Farrell, Sam remembered, digging into her memory—grinned as she settled back in the adjoining seat. If Jessica was at all awed by the luxury of their transport it didn't show and Sam suddenly felt a little better. She was setting too much store by trivialities, she realised. Reading way too much into everything that happened. Khalid's choice of transport had nothing to do with her.

'There certainly isn't.' Sam took a sip of her tea then smiled at the other woman. 'Have you been on other aid missions like this?'

'Uh-huh.' Jess swallowed a mouthful of tea. 'This is my tenth trip, although it's the first time I've been into the desert. I usually end up in the wilds of the jungle, so this will be a big change, believe me.'

'Your tenth trip? Wow!' Sam exclaimed in genuine amazement, and Jess laughed.

'I know. I must be a glutton for punishment. Every time I get back home feeling completely knackered I swear I'll never do it again but I never manage to hold out.' Jess glanced across the cabin and her expression softened. 'Peter can be so persuasive, can't he?'

'He can,' Sam agreed, hiding her smile. It appeared that Peter had a fan, not that she was surprised. Peter was such a love, kind and caring and far too considerate for his own good. He had been involved in overseas aid work ever since they had qualified, combining his job as a specialist registrar at a hospital on the south coast with various assignments abroad. Sam wasn't the least surprised that Jess thought so highly of him. What was surprising was that he and Khalid had remained such good friends when they were such very different people.

Her gaze moved to Khalid, who was sitting by himself at the rear of the plane, working on some papers. He had been polite but distant when he had welcomed her on board that morning but as he had been exactly the same with the rest of the team, she couldn't fault him for that. She had been one of the first to board and she had made a point of watching how he had treated everyone else even though she hated the fact that she had felt it necessary. They had both agreed that they had put the past behind them so what was the point of weighing up the warmth of his greeting? Nevertheless, she hadn't been able to stop herself assessing how he had behaved and it was irritating to know that he still had any kind of a hold over her. Khalid was history. Her interest in him was dead and buried. The sooner she got that clear in her head, the better.

He suddenly looked up and Sam felt her face bloom with colour when his eyes met hers. It was obvious from his expression that he had realised she was watching him and she hated the fact that she had given herself away. Turning, she stared out of the window, watching the pale glitter of sand rushing past below. She had to stop this, had to stop thinking about Khalid or she would never be able to do her job.

'Peter told me you're an obstetrician. I imagine you'll be in great demand during this trip.'

'I hope so.' Sam fixed a smile to her lips as she turned to Jess. Out of the corner of her eye she saw Khalid return to his notes and breathed a sigh of relief. Maybe he had known that she'd been watching him but so what? He must have been watching her too if he had noticed.

The thought wasn't the best to have had, definitely not one guaranteed to soothe her. Sam hurried on, determined not to dwell on it. There was bound to be a certain level of...*awareness* between them after past events. However, that was all it was, an echo from the past and not a fore-runner for the future.

'Peter emailed me a printout of the infant mortality rates and I was shocked, to be frank. They shouldn't be so high in this day and age.'

'I know. I saw them too.' Jessica grimaced. 'The number of women who die in childbirth is almost as bad.'

'I'm not sure yet what's going wrong but I suspect a lot of the problems are caused by a lack of basic hygiene,' Sam observed. 'I'm hoping to train some of the local midwives and make sure they understand how important it is that basic issues, like cleanliness, are addressed.'

'You'll find that the women are more aware of the problems than you may think. You shouldn't assume that they're ignorant of the need for good hygiene.'

Sam looked up when she heard Khalid's deep voice. He was standing beside Jessica's seat, a frown drawing his elegant brows together. His comment had sounded very much like a rebuke to her and she reacted instinctively.

'I have no intention of assuming anything. I shall as-sess the situation first and then decide what can be done to rectify the problems.' Her eyes met his and she had to suppress a shiver when she saw how cold they were. Just for a moment she found herself recalling how he had looked at her that night, his liquid-dark eyes filled with passion, before she brushed the memory aside. Maybe Khalid had wanted her for a brief time but he had soon come to his senses after that article had appeared in the newspapers. After all, what would a man like him, a man who had the world at his feet, want with someone like her?

Sam bit her lip, determined not to let him know how much his rejection still hurt. It wasn't as though it had been the first time it had happened or the last but it was incredibly painful to recall what had gone on that night. Even though she had worked hard to get where she was, she had never been able to rid herself completely of her past. Oh, she might know how to dress these days, might have refined her manners and shed her accent, but she was still the girl from the rundown estate whose mother had brought home one man after another and whose brother was in prison.

She took a deep breath and used it to shore up her defences. The truth was that she hadn't been good enough for Khalid six years ago and she still wasn't good enough for him now.

KHALID INWARDLY CURSED when he saw the shuttered expression on Sam's face. Why on earth had he said that or, at least, said it in that tone? Sam knew what she was doing. She wouldn't be here if he had any doubts about that. Peter had kept him informed of her progress over the years and Khalid knew that she was making her mark in the field of obstetrics. Sam was clever, committed, keen to learn and a lot of people in high places had recognised her potential.

Rumour had it that she would be offered a consultant's post soon and it was yet more proof of her ability.

He knew how difficult it was for women to rise through the ranks. Although most people believed that equality between the sexes was the norm in modern-day Britain, it wasn't only in countries like Azad where women came off second best. It happened all over the world to a greater or lesser degree. His own field—surgery—was one of the worst for discriminating against women, in fact. Although he knew he was good at what he did, he also knew that it helped to be male. And rich. And have the right connections.

Sam had none of those things going for her but she was making her mark anyway and he admired her for it. She had guts and determination in spades, which was why he had been attracted to her in the first place. Sam had been very different from the other women he had known.

The thought hung in the air, far too tantalising to feel comfortable with. Khalid thrust it aside, needing to focus on what really mattered. How he had felt about Sam was of little consequence these days.

'Of course. And I apologise if you thought I was criticising you,' he said smoothly. 'You are the expert in this field and, naturally, I shall be guided by you.'

She gave a small nod in acknowledgement although she didn't say anything. Khalid hesitated, wondering why he felt so unsure all of a sudden. He wasn't a man normally given to self-doubts—far from it. However, her response made him wonder if he should have been a little more effusive with his apology. He didn't want them getting off to a bad start, after all. It was on the tip of his tongue to say something else when Jess let out a yelp.

'Look! That can't *really* be what I think it is? Oh, Peter has to see this.'

Khalid moved aside as Jess shot out of her seat. Bending, he stared through the porthole, smiling faintly when he realised what had captured her attention. After the time they'd spent flying over the barren desert, he could understand why Jess had such difficulty believing her own eyes.

'It's like something out of a fairy tale. It can't possibly be real.'

The wonder in Sam's voice brought his eyes to her face and he felt a rush of tenderness envelop him. Sitting down on the recently vacated seat, he pointed to a spot a little to her right.

'Oh, it's real enough. Look over there and you'll see the lights on the runway.' He laughed deeply, feeling his chest tighten when he inhaled the lemon fragrance of her shampoo as she turned to do his bidding. It was an effort to continue when his breathing seemed to have come to a full stop. 'It looks less like a fairy-tale palace when you see the modern-day accoutrements that are needed to keep it functioning.'

'What a shame.' Sam shook her head, oblivious to the problems he was having as she studied the lights. 'It would have been nice to believe the fantasy even if it was only for a few minutes.'

She glanced round and Khalid stiffened when he saw how soft her eyes looked, their colour echoing the pale grey tones of the doves that flew over the summer palace. They had been the exact same colour that night, he recalled. A softly shimmering grey. He could picture them now, recall in perfect detail how she had looked as she had lain on the bed, waiting for him to make love to her.

The memory was too sharp, too raw even now. Khalid couldn't deal with it and had no intention of trying either. He stood up abruptly. 'We shall be landing in a few minutes. I need a word with the pilot, if you'll excuse me.'

He made his way to the cockpit and told the pilot to radio ahead and make sure the cars were standing by to meet them. There was no need for him to do so, of course. Everything had been arranged but it gave him something to do, a purpose, a reason to get away from Sam and all those memories that he'd thought he had dealt with years ago. As he made his way back to his seat, he realised with a sinking heart how wrong he had been. The memory of that night hadn't gone away, it had just been buried. He wanted to bury it again, bury it so deep this time that it would never surface, but could he? Was it possible when Sam was here, a constant reminder of what he had given up?

Khalid glanced across the cabin and felt a chill run through him as he studied the gentle lines of her profile. He had a feeling that he might never be able to rid himself of the memory of that night. It might continue to haunt him. For ever.

BY THE TIME they were shown to their accommodation, Sam was exhausted. Maybe it was the length of time it had taken to get there but she couldn't even summon up the energy to look around. Jess had no such problems, however. She hurried from room to room, exclaiming in delight.

'A sunken marble bath! And a separate wet room!' Jess opened a huge glass-fronted cabinet and peered inside. 'Oh, wow! Look at all these lotions and potions. It's like having our very own beauty salon on tap.'

'Not quite what I was expecting,' Sam observed pithily, tossing her bag onto the bed. There were three bedrooms in the guest house they'd been allocated, each decorated in a style that could only be described as lavish. Opening her case, she tipped its contents onto the umber silk spread, which matched the draperies hanging from the bed's ornate gilt frame.

'Me too. I thought we'd be camping out in a grotty old tent in the middle of the desert but this is great.'

Jess went into one of the other bedrooms and Sam heard a thud as she threw herself down onto the bed. She sighed, wishing she could share Jess's enthusiasm. If she had to describe her feelings then she would have to say that she felt…well, *cheated*. Surely Khalid hadn't brought them all this way so they could lounge around in the lap of luxury? She'd honestly thought she would be doing valuable work, making a positive contribution towards improving the lives of the desert women, but how could she do that if she was cloistered away in here?

The thought spurred her into action. Leaving her clothes in an untidy heap on the bed, she hurried from the room, calling to Jess over her shoulder, 'I'm just going to have a word with Khalid.'

'Okey-dokey. I think I'll treat myself to a bath,' Jess replied dreamily. 'No point letting all those goodies go to waste, is there?'

Sam didn't bother replying. There was no point taking the shine off things by telling Jess how she felt. Crossing the huge marble-floored sitting room, she wrenched open the door then paused uncertainly.

Night had fallen now and she wasn't sure which way to go. The female members of the team had been shown to their accommodation by one of the servants and Sam hadn't taken much notice of the route as she had followed the woman through the grounds.

She turned slowly around, trying to get her bearings, and suddenly spotted the pale gleam of the palace's towers through the palm trees to her left. There was a path leading in that direction and she followed it until she came to a ten-foot-high wall. There was a gate set into it and she turned the handle, frowning when it failed to open. She tried again, tugging on the handle this time, but it still wouldn't budge and her temper, which was already hovering just below boiling point, peaked. If Khalid had had them locked in then pity help him!

KHALID TOOK A deep breath, hoping the desert air would wash away the stresses of the day. He had honestly thought that he had been ready for what would happen but nothing could have prepared him for being around Sam again. He frowned, trying to put his feelings into context. It was bound to have been stressful to see her again—that was a given. However, he had never expected to feel so raw, so emotional. He was a master at controlling his feelings but he hadn't been able to control them today. Not with Sam. He had felt things he had never expected to feel, reacted in a way that shocked him.

It made him see how careful he would need to be in the coming weeks. He had to remember that he had nothing to offer Sam apart from a life that would stifle her as it had stifled his own mother. He wouldn't be responsible for doing that, for taking away everything that made Sam who she was. Sam was brave, kind, funny and determined and he couldn't bear to imagine how much she would change if he allowed his desire for her to take over.

The thought lay heavily in his heart as he strode along the path. The summer palace was built on the site of an oasis and the grounds benefited from an abundance of fresh water. The night-time scent of the flowers filled the air as he made his way through the grounds. Normally the richly, spicy aroma soothed him but tonight it failed to move him. The scent of Sam's shampoo still lingered in his nostrils and nothing seemed able to supplant it.

Khalid's mouth tightened as he nodded to the guard standing outside the entrance to the male guest quarters.

He had to stop this, had to remember *why* Sam was here, which wasn't for his benefit. She was here to do a job and once it was done she would go back to her own life and he would go back to his. There was no future for them together and he'd be a fool to imagine that there was.

If he had been willing to take a chance he would have taken it six years ago, made love to her and made promises that he would have kept too. He had wanted her so much, wanted her in his arms, in his bed, in his life, but he had realised after those articles had appeared in the press the damage it would cause if he had acted upon his feelings.

Maybe he had wanted her, and maybe she had wanted him too, but it wouldn't have been enough to make up for what would have happened if news of their relationship had leaked out. Sam would have been subjected to constant scrutiny by the press, her every action commented on, her family's shortcomings discussed ad nauseam. He had seen how hurt she had been, how upset, and he had known that he couldn't bear to see her subjected to that kind of pressure on top of everything else she would have had to contend with if they had stayed together.

He sighed. Sam would have had to give up such a lot, her independence, her career; give up being who she *was*, in fact, and it had been far too much to ask. Even though he spent a lot of his time working in London, Azad was his home and he always came back here. If he had brought Sam here to live, she would have had to conform to a way of life that was completely alien to her. Although changes were taking place, women in Azad still faced many restrictions. Perhaps Sam could have handled it at first even with the added strain of all the unwelcome publicity, but eventually she would have found the life too oppressive, as his mother had done.

He couldn't have stood that, couldn't have tolerated

watching her love turn to resentment, which was why he had done what he had that night. Khalid took a deep breath as he made himself face the cold hard facts. It had been better to destroy her love for him once and for all than watch it slowly wither and die.

SAM ROLLED OVER, struggling to untangle herself from the silken folds of the sheet. Reaching out, she pulled the alarm clock closer and sighed. Three a.m. and she was still wide awake. She had tried everything she could think of, counted sheep, recited poetry, thought sleep-inducing thoughts, but nothing had worked. Her body might be exhausted but her mind wouldn't slow down. It kept whizzing this way and that, yet always ending up at the same point: that moment six years ago when all her dreams had been shattered.

Tears filled her eyes but she blinked them away. She had done all the crying she intended to do and she wasn't going to start again. So Khalid had changed his mind, decided that he hadn't wanted her—so what? The world hadn't come to an end, the heavens hadn't fallen in and she had survived. If anything, it had made her stronger, made her value herself more. She had stopped apologising for her background, stopped feeling that she didn't deserve to be where she was. When it had come to breaking off her engagement last year, she hadn't hesitated. The relationship wouldn't have worked and she had known that…as Khalid must have known that *their* relationship had been doomed to failure.

Sam sighed as once again her thoughts returned to Khalid. Rolling over, she tried to get comfortable. She needed to sleep or she'd be fit for nothing tomorrow or, rather, today. Closing her eyes, she allowed her mind to drift, deciding it was easier than trying to steer it in any direction. Pictures flowed in and out of her mind: the desert they had flown over; the summer palace shimmering like a mirage in its lush green setting....

The sound of stealthy footsteps made her eyes fly open and she peered into the darkness. Was there someone in the room, Jess perhaps? Barely daring to breathe, she eased herself up against the pillows and felt her heart knock against her ribs when she saw the outline of a man silhouetted against the window. It hadn't occurred to her to close the shutters and she could feel the fear rising inside her as the figure approached the bed. Grabbing the clock off the nightstand, she held it aloft, wishing she had a more substantial weapon with which to defend herself.

'Get out or you're going to regret it!'

'Sam, it's me.'

Khalid's deep voice was the last thing she had expected to hear. The clock slid from her fingers and landed on the floor with a crash. Sam stared at him as he came closer, still not sure if he was real or a figment of her imagination.

'Khalid?' she whispered, her own voice sounding husky in the silence. 'Is it really you?'

'Yes.'

He bent so that she could see his face and her breath caught when she saw how his eyes glittered with an emotion she couldn't interpret. When he moved closer, so close that she could feel the warmth of his breath on her cheek, she almost cried out. It took every scrap of will power she could muster to lie there and not do anything, not react in any way at all. Khalid had come to her and it was up to him to tell her why.

'I'm sorry to wake you, Sam. I know how tired you must be after the journey.' His voice sounded softer, deeper, strumming her nerves like a violin bow, and she shuddered.

'What do you want?' she murmured, wishing that she sounded more certain and less unsure.

'You.' He suddenly smiled, his teeth gleaming whitely in the moonlight. 'I need *you*, Sam.'

CHAPTER THREE

'The baby's breech. It's too late to turn it or perform a C-section so we'll have to deliver it vaginally.'

Sam turned to Jess and smiled. Although the young mother, Isra, couldn't understand what they were saying, she would soon guess how serious the situation was if they showed any signs of concern. Sam could tell that the girl was terrified and it wouldn't help if they lost her confidence at this point.

'I've not delivered a breech before,' Jess murmured, following Sam's lead and smiling broadly. 'I hope you have.'

'I've done my share,' Sam assured her, washing her hands in the basin of water on the dresser. There was no point stating the obvious, that the breech deliveries she'd been involved with had been carried out in the safety of a highly equipped maternity unit. They didn't have such luxuries on tap here so they would have to manage the best way they could.

'I need a word with Khalid,' she told Jess, refusing to dwell on the negatives. She had delivered several breech babies and every single one of them had survived. There was no reason to think that this baby wouldn't survive too. 'Our biggest problem is going to be the language barrier so we'll need an interpreter.'

'OK. Anything you want me to do?' Jess asked, sponging Isra's face.

'Not really. I'll only be a moment,' Sam assured her.

She left the bedroom, frowning when she discovered that there was nobody about. After Khalid had woken her, he had led her to the servants' quarters. Isra was the wife of one of the palace cooks and she and her husband lived in the grounds. Although their house was only small, much smaller than the one she and Jess were sharing, it was spotlessly clean and tidy.

Sam peered into a kitchen, which boasted a wood-burning stove, and a tiny but well-equipped bathroom as she made her way along the passageway. From what she could see, the staff were well catered for and it was good to know that they were treated with respect. She came to the sitting room, which was also small but very attractive with brightly coloured rugs on the tiled floor and heaps of cushions on the low couches. It all looked very comfortable but decidedly empty. Where *was* everyone?

Sam stepped out of the door, waiting for her eyes to adjust to the darkness, and heard footsteps approaching. Just for a second her mind whizzed back to those moments in the bedroom when she had spotted the silhouette of a man highlighted against the window and she felt her heart race. If she'd known it was Khalid, would she have felt more afraid or less? Would it have been better to face an intruder than to face him and have to go through those seconds when she'd thought he had wanted her for a very different reason?

'How is she doing?'

Khalid's voice cut through her thoughts, cool and clear in the silence of the night, and Sam shivered. She turned towards him, taking care to maintain a neutral expression. There was no way that she was going to let him know how she had felt, definitely no way that she was prepared to admit that she had wanted him too, although not for his skills as a surgeon. It would be foolish to do that, foolish and dangerous as well. Giving Khalid licence to toy with her emotions again was a mistake she didn't intend to make.

'The baby's breech,' she informed him crisply. 'It's too late to perform a section so we're going to have to deliver it vaginally but we'll need an interpreter. The mother's co-operation is vital in this situation.'

'Of course,' Khalid agreed, frowning.

Sam's brows rose. 'Is there a problem?'

'Unfortunately, yes. The female interpreter I've hired isn't joining us until tomorrow.'

'Surely there must be someone else here who speaks English.'

'Of course. However, they are all male.'

'So?'

'So it wouldn't be right to allow them to be present at the birth.'

'Why on earth not?' Sam exclaimed.

'Because men are not allowed to be present at the birth of a child, not even the father, let alone an outsider.'

'That's ridiculous,' Sam declared hotly.

'It may seem so to you but it's a cultural issue.' He shrugged, his face betraying little of what he was feeling. If he was annoyed by her outburst it didn't show, Sam thought, but, then, why should he feel anything? Khalid was indifferent to her, as he had made clear. The thought stung so that it was an effort to focus when he continued.

'Isra would lose the respect of her husband and her family if it were to happen. It's out of the question, I'm afraid.'

'How about if you did it? I mean, you're a doctor, Khalid, so surely that makes a difference?'

'I'm afraid not. Although views are changing in the city and there are even a few male obstetricians working in the hospital, the desert people still hold fast to the old ways.'

'Then what do you suggest?' Sam demanded, in no mood to compromise. Her feelings didn't enter into this, she reminded herself. It was her patient who mattered, not how hurt she had been when Khalid had rejected her. 'I need Isra to work with me, do what I tell her to do as and when it's necessary. It's vital if we hope to deliver this baby safely.'

'The only thing I can suggest is that we erect a screen across the window. Then I can stand outside and relay your instructions to her without actually being in the same room.'

'That sounds like a plan,' Sam agreed slowly, then nodded. 'Yes. It should work so long as you're able to hear what I'm saying.'

'Oh, that won't be a problem.' He smiled faintly, his beautiful mouth turning up at the corners. 'You have a very clear and distinctive voice, Sam. I'll have no difficulty hearing you.'

'Oh. Right.'

Sam felt a rush of heat sweep up her face and was glad of the darkness because it hid her confusion. That had sounded almost like a compliment and it was something she hadn't expected. She turned away, hurrying back into the house before the idea could take hold. Khalid could have meant anything by the comment or he could have meant nothing and she would be a fool to get hung up on the idea. She quickly explained to Jess what was going to happen, half expecting the other woman to find it as ridiculous as she had done. However, Jess merely shrugged.

'I've come across it before. Some of the African tribes don't allow men to be present at a birth.'

'Really? I had no idea,' Sam admitted. She glanced round when she heard noises outside the window. 'It sounds as though Khalid is getting everything organised. We'd better get set up in here.'

She and Jess worked swiftly as they spread a sterile sheet under Isra and donned their gowns. Sam decided that she would need to perform an episiotomy to help ease the baby's passage. As it was presenting bottom first, it was harder for it to make its way out into the world and a small incision in the perineum would help enormously. It would also prevent the perineum becoming badly torn.

'Can you explain to Isra that I'm going to do an episiotomy?' she said clearly, glancing towards the window. A wooden screen had been erected across it so she couldn't see Khalid and could only assume he was there. 'If you can tell her why it's necessary, it should make it less scary for her.'

'Will do.'

His voice floated back to her, soft and deep and strangely reassuring. Although she couldn't understand what he was saying to Isra, Sam knew that his tone would have reassured *her* if she'd been in the young woman's position. It obviously did the trick because Isra stopped looking quite so scared.

Sam worked swiftly, administering a local anaesthetic before making the incision. The girl lay quite still, bearing the discomfort with a stoicism that filled Sam with admiration. 'Well done,' she told her, patting her hand.

She jumped when from the window came the sound of Khalid's voice repeating her comment. His voice sounded so warm that she shivered before she realised what she was doing and stopped herself. The warmth of his tone wasn't a measure of his regard for her but for Isra, she reminded herself.

She applied herself to the task, refusing to allow her thoughts to wander as she pressed gently on the top of the uterus to help ease the baby out. Isra's labour pains were extremely strong now and Sam decided that she needed to stop the girl pushing.

'I want you to take small breaths, like this,' she told her, panting so Isra would understand what she wanted her to do.

Khalid repeated her instructions, although Sam noticed that he didn't do the panting and smiled. Maybe it was expecting too much to hope he would mimic her. After all, he was a *prince* as well as a doctor! The thought made her chuckle and Jess looked at her quizzically.

'OK, give. What's tickled your funny bone?'

Sam knew that she should keep her thoughts to herself but she couldn't resist telling Jess. 'I was just wondering why our interpreter didn't repeat *all* my instructions,' she explained, raising her voice so that there'd be no chance of Khalid not hearing her. 'He missed out the panting.'

Jess giggled. 'Maybe not the done thing for a prince.'

'Like those mums who opt for a section because they're too posh to push?' Sam grinned. 'You could be right. He's just too posh to pant!'

KHALID FELT A rush of heat flow through him when he heard the amusement in Sam's voice. He couldn't believe how good it felt to know that he was the reason why she was laughing. She'd been so distant towards him since they'd met again, so reserved, so cold, and he hated it.

Sam possessed a natural warmth that had drawn him to her from the moment they had met. Although he was used to women fawning over him because of his position, Sam had never treated him as someone special. Her response to him had been wholly natural and he had loved that, loved seeing her eyes light up when he had walked into a room, loved hearing her voice soften, loved knowing that she had wanted to be with him for who *he* was. He might be a prince, he might be rich, he might be many things, but he had never felt more like *himself* than when he had been with her. He had never needed to pretend with Sam. Not until that last night.

The thought filled him with pain and he sucked in his breath, afraid that she would hear an echo of it when he spoke. He could hear her talking to Isra, her voice so calm and reassuring that he knew it would soothe the young mother's fears even if the girl couldn't understand the actual words. He applied himself diligently to the task of translating, doing his best to mimic Sam's tone. He didn't want to let her down; he wanted to support her in any way he could. When the reedy sound of a baby's cry drifted out to him, his face broke into a smile.

'Is it all right?' he called through the screen.

'Fine. A little battered, as is mum, but he's in fine fettle,' Sam called back, and he could hear the elation in her voice. That she was thrilled by the birth of this child was clear and it touched him that she should care so much.

'It's a boy, then?' he said levelly, doing his best to control his emotions. He had to stop letting himself get carried away, had to remember that he had no rights where Sam was concerned. How she did or didn't feel wasn't his concern.

'Yes. Jess is just weighing him…' She broke off and then continued. 'He's almost three kilos so he's not a bad weight either.'

'That's excellent,' Khalid agreed. 'I'll go and inform the father if you don't need me anymore.'

'No, we're fine.' She paused then said quickly, 'Thank

you, Khalid. We couldn't have managed nearly as well if you hadn't translated for us.'

'It was my pleasure,' he said softly, unable to keep the emotion out of his voice. Maybe it was foolish but it felt good to know that he had redeemed himself a little in her eyes.

He made his way to Isra's parents' house. Her husband, Wasim, had gone there to wait for news. He was delighted if a little overwhelmed when Khalid announced that he had a son. Having a royal prince inform him of his baby's birth obviously wasn't something he was prepared for. Khalid brushed aside the younger man's thanks and left. This was a time for family celebrations and they didn't need him there. As he made his way back to the palace, he found himself wondering if he would ever be in Wasim's position, celebrating the birth of his own child. It was what was expected of him as a royal prince and second in line to the throne. Even his father had started dropping hints that it was time he thought about settling down and starting a family, yet he had great difficulty imagining it happening. Although he had known many women—and known them in every sense of the word too—Sam was the only woman he had wanted to spend his life with.

His heart was heavy as he made his way to his suite. He had a feeling that if he did marry, whoever he chose would only ever be second best. How could it be fair to enter into marriage on that basis?

IT WAS SHORTLY before dawn by the time Sam left Isra's house. Jess had already left but she had stayed behind to make sure that there were no unforeseen complications. Thankfully, the baby seemed none the worse for his traumatic arrival and had taken his first feed. Isra seemed much happier as well and was being looked after by her mother and various female relatives. There was no reason for Sam to stay any longer so she smilingly accepted the family's thanks then made her way through the grounds, following the path that Khalid had taken the night before.

Everywhere looked very different now, the first pearly grey fingers of light lending a dreamlike quality to the scene. The palace's towers seemed to float in mid-air, shimmering above the hazy outline of the palm trees. When a horseman suddenly came into view, he seemed as insubstantial as everything else. It was only when he drew closer that Sam recognised Khalid beneath the flowing folds of the burnoose and realised it wasn't her imagination playing tricks after all.

'Have you only just finished?' he asked in surprise, tossing back the hood of his cloak as he reined the horse to a halt.

'Yes.' Sam stroked the horse's velvety muzzle, keeping her gaze on the animal rather than allowing it to linger on Khalid. Her heart gave a little jolt as the horse shifted impatiently, bringing Khalid squarely into her line of sight. He looked so different dressed in the flowing robes, a world removed from the urbane and sophisticated man she knew, that it was an effort to respond naturally. 'I wanted to stay until I was sure Isra and the baby were all right.'

Khalid frowned. 'I appreciate that but you must be exhausted.'

'I'm fine. I'm used to late nights…and early mornings,' she added wryly. 'Babies seem to prefer to keep unsocial hours.'

He laughed, patting the horse's neck when it began to paw the ground. 'It makes me glad that I opted for surgery. At least there is usually *some* structure to my working day.'

'It doesn't bother me,' Sam told him truthfully. 'I've

developed the knack of snatching an hour's sleep whenever I can.'

'That must help, but you were already tired after the journey. Are you going to try and get some sleep now?'

'I doubt I'll manage it. I'm far too keyed up,' she admitted, then wished she hadn't said anything when she saw his eyes narrow. She hurried on, not wanting him to read too much into the comment. 'It's being here in a strange place, I expect.'

'Probably,' he agreed, but she heard the scepticism in his voice and went hot all over.

Did Khalid think that he was the reason why she felt so on edge? she wondered anxiously. And was he right? Was it less the unfamiliarity of her surroundings that had left her feeling so unsettled and more the fact that she was with him? She sensed it was true and it was hard not to show how disturbing she found the idea. She didn't want to feel anything for him but it appeared she had no choice.

'If you aren't going straight to bed, why don't you come with me?'

'Pardon?' Sam looked up in surprise and he shrugged.

'If you can't sleep then come and watch the sun rise over the desert. It's a sight worth seeing, believe me.'

'Oh, but I couldn't possibly...'

'Why not?' He stared arrogantly down at her and she could see the challenge in his eyes. 'What's to stop you, Sam? Unless you're afraid, of course?'

'Afraid? Of you?' Sam shook her head, refusing to admit that he was right. She was afraid—afraid of being with him, afraid of getting too close to him; afraid of becoming attracted to him all over again.

'In that case, there's no reason why you shouldn't come, is there?' He bent down and offered her his hand. 'Come.'

Sam took a deep breath as she placed her hand in his.

She knew she was making a mistake but how could she refuse? Did she really want him to know that he still had a hold over her? Of course not.

Placing her foot in the stirrup as he instructed, she let him help her onto the horse. He settled her in front of him, putting his arm around her waist when the horse began to prance. 'Shh, Omar. There is nothing to fear.'

Drawing her back against him, he wrapped a fold of the burnoose around her, shaking his head when she opened her mouth to protest. 'It's still very cold. You'll be glad of the extra layer once we're out in the desert.'

Sam bit her lip as he turned the horse around. If she made a fuss then it would appear that she was overreacting and that was the last thing she wanted, for Khalid to suspect that his nearness troubled her. She forced herself to relax as they rode towards the gates. The guard saw them approaching and opened them, then they were outside, the lush green vegetation closing in around them. Khalid kept the horse to a walk as they made their way along the path and then all of a sudden they came to the perimeter of the oasis and before them lay the desert, shimmering like pewter in the pre-dawn light.

'All right?' Khalid asked, his voice rumbling softly in her ear.

Sam nodded mutely. She couldn't speak, couldn't seem to find her voice even. Between the raw beauty of the desert landscape and Khalid's nearness, she was awash with sensations and could barely deal with them. When he urged the horse into a canter, she clung to the pommel of the saddle. The wind rushed past, ruffling her hair and bringing with it the strangely elusive scent of the desert, yet all she could smell was Khalid's skin, a scent she would have recognised anywhere.

Closing her eyes, she gave herself up to the moment,

uncaring if she was making a mistake. Maybe it was madness but being with him was what she wanted.

Desperately.

CHAPTER FOUR

Khalid slowed the horse to a walk as they neared an out-crop of rock rising out of the desert floor. He always came to this place whenever he wanted to watch the sun rise. His parents had brought him here as soon as he had been old enough to sit astride a horse and he valued the connec-tion it gave him to his childhood. Life had been so perfect before his parents had divorced.

Sadness filled him as he reined Omar to a halt. He'd been thirteen when his mother had left Azad and although now he understood her reasons for leaving, it had affected him deeply. She had returned to England afterwards while his father had remained in Azad, so Khalid had travelled between both countries, spending time with each of them. His older brother, Shahzad, the son of his father's first wife who had died in childbirth, had tried to make it easier for him, but the constant to-ing and fro-ing had been unset-tling. In the end, Khalid had realised that he had to make a choice and had chosen to live in England.

He had won a place at Cambridge to study medicine and had thrown all his energy into making a success of his studies. Whilst he didn't regret the path he had cho-sen, there were times—like now—when he found himself wondering if he had made the wrong decision. If he had opted to live in Azad then he would never have met Sam and his life would be far less complicated now.

Khalid drove the thought from his mind as he dismounted. Having Sam here could only affect him if he allowed it to do so. Reaching up, he offered her his hand, determined that he wasn't going to let her know how ambivalent he felt. Sam had agreed to come on this mission for one reason and one reason alone: to help the desert women. If she could handle the situation then so could he.

'Take my hand,' he instructed, then sucked in his breath when she did as he'd asked. Her hand felt so small compared to his that he was struck by an unexpected rush of tenderness. He wanted to hold on to her hand, to hold on to *her*, he realised in dismay. And it was the last thought he should have been harbouring.

He quickly released her as she slid safely down to the ground. There were bound to be glitches, he told himself as he tethered Omar to a rock. Moments when his mind and his body were in conflict, but he would deal with them. He simply had to remember that being with Sam wasn't an option any more now than it had been six years ago. He had no intention of going down the same route his parents had taken, certainly didn't intend to put any children he might have through the kind of heartache he had suffered. If he kept that at the forefront of his mind, it shouldn't be a problem.

'Come. There's a path along here. It's not too steep and you shouldn't have any difficulty climbing it.' He gave her a cool smile, the sort of smile he utilised on a daily basis. Nobody looking at him would suspect that he felt far from cool inside. 'The view from the top is worth it, believe me.'

'I hope so.'

There was an edge to her voice that made him wonder if she had guessed he had mixed feelings about bringing her here. However, as it was too late to reconsider his invitation, he would have to make the best of it. He led the way, slowing his pace so she could keep up. They reached the top and stopped. Below them lay the desert, red-gold along the horizon where the sun's rays touched it, dark and mysterious closer to where they were standing. It was a sight he had seen many times before and it never failed to move him. However, it seemed to affect him even more that day, with Sam standing there beside him.

Khalid took a deep breath, trying to calm the panic that was twisting his guts as he watched the sun sail majestically over the horizon. A new day had begun and he, a man who was used to controlling his own destiny, had no idea what it would bring.

'IT'S AMAZING—'

Sam broke off, unable to put into words how the sight affected her. Wrapping her arms around herself, she shivered though not from cold. Although the temperature was still low, this shiver stemmed from the mixture of emotions she was experiencing. Sadness at what had happened in the past was mingled with joy at what she was experiencing right now; anger at the way Khalid had treated her was tempered by an unexpected acceptance. It was little wonder that she found it impossible to describe the scene so she didn't try. Anyway, it was doubtful if Khalid would be interested in her views.

She glanced at him, feeling pain tug at her heart. His heritage had never been more apparent than it was out here in the desert. It wasn't just the clothes he was wearing but his attitude. He looked every inch the desert prince, so completely at home in this bleak yet beautiful landscape that it simply highlighted the differences between them. Khalid's world wasn't her world. It never could be her world either. How could she, a Westerner with her background, become a desert princess?

'So, was I right?'

He turned to her and Sam struggled to clear her mind of everything except the need to convince him that she was over him. She had honestly thought she was, had truly believed that she had put her feelings for Khalid behind her years ago, but she was no longer sure when her heart was aching at the thought that they were such poles apart.

'Right?'

'About it being worth the climb.' He swept a hand towards the desert. 'The view from up here is magnificent, isn't it?'

'It is,' she replied coolly. 'I certainly can't fault it.'

'Did you want to?'

There was an edge to his voice that brought a rush of heat to her face. Had she been hoping to find fault with the view, to nitpick and discover flaws because it would have made it easier to find fault with him too? She sensed it was true and she hated the fact that she had been reduced to behaving in such a fashion.

'I'm sorry, Sam. Maybe bringing you here wasn't such a good idea after all.'

There was no doubt that the apology was sincere. Sam turned to look at him, seeing the sadness in his eyes. It struck her then that if she was finding it difficult to deal with this situation then it was equally hard for him. The thought shocked her so much that she didn't pause to consider the wisdom of what she was saying.

'Why did you bring me here, Khalid? Was it just so I could enjoy the view?'

'Of course. What other reasons could I have had?'

He shrugged, his broad shoulders moving lightly under the loose folds of the burnoose. Beneath it he was wear-

ing more normal clothing, although they still weren't the
clothes Sam was used to seeing him wear. Usually, Khalid
wore immaculately tailored suits, not a loose-fitting white
shirt, open at the neck so that she could see the satin gleam
of his skin through the gap. White cotton trousers tucked
into tan leather boots completed his outfit and made him
look very different from the man she had known six years
ago. Maybe that was why their relationship had foundered?
Because he hadn't been the person she had thought he was.
It hadn't had anything to do with her background after all.

The thought was far too tantalising. Sam knew that she
needed to rid herself of it as quickly as possible. It would
be foolish to imagine that Khalid's rejection hadn't had
anything to do with her past when she knew for a fact
that it had.

It had been exactly the same last year when she had
become engaged to Adam Palmer. Everything had been
fine at first; Adam's parents had seemed genuinely delighted about her joining their family. However, all that had
changed when they had discovered that her brother was
in prison. Although Sam had tried to make them understand that Michael's behaviour had nothing to do with her,
the pointed remarks about the detrimental effect it could
have on Adam's career if people found out that his future
brother-in-law was in prison had been impossible to ignore.

In the end Sam had done the only thing she could have
done and ended their engagement, given back the ring and
wished Adam well. At the time she had believed it was
the right thing to do, that it wasn't fair to expect Adam to
continually have to defend her. But had that been the only
reason? she wondered suddenly. Or had part of her known
that she hadn't really loved Adam, that she had agreed to
marry him simply because he had seemed like suitable

husband material; that her feelings for Adam could never compare to how she had felt about Khalid?

'Come. We should get back.'

Khalid touched her arm, his fingers barely making contact with her flesh, and yet to Sam it felt as though every fingertip had left an imprint on her skin. Her eyes rose to his before she could stop them and she saw to the very second when he realised what was happening.

'Sam.' His voice was low, filled with an awareness that made her heart race. Khalid might give the impression of being indifferent to her but he couldn't quite match his actions to his words, it seemed.

He took a slow step towards her and Sam found herself holding her breath. All around them the world was silent, waiting to see what would happen. Sam knew that she wanted him to kiss her, wanted to feel his mouth on hers, wanted to taste him and absorb his very essence, but was it wise? Did she really want to risk subjecting herself to that kind of heartache again? When his hand rose to touch her again, she stepped back.

'No!' She gave a harsh little laugh. 'Let's not allow the desert's magic to get to us, Khalid. There's no point creating problems, is there?'

Khalid didn't say a word, certainly didn't try to stop her as she turned and made her way down the path to where Omar was waiting patiently for them. Sam took a deep breath as she stroked the horse's neck. She was right and Khalid knew she was too. They needed to stick to the plans they had made for the future, a future that didn't entail them having another relationship. It shouldn't be that difficult. She simply had to remember that Khalid was only really interested in her skills as a doctor these days, not in *her* as a woman. Oh, maybe he had been tempted just now but it hadn't meant anything, not really. It had been

merely the instinctive response of a red-blooded male finding himself in close proximity to a woman he'd once had
an affair with.

They rode back to the palace in silence. Sam had nothing to say and it appeared that Khalid felt the same way. He
stopped outside the female guest quarters and dismounted
then turned to help her down, but this time she ignored his
outstretched hand as she slid to the ground.

'Thank you for taking me with you. The view was stu-
pendous,' she said politely, her heart aching. She was who
she was and Khalid was who *he* was; they couldn't change
that even if they wanted to. It was only in fairy tales that a
girl like her was swept off her feet by a handsome prince
and lived happily ever after.

'I'm glad you enjoyed it.' He paused and Sam found
that she was holding her breath as she waited for him to
continue, even though she knew it was silly.

'I used to imagine taking you there to watch the sun
rise,' he said, his deep voice grating. 'It was a dream of
mine and it was good to have it come true at last.'

He touched her cheek, just the barest whisper of his fingertips across her skin, before he swung himself back into
the saddle. Sam bit her lip as she watched him ride away,
watched well after he had disappeared from view. Tears
ran down her cheeks but she didn't even notice them. All
she could see was the regret in Khalid's eyes as he had
made that confession. Maybe they did intend to keep their
distance but now she understood that it wasn't going to be
any easier for him than it was for her.

THEY REACHED THE encampment shortly before noon. Khalid told the driver to park beneath the awning that had
been constructed to shelter the vehicles from the sun. He

climbed out of the powerful four-by-four and waited while the other vehicles drew up alongside.

It had been a last-minute decision to travel in three cars rather than the two he had planned on using. However, he had felt the need to be on his own as they made their way to the first of their desert camps. Being with Sam that morning had unsettled him even more and he'd needed time to get himself under control. However, as he watched her climb out of the second car, he realised that he still felt as raw and as emotional as he had done when they had watched the sun rise together. Having Sam there, in the place that was dearest to his heart, had touched something deep inside him, as his subsequent actions had proved.

'Phew! I don't think I've ever been any place so hot!'

Khalid shrugged aside the thought when he heard Jess's comment. He summoned a smile, keeping his gaze on her rather than allowing it to wander in the direction it wanted to go. He had to remember that Sam was just another member of the team and treat her as such.

'This is the hottest part of the day and normally we would avoid travelling at this time. However, I wanted to get set up so we don't waste time later on. I sent a couple of men out to spread the word that the clinic will be open this afternoon.'

'Oh, right. I see. Good thinking, boss.'

Jess grinned at him and Khalid smiled back, appreciating the fact that she didn't stand on ceremony around him. He hated it when that happened, when people couldn't see beyond his position. Sam had been exactly the same. She hadn't fawned over him either. She had treated him simply as a colleague. And a man.

The thought was too near the knuckle. Khalid blanked it out as he pointed out which tents the women would use. There were four women in the team and four men, which had made it easier when it had come to their accommodation. Although he prided himself on having a more worldly view, he had no intention of alienating his fellow countrymen by ignoring the proprieties. Men and women would be strictly segregated when it came to their washing and sleeping facilities.

Khalid turned to Peter while the women went off to explore their tent. 'I'm not sure how many people will turn up this afternoon. We could get a couple of dozen or we could get no one at all.'

'It's always the same,' Peter replied easily, mopping the sweat from his brow with a crumpled handkerchief. 'It can take several days before people drum up enough confidence to visit the clinic, I find.'

'Really?' Khalid sighed. 'It could take longer than I thought it would, then. There are so many people who need treating and I was hoping to get started as soon possible. We're only here for a matter of weeks and I hate to think that we're wasting valuable time.'

'You have to be patient,' Peter advised him. 'Once a few folk have received treatment, more will follow. It's a sort of snowball effect and gathers its own momentum.'

'I'm not sure about snowballs in the desert,' Khalid said wryly, glancing at the sky. 'I rather think they'd melt before they gathered any momentum.'

Peter laughed as he wandered off to fetch his bag. The trucks were being unloaded now so Khalid went over to supervise as the crates containing their equipment were lifted out. There was a separate tent for the clinic, another for the operating theatre and a third that would house the more fragile pieces of equipment like the ECG machine and ultrasound scanner. These would run off solar-powered generators donated by his brother.

Khalid made sure everything was put in the right place

then he and Han, the Thai male nurse, set about unpacking. It was a long and tedious job but it gave him something to do, took his mind off Sam and all the other issues. He sighed as he stowed a box of dressings on a shelf. Everything came back to Sam, didn't it? Every thought he had started or ended with her and it had to stop. Sam was here to do a job. If he said it often enough then maybe he would believe it...

And maybe he wouldn't.

SAM FINISHED UNPACKING and stowed her bag under the bed. Although the facilities were nowhere near as luxurious as those at the summer palace, she was surprised by how comfortable their accommodation was. She, Jess, Anna, the paediatrician, and Aminah, their nurse-cum-interpreter, who had arrived that morning, each had their own little cubicle containing a bed plus a locker for their clothes. There was even a bathroom leading off from one end of the tent, which sported a toilet cubicle plus a shower and a washbasin. They had everything they needed and she found herself thinking how much planning must have gone into it. Obviously, Khalid had thought long and hard about this venture.

She sighed when once again she found herself thinking about him. It was only natural, of course, but she knew how quickly one thought could lead to another and wished she could stop. Maybe it would help if she kept busy, she decided. If her mind was fully occupied then no more stray thoughts could slip in.

'I'm going to see if I can help unpack the equipment,' she told the others.

'I'd offer to come with you only I'm bushed,' Anna said, fanning herself with a magazine. She was older than the rest of them, possibly in her late forties, with bright red hair and dozens of freckles on her face. Now she grimaced. 'It's so hot I think I'm going to melt.'

Sam laughed. 'We probably all will. Why don't you try out the shower? It might cool you down.'

'Good idea.'

Anna headed for the bathroom while Sam left. She could see some men unloading one of the trucks and made her way over to them. They were taking the crates into a tent at the far end of the camp, so she followed them. There was a double entry, two openings joined by a short tunnel, which could be zipped shut at each end. Both openings were wide open and she stepped inside, pausing in amazement as she took in the sight that greeted her. That couldn't be an ultrasound scanner, not here in the middle of the desert!

'Sam?'

She spun round so fast that she overbalanced and gasped when she felt herself pitch sideways. Khalid's hands shot out, gripping her forearms as he set her back on her feet. Sam felt a rush of heat flow through her, starting at the point where his fingers were clamped around her arms, and shuddered. Looking up, she stared into his face, wishing with all her heart that she didn't react this way whenever he touched her. It had been the same that morning when they had ridden into the desert and she hated it, hated the fact that she was so vulnerable. She didn't want to feel anything for him, but it seemed she was powerless to control her emotions where he was concerned.

'Sam.'

He said her name again yet it sounded very different this time and she had to force down the lump that came to her throat. To imagine that Khalid had regrets was more than she could bear. She needed him to be *sure*, to be certain that rejecting her had been the right thing to do. If she allowed herself to believe that he wished he hadn't done it, she would never be able to cope.

'Thanks. It wouldn't have been the best start if I'd ended up flat on my face.'

She gave a little laugh as she stepped back and Khalid didn't try to stop her. Relief washed over. Maybe he did have *some* regrets but deep down she knew that he would do the same thing again.

'Were you looking for me?' he asked, his voice devoid of emotion, and she breathed a little easier.

'Not really.' She glanced at the packing cases and shrugged. 'I just wondered if I could help. Obviously there's a lot to do if we hope to be ready in time for this afternoon's clinic.'

'It's kind of you but you must be tired after your late night,' he said courteously. 'It might be better if you tried to rest before clinic starts.'

'I'm fine.' Sam's spine stiffened. Maybe he was only trying to be considerate but she resented the fact that he thought she needed his advice. 'As I explained this morning, I'm used to functioning on very little sleep.'

'Indeed you did. I apologise.'

On the surface his tone hadn't altered and yet all of a sudden Sam felt her mind wing its way back to those moments when they had watched the sun rise. Seeing Khalid then had been a revelation. Even though she had always been aware of his heritage, she had never really thought about how different his life must be from hers. It hadn't seemed important but now she could see that it had been a key factor behind his rejection of her.

As a child, Sam had grown used to being the outsider. Parents had discouraged their children from making friends with her because she'd been the 'wrong sort'. Even at high school, she had never really fitted in. The boys had heard the rumours about her mother and had pursued her in the hope that she would be the same, while the girls had been openly hostile, disliking her for her looks and her intelligence as much as for her family's reputation.

University had been her salvation. Nobody had known about her background there and for the first time in her life Sam had been able to be herself. She had made friends and had gained confidence because of it. When the truth had surfaced during her final year of rotations, there had been some who had shunned her. However, most people had been prepared to accept her for who she was and not for what her family had done. She had thought that her background had no longer mattered but she'd been mistaken. It had mattered to Khalid.

Sadness ran through as she realised that she no longer felt angry about what he had done. She should never have got involved with him in the first place and certainly never allowed their relationship to reach the stage where they had been on the point of making love. Although she'd had boyfriends before Khalid, her mother's behaviour had made her wary of having a physical relationship with them.

She hadn't slept with anyone until her engagement, in fact, and only then because Adam had expected it when they were to be married. It had been a bitter disappointment for them both. Although Sam had tried to respond, she'd been unmoved by Adam's lovemaking and had felt relieved when it was over. If she was honest, she had never wanted any man that way...

Except Khalid.

She took a deep breath. She must never forget that in Khalid's eyes she was tainted goods. Maybe he had wanted to sleep with her, but he had realised at the very last moment that it would be a mistake. And in all honesty, she couldn't blame him. Khalid could have his pick of women,

women who were far more suited to his lifestyle. What would he want with someone like her?

Maybe she had achieved a lot but she could never completely leave her past behind. Although her mother had died some years ago, she kept in touch with her brother and visited him whenever she could. Michael still had a couple of months of his sentence left to serve and she was hoping that with the right support he would make something of his life. She didn't intend to turn her back on him just because it wasn't convenient to have an ex-jailbird for a brother and anyone she met would need to understand that.

She sighed. The likelihood of her meeting a man she would fall in love with was so remote that it wasn't worth considering. There was only one man who had fulfilled that criterion and she wasn't venturing down that path again.

CHAPTER FIVE

By three o'clock everything was ready. Khalid looked around, delighted that they had achieved so much in such a short time. The clinic looked very professional with its neat little examination cubicles and shelves bearing their equipment. Once again he had taken care to observe the proprieties. The tent was divided into two sections, one for the men and one for the women. Granted, people would need to queue up together while they waited to be seen but that was acceptable. Even among the desert people changes were occurring and it was no longer considered necessary to strictly segregate the sexes.

'It's looking good, isn't it?'

'It is,' Khalid agreed, as Tom Kennedy, their anaesthetist, came to join him. 'How about Theatre? Are you happy with it?'

'It's better than I dared hope,' Tom enthused. 'The lighting is ace and as for those extractor fans to remove any dust...well, they're brilliant!'

'You can thank my brother for them. He found a supplier and told them what we needed. They weren't sure if they could deliver them on time but Shahzad managed to *persuade* them.'

Tom grinned. 'One of the perks of having royal blood,

I imagine. People are more disposed to bend over backwards and do what you want.'

Khalid sighed as Tom wandered off. There were advantages to being his father's son but there were drawbacks too. He had learned at an early age that he could never accept people at face value and that he always needed to be wary of their reasons for making friends with him. Far too many had tried to use him to their advantage. It had made him cautious about making friends. There were very few folk he trusted completely, people like Peter and Tom....

And Sam.

He frowned as he glanced over to where she was organising her desk. He had trusted Sam from the moment they had met. He had never felt wary about her motives for befriending him, never doubted her integrity, not even when his father's security team had handed him a detailed report about her background.

Checking up on the people he met was the norm for someone in his position. However, the account of her mother's numerous affairs and her brother's imprisonment for fraud hadn't fazed him. Sam possessed an innate honesty that had made him feel comfortable from the outset and he had known that he could trust her. It made him feel even worse about the way he had treated her. Even though he had done what he had for *her* benefit, he knew that he had hurt her in the cruellest way possible.

'CAN YOU ASK her if I can examine her breasts?' Sam said quietly, and then waited while Aminah translated her request. The nurse not only spoke English but a number of dialects particular to the desert tribes. Now she looked up and nodded.

'Yes, it is fine, Doctor. Please continue.'

'Thank you.'

Sam smiled reassuringly at the girl. Noor was just sixteen years of age and had recently given birth to her first child. She looked little more than a child herself with her long dark hair hanging in a thick plait to her waist. She had come to the clinic with her mother and her aunts, complaining of sore breasts, and Sam was keen to ensure that she received appropriate treatment.

Once Noor had removed her dress, Sam examined her, nodding when she discovered what she had expected to find. The girl was suffering from mastitis—inflammation of the breast tissue. Bacteria had entered her breasts while she had been feeding her baby, probably because her nipples were cracked. It was fairly common during the first month of breastfeeding but none the less painful because of that.

Sam explained that she would give Noor antibiotics to clear up the infection plus analgesics for the pain. Expressing milk would help to relieve the engorgement and make her more comfortable too. It all took time as everything needed to be translated but in the end they got there. Noor looked much happier when she left, clutching the tablets Sam had prescribed for her. Although Sam had asked her to come back so she could check on her progress, she wasn't anticipating any problems.

The time flew past and before she knew it, night was falling. Sam sighed as she flexed her shoulders after her last patient left. She had treated over a dozen women, which was pretty good considering this had been their first session. She looked up and smiled when Peter came over to her.

'We didn't do too badly, did we? How many folk did you see?'

'Six,' Peter informed her, sitting down on the edge of the desk. He frowned. 'Looks as though TB's going to be our biggest problem. Four of the men I saw were exhibiting classic symptoms of it.'

'It's difficult to treat unless you can keep on top of it,' Sam observed. 'The problem is that we're only going to be here for a limited time and it will take longer than that to clear it up.'

'I know,' Peter agreed worriedly. 'That's something I need to discuss with Khalid. I'd hate to think that we make a start on sorting people out and leave them in the lurch.'

'Difficult,' Sam said sympathetically.

She looked round when she heard footsteps and felt her heart jolt when she saw Khalid approaching them. All of a sudden she couldn't face the thought of having to speak to him. Her first clinic had gone extremely well and she wanted to focus on that, focus on the job she had come to do, rather than think about the emotional turmoil she experienced whenever he was near. She hastily gathered together her notes and stood up.

'I'd better get these filed and then I think I'll treat myself to a shower before dinner.'

'Oh, right. Good idea,' Peter agreed, looking faintly startled by the speed of her departure.

Sam made her way to the tiny office that had been set up in one corner of the tent and filed her notes. Khalid and Peter were deep in conversation when she left and she doubted if either noticed her departure. She sighed as she made her way to the women's tent. That was what she wanted, surely, that Khalid should treat her as just another member of the team, and it was ridiculous to feel ever so slightly miffed that he hadn't tried to speak to her. She showered and changed into clean jeans and a fresh T-shirt then made her way to the canteen. Jess and Anna were already there and they waved when she went in.

'Come and have a drink,' Jess instructed. 'There's no

alcohol in it but it's delicious all the same. I could definitely get hooked on it.'

'Thanks.' Sam accepted a glass of straw-coloured liquid and sipped it tentatively. Her brows rose. 'It *is* good. What is it?'

'No idea,' Anna informed her cheerily. 'It's hitting the spot, though, and that's good enough for me.'

They all laughed and that seemed to set the tone for the evening. Whether by accident or design, it ended up with the women sitting together and the men sitting at the other side of the tent. The food was excellent, some sort of vegetable stew served with rice, followed by fresh figs and yoghurt. Cups of thick aromatic coffee rounded off the meal and Sam sighed appreciatively.

'That was delicious. I don't know what I was expecting but it definitely wasn't anywhere near as good as that.'

'I'm glad you enjoyed it.'

The sound of Khalid's voice brought her head up and she felt the colour rush to her cheeks when she discovered he was standing by her chair. He smiled around the table, his gaze lingering no longer on her than it did on the others and yet Sam knew that he was as aware of her as she was of him. All of a sudden the air seemed to be charged with tension, filled with a host of feelings she couldn't even begin to decipher, and her breath caught. She could lie to herself and claim that she was over him but what was the point? She wasn't over him. Maybe she never would get over him either.

KHALID COULD FEEL the tension in the air, thick and hot and disturbing. It took every scrap of will power he could muster to act as though nothing was wrong.

'We did extremely well today,' he said, focusing on the reason why he had stopped by the women's table. His only concern was making a success of this venture, making sure that his countrymen received the treatment they deserved. It had absolutely nothing to do with Sam and this need he felt to be with her. 'Between us we saw over three dozen people, which is an excellent result for our first clinic.'

'Sam must have seen at least a dozen patients,' Jess put in.

'Indeed.' He nodded, his eyes drifting to Sam before he forced them away again. He didn't want to look at her, couldn't afford to when his emotions were so raw. If he looked at her then he might be tempted to do something he must never do. He must never forget that Sam couldn't be part of his life.

'Obviously the women are in need of all the help we can give them,' he said, struggling to ignore the pain that ripped through him at the thought. 'It makes it all the more vital that we see as many as we can while we're here and even think about setting up a permanent clinic, not only for the mothers and babies but for everyone.'

'Would that be possible?' Sam interjected. 'I mean, the people we're dealing with are nomadic and they move around a lot. It would be difficult to choose a suitable site for a clinic, surely?'

'That's true.' Khalid summoned a smile, trying not to let her see the effect she had on him. He had known many women, women who were far more beautiful than her, and yet none of them had had the effect on him that she had. It made him see how dangerous it would be to spend too much time with her while they were here.

'It will take a lot of thought before we can make any definite plans but it's something that needs to be considered.' He smiled around the table. 'Right. I'll say goodnight. Thank you all for your hard work today. I'll see you in the morning.'

Khalid left the canteen and made his way to the men's tent. Peter arrived a few minutes later and they chatted for a while before Khalid switched off his lamp. He lay in the darkness, willing himself not to think about anything except what the next day might bring, but it was impossible. Closing his eyes, he let his mind drift, unsurprised when thoughts of Sam came flooding in. For the past six years he hadn't allowed himself to think about her, but now it seemed he couldn't stop. Had he been right to end their relationship? Or had he made a terrible mistake?

Even leaving aside the matter of all the publicity that would have been generated if their relationship had become common knowledge, it had appeared that he'd had no choice. But what if they could have found a compromise? He spent at least six months of every year in England so surely they could have worked around the problem. Sam could have visited Azad but not lived here all the time. Then she could have continued her career and not had to give it up. He couldn't understand why he hadn't considered the idea before. It could have worked...or it could have done until they'd had children.

He sighed. Everything would have had to change if they'd had a child. Although his brother was next in line to the throne, Shahzad and his wife had produced only girls so far and under current laws they could never succeed their father. If he and Sam had had a son, their child would have become heir to the throne. Sam would have been faced with an impossible choice then. Either she would have had to live in Azad permanently or she would have had to allow their child to be brought up here without her.

It was the same choice Khalid's own mother had had to make and look how it had turned out. Although his parents had loved one other, his mother hadn't been able to cope with the restrictions of life in Azad. Even though the status of women in the country was improving, there was a long way to go before it reflected modern-day European standards. Maybe Sam would have coped for a while but in the end she too would have found it too constraining and left.

The thought of the heartache it would have caused not only for them but for any children they might have had was more than Khalid could bear. When he married, he would choose a woman who understood the kind of life he had to offer her. And that meant that he could never choose Sam.

SAM WAS AWAKE before dawn the next day. Surprisingly, she'd slept well and felt completely refreshed as she quietly made her way to the bathroom. Everyone else was fast asleep so as soon as she'd showered and dressed, she crept out of the tent. She shivered as the pre-dawn chill hit her, wishing that she had thought to put on a sweater. She was tempted to go back for one but the thought of waking the others stopped her. Hopefully a cup of coffee would warm her up.

She made her way to the canteen, sighing in relief when she spotted a fresh jug of coffee on the counter. She helped herself to a cup, nodding her thanks when one of the cooks offered her a dish of fruit and yoghurt. There were some tiny sweet pastries as well, dripping with honey and covered with almonds, and she accepted one of them too. She loaded everything onto a tray and carried it over to a table. She had just taken her first welcome sip of coffee when Khalid appeared.

He helped himself to coffee then looked around and Sam held her breath. Would he join her or would he opt to sit by himself? The sensible part of her hoped it would be the latter while another part hoped he would join her and she sighed. It would be so much easier if she could decide what she wanted and stick to it.

His gaze finally alighted on her and she saw him hesitate. Was it as difficult for him to decide what to do as it was for her? she wondered. If anyone had asked her how she'd felt about him a couple of weeks ago, the word she would have used to describe her feelings would have been indifferent. She had got over her anger, dealt with her pain, put it all behind her—or so she had thought. However, as she watched him walk towards her, Sam realised that *indifference* was the last thing she felt. So what had changed? Was it being with Khalid again that had re-awoken these feelings? Were they an echo from the past, a reflection of what she had felt all those years ago, ghost feelings but not actually real?

She bit her lip, praying it was so. Getting involved again with Khalid was out of the question. They'd had their chance and it would be foolish to rekindle their relationship. She knew that so why was her heart racing? Why was she finding it so hard to breathe? If she knew the answers to those questions then maybe she would know what to do.

'Good morning. You're up early.' Khalid sat down, feeling his heart hammering inside his chest. If there'd been any way he could have avoided speaking to Sam he would have done so, but it would have been too revealing if he had ignored her. He mustn't single her out. He must treat her exactly the same as any other member of the team. Now he smiled at her. 'Were you ready for your breakfast?'

'Uh-huh. I needed a cup of coffee to warm me up.' She glanced at her cup and grimaced. 'I'd forgotten how cold it is first thing of a morning.'

The comment immediately reminded him of what had happened the previous day. His hands clenched because he could still feel the imprint of her body where it had rested against him as they had ridden out to the desert. He had never taken anyone there before. It was such a special place, filled with so many precious memories that he had never wanted to share it, yet it had felt right to take Sam there.

'The extremes of temperature come as a surprise to lot of people,' he said quietly, his heart aching. Would he be able to visit that spot again or would it be too painful to stand there and watch the sun rise without her beside him? He drove the thought from his head, knowing that it was foolish to dwell on it. Sam was never going to be part of his life and he had to accept that.

'The contrast between the heat of the day and the bitter cold of the night catches a lot of people unawares. It's been the cause of several potentially life-threatening incidents in the past couple of years.'

'Really? Why? What happened?' she asked, frowning.

Khalid's hands clenched once more as he fought the urge to smooth away the tiny furrows marring her brow. He mustn't touch her, couldn't afford to do so when his emotions were so raw. Look what had so nearly happened yesterday. If Sam hadn't had the sense to stop him, he would have kissed her and heaven alone knew what would have happened then. In his heart he knew that if he kissed her, he would be lost.

'There's been several occasions when tourists have found themselves stranded in the desert and ended up spending the night out here,' he explained, confining himself to answering her question. It was safer that way, less stressful to focus on something other than his own turbulent emotions. 'Although they may have made provision for the daytime heat, they hadn't thought about how cold it gets at night. Consequently, several people have ended up in hospital suffering from exposure.'

'Good heavens!' Sam exclaimed. 'But surely any tourists should be discouraged from driving around out here on their own.'

'They should.' Khalid picked up his cup and took a fortifying sip of coffee. He had never considered himself to be an overly emotional person—just the opposite, in fact. However, when he was with Sam he couldn't seem to find the right balance and it was unnerving to realise that. It was an effort to focus on the conversation.

'In fact, my brother, Shahzad, is currently working with several of the major tour operators to make them understand how important it is that they discourage their clients from exploring on their own. Anyone wishing to drive out into the desert should do so only as part of a properly organised excursion.'

'It makes sense,' Sam agreed, picking up her pastry and nibbling off a corner. She put it back on the plate then delicately licked a smear of honey off her fingers, unaware of the havoc she was causing him.

Khalid looked away, trying to control the surge of desire that rushed through him. She hadn't done that to be provocative, he told himself sternly, but it made no difference. The vision of her pink tongue licking the sticky residue off her fingers was one that was going to stay with him for a long time to come.

He pushed back his chair, unable to cope with anything else. He needed a breathing space, time to get his emotions safely stowed away in the box where they normally resided. 'I'll leave you to enjoy your breakfast,' he said, relieved to hear that he sounded normal even though he didn't feel it. 'Clinic starts at seven this morning so I'll see you then.'

He left the canteen and made his way to Theatre. Han was already there, checking the equipment, so Khalid helped him. He had an operation scheduled for that morning, nothing too complicated, just resetting a femur that hadn't aligned properly. He and Han ran through a checklist of what he would need before the nurse left to get something to eat.

Khalid stayed on, going over the list once more even though he knew he had everything he needed. However, it was better to keep busy, better to stop his mind wandering down more dangerous paths. He would focus on his work and simply hope that one day he would be able to speak to Sam without it causing such havoc. All he needed to do was adjust the way he thought about her, see her purely as a colleague and nothing more.

He sighed as the image of her licking her fingers flooded his mind. One day. But obviously not *that* day!

CHAPTER SIX

They held two clinics: one early in the morning and one in the late afternoon so they could avoid the worst of the heat. Both were extremely busy. Sam was surprised by how many women turned up as well as by the variety of their complaints. Being used to the system in the UK, where separate ante-and post-natal clinics were the norm, it was a challenge to switch between both aspects of her job depending on what was required.

Several of the women were in an advanced stage of pregnancy and although they appeared healthy, she was keen to ensure that nothing happened to endanger them or their babies during or immediately after the birth. She decided that the best way to do this was by training the local midwives about the need for good hygiene. As soon as the last of her patients left, she sought out Khalid, knowing that she would need his help if she hoped to make a start on this very important task.

He was just leaving Theatre when she tracked him down and she waited while he deposited his gown in the hamper. Beneath it, he was wearing pale green scrubs and she felt her pulse leap as she took stock of the way the damp cotton had molded itself to his powerful chest. He turned, coming to an abrupt halt when he saw her standing in the doorway. Just for a moment his expression was unguarded

and Sam felt a rush of confusion fill her. Why was he looking at her like that? He'd been the one to end their relationship and it didn't make sense to see that desire in his eyes.

'Were you looking for me?'

His tone was cool, so cool that she realised she must
have imagined it. Khalid didn't desire her. Oh, maybe he
had done so at one time, maybe he had even felt a tiny echo
of it the other day too, but he had soon got over it. All it
had taken was that article in the tabloid press to make him
see how foolish it would be to involve her in his life on a
permanent basis.

'Yes. Is this a good time? Or would you prefer me to
leave it till later?' she asked as calmly as she could. There
was no point thinking about the past, distant or recent.
Khalid had done the only thing a man in his position could
have done and had rid himself of a potential embarrassment. And he would do exactly the same again.

'Now's fine.' He led the way, sitting down on one of
the empty packing cases that had been placed near the entrance of the tent for that very purpose. Glancing up, he
smiled at her. 'Have a seat. My office may be somewhat
informal but I hope the view makes up for it.'

'It certainly does.' Sam laughed as she sat down beside
him, feeling some of her tension melt away. Shading her
eyes against the glare of the lowering sun, she sighed appreciatively. 'I never expected the desert to be so beautiful. I mean, you see pictures on TV and get an impression
of its vastness and its emptiness but it doesn't do it justice.
There's something...well, magical about it that draws you
in, isn't there?'

'Yes. That's how I've always felt about it.' He turned
to look at her and she shivered when she saw the warmth
in his gaze. 'It's not often that people who aren't born

and raised in this environment appreciate its beauty that way, Sam.'

'No?' She shrugged, realising that she was in danger of stepping into dangerous waters. She wasn't trying to promote a bond between them, certainly wasn't trying to curry favour. She hurried on, deciding it would be safer to confine her remarks to what she wanted to speak to him about.

'Anyway, I know you're busy so I'll cut straight to the chase. I saw a lot of women today in the latter stages of pregnancy and although most of them were healthy enough, I'm keen to ensure they stay that way.'

'Of course. So what are you planning on doing?' he said smoothly.

Sam breathed a little easier when she heard nothing more than professional interest in his voice. If they could focus strictly on work, it would be so much easier. At least it would for her. The thought that Khalid might not be experiencing the same problems she was having was upsetting but she refused to think about it.

'I was wondering if it would be possible to visit some of the settlements and teach the local midwives about the need for good hygiene. I know from the research I've done that a lot of post-natal problems can be prevented if extra care is taken in the days following a birth.'

'I understand where you're coming from but I'm not sure if it's feasible,' he said slowly. 'We're aiming to hold two clinics a day and I can't see how there would be enough time to visit the camps as well, unless you worked seven days a week and that's out of the question.'

'Why?' She turned and looked at him. 'I'm more than happy to work every day, Khalid. I certainly didn't come here expecting to have a holiday!'

'I'm sure you didn't. However, you need to allow for

the fact that working under these conditions is vastly different from what you are used to.' He shook his head. 'No. There's no way that I can allow you to work every day of the week without a break. It wouldn't be right, Sam.'

'So are you going to take time off?' she demanded. Her brows rose when he didn't answer. 'Well, are you?'

'It's different for me,' he said shortly, standing up. 'I'm used to the conditions out here and I don't find it as tiring as you will do. I don't need to take time off.'

'Oh, I see. You're a super-hero, are you, Khalid? You don't get tired like we mere mortals do.' She laughed bitterly as she stood up. 'It must be wonderful to know that you are immune to all the pressures that other folk have to contend with.'

'That wasn't what I meant,' he said flatly. 'I'm as susceptible to pressure as anyone else is.'

'Really? So that's why you couldn't wait to end our relationship, was it? Because you couldn't handle the pressure of having your name linked to me, a woman with a less than perfect past!'

Sam hadn't meant to say that. When the words erupted from her lips, she felt sick with embarrassment. Her eyes rose to Khalid's in horror and she felt her heart sink when she saw the anger on his face. 'I'm sorry. I should never have said that,' she began.

'No. You shouldn't.' His voice grated, anger and some other emotion vying for precedence. 'I did what I had to do, Sam. And I did it for your sake rather than mine, although I don't expect you to believe me. Now, if that's all, there are things I need to attend to.'

He walked away and the very stiffness of his posture told her that he was deeply insulted by the accusation. Why? Once that article had appeared, he had lost no time in ending their relationship. Every word she'd said had been justified, but Khalid refused to admit it. Why was that? Because he felt guilty about the way he had treated her?

She tried to tell herself that it was the answer but she didn't really believe it. There had been more to his decision to break up with her than she had thought and it was worrying to wonder if she had misread the situation. She could accept what had happened when she had believed that she understood his reasons but it was far less easy to accept it now that doubts had crept in.

Her breath caught as she recalled what Khalid had said. He had claimed that he had done it for her benefit, which implied that he hadn't wanted to break up with her for his own sake, as she had assumed. It cast a completely different slant on what had happened, made her feel edgy and unsure and that was the last thing she needed. She couldn't afford to start wondering about his motives. It would only give rise to hope and that was something she couldn't risk. She and Khalid were never going to get back together. He didn't want it to happen and neither did she...

Did she?

KHALID WAS AWARE that he had handled things very badly. Instead of keeping his cool, he had allowed his emotions to get the better of him. As he stepped into the shower, he could feel anger bubbling up inside him. He needed to maintain his control or Sam would grow suspicious. The last thing he wanted was to have to explain why he had felt it necessary to end things with her. What if she told him that he'd been wrong, that she could have handled the media interest their relationship would have attracted? It would be so tempting to believe her and even more tempting to consider trying again.

He sighed as he rinsed the lather off his body. There

was no chance of them resuming their relationship. Even if Sam did believe she could handle the publicity, she would never cope with the restrictions of living in Azad. She was a modern woman who was used to living life on her terms and the fact that she would need to adhere to such archaic principles would only frustrate her.

Their relationship wouldn't last—it couldn't do. And there was no way that he was going to put himself in the position of having his heart broken. He had seen what it had done to his father, how his father had suffered after his mother had left, and he wasn't prepared to suffer the same kind of heartache. Getting back with Sam was out of the question even if it was what she wanted, which he very much doubted.

Peter had told him about her engagement last year. It had been a shock and an even bigger one when she had ended it a few months later. Although Khalid had no idea what had gone wrong, realistically he knew that she would meet someone else at some point, fall in love and settle down to start a family. It was what she deserved yet he couldn't pretend that he was happy at the thought of her loving another man and having his child. Not when it was what he had wanted so desperately. However, it proved unequivocally that Sam had moved on, put the past behind her and was looking to the future. And he certainly didn't feature in her future plans.

Dinner was a quiet affair. Sam wasn't sure if it was because everyone was tired after the busy day they'd had, but they seemed unusually subdued. Nobody lingered over coffee and by eight p.m. she and the other women were in their tent.

'I don't know about you lot but I'm bushed.' Jess gave a massive yawn. 'Oh, 'scuse me!'

'Don't apologise,' Anna told her, covering her own mouth with her hand. 'I'm shattered too. I don't know if it's the heat or what but I can't remember ever feeling so tired before. I feel like a limp rag.'

'I know what you mean.' Sam chuckled as she shimmied into her pyjama pants. 'I feel as though someone has wrung all the stuffing out of me! Maybe Khalid was right.'

'Right about what?' Jess queried, crawling into her bed. She tucked the sleeping bag around her then looked questioningly at Sam. 'Come on—give. What did Khalid say?'

'Oh, nothing much,' Sam muttered, wishing she hadn't mentioned it. She really didn't want to discuss what she and Khalid had been talking about earlier when it would only remind her of all the unanswered questions roaming around her head. However, there was no way she could avoid it when Jess was waiting for an answer. 'I had an idea about visiting the camps to teach the local midwives about the need for good hygiene.'

'Sounds like a good idea to me,' Jess interjected, and Sam sighed.

'I thought so but Khalid wasn't keen. He said it was too much, what with all the clinics we have scheduled.' She gave a little shrug as she wriggled into her sleeping bag. 'He didn't approve of me working seven days a week, apparently, although what I'm supposed to do with my free time is anyone's guess.'

'I suppose he does have a point,' Anna conceded. 'I mean, look at us. We're absolutely knackered and we've only done one full day!'

Everyone laughed when she pulled a wry face, Sam included. However, she couldn't help thinking that there had been more to Khalid's refusal to consider her proposal than mere concern for her wellbeing. Maybe he preferred to call the shots and not be guided by anyone else. After all this was his project and he might feel somewhat proprietorial about what happened while they were here.

Sam tried to convince herself it was that as she settled down to sleep, but she didn't really believe it. She had a feeling that Khalid had rejected her proposal mainly because it had been hers. It hurt to think that he could be so petty so she tried not to dwell on it. In a very short time the sound of gentle snoring told her that the others were asleep, although she was still wide awake.

Rolling over, she thumped the pillow into shape and tried to get comfortable. However, despite her weariness, she couldn't drop off. When the sound of hooves echoed through the tent she sat up. It sounded as though they had a visitor and at this time of the night it could only mean that someone needed help.

Climbing out of her sleeping bag, Sam dragged a sweater over her pyjamas then undid the tent flap. Low lighting had been set up around the camp and in the dim glow from the lanterns she could see a horseman talking to Khalid and Peter. It was obvious that something had happened and she wasted no time in going to see if she could help.

'What's going on?' she asked as she joined them. Khalid was speaking to the man and he barely glanced at her. Nevertheless, Sam felt the heat of his gaze like a physical touch and was glad that she had put on a sweater over her night attire. Colour touched her cheeks as she turned to Peter. Although Khalid might feign indifference, it was obvious that he was as aware of her as she was of him.

'Has something happened?' she said, trying not to dwell on the thought. It didn't matter how aware they were of each other because nothing was going to come of it.

'From what I can gather, there's been an accident at one of the settlements close to here—a fire apparently.'

Peter glanced at Khalid and grimaced. 'I don't know how many people have been injured but it doesn't look too good, does it?'

'No, it doesn't,' Sam agreed, taking note of the grim expression on Khalid's face.

Khalid finished speaking to the horseman and turned to them. 'From what I can glean, there are at least three people injured—a woman and two children. We need to see what we can do to help.'

'I'll come with you,' Sam offered immediately. She shook her head when he opened his mouth to object. All of a sudden she was determined to get her own way over this even though she didn't understand why it was so important. 'You'll need a female doctor so it may as well be me. There's no point waking the others when I'm already awake.'

'If you so wish.' Khalid gave a tiny shrug before he turned and made his way to the supply tent.

Peter frowned as he watched him go. 'He could have been a bit more gracious. What's wrong with him? I've never known him be so short with folk before.'

'Oh, he's probably anxious to get things sorted out,' Sam declared, wishing it were that simple. She sighed as she went to get ready. That Khalid didn't want her along was obvious if Peter had picked up on it, but she wasn't going to let it deter her. She had come here to do a job and do it she would. With or without Khalid's approval.

KHALID KNEW THAT he had been less than gracious but he couldn't do anything about it. As he gathered together everything they might need when they reached the encampment, he told himself that it didn't matter. He wasn't going to try and win Sam over—that was the last thing he intended to do. So what difference did it make if he had been a little...well, short with her?

He added several litre bags of saline to the growing heap then lifted a box of sterile dressings off a shelf. Details of what had happened were sketchy. All he knew was that three people had been injured when an oil lamp had exploded so he needed to make whatever provision he could. He stowed everything into a couple of cardboard boxes and headed outside, relieved to find that his driver was already waiting beside the four-by-four. He tossed the boxes into the back then looked round when Peter and Sam came to join him, doing his best to treat them both as colleagues. There was no problem about treating Peter that way, of course, but it was a different story when it came to Sam.

In a fast sweep his eyes ran over her, greedily drinking in the sight she made as she stood there in the glow from the lanterns. She hadn't stopped to brush her hair and the silky tendrils curled around her face, making his fingers itch to smooth them behind her ears. Although she was wearing trousers and a heavy knit sweater to ward off the night's chill, he could see the hem of her pyjama top peeking out below it and realised that she must have simply dragged on some clothes over her night attire. His breath caught because beneath the all-concealing layers, he knew that she would be naked...

'Right. Let's get going.' He swung round, refusing to allow his mind to go any further down that path. Thinking about Sam naked was the last thing he should be doing.

They left the camp, following the route the horseman had taken. It was pitch black, the light from the vehicle's headlamps barely enough to take the edge off the Stygian gloom. Fortunately, their driver was a local man and unfazed by the task of driving them there under such extreme conditions. However, even Khalid was relieved when he

spotted a glow of light on the horizon. Far too many people had come to grief trying to cross the desert at night for
him to be complacent about the potential dangers. They
drew up on the edge of the settlement. People were mill-
ing about, dealing with the aftermath of the fire. He could
see the remains of the tent near the centre of the compound
and inwardly shuddered as he imagined how terrifying it
must have been for the occupants to find themselves engulfed by flames.

'It must have been horrendous for the poor people who
lived in that tent.'

Sam unwittingly reiterated his thoughts and he sighed.
He didn't need any reminders about how in tune they had
always been, especially tonight when his emotions were
so near the surface.

'I'll go and see where they've taken the injured,' he said
shortly. 'Peter, if you and Sam could unload our supplies,
it will save time.'

'Will do.'

Peter hopped out of the vehicle and set about unloading
the boxes. Sam joined him, ignoring Khalid as she started
dividing everything into three piles. Khalid paused but
she didn't look up so he turned and made his way over
to where a group of men were waiting to greet him. He
couldn't have it all ways, couldn't treat her as a colleague
one minute and expect her to respond as something more
the next. It wasn't fair. He knew how he had to behave towards her and no matter how difficult it was proving to
be, he must stick to it.

SAM FINISHED SORTING their supplies, making sure that they
each had a selection of things they might need. Khalid
was still talking to the men but he glanced round, lifting
his hand to beckon her over. Picking up a box, she made

her way over to him, trying to ignore the little ache that seemed to have lodged itself in the very centre of her heart.

So what if he had been short with her—what did it matter? She was here to help the injured and how Khalid felt about her wasn't the issue. Nevertheless, it was hard to hide how hurt she felt as she set the box on the ground. Maybe she shouldn't care how he treated her but she did even though she knew it was silly.

'I want you to deal with the woman,' he told her briskly. 'Apparently, she isn't badly injured but she's pregnant and she's having pains.'

'How many weeks is she—do you know?' Sam asked quickly, forgetting her own feelings in her concern for her patient.

Khalid said something to the men. His expression was grave when he turned to her. 'Approximately twenty-eight.'

He didn't say anything else but he didn't need to. If Sam couldn't stop the woman's labour, the baby would be extremely premature. It would be worrying enough if the child was born in a highly equipped maternity unit but so much worse if it was born out here in the desert without the benefit of modern technology.

'I see.' She gave a little shrug. 'I'll go and see what's happening. Where is she?'

'In that tent over there.' Khalid pointed across the camp-site, putting out his hand to stop her when she turned to leave. 'I'll be here with Peter. If you need me then ask one of the women to come and get me. OK?'

'Fine.' Sam nodded, doing her best not to let him see how his touch was affecting her. She took a deep breath as he released her. She had always been susceptible to his touch, always responded, and it seemed that little had changed. Not even the fact that he had treated her so harshly had managed to destroy her response to him.

Picking up the box, she made her way to the tent, her heart feeling like a lead weight inside her. She had thought she was over him, had truly believed that whatever she had felt six years ago was dead, but how could it be when just the touch of his hand could set off this kind of a reaction? It made her see how careful she needed to be. She didn't want to find herself back where she'd been six years ago. She had worked too hard to get over him to welcome that scenario. No, when she returned to England she intended to be free of any such destructive emotions. She had wanted Khalid once and had suffered for it too. She wasn't about to make the same mistake again.

IT WAS A long night. By the time the sun started to edge above the horizon, Khalid was exhausted. Looking up from the makeshift operating table, he caught a glimpse of Peter's grey face and could tell that his friend was as weary as him.

'Another ten minutes and that should be it,' he said, turning his attention back to the child they were operating on. Four-year-old Ibrahim had suffered burns to his back and they had just excised the damaged tissue. Although his injuries weren't as severe as those of his elder brother, Jibril, he was suffering from shock. He was a very sick little boy and Khalid knew that the next twenty-four hours would be critical. He came to a swift decision.

'I'm going to have both the children airlifted to Zadra City. They need to be hospitalised if they're to have the best chance possible.'

'I agree.' Peter sighed. 'This little chap is going to need expert nursing if he's to pull through. And he won't receive that in the desert.'

'Exactly.' Khalid pulled off his mask as he stepped away

from the table. 'I'll make the arrangements if you're happy to finish off here.'

'Not much more I can do,' Peter said stoically. 'Are you going to check on Sam and see how she's doing? Her patient might need to be transferred as well.'

'Yes.'

Khalid left the tent, gulping in a great lungful of cold air as he stepped out of its heated confines. It had been a long night and although they had done all they could, he wasn't sure if both boys would survive. Between their injuries and shock it would be touch and go and the thought made him feel extremely downhearted even though he was a realist and accepted that he couldn't save everyone who came under his care. Still, it would have been good to know that tonight had been a success. It might have helped make him feel better about the way he had treated Sam earlier. He *had* been short with her and, try as he may, he couldn't help feeling guilty about it, but, then, what was new? He had felt guilty about the way he had treated Sam for years.

Khalid sighed as he crossed the campsite. People were already up, lighting fires to prepare their breakfasts. The scent of wood smoke filled the air, reminding him of his childhood. His father had loved to go camping in the desert and had often taken Khalid and his mother and Shahzad with him. They had been magical times when they had been able to enjoy being together as a family and forget that his father was king, with all that it entailed.

Would he ever take his own children camping in the desert? he wondered. Ever be able to forge that special bond with them? He hoped so but it all depended on what happened in the future, if indeed he ever had a family of his own. The only woman he had ever wanted to have his children was Sam, but that was out of the question.

As though thinking about her had conjured her up, she

appeared. Khalid's footsteps slowed. All of a sudden he was filled with a longing so intense that his breath caught. If he could turn back the clock then he wouldn't let her go. He would keep her with him and simply pray that somehow, *some way*, they could make their relationship work. Maybe there would have been problems, and maybe he would have suffered untold heartache, but would it have been any worse than this? Even if he had lost her in the end, at least he would have had her for part of his life. And that would have been so much better than this.

CHAPTER SEVEN

Sam took a deep breath. It had been almost unbearably hot inside the tent, the smell of the camel dung used to fuel the fire filling her nostrils to the exclusion of everything else. Glancing around, she realised in surprise that people were already going about their day. Water was being boiled for coffee and some sort of grain turned into a kind of porridge. Her stomach rumbled and she realised in surprise that she was hungry.

'How's the mother?'

Sam jumped when Khalid appeared at her side, her heart racing as she fought to get a grip. She was tired after the long night attending to her patient and emotionally raw too. It took a lot of effort to maintain an outward show of composure.

'Not too bad, all things considered. The pains have stopped and I'm hopeful that she won't go into labour just yet, but she's obviously worried about her sons. How are they?'

'Not too good, I'm afraid.' He grimaced. 'The older boy has suffered quite extensive burns and the younger one, although not as badly burned, is very shocked. I've decided that they would be better off in hospital so I just need to make the necessary arrangements to get them there.'

'Surely it would be too much to drive them across the desert,' Sam said worriedly.

'It would. I'll have them transferred by helicopter. That way they should be there within the hour. Is the mother well enough to go with them or is it too risky to move her?'

Sam shook her head. 'No. I think she would be better off going with them. Not only will it stop her worrying so much about the boys but if she does go into labour then at least she will have all the facilities on hand. The baby won't stand much of a chance if it's born out here.'

'Right. That's what we'll do, then. I just wanted to know what you thought.' He gave her a quick smile. 'I didn't want to arrange for her to be moved against your wishes, Sam.'

'Thank you.' Sam returned his smile, feeling a little glow of happiness spring up inside her. It was good to know that he valued her opinion.

It was all systems go after that. Sam returned to the tent and with the aid of one of the women who spoke a little English explained to Jameela what was going to happen. It was obvious that the idea of traveling in the helicopter alarmed her but once she knew that her sons were going as well, she accepted it. Sam checked her over once more, relieved to find that her contractions hadn't started again. It seemed that the drugs she had given Jameela had worked, or they had done for now. All she could do was hope that if Jameela did go into labour, it wouldn't happen until she was safely in the hospital.

Half an hour later the helicopter arrived. It circled the camp, looking for a place to land. Khalid and some of the men had marked out a suitable site and it set down there. As soon as the rotors stopped turning, he and Peter carried the two boys to the helicopter, where they were met by the on-board medics. Once the children were safely aboard, it was time to move Jameela. Sam held her hand while a couple of the women helped her walk to the helicopter. She could feel her trembling and squeezed her fingers.

'It will be fine, Jameela. There's no need to be scared,' she assured her, even though the poor soul couldn't understand a word she said.

Jameela smiled bravely as Sam let her go. She allowed the medics to help her on board and then the doors closed. Sam moved back out of the way, covering her face with her hands when the rotors began to turn, setting up a veritable sandstorm.

'Here.' Khalid pulled her to him, pressing her face against his shoulder as the sand swirled around them. He'd had the foresight to wrap a checked scarf around his head and he pulled it over his nose and mouth as the helicopter lifted off.

Sam clung to him, using his body as a buffer against the downdraught created by the helicopter as it rose. Her skin was stinging from the abrasive touch of the sand but at least she could breathe now that her face was pressed against his shoulder. With a final roar, the helicopter took to the skies and the air began to settle.

Sam raised her head, checking that it was safe to leave the protection of Khalid's shoulder, and found herself staring straight into his eyes. Just for a moment he stared right back at her as though frozen in time and then his head dipped as he claimed her mouth in a searing kiss that seemed to strike right to the very core of her being.

Sam knew she should push him away, knew that she should do anything necessary to stop what was happening, but she was powerless to resist the seductive taste of his mouth. It was only when she heard voices that she managed to break free but she could feel herself trembling, boneshaking tremors that racked her body from head to toe.

Turning, she made her way to the four-by-four, afraid to

stop, afraid to look back, afraid to do anything that would
acknowledge what a fool she was. She had no idea why
Khalid had kissed her but it didn't matter. The only thing
that mattered was that she had wanted his kiss, wanted it
desperately even though she knew how stupid it was. Tears
filled her eyes as she climbed into the vehicle. She wasn't
over him, as she had believed. She couldn't be. Not when
he could make her feel like this.

KHALID WAS RELIEVED when they arrived back at their camp.
He got out of the vehicle, leaving Peter and Sam to sort
out their supplies. Normally, he would have helped them,
but he couldn't face it, couldn't face the thought of making conversation with Sam after what had happened. His
mouth thinned as he strode into the men's tent. Why in
the name of all that was holy had he kissed her? He hadn't
planned on doing it, yet the moment he had looked into
her eyes he had felt this overwhelming need to feel her
mouth under his.

He cursed under his breath, aware that he had done the
very thing he had sworn he wouldn't do. He had kissed
Sam, held her close, tasted the sweetness of her lips, and it
was going to be impossible to ignore what had happened.
Even if he never mentioned it again, Sam knew how much
he had wanted her and that was the last thing he needed.
To know that *she* knew he was so vulnerable was more
than he could bear.

Khalid went into the bathroom and stripped off his
dusty clothes. Stepping into the shower, he tried to work
out what he was going to say to her. He needed an excuse,
a bona fide reason to explain why he had kissed her, but
for the life of him he couldn't come up with anything. He
could hardly admit that he had been so overcome with de-

sire that he hadn't been able to stop himself kissing her, could he?

By the time he had dressed again, their first patients were starting to arrive. Han was sorting them out, giving everyone a number so they could be seen in turn. Khalid nodded to him as he made his way to his desk. Maybe it would be best to ignore what had happened and concentrate on the job he had come to do. Explaining his actions could cause more harm than good. He looked up as his first patient approached his desk and felt his heart grind to a halt when out of the corner of his eye he saw Sam come in. She glanced across at him then looked away when she realised he was watching her.

Khalid sighed. There was no point fooling himself. It wouldn't be possible to ignore that kiss when he and Sam had to work together. He had to think of an explanation for what had happened, one that had little bearing on the truth too.

IT WAS ANOTHER busy session. By the time clinic ended, Sam was reeling from exhaustion. She gathered up her notes, smiling her thanks when Aminah offered to file them for her.

'Thank you. I think I'll go and have a lie down before lunch,' she told the other woman. 'I feel absolutely shattered.'

'It's little wonder when you were up all night,' Aminah said solicitously. 'I shall attend to the notes and restock the shelves ready for this afternoon's clinic.'

Sam thanked her again then made her way to the women's tent. Jess was already there and she grimaced when Sam went in.

'How are you? Peter told me what happened. You must be exhausted.'

'I am rather,' Sam admitted, kicking off her shoes and lying down on her bed. She sighed. 'Has Peter heard how the children and their mother are doing?'

'No, not yet.' Jess shook her head. 'He said one of the boys was very badly injured, though. It didn't sound too hopeful to me.'

'Let's just pray for a miracle,' Sam said softly.

She closed her eyes, not wanting to discuss the night's events. She wanted to forget what had happened and especially what had gone on that morning. Heat poured through her veins as she recalled the feel of Khalid's mouth on hers. It might be six years since he had kissed her but she would have recognised the taste and feel of his lips anywhere. Why had he done it, though? What had possessed him to kiss her when they both knew it wasn't going to lead anywhere? Or did he think that he could pick up where he had left off and she wouldn't object?

The thought made anger flash through her. She wasn't going to become his plaything, if that's what he hoped. She valued herself far too highly for that. And the next time she saw him she would make it clear that if he had any ideas along those lines, he could forget them.

THE DAY CAME to an end at last. Khalid gathered together his notes and took them over to the filing cabinet. He felt weary beyond belief, the busy day coming on top of the long night completely sapping his energy levels. He was the last to leave and he paused in the doorway, wondering if he could be bothered going for dinner. Although he knew that he should eat, it seemed too much of an effort, especially when he would have to face Sam.

He groaned. What on earth was he going to say to her about that kiss? The whole time he had been attending to his patients he had kept churning it over in the back of his mind, but he was no closer to finding an answer. How could he explain why he had experienced that burning need to feel her mouth under his when he didn't understand it himself?

His expression was grim as he bypassed the canteen. His tent was mercifully empty, the other occupants obviously having decided to go for dinner. Throwing himself down on his bed, Khalid stared at the canvas ceiling, wondering what to do. After all, nothing had changed. If he and Sam got involved again then she would end up getting hurt. And that was the one thing he had always wanted to avoid.

'Can I have a word?'

Khalid sat bolt upright when he recognised Sam's voice. She was standing just inside the entrance to the tent and he could tell immediately how tense she was. His heart began to race as he got to his feet because it was obvious why she had come. She wanted to know what was going on and it was up to him to find some sort of an explanation—if he could.

'Of course. Is there a problem?' he asked, stalling for time.

'I think so, yes.'

She stared back at him and Khalid felt his stomach sink when he saw the anger in her eyes. It was obvious that she had no intention of allowing him to fob her off, so he would have to come up with a really good reason to explain his actions.

'Why did you kiss me, Khalid? Was it because you thought it would be amusing to use me as your own personal plaything? Because if that's the case then you are sadly mistaken. I value myself too much to become any man's toy. Including yours.'

CHAPTER EIGHT

Sam could feel her heart racing as she waited for Khalid to answer. Maybe she could have couched the question a little more tactfully but she had no intention of tiptoeing around him. If Khalid was playing games with her then he needed to understand that she wasn't going to co-operate.

'You are getting things completely out of proportion.'

His voice was icy. Sam felt a shiver inch its way down her spine and fought to control it. She stared back at him, realising that he had never looked more unapproachable than he did at that moment as he pinned her with a look of disdain. However, if he hoped to deflect any more awkward questions by adopting that attitude, he could think again. He might be a royal prince, he might be rich and powerful beyond most people's wildest dreams, but that meant nothing as far as she was concerned. The only thing that mattered was the fact that he thought he could toy with her affections as he had toyed with them once before.

Anger surged through her and she glared at him. 'Am I indeed? So that kiss was the result of what exactly? Friendship? Lust? Old times' sake? Come on, Khalid, you're the one with all the answers so you explain it to me.'

'I don't need to explain myself.'

He stared back at her, his handsome face looking as though it had been carved from stone. In other circumstances, Sam knew she would have found it intimidating to be on the receiving end of a look like that, but not now. Not when anger was bubbling inside her like red-hot lava. It was as though all the years of injustice she had suffered because of her background had melded together, chasing away any qualms she might have had.

'I disagree.' She laughed harshly. 'I'm sorry, Khalid, but I'm not one of your *subjects*. I have no intention of bowing and scraping before you if that's what you're hoping. I asked you a simple enough question and I expect an answer.'

'It happened, Sam, and it won't happen again. As far as I'm concerned that's the end of the matter.'

He went to step around her but she put out her hand and stopped him. 'And I'm expected to be happy with that, am I?' Tipping back her head, she glared up at him. 'I'm sorry, Khalid, but it's not good enough. I want to know why you kissed me when it's the last thing that should have happened.'

'I don't know why!'

Anger flared in his eyes yet she sensed that it wasn't directed at her but at himself. Heat flowed through her veins because it was the last thing she had expected. Khalid was always so in control, always able to harness his emotions and direct them whichever way he wanted them to go. She only had to remember that last night, when they had come so close to making love, to have all the proof she needed of that. And yet all of a sudden she realised that he wasn't in control anymore, that his emotions were leading him and not the other way round, and it scared her. If Khalid couldn't control his emotions then what hope was there of her controlling hers?

She didn't try to stop him again as he shrugged off her hand and left. Something warned her that it would be too dangerous. She could feel the echo of all those feelings swirling around her and shuddered. She left the tent but instead of going to join the others, she made her way to the very perimeter of the camp.

Crouching down, she stared out into the blackness of the desert, thinking about what had happened. Even when they had been on the point of making love, Khalid had managed to draw back—he hadn't allowed his desire to dictate his actions. She could never have done that. If he hadn't stopped that night then she would have made love with him and suffered even more afterwards because of it. Was that why he had called a halt, she wondered, because he hadn't wanted to hurt her any more?

She had never considered the idea before and yet all of a sudden she knew it was true. Khalid had been trying to protect her and it cast a wholly different light on what had happened six years ago. He hadn't been trying to protect himself and his reputation, as she had believed, but her.

Sam took a deep breath, feeling the little knot of hurt that had lain in her heart for all these years unravel. To know that Khalid had cared about her to such an extent changed everything, even though she wasn't sure why it should have done.

THE REST OF the week passed in a blur. Khalid measured the days by the number of patients he saw. It seemed safer that way, less stressful to concentrate on the job he had come to do rather than to think about the mess he had made of things with Sam.

There wasn't a moment when he didn't regret that kiss, not a second when he didn't wish it hadn't happened, but there was nothing he could do about it. All he could do was try to put it behind him and hope that Sam would do the same. He certainly didn't relish the thought of her demanding to know why he had kissed her again! Not when he had made such a hash of explaining it the first time. He had come so close to allowing his emotions to take over and the thought made his insides churn. Sam must never guess just how much he had wanted her.

They packed up on the Sunday, ready to move the camp to a fresh site. It was a long and laborious job but if they were to treat as many people as possible, it was essential that they move around. It was the middle of the afternoon by the time everything was loaded onto the trucks and Khalid could tell that everyone was weary. They planned to leave straight after breakfast the following day and travel to the new site while it was still relatively cool. He came to a swift decision, sensing that they all needed a break.

'I don't know about you but I could do with some down time after all that packing. Anyone fancy a barbeque?'

'You mean here?' Peter queried, looking unenthusiastically at the remains of their camp.

'No, out in the desert.' Khalid laughed. 'It's years since I did anything like that but it should be fun. What do you say?'

'You can count me in,' Jess told him cheerfully. 'So long as I don't have to do the cooking. I'm the world's worst cook even in a kitchen so pity help you if you let me loose with a barbie!'

'Right, you're excused cooking duties,' Khalid told her with a grin. He looked around the group, his heart performing that odd tumbling movement it had started doing lately whenever he looked at Sam. It was an effort not to let her see how on edge he felt. 'What about you, Sam? Are you up for it?'

'Why not?' She gave a little shrug, making it clear that she didn't care one way or the other, and for some reason Khalid felt a tiny bit hurt, not that he showed it, of course.

Everyone else eagerly agreed that it was a great idea so in a very short time everything was organised. They packed what they needed into the four-by-fours and Khalid decided to drive one himself. It was a while since he had driven in the desert at night and it would be good to get in some practice. Jess, Aminah, Peter and Han opted to travel with him, which left Anna, Tom and Sam to go with their driver. Khalid waited while they took their seats, refusing to speculate as to why Sam had chosen not to travel with him. It was obvious why when she wanted to avoid him.

He pushed the thought to the back of his mind as they set off. Although he knew the area quite well, it didn't pay to be too complacent and he needed to concentrate. There was a wadi a few miles away that he had visited several times with his father and he headed in that direction, using the vehicle's on-board navigation system to guide him. The sun was setting now, casting deep shadows across the landscape and making it difficult to pick out familiar landmarks; however, the navigation system helped. Within a very short time they reached their destination only to discover that they weren't the only people who had chosen to spend the evening there. A group of desert tribesmen had set up camp in the wadi. Khalid drew the vehicle to a halt, knowing that it was essential to observe the proprieties.

'I'll just go and introduce myself,' he explained to the others.

'Are you sure they're happy to have visitors?' Jess asked nervously, glancing at the men. Several of them were holding rifles and it was obvious that she found the sight intimidating.

Khalid smiled reassuringly. 'The desert people are very hospitable. They will be insulted if we don't stay. Ignore the guns. It's tradition to be armed when you encounter strangers.'

'Well, if you say so.'

Jess didn't sound convinced but Khalid knew there was no reason to worry. Getting out of the car, he strode over to the leader of the group and introduced himself. It appeared that it was a stag night; the man's son was to be married in a few days' time and the men had come to the wadi to celebrate. They exchanged the usual courtesies and, as he'd expected, they were invited to join them. A fire had already been lit and a whole sheep was roasting on a spit.

Khalid went back and explained all this to the rest of the team, then he and their driver carried over the boxes of supplies they had brought with them so that everyone could share their food. He glanced around, feeling his spirits lift as he watched the members of his party mingling with their hosts. So far they had only come into contact with people who had needed their help and it would be good for them to be able to get a better idea of the nomadic lifestyle. Knowing how people lived was the key to a better understanding.

His gaze alighted on Sam, who was crouched down beside the fire, talking to the youngest member of the party, a boy in his early teens, and he felt his heart ache. Sam fitted in so well here. She seemed to have a genuine rapport with the people as well as an appreciation of the desert. It would be so easy to imagine that she could happily live here but it would be a mistake. A few months coping with this kind of life was one thing but it would be vastly different to live in Azad on a permanent basis and he must never forget that.

SAM ACCEPTED THE plate of mutton their host offered her with a smile of thanks. Night had fallen now and beyond the circle of light cast by the fire the desert was pitch black. Somewhere in the darkness an animal screamed and she jumped.

'A desert fox out hunting for prey,' a voice said beside her. 'The noise they make is really eerie, isn't it?'

She glanced up when she recognised Khalid's voice and did her best to control the thunderous beating of her heart. He looked so at home in this environment, so *right*, that she felt her senses swirl for a second before she managed to control them. She couldn't afford to be seduced by the romance of the moment. This desert prince wasn't going to sweep her off her feet and have his wicked way with her, if she had any sense!

'It is. Really eerie. It sounded almost like a child screaming,' she murmured, glad of the darkness because it helped to disguise the colour that flooded her cheeks.

She had never considered herself to be an overly romantic person; she was far too practical. However, there was little doubt that the desert seemed to be casting a spell over her. There was something beguiling about the vastness of the black velvet sky overhead, the brightness of the stars, the scent of meat roasting mingled with the sweetness of incense that stirred her senses. She felt incredibly vulnerable and it was a scary feeling in view of what had happened the other day.

Sam sighed as she bit into the succulent meat. Everything came back to that kiss. It was as though it had imprinted itself into her mind and it was impossible to shift it. Maybe it would have helped if Khalid had explained why it had happened but he seemed to have drawn a line under the event and that was it. Oh, she could try to make him explain but what was the point when he obviously wanted to forget it? The more she probed, the greater the chance that he would realise how much it had affected her, and that was the last thing she needed. She wanted him to believe that she was as indifferent to him as he appeared to be to her.

'This meat's delicious,' she said, changing the subject. 'It tastes miles better than your usual barbeque food.'

'Probably the wood they use for the fire.' He crouched down beside her, taking a piece of meat off his own plate and biting into it.

Sam looked away when she saw his strong white teeth close over the piece of mutton. She didn't need anything else to stir her senses tonight. She just wanted to get through the evening and hope that tomorrow she would be back on a more even keel. Once she was able to focus on work again, it would be that much easier to take control of her emotions. It was just out here, in the desert, with the blackness of the night forming a cocoon of intimacy around them, that it was proving so difficult.

They finished their meal and accepted the cups of coffee that were served at the end. It was thick and black and incredibly sweet but delicious despite all that. Sam put the tiny cup down on the brass tray as someone started to play some music. Leaning back on her elbows, she watched as a couple of the men began to dance. They whirled around, moving faster and faster while the rest of the party clapped and cheered. When one of the men beckoned to Khalid, inviting him to join them, she didn't expect him to comply, but he did.

Joining the group of men, he began to dance, his feet flying as he spun round in time to the music. He possessed a natural grace and Sam found that she couldn't drag her gaze away. When the music finally came to an end, her heart was pounding and her breathing was as laboured as though she had taken part as well. Khalid came over to them, grinning when Anna dryly remarked that he had kept his skills as a dancer very quiet.

'It's been years since I danced like that,' he admitted, sinking down onto the ground. 'I'm afraid I'm rather rusty.'

'You looked pretty good to me,' Anna observed. She glanced at Sam. 'I'd give him a gold star, wouldn't you, Sam?'

'I…ehem… Yes.'

Sam dredged up a smile but it was an effort. This was yet another side of Khalid that she hadn't known existed and it was worrying to discover how little she really knew about him. Thankfully, Peter provided a welcome distraction when he accepted the men's invitation to join them. His dancing was nowhere near as good as Khalid's, although he gave it his best shot. He was out of breath when he came back.

'Not really my forte,' he gasped, flopping down on the ground.

'Never mind. You can't be good at everything,' Jess assured him.

Sam saw the look that passed between them and bit back a sigh. It was obvious that Jess and Peter were growing very fond of one another and, while she was happy for them, it seemed to highlight her own single status. Her eyes drifted to Khalid, who was speaking to Tom, and she felt her heart ache.

Would she meet someone and fall in love or would her background once again prove to be the sticking point? She had honestly thought that she and Adam could make a go of things but it hadn't worked any more than it had done with Khalid. Maybe he had wanted to protect her, but at the end of the day he must have had concerns about the embarrassment it could have caused his family to have her name linked with theirs. It might be better if she accepted that she would never enjoy the kind of close and loving relationship she had always dreamt about.

THEY SET UP camp at the new site the following day. Khalid supervised as the crates containing the more fragile items of equipment were unloaded. They were quicker setting up this time, past experience helping to iron out any problems. By the time lunch was served, everything was ready.

Khalid made his way to the canteen and joined Peter and Han. Once again the women had opted to sit together and he was relieved. Last night had unsettled him even more and he needed time to get himself in hand before he spoke to Sam. They'd been too busy with the move this morning but now that everything was set up, he couldn't avoid her. After all, she was a vital member of the team and it would seem odd if he ignored her.

They were just finishing their coffee when the sound of a helicopter overhead alerted them to the fact that they had visitors. Khalid left the tent, shading his eyes as he watched it set down a short distance away. From its livery, he knew it belonged to the royal flight, although he had no idea who was on board. He smiled in delight when he saw his brother, Shahzad, alighting.

'This is a surprise,' he declared, hurrying forward to greet him. 'Welcome!' His smile widened when he saw his two little nieces being helped out as well. Bending down, he kissed them. 'How did you manage to persuade Papa to bring you to see me?'

'Mama keeps being sick,' six-year-old Janan told him importantly. 'She told Papa that she wanted to be on her own. Didn't she, Izdihar?'

Three-year-old Izdihar nodded, her thumb sliding into her mouth, and Khalid laughed. 'Well, I can understand that. Come. I shall introduce you to all the doctors and nurses then show you where we see all the sick people.'

'And make them better?' Janan put in knowledgeably.

'Hopefully, yes.' Khalid agreed, smiling wryly at his

brother as he led the girls over to where the rest of the team were waiting. He quickly introduced everyone, his heart catching when he saw how gentle Sam was with the children and how they immediately responded to her. When she offered to show them around the camp, they begged their father to let them go with her.

'They will be quite safe with Sam,' Khalid said quietly, when his brother hesitated. 'She won't let any harm come to them.'

'In that case, thank you.' Shahzad bowed to Sam as she took hold of the children's hands. He watched as they skipped along beside her as she led them to the canteen first to get a drink. Turning, he fixed Khalid with a searching look. 'Am I right to think that Sam is the woman you were involved with some years ago?'

'Yes.' Khalid changed the subject. Although he and Shahzad were close, he didn't intend to confide in him. It wouldn't help to lay out all his uncertainties for inspection; it would just confuse the issue even more. 'So, brother, delighted as I am to see you, is this purely a social visit or is there another reason for it?'

'How did you guess?' Shahzad sighed. 'I am worried about Mariam. She is pregnant again, only this time she seems to be experiencing all sorts of problems she never suffered when she was expecting the girls.'

'First of all, congratulations! I know how much you both want another child.' Khalid led the way to the men's tent and offered Shahzad the one and only chair.

'We do. We were thrilled when we discovered she was expecting another child. But she's been so ill—constantly sick and exhausted. I have to confess that I am extremely worried about her.'

'I take it that Mariam has seen her doctor?' Khalid said quietly.

'Yes, several times, but he cannot find anything wrong with her. He keeps insisting that it will pass and that she will feel better in time but she is four months pregnant now and she still doesn't feel right.'

'So what do you intend to do? Seek a second opinion?'

'Yes.' Shahzad sighed. 'However, Mariam feels that it would be unfair to cast any doubt on her doctor's capabilities. You know how quickly rumours spread and it could do him untold harm so she is reluctant to take that route. I certainly don't want her worrying at the moment so I suggested that she seek a second opinion from the obstetrician you have brought with you. If you agree, obviously.'

'Of course. I'm sure that Sam will be only too pleased to help.'

'Ah, so it is the young woman who is looking after Janan and Izdihar,' Shahzad said quietly.

'That's right. Sam very kindly stepped in when the obstetrician who was originally to accompany us had to back out.'

Khalid summoned a smile although he couldn't help feeling uneasy. Introducing Sam to his family was a step he would have preferred not to take, although not for the reasons she would undoubtedly assume. He sighed. Seeing Sam interacting with the people he loved would make it that much harder for him to view her solely as a colleague and that was what he needed to do. Desperately.

'Then can I prevail upon you to ask her if she would be willing to see Mariam? It would be a huge relief to us both to have a second opinion. It would definitely stop Mariam worrying and that is bound to ease the situation.'

How could he refuse? Even though it was the last thing he wanted, Khalid knew that he didn't have a choice. Shahzad's fears for his wife would be all the greater seeing as his own mother had died giving birth to him. It would be unforgiveable to allow Shahzad to suffer any longer if he could do something to help.

'Of course. I shall ask her when she brings the children back.'

'Thank you.'

Shahzad clapped him on the shoulder, looking so relieved that Khalid knew that he had made the right decision. At his suggestion they made their way to Theatre so that his brother could see the equipment he had so generously paid for. There was no sign of Sam and the children and Khalid was glad. He needed to get this into perspective, stop making a mountain out of a very small molehill. So Sam was going be involved with his family for a brief time—so what? It wouldn't change the status quo, wouldn't make him change *his* mind. She could never be part of his life and that was that…only it wasn't that simple, was it? Not simple at all to see her interacting with the people he loved.

SAM RETURNED HER young charges to their father, shaking her head when Shahzad asked her if they had been any trouble. 'No trouble at all,' she assured him, and meant it too. The little girls had been a positive delight, eager to see as much as they could of the camp. She laughed when they both clamoured for a kiss. Bending, she kissed their soft little cheeks, feeling a wealth of tenderness fill her. Despite their privileged background, they were lovely children and she had enjoyed spending time with them.

She straightened up, realising that it was time that she got ready for her patients. Clinic was due to begin at three and it was almost that now. She turned to leave then stopped when Khalid appeared.

'May I have a word with you, Sam?' he asked politely.

'Of course.'

Sam followed as he led the way to a spot near to the perimeter of the camp. He paused, staring out across the desert, and she had the distinct impression that he had something on his mind. Turning, he summoned a smile but she could tell how tense he was and reacted instinctively. Whatever he had to say, she had a feeling it wouldn't come easily to him.

'So what is it, Khalid? Is something wrong? Have *I* done something wrong?' she demanded, wanting to get it over as quickly as possible.

'No, of course not.' He drew himself up, his face expressionless as he looked at her. 'Shahzad's wife is expecting another child. Whilst they are both delighted, my brother is extremely worried about Mariam. She isn't at all well and although she has consulted her own doctor, who has told her not to worry, they both feel it would help to have a second opinion.'

'I see.' She shrugged, unsure where this was leading. 'Not a problem, I imagine. You told me that there is a comprehensive health care system in the cities so there must be other obstetricians your sister-in-law can consult.'

'Indeed. However, they are both keen not to cast any doubts on Mariam's doctor's proficiency.' His eyes met hers. 'In a country as small as Azad, rumours soon abound, which is why Shahzad has asked if you would be willing to examine Mariam. I told him that I would ask you.'

Sam bit her lip, unsure how she felt about the request. In other circumstances, she would have agreed immediately, subject to Mariam's own doctor's approval, of course. However, was it wise to involve herself this way, to get to know Khalid's family when he had gone to such lengths to keep her away from them? He had never introduced her to any members of his family. Although his brother and sister-in-law had visited London several times while they had been seeing one another, Khalid had made no attempt to introduce her to them. Sam had thought it rather strange at the time until she'd realised that he hadn't wanted his family to become involved with a woman like her when it could reflect badly on them. Now she looked him squarely in the eyes.

'Do you honestly believe it's wise to involve me, Khalid? What if someone finds out and decides to dig into my past? No one can claim that I appear to be the ideal candidate to give advice about a royal baby!'

'There is very little chance of anyone finding out, I assure you.' His voice was harsh, edged with an arrogance that immediately put her back up.

'You could be right. After all, you have the money and the power to call the shots, don't you?' She laughed bitterly. 'It all depends what you consider is important. Obviously this is, although our relationship—such as it was—evidently wasn't.'

'That's not fair. It's not even true,' he began, but she didn't allow him to finish. There was no point.

She held up her hand. 'Forget it. It doesn't matter now. If your brother and sister-in-law feel it would help then I shall be happy to give a second opinion, subject to Mariam's own doctor's agreement, obviously.'

'Of course.'

His face closed up, his dark eyes unreadable as he pinned her with a searching look. Sam had no idea what he was looking for and didn't waste time worrying about it either. Turning, she made her way to the clinic and got ready for her first patient. So long as her every waking thought was channelled towards her patients she would survive. And once she left Azad she could get back to normal and carry on with the life she had created for herself.

Tears stung her eyes but she blinked them away. She

wouldn't think about how much she would miss Khalid, wouldn't waste time thinking *if only*. Their relationship would never have survived the pressures that would have been put upon it. She knew that even if it hurt.

CHAPTER NINE

Khalid saw his brother and nieces off then went into the clinic. There were already patients waiting to see him so he told Han to fetch in the first one. It was an elderly man who had broken his leg in a fall. Although the fracture had started to heal, it was immediately apparent from the angle of the lower leg that it needed re-setting if it wasn't to cause the old man problems in the future.

Khalid explained what needed to be done to the man and his son, who had accompanied him. It was obvious that they were both unhappy at the thought of him having to break the leg again but he managed to convince them that it would for the best. Their nomadic lifestyle would make it extremely difficult for the father if he was left with a badly deformed limb.

He booked the man in for surgery the following afternoon and made a note to ask Tom to check him over prior to administering the anaesthetic. Once that was done, he worked his way through the rest of his patients, adding a couple more to his list of people requiring surgery. Life in the desert was harsh and accidents occurred frequently so it was little wonder that so many folk required treatment. It confirmed his decision to try to set up a permanent clinic, even though he knew how difficult it would be to get the idea off the ground. Just finding suitably qualified staff willing to work there would be a major undertaking for a start.

'That's me done.' Peter came to join him, perching on the edge of the desk. 'Several more cases of TB, as expected, plus a patient with a rather nasty cough that sounded highly suspicious.' He sighed. 'I've booked him in for a chest X-ray tomorrow, although I already suspect what it's going to show.'

'Cancer is no respecter of circumstances,' Khalid agreed quietly. Out of the corner of his eye, he saw Sam get up and leave her desk. She'd had a busy afternoon as well from the number of files she was carrying, he thought.

She glanced round and he looked away when he felt her gaze land on him. He could see the scorn in her eyes—feel it even!—and it made him feel worse than ever. Why hadn't he explained why he had ended their relationship when he'd had the chance? If he had told her the truth, that it hadn't been the damage it could cause to his family's reputation that had made him do it but the harm it might cause *her*, then maybe she wouldn't be looking at him like that right now.

He started to push back his chair then realised what he was doing. What was the point of raking it all up again? Maybe it would salve his conscience but it wouldn't change things, not really. He and Sam could never be together. She would end up resenting him for taking away everything she held dear: her career and her freedom to be the person she was. Oh, maybe it would work at first but eventually, inevitably, she would come to hate him for ruining her life and he couldn't bear that, couldn't bear to watch her love turn to loathing, not that she gave much sign of loving him these days.

Khalid sank back down onto his seat, turning so that he wouldn't have to watch her leave and be tempted to do

something he would only regret. There was no going back
and no going forward either. Not for him and Sam.

SAM FELT ON edge for the rest of the day. Maybe it was that
talk she'd had with Khalid earlier but she couldn't seem to
settle. Once dinner was over, she returned to the tent and
dug out the novel she had been meaning to read for ages
only had never found the time. It had received glowing re-
views but it failed to hold her attention. She kept thinking
about Khalid's request that she should see Mariam, churning it over and searching for a way out, but she couldn't
come up with anything plausible. His sister-in-law had
asked for her help and how could she refuse when there
was no real reason to do so? She was a doctor first and
foremost; her patients took priority over her own feelings.

By the time morning dawned, she had accepted the
inevitable and just wanted to get it over. When she saw
Khalid leaving the canteen, she hurried after him. He was
dressed in theatre scrubs, pale blue cotton trousers and a
matching top, that made his olive skin appear darker than
ever. His body was lithe and muscular beneath the lightweight fabric, the perfectly toned muscles in his chest and
abdomen making it clear that he took good care of himself.
He had told her once that orthopaedic surgery could be
physically demanding and that it required strength as well
as skill to put broken bones back together. Keeping himself
fit was all part of the job as he saw it and not merely an indulgence. The fact that he looked so good was irrelevant.

'Can I have a word?' she said hurriedly, not wanting to
get sidetracked. How Khalid looked wasn't important and
she would be well advised to remember that.

'Of course.' He stopped, waiting in silence to hear what
she had to say, and Sam felt a ripple of annoyance run

through her. Did he need to make it so abundantly clear that he had no interest in her?

'I was wondering if you'd settled on a date for me to see your sister-in-law. The sooner I examine her, the better, from what you told me.'

'Indeed. Shahzad is anxious that Mariam should stop worrying and asked if you would be available this Sunday.'

Sam laughed at the formality of the request. 'Well, I can't think of anything else I'll be doing. Of course, I shall need to check my diary but I don't think I have any dinner engagements or red-carpet functions to attend.'

'Good.' A smile curved his generous mouth, softening his expression in a way that made her pulse leap. 'I wouldn't like it to interfere with your social life, Sam. That would never do.'

'No fear of that, I assure you. My social life, as you call it, doesn't exist.' She gave a little shrug when she saw his brows rise, wishing she hadn't said that. 'Work seems to fill most of my days.'

'I see. So you aren't seeing anyone at the present time?'

'No. I've had my fill of relationships, believe me. I'm happy to be single these days—it's a lot less stressful.'

'But you did get engaged last year,' he said quietly. He must have seen her surprise. 'Peter told me, that's how I know.'

'Oh, I see.' She shrugged. 'I expect he also told you that it didn't work out and we split up.'

'Indeed. What was the reason for it?'

'We realised that we weren't suited after all.'

She spun round before he could question her further, not wanting to discuss her reasons for ending her engagement with him. She sighed as she made her way to the clinic. She had seen umpteen articles in the newspapers over the years about Khalid, linking him to various beautiful and highly suitable women, so she didn't need to enquire about his love life. There would always be women eager to be seen with Khalid…and much more.

The thought of him sleeping with all those woman was like a dagger being thrust through in her heart and she sucked in her breath. Khalid was a handsome, virile man, and even without the added lure of his wealth and status he would have attracted women by the score. There was no point her wishing that the situation wasn't so because it wouldn't change anything. Khalid was free to sleep with whoever he liked and it had nothing to do with her.

SUNDAY DAWNED, THE sun rising in a ball of fire above the horizon. Khalid stood at the perimeter of the camp and watched the desert slowly reappear from the night-time gloom. He hadn't slept. He had simply laid awake waiting for the morning to come. Maybe it was foolish to set such store by what was about to happen but he couldn't help it. Seeing Sam with his brother and sister-in-law wasn't going to be easy. That was the reason why he had shied away from introducing her to them six years ago. He had known that once there was that connection, it would be even harder to draw back. Now, today, it was going to happen and even though there was no reason to view the coming meeting as anything more than a professional obligation, he knew it was going to be difficult.

The sound of a helicopter cut through his musings. His brother had said he would send the helicopter to fetch them early and he had kept his word. Khalid swung round, meaning to go and check if Sam was ready, but she was already crossing the compound. His heart gave a small jolt then started beating faster than normal as he took stock. Her clothes were simple—white cotton jeans teamed with a pale blue shirt with a heavy knit sweater looped around

her shoulders for added warmth against the dawn chill—
but she still managed to look stunning.

She'd obviously just washed her hair because damp tendrils curled around her face, making his fingers itch to
smooth them behind her ears as she stopped beside him.
She looked so young and lovely, so fresh and desirable
that he was overwhelmed by desire. It took every scrap of
control he could muster to look calmly at her when what
he really wanted to do was haul her into his arms and kiss
her until they were both unable to think clearly.

'I take it that's our taxi,' she said, glancing skywards.

'Yes. Shahzad said he'd make it an early start and it
looks like he meant it,' he agreed, relieved to hear that he
sounded normal even if he didn't feel it.

'I imagine he's anxious to hear my opinion,' Sam observed, shading her eyes as she watched the helicopter set
down a short distance away.

'Indeed.' Khalid glanced at the helicopter, trying not
to recall what had happened when the medevac helicopter had collected Jameela and her children. It was pointless going down that route and dangerous too. He didn't
intend to kiss Sam again, not if he had any sense. Turning, he forced himself to smile politely at her. 'So, do you
have everything you need?'

'I just need to fetch my bag and that's it.'

She didn't return his smile as she made her way over to
the clinic and Khalid swallowed his sigh. The days when
Sam had smiled at him with true affection in her eyes
were long gone and it was stupid to dwell on how much
he missed those times. He went and had a word with the
pilot instead, checking that his brother was where he had
said he would be.

Shahzad and Mariam had a house on the outskirts of
Zadra City and spent most of their time there, preferring

it to the more formal surroundings of the royal palace. Although they were realistic enough to know that they couldn't ignore their status, they were anxious to ensure that their children grew up in a less rarefied atmosphere and he applauded them for it. It seemed to be paying dividends too because his small nieces were delightfully unspoiled. If he ever had children of his own, he would be more than happy if they turned out as well as the girls had done.

The thought was like a tiny dagger pricking his heart. Khalid tried to put it out of his mind as Sam came back with her case. She climbed on board and got herself settled, placing the bag on the seat next to her. Khalid took the hint and moved further back, not wanting to make an issue of it. So she wanted to sit by herself, so what? It didn't make a scrap of difference to him…only it did if he was honest.

He strapped himself in as the pilot lifted off, wishing that he could feel as indifferent as he was pretending to be. He'd never felt this way before, so edgy and unsure, so uncertain about everything he did. He was used to being in control of himself and his life but it was proving difficult around Sam. She seemed to upset his world, make even the easiest decision far more complicated than it should have been.

He sighed as the helicopter swung round in a slow circle and headed back the way it had come. His life felt very much like this, spinning in circles, and it had to stop. He had to decide what he wanted and go for it without allowing anything to distract him. It was what he had always done in the past, set himself a goal and worked towards it, so it shouldn't be that difficult. All he needed to do was to work out what he wanted to achieve in the next couple of years and not allow anything to throw him off course.

Closing his eyes, Khalid started to work out exactly

what he intended to do with his life. Although he had enjoyed working in England, he realised that he wanted to play a bigger part in improving the health of the people in his own country. It would be difficult to set up clinics to provide access to healthcare for the desert people, but it was what he intended to do. Money wasn't an issue, fortunately: his father was generous to a fault and could be relied on to provide the necessary backing. No, it was the logistics of finding suitably qualified staff to run the clinics that would be the biggest problem, but he would find a way round that.

And once that was done then he would have to think about his own life, and what he wanted from it too, decide if that family he'd thought about so often recently was a possibility. It all depended on him finding the right woman, of course, and that could prove to be the major sticking point. She would have to be very special if he planned to spend the rest of his life with her.

His eyes opened and went immediately to Sam while he felt his heart ache. Despite the number of women he had dated over the years there had only ever been one woman he had wanted that way and that was Sam.

IT TOOK LESS than an hour to reach their destination. The sun was still climbing into the sky when the helicopter touched down, gilding the pale sandstone walls of the buildings with rosy-gold light. Sam picked up her case, nodding her thanks when the pilot helped her to disembark. There was a car standing by to collect them and she followed as Khalid led the way over to it.

He opened the rear door for her, waiting while she slid into the seat. He hadn't said a word on the journey but, then, she hadn't given him a chance to do so. Now she summoned a smile, feeling that it would be easier if she at least attempted to observe the niceties. There was no point making this any more stressful than it was.

'Thank you. It didn't take as long as I thought it would to get here.'

'No?' He gave a small shrug, immediately drawing her attention to the solid width of his shoulders. 'I should have mentioned that Shahzad and Mariam live outside the city. They prefer the more informal atmosphere here to raise the girls. They don't want them to get too spoiled.'

'Well, it seems to have worked. They are lovely children,' Sam said truthfully.

'They are indeed.' He smiled at her with genuine warmth. 'They certainly took a liking to you.'

'That's nice to know.'

Sam returned his smile then made a great production out of fastening her seat belt to avoid looking at him. She let out a sigh as he closed the door and got into the front next to the driver. She had to get a grip, had to stop getting carried away each time Khalid smiled at her. Of course he was pleased that she had praised his nieces. It had been obvious the other day how fond of them he was but it didn't mean anything, not personally. About her. Khalid would have smiled just as warmly at anyone who had complimented the two girls.

It was a little deflating to have to face it but Sam knew that she couldn't allow herself to start believing things that weren't true. She stared out of the window as the driver ferried them to the house, concentrating on what she was seeing. Although it was much smaller than the summer palace where they had spent their first night in Azad it was still an imposing building with several turrets rising into the sky. The driver sounded the horn and the gates were opened then they were inside, drawing up in a small courtyard that was a riot of colour. Sam breathed in deeply as she stepped out of the air-conditioned confines of the car, her brows rising when she recognised the delicate aroma. Turning, she stared in amazement at the masses of plants, scarcely able to believe what she was seeing. Roses? Out here in the desert?

'Mariam planted them. She was brought up in England and roses are her favourite flowers. She insisted on having them in her garden when she and Shahzad had the house built. She tends them almost as lovingly as she tends her children.'

The amusement in Khalid's voice made her smile too. 'Well, they are certainly flourishing. The smell is just gorgeous.'

'It is.' Bending, Khalid plucked a delicate pale pink rose off one of the bushes and handed it to her. 'This is one of my favourites. Smell it.'

Sam buried her nose in the satiny petals and inhaled their scent, feeling the blood start to pound through her veins. It didn't mean anything, she told herself sternly, but there was no escaping the fact that it made her feel all shivery inside to have Khalid present her with the beautiful flower. It was a relief when Shahzad and the girls appeared and she was forced to focus on them rather than on what had happened.

'Welcome, welcome! It is such a pleasure to have you both here in our home.' Shahzad bowed, touching his lips and forehead in the traditional greeting.

'It's a pleasure to be here,' Sam replied, mimicking his actions before turning to greet the children. They both clamoured to be kissed so she bent down and kissed them on their soft little cheeks, laughing when they grabbed hold of her hands and started to drag her towards the door. 'Hey, I'm not here to play. I've come to see your mummy.'

'Mama is still in her room,' Janan informed her. 'She's

been sick and Papa told her that she must rest until she feels better.'

'Oh, dear.' Sam glanced at Shahzad and saw the worry in his eyes. She gently untangled herself from the children's grasp and picked up her case. 'I think I'll go and see if there's anything I can do to make her feel more comfortable.'

'You must have something to eat and drink first,' Shahzad demurred, taking his duties as their host very seriously.

'Later, thank you.' Sam smiled at him. 'There will be plenty of time for all that after I've seen your wife.'

'Of course.'

The relief in his voice told its own tale. Sam frowned as he instructed one of the servants to show her the way. It was obvious how worried he was about his wife and she only hoped that she could do something to help.

She followed the young woman inside and along an airy corridor, pausing when the girl indicated that Sam should wait while she knocked on a door. When a voice bade them to enter, she stepped into the room, surprised to discover how modern it was. There was none of the ornate gilding and lavish fabrics that she had expected to see but simple furnishings and fitments in cool neutral colours.

'What a lovely room!' she declared. She smiled at the attractive young woman seated on a daybed in front of the window, taking note of her extreme pallor. It was obvious even from a first glance that Mariam wasn't feeling well and Sam's mind began to race as she ran through a list of possible causes for her continued sickness.

'Thank you. I wanted to create a home that was comfortable for us to live in.' Mariam gave her a sweet smile. 'Whilst I appreciate the beauty of the royal palaces, they are a little too formal for my taste.'

'Well, this is perfect. I'd say you were spot on.' Sam put down her bag and held out her hand. 'Sorry. I should have introduced myself, shouldn't I? I'm Samantha Warren—Sam to my friends so I hope you'll call me that. Your husband told me that you haven't been feeling at all well throughout this pregnancy?'

'No. I haven't. I sailed through my other pregnancies so I can't understand what's wrong this time.' Tears filled Mariam's huge dark eyes. 'I am so afraid that there is something wrong with the baby even though my doctor insists that there is nothing to worry about.'

'It's only natural to worry,' Sam assured her. 'Having sailed through two previous pregnancies, you're bound to feel anxious when this one doesn't seem to be going as you expected. All I can say is that every pregnancy is different and the fact that you aren't blooming this time isn't an indication that there is something wrong with the baby.'

'You honestly believe that?' Mariam said hopefully.

'Oh, yes.' Sam smiled at her. 'I've seen it happen many times, mums who haven't experienced any problems whatsoever during previous pregnancies but who suddenly find themselves feeling dreadful. It's often caused by an imbalance of hormones.

'When you're pregnant, your body produces more of the female sex hormones, oestrogen and progesterone, as well as human placental lactogen and human chorionic gonadotrophin. If the balance isn't right then it affects how you are feeling. The key is to rule out any other potential causes and then simply accept that this time you aren't going to feel on top of the world.' She laughed. 'More often than not that helps to alleviate the problem, funnily enough.'

'Worrying about it makes it worse,' Mariam observed ruefully.

'It can do.' Sam drew up a chair. Opening her case, she

took out her sphygmomanometer. 'Now, let's start with the basics, shall we? I'll check your blood pressure then do a urine test. I take it that your own doctor is happy about you seeking a second opinion?' she asked as she wrapped the blood-pressure cuff around Mariam's arm.

'Not exactly happy, no.' Mariam grimaced. 'However, he could hardly refuse.'

'No, I don't suppose so,' Sam agreed wryly. She inflated the cuff, unsurprised when she discovered that Mariam's blood pressure was a little higher than she would have liked it to be. The stress was taking its toll on her and the sooner they sorted out what was wrong, the better.

Mariam provided a urine sample next and Sam tested that, pleased to find that there was no indication that anything was amiss. Her blood-sugar levels were fine and there was no trace of protein in her urine that could be a sign of pre-eclampsia.

'Right, so far so good. I'd like to examine you now if that's all right.'

'Of course.'

Mariam made herself comfortable while Sam carried out a physical examination. She frowned because to her mind Mariam seemed much larger than she would have expected her to be.

'How many weeks are you now?' she asked, gently feeling the position of the baby.

'Twenty.' Mariam grimaced. 'I'm much bigger than I was with either of the girls.'

'But you are certain of your dates?' Sam clarified. 'You're sure that you haven't made a mistake?'

'No.' Mariam flushed. 'I can pinpoint the exact day this baby was conceived during a trip we made to Paris so there's no doubt in my mind about that. Why are you asking? Is something wrong?'

'No. It's just that you're much bigger than I would have expected you to be at this stage.' Sam stepped away from the couch, frowning as she weighed up what she had learned. 'What did your scan show?'

'I haven't had a scan.' Mariam sat up and straightened her dress. 'I didn't have one with either of the girls either. Shahzad and I both agreed when we decided to start a family that we could never abort a child if it was found to be damaged in some way so there was no point.'

'I see.' Sam packed the sphygmomanometer in her case then sat down. She looked intently at Mariam. 'How do you feel about having a scan if it could help to solve the problem of why you have been feeling so ill?'

'You think there's something wrong with the baby!' Mariam exclaimed, pressing her hand to her throat.

'No. What I think...and I may very well be wrong...is that you're expecting more than one baby.' She took hold of Mariam's hand and squeezed it. 'That would account for the extra amniotic fluid you are carrying, not to mention the fact that you feel so sick and exhausted all the time.'

'More than one baby...' Mariam broke off, obviously stunned by the idea.

'It's possible but we shall need to confirm it. And the best way to do that is by having a scan.'

'But surely I should be able to feel if there's more than one baby growing inside me!' Mariam declared, placing her hand on the swell of her stomach.

'Not necessarily, especially if one baby is lying directly behind the other, as I suspect is the case here.' Sam laughed. 'You may find that you are about to get two for the price of one. How would you feel about that?'

'Ecstatic!'

Mariam laughed out loud at the idea. They were both

still laughing when the door opened and Shahzad appeared. He looked from one to the other and raised his brows.

'I hope you are going to share the joke with me?'

'I'll leave that to your wife.' Sam stood up. She smiled at Mariam. 'I'll get Khalid to make the arrangements, shall I?'

'Please.' Mariam returned her smile, looking so much better than she had done a short while before that Sam found herself crossing her fingers that her suspicions would prove to be correct.

She left Mariam to break the news to her husband, knowing that they needed to be on their own at this special time. Backtracking along the corridor, she went to find Khalid and discovered that he was in the courtyard, sitting on a stone bench beside the fountain. He looked up when he heard her approaching and she could see the concern in his eyes and was warmed by it. Although he might project an image of being indifferent, he truly cared about his family.

'So, do you know what is wrong with Mariam?' he asked as she sat down beside him.

'I think it's possible that she is expecting more than one baby,' Sam informed him.

'But surely her own consultant should have realised that!' he exclaimed.

'Yes. And he would have done if Mariam hadn't refused to have a scan.' She quickly relayed what Mariam had told her and heard him sigh.

'I had no idea they felt like that. If I had done then I would have urged them to have the scan done before now and save themselves all this worry.'

'It's not your fault,' she assured him. She laid her hand on his arm, feeling her skin tingle when it came into contact with his. She knew she should remove her hand but the need to touch him was just too strong to resist. For some reason she needed to feel close to him at this moment. How strange.

'Maybe not. But if I had spent more time with Shahzad then I might have been privy to his beliefs.' He gave a small shrug, causing the muscles in his forearm to flex beneath her fingers. 'It reinforces the decision I've made to spend more time in Azad. Whilst I have enjoyed working in England and appreciate how much I have learned while I've been there, I need to come back home.'

He looked up and his eyes were very dark as they met hers. 'My future lies here. In Azad.'

CHAPTER TEN

The scan confirmed that Sam's suspicions were correct. Mariam was expecting twins, one baby lying directly behind the other, which was why it had gone undetected for so long. Khalid congratulated his brother, hoping that Shahzad couldn't tell how he really felt. Oh, he was delighted by the news—there was no question about that. However, he couldn't pretend that he didn't feel upset about the way Sam had responded when he had told her of his decision to live in Azad permanently. She hadn't tried to make him reconsider, hadn't said anything really, but what had he expected? That she would beg him to stay in England, stay with her? That was never going to happen.

Once they returned from the hospital, Shahzad announced that they needed to celebrate and set about organising an elaborate dinner for them. Given the choice, Khalid would have preferred to return immediately to their camp but there was no way that he could refuse to join in the celebrations. When Sam protested that she had nothing to wear, Mariam whisked her away with the promise of finding her something suitable so there was no escape on that score. Khalid guessed that Sam was as loath to drag out the visit as he was but she too didn't want to put a damper on the evening.

He used one of the guest rooms to shower and change

into some clothes he had left behind the last time he had stayed with his brother. Shahzad was beaming with pride when he tracked him down to the salon, obviously thrilled to bits at the thought of becoming a father again not just once but twice. He handed Khalid a glass of fresh pomegranate juice, raising his own glass aloft to toast the future.

'May we both find everything we are looking for from life.'

Khalid clinked glasses, wishing with all his heart it were that simple. However, what he wanted and what he had to accept were two very different things. He glanced round when he heard footsteps and felt his senses whirl when he saw Sam come into the room. Mariam had kept her word and found Sam something to wear but it was the last thing he had expected to see her dressed in.

In a mesmerised sweep he drank in the picture she made as she stood in the doorway, the azure-blue folds of a traditional Arab dress falling softly around her. She was even wearing a headdress, a lightweight veil trimmed with the same elaborate beading that edged the neckline of her dress. She looked so beautiful that for a moment he couldn't think let alone speak and was grateful for the fact that his brother saved him from standing there looking as though he had been struck dumb.

'You look beautiful, both of you.' Shahzad stepped forward, taking Sam's hand and kissing it.

'Thank you.' Sam smiled but Khalid could tell how tense she was as she came further into the room. She stopped beside the tray of drinks and he hurriedly gathered his wits. It was up to him to make this as stress-free as possible for her. After all, it was just one night, a few short hours to get through before they returned to their camp in the morning. He had endured far worse than this!

'Would you like a drink?' He picked up the jug of pome-

granate juice. 'My brother doesn't drink alcohol but this
is delicious if you'd like to try it.'

'Thank you.' Sam accepted the glass and took a sip of
the ruby-red liquid. 'Mmm, you're right, it *is* delicious.'

'Good.' Khalid topped up his own glass then glanced at
Mariam and Shahzad, swallowing a sigh when he realised
that they were so wrapped up in their news that they were
oblivious to everything else. It was up to him to play the
host and it was a job he would have preferred not to do,
only good manners dictated otherwise.

'Would you like to take a walk in the rose garden? The
scent of the blossoms is stronger at night and I'm sure
you'd enjoy it.'

'You don't have to entertain me, Khalid,' Sam said
sharply. Her eyes rose to his and he saw the hurt they
held and silently cursed himself for making his reluctance
so apparent.

'I know I don't.' He touched her hand, unable to lie,
even though he knew how dangerous it was to admit the
truth. 'I asked you because I can't think of anything I
would like more than to enjoy the garden with you, Sam.'

'Oh.'

She didn't say anything else; however, he could tell that
she was surprised and wished he had managed to keep his
feelings to himself. He led the way, opening the French
doors at the far end of the salon that gave direct access to
the rose garden. Night had fallen and apart from the light
from the torches placed alongside the path, everywhere
was dark. It added an air of intimacy, which was heightened by the fact that they had to rely more on their other
senses and less on sight.

Khalid breathed in deeply, inhaling the delicate yet potent scent of the roses. Somewhere a frog began to croak,
an insistent rhythm that drummed inside his skull and

made it difficult to think. His mind seemed to be awash
with sensations, with all the things he couldn't afford to
feel, but he was powerless to resist their appeal. When Sam
stopped and turned to him he acted instinctively, unable
to weigh up the dangers of what he was doing when all he
was aware of was this need burning inside him.

'Sam.' He said her name so softly that he wondered if
he had actually spoken it out loud. Her eyes rose to his and
his heart leapt when he saw an answering need reflected
in their depths. She didn't try to pull away when he drew
her to him, didn't resist in any way. She wanted this kiss
as much as he did, needed it just as desperately too.

The thought was the final key that unlocked his restraint. Khalid placed his mouth over hers and shuddered
when he felt her immediately respond. When he pulled her
to him, holding her so close that he could feel the swell of
her breasts pushing against his chest, it felt as though he
had come home after a long and tiring journey. *This* was
what had been missing from his life, this feeling of completion. With Sam in his arms he felt whole; without her
it was as though something vital was missing.

SAM COULD FEEL her heart beating, its rhythm marking time
with Khalid's, and shivered. It was almost too much to
realise that their bodies were so perfectly attuned. Pressing herself even closer against him, she twined her arms
around his neck and drew his head down so she could
deepen the kiss, wanting...*needing*...this moment to continue for as long as possible. She wasn't stupid. She knew
that it would have to end, but for now it was enough that
she could feel his need of her. Maybe they couldn't be together for ever but for this moment Khalid wanted her,
her and nobody else!

They were both breathing hard when they broke apart,

both shaken by the depth of their desire. Khalid cupped her cheek and she could feel his hand trembling and was overwhelmed by tenderness. Even though he projected an image of cool indifference, she knew otherwise. He was neither cool nor indifferent. Not when he held her in his arms and kissed her at least.

'I shouldn't have done that,' he said, his deep voice grating in the silence.

'Maybe not but it's what we both wanted, Khalid.' She tilted her head and looked him in the eyes because she refused to lie. 'If I hadn't wanted you to kiss me I would have stopped you.'

'It can never lead anywhere. You understand that, Sam, don't you?'

'Oh, yes. I'm under no illusions.' She gave a discordant little laugh. 'I'm not the sort of woman a man like you wants in his life. I'm fine for a fling but that's all!'

'That wasn't what I meant!' He caught hold of her by the shoulders, bending so he could look into her eyes, but Sam wasn't about to be persuaded. She needed to face the facts and not be swayed into believing what patently wasn't true.

'If you say so.' She gave a little shrug as she pulled away, deliberately setting some distance between them because she couldn't trust herself. It would be only too easy to allow him to convince her that her past didn't matter but it did. It had mattered six years ago and it still mattered now.

'Ah, so there you are. Mariam sent me to find you. Dinner is ready.'

Sam was glad of the interruption when Shahzad appeared. She could see the curiosity in his eyes as he glanced from her to Khalid. Obviously, he had sensed that something was going on but it wasn't up to her to explain—she would leave that to Khalid. No doubt he would

appreciate hearing his brother's opinion, especially if it reinforced his own view, as she suspected it would. Despite
how welcoming Shahzad had been, he would be equally
loath to allow his family to become involved with someone from her background.

Swinging round, she made her way inside, summon-
ing a smile when she found Mariam waiting for them.
Although Mariam still looked a little pale, Sam could tell
how much better she was feeling now that her worst fears
had been alleviated. 'Feeling better, are you?'

'Much.' Mariam smiled her sweet smile as she came
over and kissed Sam on the cheek. 'Thank you so much for
persuading me to have that scan. I only wish that I'd agreed
to have it done sooner and saved myself and Shahzad all
that heartache.'

Sam gave her a hug. 'It's easy to be wise after the event,'
she said sympathetically, glancing round when she heard
Khalid and his brother come into the room.

Her heart ached as the truth of that statement hit her.
She should never have allowed Khalid to kiss her just now,
certainly shouldn't have responded the way she had done.
Now she not only had to contend with her own emotions
but with the knowledge that he still desired her. It would
make it that much more difficult to keep him at arm's
length as she had to do if she wasn't to find herself right
back where she'd been six years ago: her heart broken and
her life in tatters.

The thought lay heavily in her heart as she followed
Mariam to the dining room. Once again the furniture and
fitments were understated and ultra-modern, the only indication of the couple's extreme wealth apparent in the exquisite china and beautiful cut-glass stemware that adorned
the table. Candles had been lit and the glow from them
should have added to the feeling of celebration, yet Sam

found it difficult to get into the right frame of mind. She kept thinking back to what had happened in the rose garden, how Khalid had stated with such certainty that there was no future for them, and it hurt. It really hurt even though she had expected nothing else.

She glanced at him over the rim of her glass, watching how the flickering candlelight highlighted the strong planes of his handsome face. Khalid would never be hers and she would never be his. The future was already mapped out and it wasn't about to change.

SOMEHOW KHALID GOT through the evening but it was touch and go. He had to force himself to concentrate on the conversation because his mind kept skipping this way and that, always returning to those far-too-brief moments in the rose garden. He knew he should never have kissed Sam, knew that if he could go back in time he would resist temptation somehow, but for some inexplicable reason he didn't regret it. Holding her in his arms, feeling her lips so sweet and responsive under his, was a memory he would cherish. What he *did* regret was the fact that he had hurt her.

The thought plagued him. It was a relief when the evening ended and he could escape to his room. Unlike the royal palaces, his brother had opted for a more relaxed approach when it came to housing his guests. Men and women weren't segregated in separate areas and he discovered that his suite was right next to the one Sam was using. He went in and closed the door, forcing himself to think about nothing more than necessities. They would need to leave extra early the following morning if they weren't to miss the start of clinic…

The sound of the terrace doors being opened in the adjoining suite made his thoughts tail off. He held his breath, his heart jerking painfully when he heard footsteps crossing the terrace. This section of the house overlooked the desert so was Sam taking the chance to enjoy the night-time peace and quiet, hoping that it would soothe her, comfort her, possibly make her feel that bit less hurt?

Knowing that he was responsible for how she felt made him feel worse than ever but there was nothing he could do, no words that he could say that would make the situation better for her. Or for him. If he offered her a future that was linked to his then, inevitably, she would suffer even more, and that was something he couldn't tolerate. He had to protect her, protect himself too because he couldn't bear the thought of suffering the same kind of heartache if he lost her.

'Oh!'

The cry brought him to his feet. Crossing the room, Khalid flung open the terrace doors. Sam was standing at the edge of her terrace, her hand pressed to her throat. Although she had removed the headdress, she was still wearing the dress Mariam had lent her. Even though Khalid was more concerned about what had happened to make her cry out like that, he found himself thinking once again how much it suited her.

'Are you all right?' he demanded, struggling to confine his thoughts to areas where they needed to remain. 'What happened? Why did you cry out like that?'

'It was a lizard. I didn't see it until it ran over my foot.' She gave a little shudder then made a determined effort to collect herself. 'Sorry. I didn't mean to disturb you.'

'It doesn't matter. So long as you're all right, that's the important thing.' He half turned then realised that he couldn't leave it like this. He had to try to repair some of the damage he had caused at the very least. 'About tonight, Sam,' he began, turning back.

'Don't! Please don't apologise. I... I don't think I could bear it.'

Her voice broke as she turned away but not before he had seen the tears that welled into her eyes. Khalid cursed under his breath as he leapt over the ornate iron railing that separated the terraces. Drawing her into his arms, he held her against him, hating himself when he felt the sobs that wracked her slender body. He had done this to her. Him. Nobody else.

'I'm so sorry,' he murmured, stroking her hair. The silky blonde strands twined around his fingers, binding her to him in the sweetest way possible, and his heart ran wild. If he could be granted one wish, it would be to bind her to him for ever, never to let her go, to keep her at his side for eternity. It was at that moment that he finally acknowledged what he had known in his heart for a long time: he loved her. He always would even though he could never have her.

Whether it was that thought, that final uncompromising admission that made him do what he had sworn he must never do, he wasn't sure. But all of a sudden Khalid knew that he had to make love to her, that he couldn't live out the rest of his life without that memory to keep him sane. Tilting her face, he looked deep into her eyes, knowing that he must make it clear what he was asking, offering.

'I want us to make love, Sam, but only if you understand that it can never lead anywhere. You said before that I wouldn't want a woman from your background in my life and it's true, although not for the reasons you believe.' He cupped her face between his hands, wiping away her tears with his thumbs. 'The media interest would be unbearable for you. Your past would be raked up time and time again, every little thing that had happened to your family laid out for public consumption. It wouldn't matter if half of it weren't true—that wouldn't stop them. It would be a nightmare for you.'

'And for you.' She met his gaze, met and held it. 'It wouldn't help you, Khalid, to be linked to a woman like me, would it?' The laugh she gave was filled with such scorn that he flinched. 'When the news first broke you couldn't wait to get rid of me, could you? It must have come as a nasty shock to discover that my mother was just a step away from being a prostitute and that my brother was in prison.'

'It wasn't a shock. I already knew all about your background.'

'You knew! But how could you?'

He heard the disbelief in her voice and realised that he had to explain. 'Because my father's security team had run a background check on you when we first met.' He gave a little shrug. 'They do it whenever I meet anyone new. They checked up on Peter as well.'

'But that's terrible! It's an infringement of a person's rights.'

'I agree, but it's something that happens all the time and not just in countries like Azad. Your own government is very good at checking into the backgrounds of various people,' he added dryly.

She shook her head. 'I still don't think it's right but that's not the point, is it? If you knew about my past then why did you get involved with me? I would have thought you'd have run a mile rather than have your name linked to mine.'

'Why did I get involved with you? Well, that's easy.' He took hold of her hands and held them lightly, willing her to believe him. He wouldn't force her to accept what he had to say; she had to believe it in her own heart for it to mean anything. 'Your past didn't matter to me. The only thing I cared about was you, Sam. *You*. The person you were.'

He took a deep breath but there could be no holding back, no attempt to safeguard his pride at this stage. He had to tell her the truth or be damned.

'It's still the only thing that matters to me. I don't care about anything else. I only care about you and about making sure that you don't get hurt again. That's why I need you to think hard about what I am suggesting. I may want to make love with you, want it more than I've wanted anything in my life, but not if it means that you are going to suffer afterwards.'

CHAPTER ELEVEN

Candlelight lit the room, its soft glow casting shadows over the bed. Sam lay on the cool, silk spread and waited while Khalid closed the shutters. Placing her hand on her heart, she felt it pounding beneath her palm.

She had been here before. Six years ago she had been in this very position, waiting, dreaming, *wanting* to make love with Khalid. The memory of her shock when he had told her that he had changed his mind was still so vivid that she closed her eyes, praying it wouldn't happen a second time. She didn't think she could bear another rejection.

The sound of his footsteps approaching the bed seemed unnaturally loud but Sam didn't open her eyes. She was afraid to do so, afraid to face what might happen a second time. She heard him pause but still she couldn't look at him—she was too scared.

'Sam, look at me.'

His voice was low, filled with understanding, and her lids slowly lifted. He sat down on the side of the bed, lifting her hand and pressing a kiss to her palm. 'Don't be scared. If you've changed your mind then I understand. I don't want you to do anything you might regret.'

Relief poured through her, swamped her. 'I haven't. Changed my mind, I mean. I was just afraid that you might have done, like last time...'

She broke off, not wanting to rake over the past at that moment and spoil it.

'Oh, sweetheart, I'm so sorry. I should have realised.'

He gathered her to him, his lips painting a line of tender kisses down her cheek. He reached her jaw and lingered, his mouth resting on the tiny pulse that was beating there with such frenzy before he straightened. His voice sounded strained when he continued, hinting at the effort it had cost him to call a halt, and she felt reassured. This wasn't going to be a repeat of the last time. There was no danger of that!

'I haven't changed my mind. If it's what you want then it's what I want too. Desperately.'

'It is what I want, Khalid. I'm absolutely sure about that.'

Reaching up, she drew him down towards her, pressing her mouth to his, and heard him sigh. The kiss they shared was one of tenderness and understanding, of acceptance even, and it helped to dispel the very last of her fears. Maybe this night had to be a start, a middle and an end, but it would be worth it to have its memory stored in her heart. She could take it out whenever she needed to, remember how it had felt to have Khalid love her.

She closed her eyes, savouring the taste and feel of his lips as he scattered kisses over her face. He reached her throat and skated down it, pushing aside the folds of her dress so he could kiss the upper swell of her breasts. Mariam's underwear had proved to be far too large for her so Sam had opted not to wear any that night. There'd been no real need as the flowing folds of the gown had protected her modesty. Now there was very little separating Khalid's seeking mouth from her breasts and that was soon dispensed with.

'You are so beautiful. So perfect...' He couldn't continue because he was too busy lavishing her breasts with kisses to speak.

Sam groaned as he drew her nipple between his lips. Admittedly her experiences of lovemaking were limited, but not once had she felt this need growing stronger and stronger inside her. It was as though it was consuming her totally so that she could no longer think, only feel, but that was probably for the best. She didn't want to think and maybe start having doubts. She wanted this night to be perfect.

His hands returned to the row of tiny buttons down the front of her gown as he worked the rest of them free. Sam heard him suck in his breath as he parted the silky folds of cloth, exposing her naked body to his gaze, and shivered with anticipation. It really was going to happen. Tonight they were finally going to make love.

Khalid stood up and slid off his robe, letting it fall in a heap on the floor. His body was lean and fit, the taut muscles in his chest and shoulders flexing as he lay down beside her on the bed. Sam reached out and ran her hand over the smooth olive-toned skin on his chest, loving the way it slid beneath her palm like the purest silk. He had said that she was beautiful but he was beautiful too in his blatant masculinity.

Her hand glided on, down his chest, over his flat stomach until she reached the thatch of crisp black hair that delineated his masculinity. That he was deeply aroused was obvious and she paused, the colour flooding to her cheeks because all of a sudden she was overcome by shyness. The few times she had made love hadn't prepared her for this. She wasn't sure if she had the experience to make tonight as wonderful for him as she wanted it to be. The thought that she might disappoint him was like a heavy weight suddenly filling her heart.

'What is it? Tell me, my love.' His voice was soft and low, filled with such tenderness that Sam found herself blurting out the truth.

'I'm afraid that you will be disappointed.' She paused then hurried on. 'I… I'm not very experienced when it comes to making love, you see. You…well, you could re-gret it.'

'Never.' He lifted her hand and kissed her fingers, one by one. His eyes were very dark as they met hers. 'Noth-ing you do can ever disappoint me, Sam. Remember that.'

Bending, he kissed her on the lips, his mouth gentle at first then quickly becoming more demanding. Sam re-sponded immediately, kissing him back with a hunger that she didn't try to hide. Maybe she lacked his experience but she loved him so much and that would make up for it.

It was the first time she had admitted how she truly felt and it was both exhilarating and terrifying to have to face the fact that she still loved him. Sam drove the thought from her mind. She couldn't deal with it right now, not when Khalid was making her body hum with desire as he stroked and caressed her. Everywhere his hands touched, it felt as though she was on fire, burning up with this in-satiable need for him. One caress wasn't enough, neither were a dozen. She wanted more and more, wanted the feel-ings he was arousing inside her to never end.

'Sam!' He cried out her name, his voice hoarse with pas-sion, and she held him close, feeling her own body grow tense as all the sensations suddenly erupted into one huge conflagration.

Sam closed her eyes, seeing the flames licking behind her lids, *feeling* them pouring through her body. This was how it felt to make love, she thought as she slid over the edge into oblivion. This was how it was meant to be. But even as passion swept her away, she knew that it was only with Khalid that she would experience this depth of feeling, only with him that she would ever know how it really felt to be a woman. It was only Khalid who she would ever love this way.

Soft morning light filtered into the room, chasing away the night's shadows. Khalid lay on his back and watched as the dawn broke. He wished he could stop it happening. Wished he could turn back the clock and keep time in abeyance but he didn't have that power. The minutes would keep ticking past, the hours would keep on stacking up, and a new day would begin.

Last night had been the most wonderful experience he had ever known but it wouldn't last. It couldn't. It couldn't be repeated either. It had been a one-off, a night that he knew would influence his life from now on. Making love with Sam had been everything he had dreamt it would be and so much more. Nothing that happened from here on could match it. Ever.

'What's wrong?'

The gently spoken question alerted him to the fact that Sam was awake. Rolling onto his side, he studied the delicate lines of her face. Her huge grey eyes were still heavy with sleep but he could see remnants of the passion they had shared lingering in their depths. That she had been as moved by the whole experience as he had been wasn't in doubt and he suddenly found himself wishing that it hadn't been so wonderful, so all-consuming for both of them. Maybe it would have been easier to do what needed to be done if they hadn't found such delight in each other's arms.

'Nothing.' He leant forward and kissed her lips, felt her shudder, and drew back. He couldn't afford to make love to her again, couldn't allow temptation to lead him from the path he had to take. For Sam's sake he had to be strong and resist. Tossing back the sheet, he went to get out of bed but she stopped him.

'Don't lie, Khalid. I can tell that something is troubling you.'

He sighed as he sank back onto the mattress and took her in his arms. 'I'm just feeling a little sad because the night has ended. That's all it is.'

'Is it?' She drew back and looked at him. 'It's not because you regret what happened?'

'No!' He pulled her to him, held her close, willed her to believe that regret was the last thing he felt. He didn't regret what they had done; his only regret was that it could never happen again. 'I don't regret it, Sam. How could I when it was everything I had dreamt it would be?'

He kissed her softly, letting his lips linger this time as he didn't have the strength to resist. He could feel her trembling when he raised his head, see the passion that had ignited in her eyes again, and felt his own desire start to flow hotly through his veins. Maybe they couldn't have for ever but they had now and that was something special. Magical.

They made love and once again it was perfect. Each kiss, each caress seemed to take on a depth and meaning he had never experienced before. Khalid's heart was racing, aching, as he drove them both to fresh heights. He had never felt this kind of completion before, never known how it could feel to give and to receive love like this. It was only Sam who could arouse him this way, only Sam he wanted. They were both completely spent when they broke apart, both exhausted by such an outpouring of their passion. When Sam raised his hand and pressed a kiss to his knuckles, he trembled with need, with desire, with love for her.

'I had no idea it could feel like this, Khalid. No matter what happens, I shall never regret what we've done. I want you to know that.'

'I shall never regret it either.' He squeezed her fingers and his heart was heavy as he forced himself to let her go. 'I'd better return to my own room. I wouldn't want to shock the servants.'

'Of course not.' She sat up as he got out of bed, modestly drawing the sheet around her. 'We shall need to leave soon if we don't want to miss the start of clinic.'

'I'll make sure that Shahzad has organised the helicopter as soon as I'm dressed.' He summoned a smile but it wasn't easy as the demands of the day started to press down on him. Last night may have been wonderful but he was all too aware that it was over. It had been a tiny oasis of time, a few precious hours that could never be repeated. From this moment on he would have to get on with his life as Sam would have to get on with hers.

'There will be time for something to eat before we leave,' he said as steadily as he could when it felt as though his heart was in shreds. 'Would you like me to get one of the servants to bring you a tray?'

'If it isn't too much trouble.'

The flatness of her tone told him that she too had realised that this was it, that the night was over and that from this moment on they had to be sensible. Khalid wished he could make the situation easier for her but there was nothing he could do. Despite his joy in their lovemaking, he was still convinced that he had to let her go.

He went back to his room and showered and dressed then went to find his brother. Shahzad was in the rose garden and Khalid could see immediately how much better he looked now that he had stopped worrying about Mariam. How he envied him! Envied him for having found the woman he loved and for being able to share his life with her and their children. Maybe he was being foolish. Maybe there was a way that he and Sam could be together. If she was willing to adapt to life in Azad it could work…

And it could fail miserably too.

'Good morning. And it is a beautiful morning, isn't it?' Shahzad greeted him with undisguised delight and Khalid did his best to shake off the feeling of despondency that threatened to overwhelm him.

'It is indeed.' He dredged up a smile. 'How is Mariam this morning? Feeling better, I hope.'

'Much. Discovering the reason why she has felt so ill lately has improved things a hundredfold. She is thrilled at the thought of having twins, as I am.' Shahzad enveloped him in a brotherly hug. 'Thank you, Khalid, for bringing Sam here. I doubt we would have got to the bottom of the problem if it weren't for her.'

'I'm sure Mariam's own doctor would have realised what was wrong eventually,' he demurred.

'Perhaps and perhaps not.' Shahzad sighed. 'Sometimes our royal status can be a hindrance, can't it? People are less inclined to put forward their opinions and insist on a course of action than they might do otherwise.'

Khalid knew it was true. 'Fortunately Sam doesn't view life that way. She's unimpressed by wealth or status.'

'Which is why you were attracted to her, I imagine.' Shahzad's gaze was searching. 'I expect you knew all about her background before the media latched on to it, but it didn't concern you, did it, brother?'

'No,' Khalid replied truthfully. 'It didn't matter a jot to me.'

'Yet you two split up shortly after the newspapers ran the story?' Shahzad smiled when Khalid looked at him in surprise. 'Oh, yes, I know that you two were seeing one another. There's little that either of us do that doesn't get reported.'

Khalid recognised the truth of that statement. As a member of the Azadian royal family, he should have known that his affairs were being closely monitored. 'Yes, it's true. Sam and I were close at one time. However, after the papers ran that story I knew that we would have to split up. I wasn't concerned about the effect it would have on me—I'm used to being the subject of speculation. However, I realised how hurt and upset she'd have been if her family's shortcomings were continually raked up.'

'I see. And that's why you decided to end your relationship?'

'That plus the fact that I didn't want her to end up regretting getting involved with me. Sam would have had to give up so much if we had married—her career, her dreams, everything she has worked so hard to achieve. I couldn't do that to her, couldn't take away everything that makes her who she is. She would have ended up resenting me, *blaming* me even, just like my mother ended up blaming our father, and that was a risk I wasn't willing to take.'

He took a deep breath, determinedly ironing any trace of emotion from his voice. 'It's a risk I am still not prepared to take. Once this mission is completed I have no intention of seeing Sam ever again.'

SAM CAME TO an unsteady halt when she heard what Khalid had said. It was no more than she should have expected and yet it hurt unbearably to hear him state it out loud. It made what had happened the previous night seem somehow tawdry. Shameful. Khalid had made love to her and she had truly thought it had meant something to him, but had it? Really?

It was all she could do not to turn tail and scurry back

inside but once she did that then it would be even harder to face him in the future. She squared her shoulders, knowing that she had to brazen it out. Khalid had made no promises. On the contrary, he had told her that they didn't have a future. It was her own fault if she had read too much into what had happened last night. It had been sex and that was all. One night of glorious, mind-blowing sex. Most women her age would think nothing of having indulged in such an experience.

'There you are.' She fixed a smile to lips that were inclined to tremble if she let them. However, this new Sam, the one who now understood the joys of sleeping with an experienced partner, wasn't about to show any sign of weakness. 'I was just coming to find you. Are we ready for the off?'

'Just about.' Khalid's tone was cool, the look he gave her equally so, and she was glad that she had managed to keep control of her emotions. He wouldn't thank her for making a scene, certainly not. He turned to his brother. 'Is the helicopter ready to fly us back to camp?'

'Whenever you wish.' Shahzad smiled at them both. 'Mariam will want to see you off, though. I shall go and fetch her.'

He disappeared inside, leaving behind a small silence. Sam wished she could think of something to say but her mind was blank. Had it been purely sex for Khalid? All those magical kisses, those delicately sensual caresses that had turned her bones to liquid fire? Had it been less emotion than experience that had made him seem like the perfect lover?

A sob caught in her throat and she hurriedly turned it into a cough when she felt him look at her. All that was left to her now was pride and if she lost that then heaven knew how she would cope. There was another month to get through, four more weeks of working with Khalid, and it would be unbearable if he suspected how devastated she felt. Maybe he hadn't rejected her last night but she wished he had. It couldn't have felt any worse than this!

Mariam and Shahzad came hurrying out to say their goodbyes. The girls were with them and in the flurry of farewells it was easier to hide her feelings.

'Thank you so much, Sam. To discover I am carrying twins has come as the most wonderful surprise and I am truly grateful to you.' Mariam hugged Sam then smiled at Khalid. 'And thank you for bringing her. Knowing what a doting uncle you are, I'm sure you must be thrilled too, although it's time that you thought about starting a family of your own, isn't it?' She turned to Sam and laughed. 'We're all looking forward to the day when Khalid finally relinquishes his bachelor ways and settles down!'

Sam couldn't think of anything to say. She dredged up a smile, her heart aching at the thought of Khalid marrying and having a family, as indeed he would at some point. It was what was expected of him, after all, that he would find a suitable bride and have children to carry on the royal bloodline. The thought was almost too painful to bear but she had to face facts and not allow herself to imagine that she could fulfil that role. She could never be Khalid's wife and the mother of his children, not someone like her, a Westerner without the right connections.

Her heart was aching as she kissed the children and promised that she would come back and visit them again even though she knew it wasn't going to happen. Once she left Azad, that would be it: she wouldn't return.

The helicopter was waiting for them so they climbed on board. Sam fastened her seat belt, turning to stare out of the window as they lifted off. Tears pricked her eyes as she watched the villa disappear from view. She had dis-

covered the real meaning of what it meant to be a woman
in that villa and it was sad to think that she would never
go there again but inevitable, given the circumstances.
Now she just had to get through the next few weeks and
that would be it. She would go back to her own life and
put what had happened behind her.

Just for a moment her heart shrank at the thought before she took a deep breath. She had done it before and
she could do it again.

CHAPTER TWELVE

The following month passed in a blur. News of the clinic had spread throughout the desert communities and each time they pitched camp they were inundated with patients. Everyone worked flat out but Khalid was very aware that they were only touching the very tip of the iceberg. There was still so much work to be done, far too much to complete in the time he had allotted for this mission.

It made him see that he needed to instigate the tentative plans he had made to set up a chain of permanent clinics. Between working out the logistics of doing that and seeing patients, he didn't have a minute to himself but he was glad. The less free time he had the better if it meant he didn't keep thinking about Sam and what had happened.

Their final day arrived and everyone was in high spirits as they packed up. Khalid supervised the packing of the more delicate pieces of equipment, which would be needed when his plans reached fruition. Peter offered to help him, an offer he accepted with alacrity. Peter was crucial to his plans and he wanted to have word with him.

'How would you feel about moving out here on a permanent basis?' he asked, not wasting any time. He helped his friend stow some particularly fragile pieces of technology into one of the crates then looked up. 'I've decided to set up a chain of permanent clinics and I need a director who knows what he's about. Would you be interested?'

'Yes. I would.' Peter's face turned pink with pleasure. 'I was wondering how best to approach you about doing something like that. There's a desperate need for a more permanent source of healthcare out here, isn't there?'

'There is.' Khalid clapped him on the shoulder, unable to hide his delight that Peter was keen to come on board. Normally, he would have opted for a much cooler approach but since *that* night he'd found it far more difficult to hide his feelings. He hastily dismissed the memories that rushed to the forefront of his mind, pictures of Sam's body naked to his gaze and the passion in her eyes. He needed to focus on his plans or he would drive himself mad.

'Obviously it will take some time to get everything organised but I don't want there to be too long of a delay. I'm aiming for three months maximum for the first clinic—would that be too soon for you?'

'Not for me, no. But I may need to convince Jess that it's a good idea.' Peter blushed even more. 'Jess and I... well, we have an understanding, you see. I hope I can persuade her to come with me.'

'So do I. Congratulations! She's a great girl. You couldn't have found anyone better suited to you,' Khalid told him sincerely.

'Thanks.' Peter looked up and grinned. 'Oh, hi there. Has Khalid managed to persuade you to sign up as well? I hope so. It would be great to have as many of the old team together as possible.'

Khalid glanced round to see who Peter was talking to and felt his heart sink when he saw Sam. By tacit consent they had kept any conversations they'd had confined to work during the past few weeks. He guessed that Sam was as wary as he was of getting into difficult territory. Peter would be mortified if he realised that unwittingly he had taken them down a route neither of them wished to explore.

'I'm not sure what you mean,' Sam replied as she joined them. She looked from Peter to Khalid and raised her brows. 'What's going on?'

'I've decided to make a start on setting up those clinics I was thinking about.' Khalid shrugged, feigning an insouciance he wished he felt. It would have been the icing on the cake if he could have asked Sam to come on board but he didn't dare. It was too risky, too tempting, too *everything*! 'Peter's just agreed to take on the role of director.'

'Really? Congratulations. You couldn't have found anyone better.'

Sam stepped forward and hugged Peter. She looked genuinely delighted but Khalid could see the pain in her eyes and knew that beneath the surface she was mulling it over, assessing why he hadn't offered her a role. He wanted to, wanted it more than anything, but surely she could see how impossible it would be if they had to work together on a long-term basis?

'I would have suggested that you join us but it wouldn't be fair, would it, Sam? Not at this stage in your career. You're in the running for a consultant's post, I believe, and that's more important than anything else.'

'Of course.' She glanced at him and he saw the scorn in her eyes that told him emphatically that she didn't believe him. It stung but there was nothing he could do but stick to his story. 'Anyway, I just wanted to let you know that the clinic is all sorted. Everything's boxed up and clearly labelled so it should be simple enough to unpack whenever you need anything. What time are we leaving?'

'One-thirty.' Khalid checked his watch. There were still four hours to go before the plane was due to take off, more than enough time to get everyone to the airport. He

came to a decision, needing to bring things to a swift conclusion when he didn't trust himself not to do something
foolish. 'Why don't you and the rest of the women set off
now? You can do some shopping at the airport before your
flight takes off.'

'Why not indeed?' Sam flicked him an icily polite
smile. Her expression warmed up considerably as she
turned to Peter. 'It's been great working with you, Peter.
Best of luck with the new project.'

They exchanged kisses before she left. Khalid went
back to his packing, trying his best to focus on what he
was doing, but it was a losing battle. Sam was leaving and
he wouldn't see her again. How could he bear it? But how
could he not?

THE FLIGHT TO England seemed never-ending. Sam tried
to sleep to while away the time but her mind was too
busy to relax. Khalid could have stopped her leaving. He
could have said something, *anything*, and she would have
stayed. Even though it would have raised a lot of eyebrows
in such a conservative country as Azad, she would have
stayed with him on any terms, but he hadn't said a word,
had he? He didn't want her to stay for the simple reason
that he didn't want *her*. Not now that he had finally made
love to her.

It was a relief to land at Heathrow. In the flurry of farewells nobody noticed her distress and, more importantly,
asked her what was wrong. She had been intending to stay
overnight in London but she decided to take the next available flight back to Manchester. She wanted to go home
to her flat and close the front door so she could lick her
wounds in private. That they were wounds she had helped
to inflict on herself was something she would have to come

to terms with. One thing was certain: she refused to let what had happened ruin her life.

SAM THREW HERSELF back into her work with gusto. There'd been several changes while she'd been off, staff had left and new people had been hired so it took her longer than expected to get back into the flow. Added to that, she felt unusually tired but put it down to the fact that she had been working non-stop for months. When her tiredness didn't improve by the time she had been home for six weeks, she started to wonder if she was maybe anaemic and bought herself some iron tablets from the hospital's pharmacy but they didn't improve matters. It was only when she got up one morning and was violently sick that the penny finally dropped with a resounding clang. Was it possible that she was pregnant?

It was too early to go to the shops so Sam went straight into work and took a pregnancy testing kit out of the cupboard. She went into the bathroom and peed on the plastic stick as per instructions then waited for the results. When the word 'PREGNANT' appeared on the screen she groaned out loud. What a fool she was not to have thought of this before. It was her job, so help her; she dealt with pregnant women every day of her working life and understood better than anyone the mechanics of how it happened! Yet she had blithely slept with Khalid without a thought for the consequences. Now she had to decide what to do, although there was no chance of her terminating the pregnancy. She was sure about that.

She placed her hand on her stomach, imagining the tiny life growing inside her, a life that she and Khalid had created. They were both responsible for this child's conception and she had to tell him, no matter how shocked or how angry he was, because he certainly wouldn't have chosen for this to happen, would he? Not a woman from a background like hers carrying his child, a child who had royal blood.

Sam squared her shoulders. Even if he was furious, he still needed to be told, not for his sake or for hers but for the sake of their child. She wasn't going to allow her son or daughter to grow up feeling ashamed, feeling that they had to apologise for their very existence. She knew how that felt and she refused to let her child suffer that kind of heartache. No matter how Khalid felt, this baby would know from the outset who its father was, even if Khalid refused to acknowledge him or her!

SETTING IN MOTION his plans for the clinics proved to be easier than Khalid had imagined. His father, King Faisal, proved to be an enthusiastic ally, offering both practical and moral support. His father railroaded the more conservative members of his government and obtained their agreement so that within a remarkably short space of time Khalid was told that he had the go-ahead and that funding would be found to pay for whatever was needed.

Three months later, the first clinic opened. Peter had proved to be invaluable at finding experienced staff to work for them. Although most people were hired on short-term contracts, the excellent pay plus all the other benefits had attracted a lot of interest. Khalid found himself in the enviable position of being able to pick and choose who they hired.

Once the clinic opened, he decided that he could afford to take some time off. He had been working flat out and he needed some down time. It was just the thought of spending his free time thinking about Sam that made him hesitate. He couldn't bear to keep going over and over what had happened when he knew in his heart that he had done the right thing. The only thing. Sam would have wilted and died if she'd had to conform to Azadian standards, even if they were improving.

He decided that he would spend some time endurance riding. He hadn't been able to indulge his interest in the sport for some time. Riders crossed the desert on horseback, setting time limits for the distances they travelled. It was a gruelling and demanding hobby that required a great deal of physical and mental strength from the riders. Although the horses were changed frequently, the riders had to complete the course no matter what. It was almost guaranteed that he wouldn't have time to think about much else, including Sam, hopefully.

He set off at dawn a few days later, accompanied by several friends who also enjoyed the challenges of the sport. They covered a lot of ground and he was delighted with what they had achieved when they stopped for the night. The next leg promised to be the most taxing so they were up before dawn and set off as soon as the sun rose. By mid-morning they were halfway to their destination and on schedule to complete the next leg on time.

It was only when they stopped to change horses that he became aware of a potential problem and his heart sank. The sky was rapidly turning dark, showing all the signs that a major sandstorm was approaching. As they gathered the horses and equipment together and hunkered down to ride out the storm, he found himself thinking about Sam.

Maybe he should have done the same, ridden out any storms that may have occurred in their relationship, fought for that happy ending he wanted so desperately. There were no guarantees in life, apart from the fact that he loved her. He should have fought for what he wanted, he realised. He should have fought for Sam.

THE FLIGHT TO Azad seemed to take for ever. It wasn't a private jet this time but a scheduled flight with all the attendant delays. Sam was exhausted when they finally touched down. She had booked a room at a hotel close to the airport and found a taxi to take her there, aware that this had been the easy bit. She still had to contact Khalid and make arrangements to see him.

Her heart jolted at the thought of his reaction to what she had to tell him but she was determined to do the right thing for this baby. She and Jess had kept in touch so as soon as she got into her hotel room she texted her friend to let her know that she had arrived. Jess had moved out to Azad to be with Peter, although they were observing the proprieties and not actually living together. As Jess had told her, it would make it even more special when they got married, which they planned to do very shortly.

Jess texted her back immediately, offering to meet her for breakfast the following day in the hotel. Whilst two women breakfasting together without a male companion wouldn't raise any eyebrows in the cosmopolitan confines of the hotel, Sam knew that it would be frowned upon outside. The last thing she wanted was to cause a fuss; she had too much else to worry about.

By the time the receptionist phoned to tell her that Jess had arrived the next morning, Sam was all ready. Despite her exhaustion, she hadn't slept and it showed in the dark circles under her eyes. She studied her reflection in the mirror for a moment before practising her smile. She hadn't told Jess why she had come back to Azad. Although she had no intention of keeping it a secret, it didn't seem right to tell anyone about the baby before she told Khalid. She had opted instead for the rather flimsy excuse that she had a few days free and wanted to see how the plans for the clinics were progressing.

Thankfully, Jess seemed to have accepted that but she would soon grow suspicious if Sam appeared with a glum face, hence the smile. However, when she went downstairs and saw Jess waiting for her, it was her friend's expression that worried her most of all. What on earth was wrong with Jess?

'What is it?' Hurrying over, she squeezed Jess's hands. 'It isn't Peter, is it? You two haven't had a row, have you?'

'No. Peter's fine.' Jess gripped Sam's hands and her face was filled with compassion. 'It's Khalid. I don't know how to tell you this, Sam, but he's missing.'

'Missing. What do you mean?' Sam's heart sank like a stone. She could feel it plummeting all the way down to her feet and was glad that Jess had hold of her because she was afraid that she might keel over.

'Apparently, he was out in the desert with some friends. Endurance riding or some such thing—I dunno 'cos I've never heard of it before. Anyway there was a sandstorm, a really massive one, and one of the men was badly injured. Khalid insisted that it was too dangerous to move him so once they'd dug out the truck, most of the party set off to fetch help. Khalid stayed behind with the injured man and one of the grooms to look after the horses. The rest of the group had taken a GPS reading so they thought it wouldn't be that difficult to find their way back but something must have gone wrong with the GPS.'

Jess gulped. 'To put it bluntly, they can't find Khalid and the other men. They seem to have disappeared off the face of the earth. There are people out searching for them, but although no one has actually come out and said so, it's obvious that they think they're probably dead!'

KHALID TILTED THE canvas awning to try and deflect the worst of the heat off his friend. It was midday and the temperature was horrendous. Basir was rambling under his breath again and Khalid frowned. There was no doubt that his friend's condition was worsening despite the drugs he had given him to fight off any infection. He desperately needed to get him to hospital so that the displaced fracture to Basir's left femur could be repaired properly. He had done all he could with what limited supplies they'd had with them, but he certainly hadn't been able to do all that was necessary. If help didn't arrive soon, he couldn't guarantee that there would be a happy ending to this story.

Mohammed, the groom, came to tell him about the horses. The man bowed low then explained that they were all well but that water was running short. They had enough to last them another day but after that…well.

Khalid thanked him, trying not let the older man see how worried he was. He checked his watch. It was three days since the rest of the party had left to fetch help so where were they? He could only assume that they had encountered some kind of a problem, although he tried his best not to dwell on the thought. He had to stay positive, believe that help would arrive, believe that they would survive; believe that that he would see Sam again. If he stopped believing, especially that last bit, he would give up.

Closing his eyes, he summoned up her image, unsurprised when within seconds there she was, inside his head. A smile curved his mouth. If the thought of seeing her again wasn't the biggest incentive of all to remain positive, then heaven alone knew what was!

JESS TOOK SAM to see Peter, who was based at the largest of the clinics. It was almost an exact replica of the one Sam had worked in and her heart ached as she recalled everything that had happened during her time there. She pushed the memories aside because she couldn't afford to think about the past. It was the present that mattered and that meant finding Khalid.

Peter greeted her warmly but it was impossible not to see how worried he was. He sat her down and quietly explained what was happening. There were helicopters out searching for the missing men, plus people on the ground, scouring the desert around where they were believed to have last been seen. It all took time but Khalid would be found, Peter assured her, although Sam suspected that his assurances owed more to wanting to spare her feelings than anything else. They both knew how difficult it would be to find anyone in the vastness of the desert.

The wait was almost unendurable. Sam had nothing to fill the time and spent it worrying. When Jess came racing into the tent to find her, Sam couldn't understand what she was saying at first.

'What is it?' she demanded, leaping to her feet. 'Has something happened?'

'They've found them!' Jess grabbed hold of her and whirled her round in a victory dance. 'They've only gone and found them!'

Sam gazed at her in shock for a second before her vision suddenly blurred. Jess hastily lowered her onto a seat and pushed her head between her knees.

'Sit there while I fetch you some water. You'll feel better in a moment.'

Sam breathed slowly, forcing the faintness away. By the time Jess returned with the water she was able to sit up and take the glass from her. 'Thanks. Sorry about that. It was the shock, I suppose.'

'Just the shock?' Jess gave her an old-fashioned look and it was obvious that she had guessed the real reason for what had happened.

Sam sighed softly. 'OK. Yes, I'm pregnant. And, yes again, Khalid is the baby's father.'

'I thought there must be more to this visit than you were letting on.' Jess sat down beside her and her expression was grave. 'Does he know about the baby?'

'Not yet. That's why I'm here, to tell him.' Sam smiled thinly. 'I'm not expecting him to be pleased but he needs to know.'

'I don't know about him not being pleased. From what Peter's said, I don't think he will be too upset, shall we say. But that's your business, not mine. What I will say, Sam, is that you're doing the right thing, no matter what happens. Khalid needs to know that you're carrying his child. Right. Now let's see about getting you to the hospital. According to Peter, Khalid should be there by now and I'm sure you will want to see him a.s.a.p.'

Sam was grateful for Jess's understanding. Within a very short time everything was organised and Peter had volunteered to drive her into the city. He led the way once they reached the hospital, obviously familiar with the modern, hi-spec building. Khalid had a private suite on the ninth floor and the state-of-the-art lift swiftly conveyed them up there. There was a guard outside but he bowed when he saw Peter and allowed him to knock on the door, which was opened almost immediately by a white-coated manservant. They were ushered into what was obviously a sitting room and offered refreshments, which they both refused. Sam didn't want refreshments: she wanted to see Khalid!

Five minutes later her wish was granted. Sam's breath caught as they were led into a room that contained all the equipment she would have expected to see in a highly equipped hospital unit. Her eyes skated over the familiar monitors and other equipment before coming to rest on the man lying on the bed. There was a tube attached to his arm, undoubtedly feeding him much-needed fluid. After spending so much time out in the desert, he would be dehydrated, although there could be many other things wrong with him as well.

Her gaze moved on, searching for clues as to his condition, but she couldn't see any sign of injury and breathed a little easier. Maybe he wasn't too badly hurt, not so badly hurt that he was in danger at least.

The thought triggered another bout of faintness and she swayed. Peter must have noticed her reaction and unceremoniously bundled her into a chair.

'Sit there and I'll get you some water,' he told her, hurrying over to fill a glass from the carafe standing on the bedside table.

Sam slowly raised her head, her face colouring when she discovered that Khalid was watching her. She thanked Peter for the water and forced herself to sip it slowly and not gulp it down as she felt like doing. Khalid was bound to be surprised to see her but was it only that? Surely it wasn't possible that he had guessed why she had come, like Jess had done?

'So, how are you?' Peter checked the monitors and nodded. 'Your vital signs appear to be normal, if it's any consolation.'

'I'm fine.' Impatience laced Khalid's voice and Sam's skin prickled. She knew what lay behind it, that he had questions he wanted to ask her and didn't welcome the delay. 'My doctor is erring on the side of caution, erring too far in that direction in my opinion. He insisted on the drip and the monitors even though they aren't necessary. I know how I feel and I am perfectly well.'

As though to emphasise the point, he removed a couple of leads, causing the monitor to beep out a noisy warning. Sam breathed in sharply, her head spinning with the sound. The door was flung open and a couple of nurses appeared. They fussed around when they spotted the loosened leads but Khalid shook his head when they tried to re-attach them.

'Leave them,' he ordered regally. 'And while you are here, you can remove the drip as well. It isn't necessary.'

It was obvious that they were unhappy about that idea. The older woman muttered something before they both hurriedly retreated. Sam suspected that they were going to find the doctor and leave the decision to him, not that she blamed them. In their shoes, she would have wanted some backing if she'd been ordered to countermand instructions, even if it was someone of Khalid's standing issuing them.

The thought that he was playing on his royal status to get his own way annoyed her. She glared at him. 'Throwing your toys out of the pram because you can't do what *you* want doesn't exactly show you in a good light, Khalid.'

His head reared up when he heard the scorn in her voice. 'I am a doctor. I know if I'm ill and need all this equipment or not.'

'Perhaps.' She shrugged. 'Although to my mind you aren't in a position to make rational decisions. Not after being out in the sun for so long.'

'You think I am suffering from sunstroke and unable to know my own mind?' he shot back.

'Something like that,' she countered, oddly exhilarated by the spiky exchange. She had spent the past few weeks first brooding about sleeping with him, then missing him, and then worrying about his reaction when she told him she was pregnant. It was a relief to be able to let loose some of the turbulent emotions that filled her.

'Now, now, children. Let's not squabble.' Peter looked from one to the other with undisguised amusement.

'You've both had a shock and my advice is to let things settle before you go tearing strips off each other.' He gave them a moment for that to sink in then went to the door. 'I'm off to find myself a cup of tea. Try to be good while I'm away, won't you?'

Sam watched the door close behind him. Her heart was pounding because she was very aware that now they were alone she would have to tell Khalid why she had come. Maybe she could put it off a while longer but why bother? He had said that he was fine and there was no reason to delay.

'Khalid...'

'I'm sorry, Sam. I have no idea why I behaved that way when I have been longing to see you.' He cut her off but she didn't mind, not when she heard what he said.

'Have you?' she asked huskily.

'Yes. It was the thought of seeing you that kept me going these past few days.' He held out his hand, palm up. 'Seeing you and touching you.'

Sam didn't need to hear anything more. She was across the room in a trice, placing her hand in his and gripping it so tightly that it was a wonder his fingers didn't go numb. 'I've been longing to see you too. See you and... and touch you.'

'My love.'

He pulled her down to him, his mouth claiming hers in a kiss that was an explosion of so many emotions that her heart ran wild. Passion and tenderness, desire and need were all mingled together in one huge surge of feelings that cleared her mind of everything else. It was hard to gather her thoughts when they broke apart but Sam knew that she had to tell him about the baby before they went any further.

'I have something to tell you, Khalid. Something that

you may not want to hear but which you need to know. I'm pregnant with your child.'

Khalid felt the world grind to a stop. It was as though it was suddenly teetering on its axis, brought to a halt by the announcement. He stared at Sam, seeing the worry in her eyes as well as the determination. How much courage it must have taken for her to come here and tell him that after the way they had parted, he couldn't imagine, but he was filled to the brim with admiration for her. Filled with that along with so many other emotions he could barely make sense of them all. Then one single thought rose to the surface: She was carrying his child.

'Oh, my sweet!' He pulled her into his arms, held her to his heart and rejoiced. It was something he had longed for yet had never allowed himself to hope it would happen. Now that it had, he knew that he would make it work. Somehow. Some way. *Any way at all!* No matter what problems they encountered, he and Sam would love and care for this precious child. Together.

He kissed her again and it was a kiss that held a promise for the future. Drawing back, he looked deep into her eyes. 'I can't tell you how thrilled I am. It's what I have dreamt about but never thought would happen.' He placed his hand on her stomach, imagining the new life growing inside her womb. 'Having you and a baby was my dearest wish but I was afraid it couldn't be.'

'It was my wish too.' Her tone was flat all of a sudden and it worried him.

'Was? It isn't what you want now?'

'Yes, it's what I want. However, I am realistic enough to know that we can't always have what we want.' She looked round when a knock on the door heralded the return of the nurses. 'We need to talk, Khalid, but we can't do so here. Peter knows where I'm staying—you can get the details from him when you're ready to meet up and discuss where we go from here.'

'I thought that was obvious,' he shot back, unbearably hurt by her attitude. Didn't she want him in her life—was that what she was saying? Had telling him about the baby been purely a token gesture born out of a sense of duty and nothing more? The thought turned his flesh to ice.

'Nothing is obvious in this situation,' she said quietly. 'We just have to do what is right for all of us, and especially what is right for our child.'

She stood up and went to the door, ignoring him when he ordered her to stop. The two nurses, closely followed by his doctor, hurried into the room as Sam left. Khalid allowed them to fuss around him, re-attaching the leads, checking the monitors, performing all the tasks that he would have insisted on in their position. It was less giving in gracefully than lack of interest that made him so compliant. He didn't care what they did; he only cared about Sam and what she was thinking. Feeling. Planning. He couldn't bear the thought that his whole future might lie in her hands and that there was nothing he could do about it!

He took a deep breath after the medics left then calmly detached all the leads once more. Ignoring the monitor, which was beeping like crazy, he got out of bed. He wasn't going to lie here and wait for Sam to reach a decision. No way! He was going to fight for what he wanted. Fight for her and his child and fight tooth and nail too. Sam could find that she had a bigger battle on her hands than she had anticipated but so long as she was happy with the outcome they would both be winners.

CHAPTER THIRTEEN

Sam went straight to her room after Peter dropped her off at the hotel. Jess had wanted her to go home with her but Sam had refused the well-intentioned offer. She needed to be by herself so she could work out what she should do. It would be so easy to get carried away by Khalid's declarations but deep down she knew it wasn't that simple. Yes, she loved him, and, yes, it appeared that he loved her too; however, she needed to think very carefully about the repercussions it could cause if she agreed to stay with him.

She made herself a cup of coffee and sat by the window to drink it, watching the sunlight reflecting off the modern high-rise towers that comprised this part of the city. Khalid had told her that Azad was changing and it was, but the old values still held firm. How would it affect Khalid if they married and the Azadian people found out about her family? Would it blight him in their eyes, make his position as a member of the ruling family untenable?

He hadn't mentioned marriage, granted, but she knew he would and that was something else she needed to think about. Khalid had a strongly developed sense of honour, so how could she be sure that he wouldn't offer to marry her simply because she was carrying his child? She couldn't bear to think that his life might be blighted because he wanted to do the right thing, couldn't bear to know that his feelings for her weren't as all-encompassing as hers were for him. It would be better for them to part than to live her life knowing that he was with her out of a sense of duty.

Sam's heart was heavy as she stood up and put her cup on the table. She had done what she had set out to do and told Khalid about the baby. There was no reason for her to stay.

As soon as Khalid was dressed, he phoned Peter and asked him where Sam was staying. Once he had the address, he summoned his driver and told the man to take him to her hotel. His impromptu departure from the hospital caused an uproar but he brushed aside the doctor's protests. This was far more important than anything else, far more urgent. Maybe he was mistaken but he had a nasty feeling that if he didn't go and find Sam immediately, she would do something stupid.

He sat on the edge of his seat as the car swept through the busy downtown traffic. When they drew up in the hotel's forecourt he had the door open before his driver could stop the engine. He strode across the foyer and made his way straight to the reception desk. The receptionist blanched when she recognised him but Khalid ignored her discomfort as he demanded to know which room Miss Warren was in. His heart sank when the woman haltingly explained that Miss Warren had checked out and was on her way to the airport.

Khalid returned to his car and told the driver to take him to the airport. Peter had given him Sam's mobile phone number so he tried calling it but it went straight to voice mail. He tried the airlines next and discovered that there was a flight leaving for London in less than an hour's time. He could only assume that she was booked on it.

The drive to the airport seemed never-ending. Khalid could feel his tension mounting as the minutes ticked past. When they finally arrived, he could barely contain himself as he leapt from the car and ran into the terminal. International flights went from Terminal Two so he raced across the concourse, taking the escalator steps two at a time. Sam's flight was boarding and once she got on the plane that would be it; he wouldn't be able to follow her unless he had a ticket...

Cursing his own stupidity, he veered off towards the booking hall. Thankfully, there wasn't a queue and he was able to purchase a first-class ticket for the London flight. A glimpse of his passport immediately afforded him VIP status and he was rushed through the various channels. Five minutes later he was boarding the plane. Now all he had to do was find Sam and talk to her, make her understand that they could work this out.

He grimaced. That was all?

SAM WATCHED AS the ground fell away. Tears were stinging her eyes but she blinked them away. She had done the right thing even though it didn't feel like it at this moment. If she had stayed and allowed Khalid to persuade her they could have a future together, she would have regretted it. She loved him too much to risk hurting him. It was better to let him go than live with that constant fear in her mind. She would let him see the baby—there was no question about that. However, she wouldn't tie him to her, wouldn't allow his life to be adversely affected in any way.

The plane levelled off and people started to move about when the seat-belt sign went out. When someone stopped beside her seat, Sam didn't look up, simply assuming that it was a passenger wanting to retrieve something from the overhead locker.

She wasn't prepared in any way when a familiar deep voice said quietly beside her, 'Hello, Sam.'

'Khalid!' Sam's hand flew to her mouth to stifle her gasp as she stared up at him. He smiled thinly but she could see the anger in his eyes and knew that he was less than pleased by her hasty departure.

'The very same. Obviously you didn't expect to see me so soon. I apologise if I've upset your plans.'

'What are you doing here?' she asked, her voice quavering with shock. She took a steadying breath but it didn't help, didn't do anything to quieten her racing heart. Maybe it was foolish but the fact that Khalid had followed her had to mean something, surely?

'You said we needed to talk and I agree with you.' He gave a little shrug. 'I didn't imagine we were going to have that conversation on a plane but needs must.'

Sam glanced along the row of seats and flushed when she realised that they were attracting a great deal of interest. It was obvious that several of the passengers had recognised Khalid and that was simply exacerbating the problem. The thought of them having an in-depth discussion about the baby with all these people listening was more than she could bear.

'This is hardly the best place to talk,' she began but he cut her off.

'I agree. It isn't.' He stepped back, his brows arching as he nodded to the first-class cabin. 'Come. There's more room up there. We can talk in private.'

'Oh, but I haven't got a ticket for First Class,' she protested, desperately playing for time. It had been such a shock to see Khalid and she needed to work out what she should say to him, muster up all the arguments she could to make him understand that it wasn't possible for them to be together.

'That isn't a problem. I shall take care of it.'

Sam could tell from his tone that he wasn't going to be deterred. He intended to talk to her about the baby and what would happen in the future and nothing she could say would stop him either. She stood up and followed him into the first-class cabin, sitting down where he indicated without a word. There was no point wasting her breath by objecting to his high-handed manner, not when she would need every scrap of breath to put across her reasons for them not being together. She knew Khalid too well to imagine that he would accept her decision without a fight. The thought filled her with dread.

Khalid spoke briefly to the flight attendant then sat down beside her. 'So why did you run off when you knew that we needed to talk?'

'I realised that there wasn't anything else we really needed to say.' She gave a little shrug. 'I'd told you about the baby and that was the main thing.'

'I see. So the fact that we haven't made any decisions about the future isn't important?'

His tone was silky, smooth, but Sam shivered when she heard the underlying thread of steel it held as well. Khalid wasn't going to be fobbed off by half-truths; she would have to be completely honest with him.

'Of course it's important but we need to think about the situation and not rush into something we will regret.'

'And you believe that we will regret making a commitment, regret it if we get married, regret making a life for us and our child?'

It was what she wanted so much but she knew that it could never happen, that the cost was too great. 'I… Yes.' Her voice caught but she forced herself to continue. 'You will regret it, Khalid. I'm certain of that.'

'You are so wrong, so very wrong, my love.' He took

her hand and raised it to his lips. 'The only thing I shall ever regret is that I let you go six years ago. I did it with the very best of intentions, because I was afraid of you getting hurt if our relationship became public knowledge, with all the attendant publicity it would have aroused. I was also afraid that you would come to hate me one day for ruining your life.'

'Ruin my life?' she repeated, staring at him in surprise. 'What do you mean by that?'

'That if we had got married and you had moved to Azad to live, your life would have had to change drastically. Although it's easier for women these days than it was when my mother lived there, there are still far too many restrictions on what a woman can do.'

He ran the pad of his thumb over her knuckles and Sam trembled when she felt the light caress. It was all she could do not to tell him that it didn't matter, that she didn't care how her life would be affected, but she knew that she mustn't do that, that she had to listen to what he had to say because it was important to him that she understood.

'What sort of restrictions?' she asked quietly.

'You might not have been able to continue with your career in medicine, for a start, although, thankfully, that isn't such an issue nowadays. There are far more women doctors working in our hospitals and clinics then there used to be.'

'That's good,' she said softly.

'Yes, it is.' He smiled at her with such tenderness that her breath caught. 'Nevertheless, it will be some time before our women doctors achieve the same degree of equality as their male counterparts. Consultants' posts tend to be offered to men, I'm afraid.'

She gave a tiny shrug. 'It will happen eventually. And

let's be realistic. Men tend to get boosted up the career ladder far faster than we women even in the UK.'

'That's true,' he agreed, then sighed. 'However, as the wife of a member of the ruling family, you would be expected to conform to traditional values—home and family first, with your career way down the list of priorities.'

'I understand. Obviously it would take some getting used to but if, as you say, things are changing then it would only be for a limited period, surely?'

'Perhaps. But I know from experience the effect it could have. My mother trained as a barrister but she gave up the law when she married my father. It was fine at first but eventually the fact that she couldn't do the job she loved was too much for her.' He shrugged. 'She and my father divorced when I was in my early teens, not because they didn't love one another but because my mother couldn't cope with life in Azad any longer.'

'How sad. It must have been very difficult for you.' She turned her hand over and squeezed his fingers. 'I can understand how it must have affected you, Khalid, but just because your mother couldn't cope with life in Azad, it doesn't mean that I couldn't cope with it.'

She took a quick breath, knowing that she had to be as honest as he had been. 'No, my biggest fear is the damage it could cause to you and your family if people found out about my background. That's something I couldn't bear. You said that I might come to hate you for ruining my life but it works two ways. You could come to hate me for tarnishing your family's reputation.'

'No. That would never happen.' His fingers closed around hers, holding her fast when she tried to pull away. 'I could never hate you, Sam. Never in a thousand years.' He bent and kissed her, his lips clinging to hers for a mere heartbeat, but she felt the passion they held and shivered.

It would be so easy to believe him but she had to be strong and do what was right.

'You can't make promises like that, Khalid. Nobody can.'

'I know how I feel.' He pressed her hand to his chest so she could feel the steady pounding of his heart. 'I know that I could never hate you for any reason. I love you too much, just as I shall love this child we have conceived. That's why I came after you, to make you understand that we need one another.'

'I don't need you, though,' she muttered in a desperate attempt to be sensible.

'Don't you?' He brushed his mouth over hers again then drew back and looked at her. 'Not even a little bit?'

'I... No,' she whispered, trying to stem the shudder that was working its way down her spine.

'Are you sure?' His mouth touched hers once more and lingered so that she could both feel and hear the words. It made it that much harder to stick to what she knew was right. 'Absolutely certain?'

'Yes,' Sam whispered, although she could feel her resolve melting and desperately tried to hold on to what little remained.

'I see.' He sighed throatily as his hand slid up her arm, caressing her skin through the thin fabric of her blouse. 'That's a real shame because I need you. So much. You and our baby. If I'm honest, I can't imagine how I shall live the rest of my life without you both.'

His hand slid up then down, the light pressure of his fingers making her shudder with need, with longing, with far too many things. When he drew her to him and held her against his chest, Sam tried to be strong, tried her best to remember that she mustn't allow this to happen, but her resolve seemed to have disappeared completely.

When Khalid tilted her chin and kissed her, she didn't push him away, didn't even attempt to stop what was happening. How could she when it was what she wanted so desperately?

The kiss seemed to last for an eternity and yet at the same time it was over far too quickly. Sam clung to him afterwards, needing the solid support of his body to hold on to as her determination faded into nothing. She loved him so much and if he wanted her to live with him then she would do so and face whatever the future held.

'I love you, my darling.' He stroked her hair, repeating the words in his own tongue, and she sighed softly.

'I love you too. So very much. So much that I can't bear the thought of you getting hurt.'

'As I can't bear the thought of you getting hurt either.' His expression was grave. 'It isn't just the unwelcome attentions of the press you would have to contend with, Sam, but the vastly different lifestyle you would lead in Azad. Could you bear it, bear to have restrictions placed upon what you do?'

'I don't know,' she said honestly. 'All I can do is give it a go and see what happens.'

'Or I could move to England on a permanent basis.'

'You'd do that?' She drew back and looked at him in surprise.

'Yes.' He smiled. 'If it was a choice between that and losing you then I would do it. Willingly too.'

'I don't know what to say...' She broke off and swallowed, unbearably moved by the offer. 'Thank you so much. I know how you feel about Azad and that you are willing to give up living there for me is more than I could ever hope for.'

'I'd be doing it for us—you, me and our child.' He kissed her hand. 'That would make any sacrifice worthwhile.'

'I feel the same. Maybe it will be very restricting to conform to Azadian mores but I can handle it so long as I have you.'

He sighed. 'I hope that's true. I saw how hard it was for my mother and how frustrated she became at having to adhere to a way of life that was alien to her.'

'But a lot has changed since then, hasn't it? And it's still changing.'

'That's very true.' He smiled. 'Maybe we can help to make those changes happen sooner than they might have done. You will soon charm my fellow countrymen, the way you have charmed me!'

'I doubt that,' she denied, laughing up at him. She sobered abruptly. 'The press will have a field day once the news of our relationship gets out. Are you sure it won't upset you, Khalid?'

'Only if it hurts you.' His gaze was tender. 'I love you, Sam, and I don't care about your background. It's important only in as much as I know how hurt you were when the story was raked up that last time.'

'It did hurt. It hurt to be made to feel that I was somehow to blame for my family's mistakes.' She bit her lip. 'One thing you need to understand, Khalid, is that I love my brother despite what he's done and I refuse to turn my back on him.'

'It's no more than I would have expected.' He kissed her lightly. 'Maybe we can both help him to make a fresh start, if he's willing.'

'That would be wonderful!' She returned his kiss then sat back in her seat. 'I wish we weren't on this plane. It will be ages before we land and we shall have to observe the proprieties.'

'Hmm. No mile-high club for us,' he teased her. He took her hand and held it lightly in his. 'We shall book into one

of the airport hotels as soon as we reach London and celebrate our engagement in the appropriate manner. Until
then we shall be the very models of decorum. Agreed?'

'Yes. So long as you don't look at me *that* way!'

Khalid laughed as he bent and dropped a kiss on the tip
of her nose. The flight attendant stopped by their seats just
then and offered them coffee, which they both accepted.
Sam drank hers slowly, savouring its richness. It was the
best cup of coffee she had ever tasted, although she suspected that it was the thought of what was to happen when
they reached London that had enhanced its flavour.

She glanced at Khalid and felt a rush of love consume
her when he smiled at her. In that moment, she knew that
it was going to be fine, that they would deal with whatever
problems they encountered. They loved one another and
nothing would stop them being together from this moment
on. Happiness filled her as she rested her head against the
back of the seat and closed her eyes. She and Khalid had
a wonderful future to look forward to with their child.

EPILOGUE

Three years later

'Are you ready, my darling?'

'Almost. I just need to finish brushing Jasmina's hair.' Sam looked up and smiled as Khalid came into the room, thinking that she would never tire of seeing him. She loved him so much and made a point of telling him that each and every day.

They had been married for three glorious years and tonight they were throwing a party to celebrate their third anniversary. She also had something to tell him, news that she knew would thrill him, but she would wait until they were on their own. Now she finished brushing their daughter's hair and gave Jasmina a kiss.

'Go and show Daddy how pretty you look, darling,' she told the little girl.

She watched as Jasmina ran over to Khalid and held up her arms to be picked up. Jasmina had inherited her fair colouring and looked a picture in the pale pink dress that her aunt Mariam had bought for her. Everyone adored her and there was never a shortage of volunteers if Sam needed a babysitter when she was working.

The status of women in Azad had come on in leaps

and bounds, thanks to Khalid's determination to improve matters. Sam had returned to work on a part-time basis when Jasmina was a year old and loved her job at the hospital, working with expectant mothers. Although much had been made of her background when she and Khalid had married, these days it was rarely mentioned. Maybe it was the fact that she and Khalid were so obviously in love but most people ignored the difference in their social standing. Even Khalid's father had accepted her and was proving to be a doting grandparent; Jasmina could twist King Faisal round her dainty little finger by all accounts! Life was working out extremely well and it would only get better after she told Khalid her news.

Suddenly, Sam knew that she couldn't wait a second longer to share it with him. Standing up, she went and kissed him on the cheek. 'I wasn't going to tell you this till later but I can't keep it to myself any longer. I'm pregnant.'

'What?' Khalid stared at her for a moment before his face broke into a delighted smile. Setting Jasmina down, he took Sam into his arms and hugged her. 'When did you find out?'

'This afternoon for certain, although I've had my suspicions for a few days now.' She laughed. 'I wanted to be absolutely sure before I told you.'

'And you are? There's no mistake?'

'Nope! In seven months' time you are going to be a daddy again. What would you like this time, a girl or a boy?'

'I don't care.' He kissed her lingeringly then laughed. 'I don't care what it is. I shall love it with all my heart, just as I love Jasmina and her mother!'

He kissed her again, putting the seal on their happiness. Sam kissed him back, knowing how fortunate she was. Not only had she found the man she loved with all her heart but they had a wonderful future to look forward to together with their family. She couldn't have wished for anything more than what she had.

* * * * *

Seducing His Princess
Olivia Gates

MILLS & BOON

Books by Olivia Gates

Harlequin Desire

The Sarantos Secret Baby #2080
***To Touch a Sheikh* #2103
A Secret Birthright #2136
Ω*The Sheikh's Redemption* #2165
Ω*The Sheikh's Claim* #2183
Ω*The Sheikh's Destiny* #2201
§*Temporarily His Princess* #2231
§*Conveniently His Princess* #2255
Claiming His Own #2265
§*Seducing His Princess* #2290

Silhouette Desire

**The Desert Lord's Baby* #1872
**The Desert Lord's Bride* #1884
*The Desert King #1896
Δ*The Once and Future Prince* #1942
Δ*The Prodigal Prince's Seduction* #1948
Δ*The Illegitimate King* #1954
Billionaire, M.D. #2005
In Too Deep #2025
    "The Sheikh's Bargained Bride"
**To Tame a Sheikh #2050
***To Tempt a Sheikh* #2069

*Throne of Judar
ΔThe Castaldini Crown
**Pride of Zohayd
ΩDesert Knights
§Married by Royal Decree

Other titles by this author
available in ebook format.

OLIVIA GATES

has always pursued creative passions such as singing and handicrafts. She still does, but only one of her passions grew gratifying enough, consuming enough, to become an ongoing career—writing.

She is most fulfilled when she is creating worlds and conflicts for her characters, then exploring and untangling them bit by bit, sharing her protagonists' every heart-wrenching heartache and hope, their every heart-pounding doubt and trial, until she leads them to an indisputably earned and gloriously satisfying happy ending.

When she's not writing, she is a doctor, a wife to her own alpha male and a mother to one brilliant girl and one demanding Angora cat. Visit Olivia at www.oliviagates.com.

Dear Reader,

When I wrote my very first Harlequin Desire novel, *The Desert Lord's Baby,* I created Judar, the desert kingdom that was the cornerstone of my sheikhdom universe. And in those first magical three books about those irresistible brothers, one figure stood in the wings, talked about but never present. It was the Aal Masood princes' youngest sibling, their only sister, Jala.

For years, she'd refused to tell me her story. But she was so adamant in escaping my curiosity that I started to suspect her secrets were deep, dark and painful. And that made sure I'd never forget about her, and that I'd keep after her until I could discover her past trauma, and be there for her future happily every after.

But for years, I didn't know how to do that!

Enter Mohab Aal Ghaanem. Like a desert storm, he swept back into her life against all odds, even against her will. Their turbulent past stood like an insurmountable barrier, blocking the way to even mere forgiveness. Not that that could have stopped him. Mohab was an unstoppable force to Jala's immovable object. And I delighted in documenting their passionately explosive and emotionally tempestuous journey back to each other and to happiness. I hope you enjoy it as much!

I love to hear from readers, so email me at oliviagates@gmail.com, and please follow me on Facebook at my fan page, www.facebook.com/oliviagatesauthor, on Goodreads under Olivia Gates and on Twitter: @OliviaGates.

Thanks for reading!

Olivia

DEDICATION

To my endlessly loving and supportive mother.
Thank you for being there for me always.
Love you, always.

PROLOGUE

Six years ago...

A fist of foreboding squeezed Mohab Aal Ghaanem's heart.

Najeeb was back. And Jala had gone to see him.

Although he had contrived to keep her from seeing Najeeb for months now as part of his original mission to keep them apart, when Najeeb had returned in spite of all his machinations, there'd been nothing further Mohab could do. Nothing but demand Jala not see Najeeb.

And what reason could he have given for asking her not to see his cousin and crown prince? That he was jealous?

She would have been shocked by the notion. At best, this would have made her think he didn't trust her, or that he wasn't the progressive man she thought him to be. Personal freedom and boundaries were very touchy subjects with her, and she had serious issues with the "repressive male dinosaurs" prevalent in their culture.

At worst, she might have suspected that he had other motives for wanting to prevent that meeting with her "best friend," motives that went beyond simple possessiveness. As he did.

So he'd stood back and watched her leave for that dreaded yet inevitable rendezvous. And she hadn't returned.

Not that she'd said she would. Having an early business meeting the next day close to her house in Long Beach, it made sense for her to spend the night at her home. He wished he could have waited for her there, but though she'd given him keys, the gesture had been only as a token of trust. She'd been adamant about not making their relationship public knowledge before she was ready to do so. He was probably working himself up for nothing but...

B'Ellahi... What was he *thinking?* It *was* for nothing. Jala had agreed to marry him. She was his, body and heart. He'd been her first, and he'd always be her only. He should have stopped worrying about how their relationship had started long ago, shouldn't have tried to keep Najeeb away once his...purpose had been achieved—even if the way it had been had taken him by surprise. He'd already been attracted to Jala, but he surely hadn't imagined when he'd first approached her that he'd fall for her that hard, that totally.

Emptying his lungs, he strode away from the window. He could barely make out anything from sixty floors up anyway.

Though he was sure he would have seen her.

Since he'd first laid eyes on her, she'd been the only one he ever truly saw, even when others should have been in his focus. As on the day of the hostage crisis, when he'd been sent to save Najeeb and had saved Jala, too.

Najeeb. Again. Everything always came back to him.

Mohab had kept his cousin away from New York, away from Jala, for as long as possible. Any more contrivances would have made Najeeb suspect he was being manipulated. And since there were only a handful of people who had enough power to keep the crown prince of Saraya jumping—his father, King Hassan, his brothers and

Mohab himself—Najeeb would have eventually drawn the proper conclusions.

By elimination, only Mohab, as the kingdom's top secret-service agent, had the skills and resources to invade Najeeb's privacy, to rearrange his plans, to nudge him wherever he wanted. The next step would have been finding out *why*.

So Mohab had been forced to let his cousin come back. To let Jala go to him. At nine o'clock this morning. That had been eleven hours ago.

What could be taking her so long?

Kaffa. Enough. Why not just call her instead of having a full-blown obsessive episode?

So he did. And it went straight to voice mail. Time and again.

When another hour passed and she hadn't called back, he tore out of his penthouse, numb with dread.

By the time he arrived at her house his nerves had snapped, one at a time. What if she was lying unconscious or unable to reach her phone? What if she'd been mugged… or worse? She was so beautiful, and he'd seen how men looked at her. What if someone had followed her home?

He barged inside and was hit at once with the certainty. She was there. Her presence permeated the place.

He ran upstairs, homing in on her. As he approached her bedroom, he heard sounds. To his distraught ears, they sounded like distress. Coming from the bathroom.

He tore inside. And there she was. In the shower cubicle. Facing the door. She saw him as soon as he saw her.

At his explosive entry, she lurched, her steam-obscured face contorting, her lips parting. He assumed she'd gasped or even cried out. He could hear nothing now above the cacophony of his own turmoil and the spray of water. All he knew was that she was here. She was safe.

And he was tearing off his clothes, his only need to prove to himself both facts.

Then he was inside the cubicle, dragging her into his arms, groaning as he felt her warm resilience slamming against his aching flesh, her cry shuddering through him as he drove trembling hands into her soaked tresses, his feverish gaze roaming her water-streaked face. That face, that body, that essence, had taken control of his fantasies from the instant he'd seen her, from the very moment he'd claimed her. And she'd claimed him right back. Throughout these past five months, with each caress, with each passion-filled encounter, he found himself craving her more and more. His hunger for her knew no bounds.

"Mohab…"

He swallowed her gasp, drove his tongue inside her fragrant, delicious depths and she started squirming, building his fire higher. He needed to be inside her, possessing her, pleasuring her. Reassuring himself she was whole and all his.

His hand glided between her smooth thighs, sought her core. His fingers slid between her slick folds, and his head almost burst with the sledgehammer of arousal. Knowing she would love his urgency, that the edge of discomfort his ferocity would cause would amplify her pleasure, he cupped her perfect buttocks and opened her silky thighs around his hips. Capturing her lips again and again in ravaging kisses, he sought her entrance, flexed then sheathed himself in her molten tightness in one long, forceful thrust.

The sharpness of her cry, a testament to the intensity of her enjoyment, heightened his frenzy, her hot gust of passion expanding in his own lungs. Then he withdrew and pistoned back, needing to merge with her, dissolve in her, knowing it would send her berserk. It was unraveling him, too—acute sensations layering with every plunge,

ratcheting with each withdrawal. The carnal groans torn
from their depths rode him higher and higher. He felt his
climax hurtling from his very essence, felt her shuddering uncontrollably, heard the sound of her tortured squeals
telling him she'd explode in ecstasy if he gave her the ca-
dence and force she needed.

Unable to prolong this torment a second more, he gave
it to her, his full force behind his jackhammering thrusts,
until she convulsed in his arms and her shrieks of pleasure snapped his own tension. He all but felt himself deto-
nate in a violent release, the most intense he'd ever felt, his
seed burning through his length, jetting into her depths to
mingle with her own gushing climax.

At last, the severity of sensations leveled, leaving him
so satiated, so depleted, he could barely stand. She collapsed in his arms as she always did. Taking her down to
the floor, he soothed her, and she surrendered to his min-
istrations, letting him fondle and suckle her, pour wonder
and worship all over her.

Then he carried her out of the shower and dried them
both off. As he bent to take her to bed, she pushed out of
his arms, unsteadily waddling away to fetch her bathrobe.

He winced. How insensitive could he be? He'd scared
her witless bursting in here, made her limp with satiation
for hours and could only think of continuing their inti-
macies?

He put on his pants as she turned to him, wrapped in the
stark white bathrobe, her golden flesh glowing in contrast.
The need to ravish her again almost overpowered him.

"What was *that* all about?"

He saw the hardness in her eyes before he heard it in
her tone. Something he'd never been exposed to before.

Suddenly wary, he shrugged. "Wasn't it self-evident?"

"Not to me. What brought you here in the first place?"

Disturbed by her coldness, especially after the inferno they'd just shared, he told her what he could. At the tail end of his account, he released a breath he hadn't realized he'd been holding. "And then I found you in there and all I could think was that you're safe. And I was, as always, starving for you." He tried a coaxing smile. "Finding you already unwrapped was most opportune."

"So you thought it was okay to barge in here and just have your way with me?"

The harsh accusation hit him between the eyes. She'd never been angry with him before. And to be so for the first time today, of all days, jarred him.

He found his own voice hardening. "You loved every second. You came so hard you blew my brains out."

She shrugged, not contesting that truth, those molten-gold eyes growing harder. "The point is, you disregarded my choice. Your overriding tactics have become a pattern."

"What 'overriding tactics'?"

"All your manipulation, ending with trying to keep me from seeing Najeeb. You think I'm so oblivious I didn't notice? Oh, I noticed, all right…every time you nudged and cajoled. Every time you artfully overruled me. You're almost undetectable, but I've had enough time and proximity to decipher your methods."

So she'd caught on.

Either he'd underestimated her astuteness…or he couldn't keep a cool enough head around her to maintain the seamless subterfuge he normally employed in his professional life.

Coming clean wasn't an option, though. He couldn't let her know why he'd originally approached her, or how he'd kept Najeeb away, or why. He couldn't risk that she might suspect the genuineness of his current involvement. They already had too much working against their relationship to introduce internal strife. The feud that had long raged between their families was enough of an obstacle on its own. He had to deny any culpability. There was just too much at stake.

"Why would I want to stop you from seeing Najeeb?"

She glared up at him, then turned and walked out.

Unable to believe she'd turned her back on him, he watched her, that fist of foreboding squeezing his insides again.

Mohab finished dressing, then followed her into her bedroom. His mind churning, he approached her where she stood across the room in jeans and a T-shirt, raven hair starting to dry into a waterfall of gloss, looking heartbreakingly perfect.

"I'm sorry I got carried away in there," he started. "I didn't think you'd mind…didn't think at all. I've never been so frightened in my life, and I overreacted…."

"I could have said stop. I didn't. So let's drop it."

"Let's not. If you're angry with me, don't just freeze me out." He stopped before her, ran a finger down her velvet cheek. "I beg your forgiveness, *ya habibati,* if you felt I was disregarding your choices. I didn't mean to, and I—"

"Don't." Her interruption was exasperated this time. "It doesn't matter. I actually think it's a good opportunity to finally tell you what I've been putting off for too long."

"Tell me what?"

"That I wasn't in any condition to make a rational decision when I accepted your marriage proposal."

His heart faltered. "What do you mean?"

"I was experiencing a postsex high for the first time, which was heightened by the fact that I was already indebted to you for saving my life during the hostage crisis. So when you hit me with your proposal, I found myself saying yes. I've tried to take it back ever since, but you wouldn't let me."

"You did no such thing." Denial rasped out of him. He shook his head, as if to snap out of the nightmare. "Is this why you kept putting off telling anyone about us? Not because you were afraid our families' feud would impact our relationship, but because you were having second thoughts?"

"I'm not just having second thoughts. I'm *certain* I don't want to get married."

That was it? A case of commitment phobia? That was something he could deal with.

He drew a breath of relief into his tight chest. "I can understand your wariness. You struggled for your independence. You might think you'd lose it with marriage. But I'll never encroach on your freedoms…." At her baleful glance, he insisted, "Whatever my transgressions, they were unintended. Guide me in navigating your comfort zones and I'll always abide by them. If I pushed you into a commitment too soon, I'll wait until you're ready."

"I'll never be ready to marry *you*."

He stared at her, beyond shocked, the ferocity of her rejection an ax cleaving into his heart.

Just yesterday, he'd thought everything was perfect between them. And she'd had all this resentment seething inside her? How had he been so oblivious?

This led him to the only possible explanation. A dreadful one. "Have you received a better offer?"

At his rough whisper, she turned away again. He wanted to pounce on her, to roar that she couldn't do this to him, to them. He remained paralyzed, sick electricity arcing in his clenched fists, jumbling his heart's rhythm.

He forced more mutilating deductions from numb lips.

"Since this is coming right after you visited Najeeb, I assume he finally popped the question."

She bent to pick up her laptop, as if she'd already dismissed him from her life. Heartache morphed into fury, all his early, long-forgotten suspicions about the nature of her relationship with Najeeb crashed into his mind.

"That's why you wheedled into his life, isn't it? But then he left, and you thought he wouldn't come through, and you were…what? Keeping me as plan B in case he didn't propose? And now you got the offer you were after all along, the one where you become a future queen, and I'm suddenly redundant?"

She turned the eyes of a total stranger to him. "I'd hoped we could part on civil terms."

"Civil?" His growl sounded like a wounded beast's. "You expect me to stand aside and let you marry my cousin?"

"I expect you to know you have no say in what I do."

And he went mad with pain and rage. "You can't just toss me aside and hook up with him. In fact, you can forget it. Najeeb will withdraw his offer as soon as I tell him how I made you…ineligible to be his princess. Regularly, hard and long, for five months. That I even took you after you said yes to him."

Her eyes filled with something he'd never dreamed he'd see in them. Loathing. "And I expected you to take my decision like a gentleman. But I'm glad you showed me how vicious and dishonorable you can be when you're thwarted. Now I know beyond a shadow of a doubt that I was right to end this."

His blood congealed as she turned away. "You really think you *can* end it…just like that?"

Hearing his butchered growl, she turned at the door.

"Yes. And I hope you won't make it uglier than it has already become."

His feet dragged under the weight of his heart as he approached her. "*B'Ellahi*...you loved me.... You said so.... I *felt* it."

"Whatever I said, whatever you think you felt, it's over. I never want to see you again."

He caught her, the feel of her intensifying his desperation. "You might think you mean it now, but you're mine, Jala. And no matter how long it takes, I swear to you, I will reclaim you. I will make you beg to be mine again."

"I was never yours. If you think you have a claim on me, I *will* repay you for saving my life one day. But not *with* my life."

His fingers sank into her shoulders, as if it would stop her from vanishing. "I don't care who Najeeb is. I'll destroy him before I let him have you. I'll destroy anyone who comes near you."

The disdain in her eyes rose. Everything he said sent her another step beyond retrieval.

"So now I know why you're called *Al Moddammer*." The Destroyer. The label he'd earned when he'd decimated conspiracies and terrorist organizations. "You annihilate anyone who becomes an obstacle to your objectives. Not to mention anyone who comes close to *you*."

His heart seized painfully. He'd never thought she'd ever use *that* knowledge against him. What else had he been wrong about?

Her disgust as she severed his convulsive grip told him this was it. It was over. Worse still, it might never have been real. Everything they'd shared, everything he'd thought they'd meant to each other might have all been in his mind.

Before she receded out of his life, she murmured, "Find yourself someone else who might have a death wish. Because I don't."

CHAPTER ONE

Present day...

"Do you have a death wish?"

Mohab almost laughed out loud. A bitterly amused huff did escape him as he rose to his feet to meet the king of Judar.

What were the odds? That these exact words would be the first thing Kamal Aal Masood said to him when they'd been the last thing the man's kid sister had flung at Mohab?

Guess it *was* true what was said about Kamal and Jala. That the two youngest in the Aal Masood sibling quartet could have been identical twins—if they hadn't been born male and female and twelve years apart. Their resemblance *was* uncanny.

With the historical enmity between their kingdoms, Mohab had only seen Kamal from afar. He'd last beheld him at the time of his *joloos*—as he'd sat on the throne, five and a half years ago. Not that Mohab had manipulated his way into Judar that night to see him. Jala had been his only objective. But *she* hadn't attended her own brother's wedding. Yet another thing he'd failed to predict where she was concerned.

Something else he'd failed to predict was how it would

feel seeing this guy up close. Kamal looked so much like Jala, it…ached deep in his chest.

It was as if someone had taken Jala and turned her into an older, intimidating male version of herself. They shared the same wealth of raven hair, the same whiskey-colored eyes and the same bone structure. The only differences were those of gender. Kamal's bronze complexion was shades darker than Jala's golden flawlessness, and at six foot six, the king of Judar would tower over his sister's statuesque five-nine, just as *he* once had. Her big brother was also more than double her size, but they shared the same feline grace and perfect proportions. While all that made her the embodiment of a fairy-tale princess, Kamal was the epitome of a hardened desert raider, exuding limitless power. And exercising it, too.

At forty, Kamal was one of the most influential individuals in the world, and had been so even before his two older brothers had abdicated the throne of Judar to him in a chain reaction of court drama and royal family scandals that still rocked the region and changed its course forever.

Now Kamal's lupine eyes simmered with the trademark menace famous for intimidating anyone he seared with his gaze. "Anything you find particularly amusing, Aal Ghaanem?"

"Your opening remark revived a memory of another… person mentioning death wishes." At Kamal's fierce glower, Mohab's smile spread. "What? You think I find you, or being escorted here like a prisoner of war, amusing?"

He'd expected worse arriving in Judar, with tensions between Saraya and Judar at a historic high. In fact, just yesterday, his king had all but declared war on Judar during a global broadcast from a UN summit. For Mohab, a prince of Saraya second in rank only to the king and his heirs, to land uninvited on Judarian soil in these fraught times was cause for extreme concern. Especially when said prince also happened to be the former head of Saraya's secret service. He'd expected to be put on the first flight out of Judar. Or even to be taken into custody.

In a preemptive bluff, he'd asserted he had time-sensitive business with King Kamal and the king would punish whoever detained him. That sent border security officials at the airport scrambling for orders from the royal palace. Mohab had half expected his gamble to fall through, that Kamal would have him kicked out of the kingdom. But within minutes, a dozen of Judar's finest secret-service men had descended on Mohab, breathing down his neck all the way here.

Apparently they considered him that dangerous. He was flattered, really.

"So you find death wishes a source of amusement? A daredevil by nature, not only by trade, eh? Figures. But aren't you also supposed to be meticulous and prudent? I thought that's why you're still in one piece after all the crazy stunts you've pulled. Isn't it the first thing you're taught when you're hatched in Saraya—that Judar doesn't sustain life for your species?"

His species. The Aal Ghaanems. The Aal Masoods' mortal enemies. *Aih.* There was *that* stumbling block, too.

"So again...*do* you have a death wish? Don't you know that, now more than ever, a high-profile Sarayan like you at large in Judar could have been targeted for any level of retribution?"

Mohab flattened a palm over his heart. "I'm touched you're concerned about keeping me in one piece. But I assure you, I behaved in an exemplary fashion, antagonizing no one."

"No one but me. Arriving unannounced, terrorizing my

subjects, forcing me to drop everything to investigate your incursion. Is this your king's last hope now that he's put his foot in his mouth on global feed? Is he afraid I'll finally knock him off his throne, as I should have long ago? Has he sent his wild card to deal with the crisis...at the root?"

"You think I'm here to...what? Assassinate you?" A huff of incredulity burst from Mohab. "I may be into impossible missions, but I'm not fond of suicidal ones. And I was almost strip-searched for anything that could even make you sneeze."

Kamal's laserlike gaze contemplated Mohab's mocking grin. "From my reports, you can probably take out my royal guard stripped and with both hands tied behind your back."

"Ah, you flatter me, King Kamal. I'd need one hand to go through them all."

The other man's steady gaze told him Kamal believed Mohab was capable of just that—and more—and wasn't the least bit fooled by his joking tone. "I have records of some true mission-impossible scenarios that you've pulled off. If anyone can enter a maximum-security palace with only the clothes on his back and manage to blow it up and walk away without a scratch, it's you."

Mohab's lips twitched. "If you believe I can get away with your murder, why did you agree to see me?"

"Because I'm intrigued."

"Enough to risk letting such a lethal entity within reach? You must be bored out of your mind being king."

Kamal exhaled. "You don't know the half of it—or how good *you* have it. A prince who is in no danger of finding himself on a throne, a black-ops professional who had the luxury of switching to a freelance career...emphasis on the 'free' part."

"While *you're* the king of a minor kingdom you've

made into a major one, and a revered leader who has limitless power at his fingertips and the most amazing family a man can dream of having."

"Apart from my incomparable wife and children, I'd switch places with you in a heartbeat."

Mohab laughed out loud. "The last thing I expected coming here is that I'd be standing with you, in the heart of Aal Masood territory, with us envying each other."

"In a better world, I would have offered you anything to have your skills at my disposal and you at my side. Too bad we're on opposite sides with no way to bridge the divide."

Mohab pounced on the opening. "That's why I'm here. To offer not only to bridge that divide, but to obliterate it."

Kamal frowned. "You deal in extractions, containments and cleanups. Why send you to offer political solutions?"

"I'm here on my own initiative because *I'm* the solution."

His declaration was met by an empty stare.

Then Kamal drawled, "Strange. You seem quite solid." Mohab chuckled at Kamal's unexpected dry-as-tinder wit, drawing a rumble from Kamal. "I have zero tolerance for wastes of time. If you prove to be one, you will spend a few nights as an honored guest in my personal dungeon."

"Is this a way to talk to the man who can give you Jareer?"

Kamal clamped his arm. "*Kaffa monawaraat wa ghomood*...enough evasions and ambiguity. Explain, and fast, or..."

"Put down your threats. I *am* here to mend our kingdoms' relations, and there's nothing I want more than to accomplish that as fast as possible."

"*Zain.* You have ten minutes."

"Twenty." Before Kamal blasted him, Mohab preempted him. "*Don't* say fifteen."

Kamal's gaze lengthened. "As an only child you missed out on having an older sibling kick your ass in your formative years. I'm close to rectifying your deficiency."

Mohab grinned. "Think you can take me on, King Kamal?"

"Definitely."

And Mohab believed it. Kamal wasn't a pampered royal depending on others' service and protection. This man was a warrior first and foremost. That he'd chosen to fight in the boardroom and now in the world's political arenas didn't mean he wouldn't be as effective on an actual battlefield.

Before Mohab made a rejoinder, the king turned and crossed his expansive stateroom to the sitting area. Mohab suspected it was to hide a smile so as not to acknowledge this affinity that had sprung up between them.

Kamal resumed speaking as soon as Mohab took a seat across from him. "So why do you think *you* can give me Jareer…when I already have it, Sheikh Prince Solution?"

A laugh burst out of Mohab's depths. That clinched it. He didn't care that other people thought Kamal scary or boorish. To him, the guy was just plain rocking fun.

Kamal's lips twisted in response, but didn't lift.

"There is no law prohibiting an Aal Masood from smiling at an Aal Ghaanem, you know."

Kamal's lips pursed instead. "I may issue one prohibiting just that. The way you're going, you might end up making the dispute between Judar and Saraya even more… insoluble."

Mohab sighed. "So… Jareer, euphemistically referred to as our kingdoms' *contested region*…"

"*And* currently known as our kingdoms' *future war zone,*" Kamal finished.

Not if Mohab managed to resolve this.

Jareer used to be under Saraya's rule. But the past few Sarayan monarchs had had no foresight. They'd centralized everything, neglecting then abandoning outlying regions. Jareer, on the border with Judar, had always been considered useless, because it lacked resources, and traitorous, because its citizens were akin to "enemy sympathizers." So when Judar had laid claim to Jareer, with its people's welcome, Mohab's grandfather, King Othman, had considered it good riddance.

But when Mohab's uncle, King Hassan, sat on Saraya's throne, he'd reignited old conflicts with Judar. His favorite crusade had been reclaiming Jareer. Not because he'd suspected its future importance, but to spite the region's inhabitants—and because he wanted more reasons to fight the Aal Masoods.

Then, two months ago, oil had been discovered in Jareer. Now the situation had evolved from an idle conflict between two monarchs to a struggle over limitless wealth and power. In a war between the two kingdoms, Saraya would be decimated for generations to come.

Only Mohab had the power to stop this catastrophe. Theoretically. There was still the possibility that Kamal would hear his proposition and reward his audacity by throwing him in that personal dungeon before wiping Saraya off the face of the earth.

One thing made Mohab hope this wouldn't happen. Kamal himself. He was convinced that, though Kamal had every reason to crush Saraya, he would rather not. He hadn't become one of the greatest kings by being reactionary—or by achieving prosperity for his kingdom at the cost of another kingdom's destruction.

At least, Mohab hoped he was right. He *had* read Kamal's "twin" all wrong once before after all....

"I will be disappointed if, after all this staring at me, you can't draw me from memory."

Jarred out of his thoughts by Kamal's drawl, Mohab blinked at him. "You just remind me of someone so much, it keeps sidetracking me."

"The same someone who made the death wish comment, eh?"

Not only brilliant, but intuitive, too. Mohab nodded.

"And there I was under the impression I was unique."

Mohab sighed. "You are...both of you. Two of a kind."

Kamal sat forward, ire barely contained. "As charmed as I am by all this...*nostalgia* of yours, I have a date with my wife in an hour, and I'd rather be late for my own funeral than for her. I might make you early for yours if you don't talk. Fast."

"All right. I am the rightful heir to Jareer."

Kamal's eyebrows shot up. He hadn't seen this coming. No one could have.

Mohab explained. "For centuries, Jareer was an independent land, and my mother's tribe, the Aal Kussaimis, ruled it up till a hundred and fifty years ago. But with my great-great-grandmother marrying an Aal Ghaanem, a treaty was struck with Saraya to annex the region, with terms for autonomy while under Sarayan rule and with provisions for secession if those terms weren't observed.

"When Jareer found itself on its own again under my grandfather's rule, it saw no reason to enforce the secession rules, as it was effectively separated from Saraya anyway. Then Judar offered its protection. But in truth, Jareer belongs to neither Judar nor Saraya. It belongs to my maternal tribe. I would have brought you the records of our claim for as far back as a thousand years, but after yesterday's fiasco, I had to rush to intervene before I could get everything ready. However, rest assured, the claim is heavily documented by the tribe's elders and historians."

Kamal blinked as if emerging from a trance. "That's your solution? Inserting the Aal Kussaimis as preceding claimants? Widening the dispute and adding more fuel to the fire?"

"Actually, I am ending the dispute. The Aal Kussaimis' claim trumps both the Aal Ghaanems' and the Aal Masoods'. Any regional or international court would sanction that claim."

Kamal's eyes burned with contemplation. "If all this is true, shouldn't I be talking to the tribe's elder? Who can't be you since you're…how old? Thirty?"

"Thirty-eight. But while it's true I'm not the tribe's elder, I am the highest-ranking tribe member by merit. I was elected the tribe's leader years ago. Which effectively makes me the king of Jareer."

Kamal's lashes lowered. A testament to his surprise.

When his gaze rose again, it was tranquil. That didn't fool Mohab for a second. He could almost hear the gears of Kamal's formidable mind screeching.

"Interesting. So you're claiming to be *King* Solution. Even if you prove to be the first, how do you propose to be the second?"

"Proving my claim is a foregone conclusion. The second should be self-evident."

"Not to me."

Jala's exact words that fateful night. Said in the same tone. Kamal's likeness to her had suddenly ceased to be reminiscent and had become only grating.

Mohab gritted his teeth. "My uncle assumed I would never invoke my claim, that I would always let him speak for me concerning Jareer's fate. And he was right—I didn't have time to be more than an honorary leader and had no desire to upset a status quo my people were perfectly content with under Judar's protection. But now things have changed."

Kamal huffed. "Tell me about it. Just two months ago, you were the 'rightful heir' to a stretch of desert with three towns and seven villages whose people lived on date and Arabian coffee production, souvenir manufacturing and desert tourism. Now you're the king of a land sitting on top of one of the biggest oil reservoirs ever discovered."

"I have no personal stake in Jareer's newfound wealth. I'm not interested in being richer, and I never wanted to be king. However, my people are demanding I declare Jareer an independent state and that I become their full-fledged ruler. But business and politics aren't my forte. So while I will do my people's bidding, I think it's in their best interests to leave their new oil-based prosperity to the experts."

"By experts, I assume you mean oil moguls."

"With you in charge of every step they take into Jareer."

Kamal raised one eyebrow. "You want me to run the show?"

"Yes."

Kamal digested this. "So that's Judar and Jareer and the oil companies. What about Saraya?"

"As a Sarayan, too, and because I admit the treaties with Saraya were never properly resolved before entering into the new ones with Judar, I will recognize its claim."

"So you claim Jareer, and split the cake between us all. Why do you assume I'll consider it? If I can have the whole cake?"

He sat forward, holding Kamal's gaze. "I do because you're an honorable man and a just king. Because I believe you'll do everything in your power to avoid escalating hostilities between our kingdoms. Before, it was about family feuds and pride. Now we're talking staggering wealth and power. If you decimate my claim and take all of Jareer, those who stand to lose that much would cause unspeakable damage. I regularly deal with situations that rage over way less, and believe me, nothing is worth the price of such conflicts."

"So how do you propose we split the cake?"

"For its historical role and ties to Jareer, and because both Judar and Jareer will need its cooperation, Saraya will get twenty percent of Jareer's oil. In recognition of Judar's more recent claim and its much bigger role in Jareer till this day, Judar gets forty percent. Jareer gets the other forty percent. Plus, its inhabitants would be first in line for all benefits and job opportunities that arise, and you will also be responsible to provide training for them."

"You've got it all worked out, don't you?"

"I have been working on my pitch since the oil's discovery. I was far from ready, but my uncle's theatrics at the UN yesterday forced my hand prematurely."

"What if I don't like your percentages or terms?"

"I would grant you whatever you wish."

"Even if you wanted to, as kings, we're not omnipotent. Why would your people agree to let you be so generous with their resources?"

Here it was. Moment of truth. The point of all this.

He took the plunge. "They would because it would be the *mahr* of your sister, Princess Jala."

Kamal rose to his feet in perfect calmness. It screamed instantaneous rejection more than anything openly indignant would have.

"No."

The cold, final word fell on Mohab like a lash. As Jala's rejection once had.

He resisted the urge to flinch at the sting. "Just no?"

"Consider yourself honored I deemed to articulate it. That you dared to voice this boggles the mind."

"Why?"

Kamal glared down at him. "I'll have my secretary of state draw you up an inventory of the reasons."

"Give me the broad lines."

"How about just one? Your bloodline."

"You'd condemn a man by others' transgressions?"

"We do inherit others' mistakes and enmities."

"And we can resolve them, not insist on regurgitating hatreds and spawning warring generations."

"The Aal Masoods aren't angels, but there is good reason why we abhor you, why all attempts at peacemaking fell through for centuries. Surely you remember the last marriage between our kingdoms and what your great-grandfather did to my great-aunt. I'm not letting my sister marry a man who comes from a family where the men mistreat their women."

"My great-grandfather and uncle don't represent the rest of us. *I* am nothing like them. You can investigate me further. And then consider the merits of my proposal. Once I claim Jareer, my uncle can retreat from his warpath. We'd appease his pride while going over his head in forging peaceful relations between all sides, to the benefit of all our people." Mohab rose to his feet to face him. "What I'm proposing is the best solution for all concerned, now and into the far future. And you know it."

After a protracted stare, Kamal finally exhaled. "We can forge peace with other kinds of treaties. Why bring marriage into this? And more important, why Jala? If you want to solidify the new alliance in the oldest way in the book, and the most enduring in our region, the Aal Masoods have other princesses who would definitely be more acceptable to your stick-in-the-mud family."

"My family has nothing to do with it. Jala is *my* choice." Kamal's astonishment made Mohab decide to come clean, as much as it was prudent to. "I had a…thing for Jala years ago, and I thought she reciprocated. It didn't end as I hoped. Now, years later, with both of us still unattached, I thought it might be fate's way of telling me I had to make another attempt at claiming the one woman who captured my fancy…and wouldn't let go. So while resolving our kingdoms' long-standing conflicts would certainly be a bonus, she's always been my main objective."

Expecting Kamal, as Jala's brother, to be offended—or at least to grill him about the nature of the "thing" he'd had for Jala—Kamal surprised him again, a hint of a smile dawning. "You mean discovering oil in Jareer and the crisis that ensued just presented you with the best bargaining chip to propose? And you didn't propose before because you never had enough leverage?"

Mohab shrugged, tension killing him. "Do I have enough now?"

Kamal's smile became definite. "If I disregard the stench of your paternal lineage and consider you based on your own merits, this might be a good idea. A perfect one, even. Knowing Jala, she'd never marry of her own accord and I hate to think she'll end up alone. And you, apart from the despicable flaw of having the Aal Ghaanem blood and name, seem like a…reasonably good match for her."

"So you're saying yes?"

"A yes isn't mine to say. I can't force her to marry you and wouldn't even if I could. Clearly this marriage quest of yours is hardly a done deal, since you require my intervention to even reach her. I won't ask what earned you a place on Jala's viciously strict no-approach list. *Ullah* knows I'm the last man to go all holier-than-thou on you for whatever transgression you committed to deserve this kind of treatment."

What would Kamal say if Mohab told him he didn't know exactly why he'd deserved that till this day?

Kamal gazed into the distance as if peering into a distasteful past. "I once did unforgivable things to the one woman who'd captured *my* fancy and wouldn't let go, and it took the intervention of others to give me that second chance with her."

"So you're paying it forward."

Kamal's eyes returned to his, the crooked smile back. "I am. *But* if she agrees to marry you, I'll take *sixty* percent as her *mahr*. If she refuses, the whole deal is off—and we'll draw up another treaty that saves your king's face so he can go sit in his throne and stop throwing war-agitating tantrums."

Mohab's first impulse was to kiss Kamal on both cheeks. This was beyond anything he'd come here expecting.

He extended his hand to Kamal instead, his smile the widest it had been in…six years. "Deal. You won't regret this."

Kamal shook his hand slowly. "You were wrong when you said you don't know much about business. You know nothing. You could have gotten me to agree to thirty percent. You're holding all the cards after all."

Mohab's smiled widened more. "I'm not so oblivious that I don't know the power I wield. But I would never haggle over Jala's *mahr*. If my decision didn't affect millions of people in both Saraya and Jareer, I would have given you the whole thing."

"You got it that bad?" Kamal drilled him with an incredulous gaze. "Do you *love* her?"

Love? He once had…or thought he had. But now he

knew it hadn't been real. Because nothing real could ever exist for a man like him. He only knew he couldn't move on. And that she hadn't moved on, either. He was still obsessed with their every touch, had starved for her every pleasure. Love didn't enter into the equation. Not only was it an illusion, it was one he couldn't afford.

But the pact he'd struck with Kamal was real. As was his hunger for Jala. That was more than enough. In fact, that was everything.

Kamal waved his hand. "Don't answer that. I don't think you *can* answer. If you haven't seen her in years, whatever you felt for her back then might be totally moot once you come face-to-face with each other again. So I won't hold you to this proposal for now. But since Jala is the most intractable entity I have the misfortune to know and love…" At Mohab's raised eyebrow, Kamal sighed. "*Aih,* she takes after her older brother, as Aliyah tells me."

Mohab did a double take. It was amazing, the change that came over Kamal's face as he mentioned his wife and queen. It was as if he glowed inside just thinking of her.

Kamal went on. "But for this to have a prayer of working, I need to give you much more of a helping hand than putting you in the same room with her. I need to give *her* a shove. I'll make it sound as if refusal isn't an option. Of course, if she *really* wants to refuse, she will, no matter what." His lips spread into a smile again. "All I can hope is that if I make things sound drastic enough, it'll give you that chance to make your approach. The rest… is up to you."

CHAPTER TWO

"You...*what?*"

Jala stared at Kamal, her shrill cry ringing in her own ears.

Staggering, she collapsed on the nearest horizontal surface, gaping up at Kamal who came to stand over her.

"I lied."

Ya Ullah. She *had* heard right the first time.

Another cry of sheer incredulity scratched her throat raw. "How could you do this to me? Are you *insane?*"

Kamal shrugged, not looking in the least repentant. "I had to get you here. Sorry."

"*Sorry?* You let me have a thousand panic attacks during the hours it took me to get here, thinking that Farooq was lying in hospital, critically injured, and you say... sorry?"

Even now that she knew Farooq was safe, the horror still reverberated in her bones. She'd never known such desperation, not even when she'd been held hostage and thought she'd die a violent death.

Fury seethed inside of her. "Don't you know what you did to me? As I thought of beautiful, vital Farooq lying broken, struggling for his life, how I wept as I thought how much he had to live for, as I thought of Carmen losing her soul mate, of Mennah growing up without her father.... You're a monstrous *pig,* Kamal!"

Kamal winced. "I said he was injured but that he was stable. I wanted you here, but didn't want to scare you more than necessary. How am I responsible for your exaggerations?"

"How? *How?*" She threw her hands up in the air in frustration. "How does Aliyah *bear* you?"

Kamal had the temerity to flash her that wolfish grin of his. "I never ask. I just wallow in the miracle of her, and that she thinks I'm the best thing that ever walked the earth."

"Then Aliyah, although she *looks* sane, is clearly deranged. Or under a spell...."

"It's called love." Kamal raised his hands before she exploded again. "I *am* sorry. But you said you'd never set foot here again, and I knew you wouldn't come unless you thought one of us was dying."

"I know you're ruthless and manipulative and a dozen other inhuman adjectives but...argh! Whatever you needed to drag me here for, you could have tried telling me the truth first!"

Kamal smirked. "*Aih,* and when that didn't work, I would have tried the lie next. I *would* have ordered you to come, but knowing you, you would have probably renounced your Judarian citizenship just so I'd stop being your king. If you weren't that intractable I wouldn't have had to lie, and you wouldn't have had those harrowing sixteen hours."

"So it's now my fault? You—you humongous, malignant rat! What could possibly be enough reason for you to drag me back here with this terrible lie?"

"Just that Judar is about to go to war."

She shot back up to her feet. "*Kaffa,* Kamal…enough. I'm already here. So stop *lying.*"

His face was suddenly grim. "No lie this time." He put his hand on her shoulder, gently pressed her down to the couch, coming down beside her this time. "It's a long story."

She gaped at him as he recounted it, plunging deeper into a surreal scape with every word.

But wars did erupt over far less, especially in their region. This was real.

When he was done, she exhaled. "You can't even consider war over oil rights, no matter how massive. Aren't you the wizard of diplomacy who peacefully resolves conflicts to every side's benefit?"

"Seems you're not familiar with King Hassan." A scoff almost escaped her. Oh, she was *so* very familiar with King Hassan. "Some people are immune to diplomacy."

"And *you're* not posturing and allowing your council to egg you on with hand-me-down rivalries and vendettas?"

It was Kamal's turn to scoff. "Give me some credit, Jala. I care nothing about any of this bull. *I* don't have an inflamed ego and don't borrow others' enmities."

"Yet you're letting someone who has and does drag you down to his level, when you should contain him and his petty aggressions." She exhaled her exasperation. "No wonder I did everything I could to get out of this godforsaken region and had to be told my oldest brother was dying to set foot here again. All this feudal backwardness is just…nauseating. You'd think nothing ever changed since the eleventh century!"

"War over oil rights is *very* twenty-first century."

"Congratulations to all of you, then, for your leap into modern warfare. I hope you'll enjoy deploying long-range missiles and playing high-tech war games." She muttered something about monkeys under her breath. "I still don't get why you conned me back here. You want me to have a front row seat with you lunkheads when the war begins?"

He reached for her hand, his eyes cajoling. Uh-oh.

"You actually play the lead role in averting this catastrophe."

"What could I possibly have to do with resolving your political conflicts?"

"Everything really. Only you can stop the war now, by marrying an Aal Ghaanem prince."

"What?"

"Only a blood-mixing union will end hostilities and forge a long-lasting alliance."

She snatched her hand from his grasp, erupting to her feet. "Did I say you were stuck in the eleventh century? You've just stumbled five more centuries backward. *Not* so good seeing you, Kamal. And don't expect to lay eyes on me for a long while. Certainly never in Judar again."

Kamal gave her that unfazed glance that made her want to shriek at the top of her lungs. "It's this or war. The war you know full well would come at an unthinkable price to everyone in Judar—and in Saraya and Jareer, too."

Wincing at the terrible images his words smeared across her imagination, she gritted out, "Let's say for argument's sake that I don't think you're all insane to be still dabbling in marriages of state to settle political disputes. The Aal Masoods have many princesses who're just right for the role of political bride. In fact, some have been born and bred for the role. So how are any of you foolish enough to consider *me*—aka the Prodigal Princess?"

Lethal steel came into Kamal's eyes. "Others' opinions are irrelevant. You're *the* princess of Judar. Only your blood could end centuries of enmity and forge an unbreakable alliance. So it's not a choice. You are getting married to the Aal Ghaanem prince."

"Wow. If you wore a crown, I'd think it got too tight on your swelling head and gave you brain damage. Anyway, if you think you can sacrifice me at the altar of your tribal reconciliations, you're suffering from serious delusions."

"We all offer sacrifices when our kingdom needs us."

"What sacrifices?" She coughed a furious chuckle. "To remain married to Carmen, Farooq tossed his crown-prince rank to Shehab when our kingdom needed him. Shehab did the same with you, to marry Farah. You grabbed the rank and *sacrifice* only because it got you Aliyah in the bargain. You're all living in ecstatic-ever-afters because you did exactly what you wanted and never sacrificed a thing for 'our kingdom.'"

"Farooq and Shehab had the option of passing on their duty. I didn't, like you don't now. And I thought it *was* a sacrifice when I accepted my duty."

"No, you didn't. You knew nothing less than another threat of war would get Aliyah to say good-morning to you again. You pounced on the 'duty' that would make her your queen and pretended to hate your 'fate.'" At his raised eyebrows, she smirked. "I can figure things out pretty good, *ya akhi al azeez*. So spare me the sacrifice speech, brother dear. You're out of your mind if you think you can sway me into this by appealing to my patriotism."

"Then it will be your steep humanitarian inclinations. You've been in war zones. You know that once war starts, there's no stopping the chain reaction that harvests lives in its path. As a woman who lives to alleviate the suffering of others, and who can stop this nightmarish scenario, you'll do anything to abort it, even if you abhor Judar and the whole region. And the very idea of marriage."

The terrible knowledge that he was right, if there was

no other choice, seeped into her marrow. "So now what? You'll line up Aal Ghaanem princes and I'll pick the least offensive one? And the one I pick would just accept being sacrificed for his kingdom's peace and prosperity?"

"If a man considers marrying you a sacrifice, he must be devoid of even a drop of testosterone."

"You won't appeal to my feminine ego, either. Any man in the region would rather jump out of a ten-story window than marry a woman like me, *the* princess of Judar or not."

"A woman like you would be an irreplaceable treasure to any man in any region."

"Blatant brotherly hyperbole aside, no, *a woman like me* wouldn't. A woman living alone in the West since she was eighteen is the stuff of region-wide dishonor around here. It had to be something as dire as the threat of war and the promise of unending oil to sweeten my scandalous pill for one of those stuck-in-the-dark-ages princes."

"The new generation of princes are nowhere as bad as that."

"The only one I know who isn't is Najeeb. But I bet *he* won't be joining the lineup." Her lips twisted with remembered bitterness. "King Hassan would never sacrifice his heir to such a fate as me, no matter the incentives."

Kamal waved his hand. "You won't suffer the discomfort of a lineup. The Aal Ghaanem prince has already been chosen."

She almost had to pick her jaw off the floor this time. "How can I express my gratitude that you've gone the extra mile and abolished whatever choice I had in this antiquated process?"

Kamal's lips twitched. "Let me rephrase my extremely misleading statement. The Aal Ghaanem prince volunteered. And he is already here. But he had the consideration to let me prepare you before he came in. So shall I send him in…or do you need some more time before you meet your groom-to-be?"

She sank back onto the couch, objections and insults swarming so violently it was impossible to pick one to voice.

Calmly disregarding her apoplectic state, Kamal bent and kissed her cheek. "Give this a chance, and it'll all work out for the best. You have me as the best example for *assa ann takraho shai'an wa hwa khairon lakkom.*"

You may hate something and it's for your best.

Before she could do something drastic, like poke him in the eye, he straightened, turned on his heel and walked away.

She watched him disappear, all her mental functions on the fritz.

What had just happened?

Was she really back in Judar? Only to find herself being pushed into a far worse cage than anything her previous life here had been? Could it be true that refusal wasn't an option?

Suddenly a suspicion cleaved into her brain.

The logical progression to this nightmare.

The identity of this "volunteer."

The man who was the reason she'd sworn never to return to this region. He *was* an Aal Ghaanem prince, even if the world forgot that most of the time.

But he would never volunteer to…to…

You're mine, Jala. And no matter how long it takes, I swear to you, I will reclaim you. I will make you beg to be mine again.

The promise…the *threat*…that had circulated in her being for six long years, burning her to the core with its malicious arrogance and possessiveness, reverberated in her bones.

No. He'd just said that out of spite, to poison whatever reprieve walking away would grant her. He hadn't really wanted to reclaim her. Not when he'd only claimed her as a means to an end. An end he must believe he'd long achieved....

Her heart kicked, had her pitching forward to the edge of her seat. The door of the reception room was opening.

The next moment, her heart battered her ribs. Time ceased. Reality fell away. Everything converged on one thing. The shadow separating from the darkness. A shape she remembered all too well.

Him.

No. *No.* Not when she'd finally managed to purge his malignant memory. She must stop this confrontation from coming to pass, flee...*now.*

She didn't move. Couldn't. Could only sit there, her every nerve unraveling as soundless steps brought him into the circle of light where she sat exposed, besieged.

His eyes were the first things that emerged out of the gloom. Those fire pits had haunted her dreams and tormented her waking hours since she'd last seen them.

But the tremors arcing through her weren't from what she saw in them, or the blow of his presence or its implications. It was the awareness that had swept her from the first moment she'd ever encountered him. Even amidst the terror of the hostage crisis, it had yanked her out of reality, plunged her into a stunned free fall where only he existed. For that same feeling to mushroom again now, after all that had happened...

He blinked, and the vice garroting her snapped, propelling her to her feet and to the French windows.

Her steps picked up speed as her exit to the palace gardens neared...then it disappeared. Behind a wall of muscle and maleness. It was as if he'd materialized in her path.

He didn't try to detain her, didn't need to. His very aura snared her. And that was before her gaze streaked up, found him looking at her with that trance-inducing intensity.

Finding him so near, after all these years, after what he'd cost her....

Her grip on consciousness softened. The world swirled as she stared up at him, a prisoner to her own enervation. And again the sheer injustice of it all hit her.

No one should be endowed with all this. He was too... everything. And even in the subdued lighting and through the veil of her own wavering senses she could see he was even more than she remembered. Six years had taken him from the epitome of manhood to godlike levels.

He towered over her, even though she was six feet in her heels, his physique that of an Olympian, his face that of an avenging angel, every inch of him composed of planes and hollows and slashes of power and perfection. Adding to his lethal assets, his wealth of sun-gilded mahogany hair was now long enough to be gathered at his nape, the severe scrape emphasizing the ruggedness of his leonine forehead and the vigor of his hairline. A trim new beard and mustache accentuated the jut of his cheekbones and the dominance of his jawline and completed the ruthless desert raider image. Maturity had added more of everything to that supreme being of bronze and steel who'd taken her breath away and had held it out of reach for as long as he'd had her under his spell. Something she'd thought she'd broken.

But if, after all she'd been through, all the maturation she'd thought she'd undergone, he could still look at her and take control of her senses, then the spell couldn't *be* broken.

But this unadulterated coveting in his eyes… She couldn't be reading it right.

Still, when he took a step closer, he vibrated with something that simulated barely checked hunger. Which would be unleashed at the slightest provocation—a word, a gasp….

But she was incapable of even those. She'd expended all her power in her escape effort. Now she was caught in stasis, waiting for his next move to reanimate her.

None came. He stared down at her, as if her nearness affected him just as acutely. When *he'd* been the one who'd planned this ambush, who'd been lying in wait for her.

The barricades around her resentment melted, shattering her inertia, imbuing her limbs with the steadiness of outrage as she put the distance he'd obliterated back between them.

"Guess your memory must be patchy from all the head blows I hear is an occupational hazard in your line of work. Your presence can only be explained by partial to total amnesia."

Another blink lowered his thick, gold-tipped lashes, eclipsing the infernos of his eyes and his reaction. Then they swept up, exposing her to a different kind of heat. Surprise? Challenge? Humor?

Just the idea that it could be the latter poured acid on her inflamed nerves. "Let me fill one paramount hole in your recollections. What I last said to you remains in full force now. I never want to see you again. So you can take whatever game you think you're playing and go straight to hell."

She swept around then, desperation to get away from him fueling her steps…and her arm was snagged in a hard, warm grip.

Before she could fully register the bolt that zapped her, a tug swirled her around smoothly, as if in a choreographed dance, and brought her slamming against him from breast to calf.

Before she could draw another breath, one of his hands slipped into the hair at her nape, immobilizing her head and tilting her face upward. The other hand trailed a heavy path of possession down to her buttocks. Then, as he held her prisoner, exerting no force but that of his will, he let her see it. The very thing she'd once reveled in experiencing—the lethal beast he kept hidden under the civilized veneer. Its cunning savagery had assured his survival in the dangerous existence he'd chosen, his triumph over the most deadly enemies. That beast appeared to be starving—and she was what would sate its cravings.

Holding her stunned gaze, his own crackling with a dizzying mixture of calculation and lust, he lowered his head.

Feeling she'd disintegrate at the touch of his lips, she averted her face at the last moment.

His lips landed at the corner of her mouth, plucking convulsively at her flesh. The familiarity of his lips, the unfamiliarity of his facial hair, sparked each nerve ending individually. The gusts of his breath filled her with his scent, burying her under an avalanche of memory. Of how it used to feel to lose herself to the ecstasy of his powerful possession.

The hand on her buttocks pressed her closer, letting her feel his arousal, wringing hers from her depths. Before she could deal with this blow, the hand holding her head combed through her hair. Each stroke sent delight cascading from every hair root, spilled moans from her depths in answer to the unintelligible bass murmurings from him. Then his other hand caressed its way beneath her jacket, freeing her blouse from her skirt…and delving below.

A gasp tore out of her as those calloused fingers splayed against her sizzling flesh, imprinting it like a brand, mak-

ing her instinctively press closer. And then he took his onslaught to the next level.

Yanking up her skirt, he slipped below her panties to
cup her buttocks, kneading her taut flesh hungrily before
hauling her against him. Weightless, in his power, she
keened as the long-craved steel of his erection ground
against her core. A scalding growl rolled in his gut as he
tugged one thigh, opening her around his hips, spreading
her for his domination, while the hand at her back plastered her heaving chest against his. Her breasts swelled
with each rub against his hard power, the abrasion of their
clothes turning her nipples to pinpoints of agony.

She writhed in his hold as he singed kisses down her
neck, ravaged her in suckles that would mark her skin,
sending vicious pleasure hurtling through her blood, lodging into her womb with each savage pull.

All existence converged on him, became him—his body
and breath, his taste and feel, his hands and mouth—as
he strummed her flesh, reclaimed her every inch and response. With just a touch, she'd ceased to be herself, becoming a mass of need wrapped around him, open to him,
his to exploit and plunder…to pleasure and possess.

She could no longer hear anything but her thundering
heart and their strident breathing as he raised her up and
slid her down his body in leisurely excursions. He had
her riding his erection through their clothes. He dipped
his head to capture her nipple through her bra in massag-
ing nips, sending never-forgotten ecstasy corkscrewing
through her every nerve ending.

Her moans droned, interrupted only by sharp intakes
of breath. The flowing throb between her thighs escalated
into pounding, tipping from discomfort into pain until she
cried out. At her distressed if unmistakable demand, he
shuddered beneath her, snapping his head up. Then, eyes

glazed with ferocity, he crashed his lips onto her wide-open mouth and thrust deep.

She plunged into his taste, fierce wonder spreading in her flickering awareness. How did she remember it so accurately, crave it so acutely still?

Then everything ceased as his tongue invaded her, commanded hers to tangle and duel and drink deeper from the well of passion she'd once drowned in.

Then something stirred in her, shutting down her mind; something cold and ugly tore through the delirium. A realization.

This had happened before. This had been what he'd done to her that last time. He'd taken over her senses, exploited her responses, inundated her with physical satisfaction…and almost decimated her soul and psyche in the process.

Now he'd taken her over again, as if a mountain of pain and resentment didn't exist between them. She was letting him pull her strings again when he only ever saw her as a means to an end. Having an even bigger end this time, he'd decided to go into all-out invasion mode from the get-go. And she was letting him. *No.*

Anger and humiliation shattered the spell, had her struggling in his arms as if fighting for her life.

Stiffening for a long moment, as if unable to make up his mind whether that was an attempt to get away or to press closer, he finally tore his lips from hers and slid her down his body and back to the ground.

Every muscle burning from the slow poison of need with which he'd reinfected her, she staggered, groping for equilibrium. She'd taken barely a step away when his hands descended on her shoulders and pulled her back against him.

She couldn't even tremble, the control she'd long struggled for shattered, leaving her drained. She could only lean back against him limply, her head rolling on his shoulder.

Taking this as consent, he cupped her breasts, pressing against her as he groaned in her ear. "I didn't intend to do this. I still have no control over what I'm doing right this second. I walked in here and it was as if time hit Rewind, as if we'd never been apart. And just like you always do, you overrode my every rational thought and impulse with a look, a word. Then I touched you and you responded… like you're responding still…."

This zapped her with just enough energy to push out of his arms. "Sure. It's my fault."

He let her put distance between them this time. "There's no fault here. Just the phenomenon that exists between us, this absolute physical affinity we share. But I really didn't intend to kiss you."

"*Kiss* me? That's what you call a kiss?"

A rough huff of self-deprecation escaped him. "So I almost took you standing up, probably would have, not giving a second thought that we're in the middle of your brother's stateroom, if you hadn't stopped me. You have that effect on me. I see you and I can only think of pleasuring you."

Once she'd believed his every word. She'd been certain that what they did share *was* a phenomenon, as undeniable and unstoppable as a force of nature. Then she'd found out the truth. It was clear he thought she didn't know, that he didn't need to invent a new deception.

He approached her again, one of those hands stroking a gossamer touch down her cheek. "But you're wrong. About the last thing you said to me. No matter how many blows to the head I sustain, nothing could make me forget it. You said, *Find yourself someone else who might have a death wish. Because I don't.*"

He remembered. Word for word.

Figured. He was said to possess a computerlike mind, always archiving, networking, extrapolating. On top of his fighting prowess and weapons mastery, it was what made him the ultimate modern warrior and strategist in this information age.

She pulled away from the debilitation of his touch. "And that statement has been solidified by the passage of time and reinforced by this new stunt. So, since you have a flawless memory, what else is wrong with you? Haven't I already turned down your marriage proposal once before?"

Perfect teeth sank into his lip, making her feel they'd sunk into hers again. "I prefer to dwell on when you said yes."

She ignored the tingling of her lips. "Only to follow it with a resounding no, when I came to my senses. Now you're using an impending war to reintroduce the subject? Since it's not faulty memory, I assume these are your new orders?"

Something blipped in his gaze. It was gone before she could fathom it. But even that much from him was telling. He was taken aback and clearly had no idea that she was onto him.

Infusing her tone with all the cool derision she could, she cocked her head at him. "This surprises you? Hmm, maybe I must reconsider all I heard about your reputation as a know-it-all spymaster. Anyway, if you're still not sure what I mean… Yes, I do know. Everything."

CHAPTER THREE

She knew. Everything.

For stunned moments that was all that filled Mohab's mind. Then alarm diminished and questions crowded in its place.

What was "everything" according to her? Whatever she thought that was, could that be the reason behind her sudden rejection six years ago?

He stared at her as she stood safe feet away, tall and majestic in a cream skirt suit that made her skin glow, still the most magnificent thing he'd ever seen. Even more than he'd remembered. And he'd thought he remembered everything about this woman whose memory had refused to relinquish its hold over him, whose feel still seethed beneath his skin, whose taste still lingered on his tongue.

But he'd come here today hoping what he remembered had been exaggerated, that his many sightings of her during the past years had perpetuated the delusion, that one up close look would dissipate it.

Then he'd walked into Kamal's stateroom, and one look at her had dashed any hopes he'd ever entertained of finally purging her from his system. Everything he'd remembered about her had been diluted. Or maturity had only intensified her effect on him. He *hadn't* meant to drown in her. But the years of separation, instead of dampening his responses, had only made it impossible for him to ration them.

His gaze swept her ripe curves. His every inch ached, remembering how they'd fit against his angles, how her supple softness had filled his hands, cushioned his hardness, accommodated his demand. His fingers buzzed as they relived skimming her warm, velvet skin, overflowing with her resilient flesh, winding in her silky, raven tresses. His lips and tongue stung with the phantom sensations of feeling hers again, hot and moist and fragrant, surrendering to his invasion, demanding his dominance.

He'd almost taken her, in a near-literal reenactment of their last time together, before saying one word to her. And how she'd responded. He'd felt her every inch vibrate to his frequency, every nerve resonate with his urgency. Even now, after she'd collected herself and retreated behind a barricade of cold contempt, he could still feel it seething. Her mind was another matter, though. If outrage could flay, he'd be minus skin now. He certainly felt as raw as if he was.

So was her rage a reaction to his incursion, or did the developing situation only pile on top of the "everything" she claimed to know?

He could ask, since she seemed to be forthcoming all of a sudden. But he wasn't here to dredge up the past. And if he could still just touch her and they'd both go up in flames, that was all he needed to know.

All he needed, period.

But she was waiting for him to make some kind of response to her revelation. He'd give her one, all right. Just not what she might expect.

He walked back to where she'd retreated. "So you know everything?" At her curt nod, he shoved his hands into his pockets so they wouldn't reach for her again. "Let's test this claim, shall we?"

That twist surprised her. *Zain*. Good. He shouldn't be the only one not knowing if he was coming or going here.

He cocked his head at her. "Do you know that I committed a cardinal sin during that hostage crisis?"

The tangent seemed to confuse her.

When she answered, the modulated voice that had sung its siren song in his ear for years was lower, huskier. "If you mean killing, I know all too well. Those moments, when you stormed the conference hall with your black-ops team and took out our captors, is forever branded in my memory. I watched you…terminate six of our captors single-handedly, with a precision I only thought happened in movies." Those slanting, dense eyebrows he'd loved to trace and lips drew together. "But I didn't think you considered killing a sin. Not in your line of work."

"Killing *is* my line of work. At least, it's part of the job description. Though 'killing' isn't what I call it. I prefer 'eliminating lethal threats to innocents.'"

Her eyes turned a somber cognac as she nodded. She didn't contest that he spoke the simple truth, that people like him were a necessity to control the monsters who roamed the earth. She'd obviously seen enough in *her* line of work to know that his extreme measures were indispensable at times. Just as they had been that day when she'd been taken hostage with five hundred others at that conference in Bidalya.

But she could have contradicted him to score a point. That she didn't, that she remained objective even to the detriment of her own attack, thrilled him.

He sighed. "But the sin I committed had nothing to do with the violence I perpetrated. I committed the cardinal sin of my line of work."

"How so?"

"I deviated from the plan, improvised. I could have gotten so many killed."

Again, counter to his expectations, her eyes grew impassioned as she contradicted him, in *his* defense. "But you saved hundreds, all of us who remained. And you didn't seem to be improvising. You acted with such certainty, such efficiency, it was as if everything had been rehearsed. To the point that it felt as if the captors themselves were playing an exact role in the sequence you designed."

"If it seemed like that to you, it was because of my men's outstanding skills, and because I managed to compensate on the fly. But that doesn't mean I didn't make a huge mistake." Her eyes were puzzled but engrossed. He could tell that she couldn't wait to see where he was taking this. "Do you remember what I did when we stormed in?"

She nodded stiffly, as if it still pained her to think of that harrowing time. And who could blame her? She'd watched three people get killed in cold blood as proof of their captors' resoluteness. She'd once told him that knowing the true meaning of helplessness, failing to protect those people, had damaged her more than her fear of meeting the same fate.

"What do you remember?"

Her exquisite features contorted with the reluctance to conjure up the memories. Still, she answered, "It was so explosive, but I remember it frame for frame. You burst in while one of them was threatening Najeeb that he'd start blowing parts off him. Then I met your eyes across the distance and…and…"

"Go on."

She swallowed. "You streaked toward me, blowing away those men left and right, and then you were in front of me—shielding me—as you and your team finished off the rest."

"And that was my sin. *Najeeb* was my mission. And I took one look at you across that hall and made the instantaneous decision to save you first."

Her eyes widened; her lips opened on a soundless exclamation. She'd evidently never thought to question what he'd done.

When she finally talked, her whisper was impeded. "But you blasted away the one who was threatening him as you ran to me. You gave no one a chance to use him as shield or to harm him."

"I should have run *to* him, should have shielded *him*. As my crown prince, he should have been my only priority. Instead, I made that you."

"But you managed to save him and everyone else."

"Only because I managed to compensate, as I said. Najeeb could have gotten shot before I ended the threat to him. And knowing full well the widespread damage his injury or death would have caused, retaliations that would have reaped far more than five hundred lives, I still risked that."

Time seemed to stretch as bewilderment glimmered in her gemlike eyes.

She let out a shaky breath. "So what are you saying? That you took one look at me and were so bowled over you decided to risk everyone's lives—including your own—for *me*?"

"No. That's not what I'm saying. I was…bowled over a bit before that."

He watched her mouth drop open. This was news to her. He'd never intimated that he'd seen her before that day. But he'd seen her over two years earlier, had searched her out many times afterward.

"But it was the first time I'd seen you!"

"I saw no upside in letting you see me, or in acting on my interest. You were, as you pointed out so many times when we were together, an Aal Masood…and I was an Aal Ghaanem. The Montagues and Capulets didn't have a thing on our moronically feuding houses. I also didn't think it would be wise or fair to ever involve a woman in my crazy existence." He exhaled. "Then I saw you in danger and every rational thought flew out the window."

Her eyes filled with so much; he struggled not to drag her to him and kiss them closed.

Then they emptied of everything, leaving only hardness. "Why are you telling me this now?"

He shrugged. "I am testing your claim that you know everything. I just proved that you don't."

"You proved only that you spin a good yarn. As I already knew you did. Is this one supposed to appeal to my ego?"

A mirthless huff escaped him. "You think I'm making this up? Why? To butter you up for my current purposes? I wish. As someone who knows what a bullet feels like ripping through my flesh, I would have preferred one to admitting how fallible I am, how unprofessional I was, how I risked everyone's lives to protect a woman who didn't know me…whom I believed could never be mine."

Steel mixed with gold in her gaze, clearly not buying his admissions. Funny. If he'd ever thought he'd confess this to her, he wouldn't have dreamed this would be her reaction.

Might as well confess the rest, let her make whatever she wished of it. "When I burst in and I met your eyes, saw that mixture of terror and courage and fury… I couldn't imagine I wouldn't be able to look in those eyes again, to get the chance to know you. My instincts took over…and I let them."

She averted those eyes, depriving him of their touch. "Yet after you went to such lengths to save me, you didn't follow up on your wish to 'know' me. Not for over a year."

He exhaled heavily. "I might have saved the day, for you and for everyone else, but *I* knew how badly I messed up. I guess I was punishing myself for failing to fulfill my duty and couldn't reward my failure by giving myself the gift of knowing you, the one behind my lapse."

She raised her eyes, that derision back in full force. "So was it guilt that stopped you from giving yourself the 'gift' of knowing me, or was it that you didn't think it 'wise or fair' to involve a woman in your crazy existence?"

"Both. And the family feud. Everything."

"Then, a year later, you just decided to disregard all those overpowering reasons you had not to approach me. Once you made that first contact, you relentlessly courted me all the way to your bed. Then, before I could catch my breath, you pushed for marriage. And when I tried to slow things down, you pushed harder. And when I decided to put a stop to it, you threatened you'd slander me and destroy any man who came near me."

He gritted his teeth on the memory of his despair, when he'd felt her slipping through his fingers. "These were my most indefensible moments. Trying to hang on to you, then going almost berserk when I couldn't."

"Yeah, sure," she scoffed. "You lost control out of sheer emotion. That coming from the ice-cold man they sent after the Mata Haris of the world, to seduce, entrap and destroy them."

It was his turn to blink in surprise. She knew that? How?

She elaborated on just how much she knew. "I've been told how you are the man to rely on when a woman is involved, the incomparable undercover agent no female can resist. You're not only known as *Al Moddammer,* but *Qatel an-Nesaa*—the lady-killer. And you're claiming you took one look at the twenty-year-old nobody I was, an obscure member of your family's hereditary enemies, and couldn't think straight on account of my irresistibility?"

He exhaled. "That does about sum it up."

"Tut."

That click of her tongue shot straight to his loins. Any second now he was going to ravish her again, come what may.

Unaware of his state, she went on, "I expected better from the ultimate secret-service weapon that you are. Some airtight premise, at least something more plausible. Seems I have to revise many things I believed about you. You do remember I prefaced this unfortunate encounter, before you took that detour into badly scripted drama, by mentioning that I know everything, don't you?"

"Again I say I wish it was anything but the pathetic truth. So, against all my intentions, I find myself forced to ask, according to you, what *is* everything?"

Her eyes became icy embers. "Everything from the moment I went to meet Najeeb and found you waiting for me instead."

JALA WATCHED THOSE eyes of his blaze at her declaration.

She'd never been able to decide when they were most hypnotic: when they glowed with a constant flame or when they fluctuated—as they'd been doing throughout this confrontation—their pupils expanding and constricting, giving the intense tawny irises the illusion of burning coals.

She'd dreamed of those fiery eyes, his voice, his touch, for over a year after the hostage crisis. And it had had nothing to do with his saving her life. He'd just…overwhelmed her. He'd melted her just by looking at her, just

by being near. When feeling that way had been totally out
of character for her. She'd been too mature for her age, as
her brothers had always told her. Cerebral, almost jaded.

But Mohab...he *had* bowled her over. For over a year,
she'd relived every single second of being pressed against
the body he'd fearlessly offered as her shield. She'd suffocated with remembered terror that a bullet could tear
through his perfection. Then she'd relived every second
as he'd sheltered her away from the scene of carnage. But
before she could have even a word with him, the Bidalyan
government had bundled all the hostages, sending them
back to their countries to close that case as quickly as
possible.

For months afterward, she'd gone crazy trying to find
out who he was. Until Najeeb, her fellow hostage, had
sought her out.

Najeeb had been magnificent during the crisis. Levelheaded, fearless, shrewd, he'd managed their captors like a
veteran used to being under fire. It was certain more people
would have died if not for his intervention. He'd recognized her as the only one he could depend on and they'd
forged an instantaneous bond, as if they'd always worked
together, minimizing damages for two agonizing days.

Then one of their captors had cracked, started shrieking he'd blow bits off Najeeb, as the highest-ranking royal,
so his father would pressure the Bidalyans to meet their
demands faster. But just as the situation had escalated,
Mohab had exploded onto the scene.

It had surprised her to find out from Najeeb that their
savior had been the head of Saraya's special forces, not Bidalya's. Turned out Bidalya had ceded control of the hostage retrieval to Mohab so he'd be responsible for his crown
prince's fate, and because he was the best at what he did.

But finding out he was also Najeeb's older paternal

cousin had dashed even her fantasies. Najeeb could be her friend in spite of their families' enmity. But friendship wasn't what she'd wanted from Mohab. Not that she'd thought she'd see him again.

Then, one day, he'd just appeared, instead of Najeeb, to escort her to her first award ceremony. She'd been so delirious with this windfall she hadn't questioned how or why. Even when Najeeb had called, explaining the emergency that would keep him away for months and hadn't mentioned sending Mohab, she hadn't thought it odd. She'd taken everything Mohab had said as uncontestable truth.

That first evening had been magical, and he'd been the perfect companion. He'd suggested lunch the next day and she'd jumped at his invitation, had continued to grab every opportunity to be with him for the next two months, with Mohab showing her more facets of himself, each impossible to resist.

Not that resisting had been a consideration. Then, as if he'd known just when she'd become ready for more, he'd taken her to his penthouse, and then he'd taken her....

"Will you answer my question, or will you keep the 'everything' you know a mystery?"

His taunt pulled her out of the plunge into the past, which appeared to have been only a moment in real time.

She was loath to dredge up the sordid past, but she'd cornered herself into doing just that.

What the hell.

She leveled her best denigrating gaze on him. "How is it a mystery when we both know you only entered my life to eliminate me from Najeeb's? That I was just another mission to *Qatel an-Nesaa?*"

CHAPTER FOUR

Jala watched his pupils expand until it looked as if his eyes were being engulfed by black holes.

He finally inhaled. "What's the source of your info?"

"What do you think?"

"Najeeb." It was a statement. "What did he tell you?"

"The truth."

A long exhalation, then Mohab moved, brushing past her on his way to the couch. He sat down in one of those movements of pure power and grace. "I injured my knee in my last mission, so standing isn't a favorite activity at the moment." When she only stared down at him, he sighed. "I also pulled a muscle in my neck."

His perfectly formed hand caressed the space beside him, enticing her to fill it, making her feel it over her back, below her panties, kneading and owning all over again.

She gritted her teeth against the resurgence of lust. "And I should care about your discomfort? The man who's responsible for dragging me back to this godforsaken region and behind this farce that's causing me nothing but discomfort?"

"Point taken. But this will take longer than I expected and it would alleviate at least your physical discomfort if you sit for the duration."

"Actually, this won't take *any* longer. I already told you

to go to hell. I'm sure you chest-thumping males will find another way to settle your war once you give up on me as a convenient chess piece in your backward power games."

She thought she was safely out of his range, but when she turned away it was her hand he snagged this time. Her balance was so compromised she needed only a coaxing tug to tumble over him.

Breath burst from her lungs as her body impacted his, even when it did so softly. His effortless power supported most of her weight in midplummet, arranging her to land across his body, one arm cushioning her back, the other gathering her thighs over his lap.

Before she could even recoil, he flattened her breasts to the expanse of his chest, swamping her in the intoxication of his scent and heat. "I'm a breath away from picking up where we left off, Jala. This time, neither of us will be able to stop. So if you don't want me to make love to you right here on your brother's couch, distract me."

She hated him, but herself more, for knowing he'd only spoken the truth. All her pleasure centers were revving, her body readying itself for him. Craving *had* been seething beneath her skin all this time. She had to end this before he exploited that weakness. More than he already had.

"Would a poke in the eye be distracting enough for you? Or do you prefer something bitten off?"

"I'd take any voluntary touch from you, but—" he released her thighs and scooped her hands into his palms "—I'd prefer not to add to my injuries right now. There's another thing that would dampen my arousal. Having this out at last. Talk to me."

"I already said all I had to say, then and now."

"All right. I'll do the talking. So Najeeb told you 'the truth.'" She nodded, hoping to lull him enough so she'd be able to squirm away with as little indignity as possible. He sighed, pressing his chest harder into her. "Truths are over-rated, points of view and perspectives at best. So tell me his version, what you sanctioned as the only one there is."

"I'll play your aggravating game on one condition."

"Let you go?" Her glare said that didn't deserve the oxygen it would take to say yes. He sighed deeper. "I doubt anything you say can be worth not holding you like this."

A growl rolled in her gut. "I would have preferred to end this with your dignity and appendages intact, but at this point, I'm not against screaming bloody murder to get rid of you. The royal guard won't care who you are. By the time I pull them off you, you'll have more than a creaking knee and neck."

The smile playing across his cruelly sensuous lips became a full-fledged grin, as if she'd just made him a delightful promise. "I had this discussion with your brother a few days ago, about who'd win in such a confrontation—his royal guard or me with my hands tied behind my back."

And the worst part? She could believe the odds *would* be in his favor. Damn him.

"But since I can't risk your brother's current goodwill if I damage his soldiers, I'll pass on a demonstration."

He released her, oh, so slowly, and she felt nerves spooling inside every inch that separated from him. Even withdrawing his touch was as exquisite as bestowing it.

Ya Ullah...why was she so afflicted? Why was he the only man who'd ever accessed her controls and so...uncontrollably? How was her mental and emotional aversion so divorced from her sensual response? Why was it so absolute?

And he knew exactly what he was doing to her; he was playing her responses like a virtuoso. A ruthless expert in manipulating the female body and psyche.

Najeeb had told her Mohab had played many women

before her. As, no doubt, he had countless others after her. Probably during. Not ones like the inexperienced and already infatuated young woman she'd been, but cunning, jaded women who'd seen and done it all, even hardened criminals and spies. Yet he'd still taken them in with his overwhelming sexuality and perfectly simulated charm and chivalry. She hadn't had a chance.

A new wave of mortification poured strength into her limbs as she pushed away from him. He didn't help her this time, forcing her to dip with all her weight into his unyielding power for support. The way he threw his head back against the back of the couch, his rumble of enjoyment as her fingers sank into his muscles, the way his heavy lids lowered, turning his eyes to burning slits as he watched her struggle up, assailed her with the memory of all the times he'd looked and sounded like that as she'd ridden him to oblivion….

Severing contact, she thought she'd managed to escape his compulsion when he ensnared her again.

Holding her head in the cradle of his hands, striking her immobile with his very gentleness, he exhaled softly. "Just one more."

Then he took her lips in a kiss that all but extracted her soul.

She took it all, helpless to do anything but let him invade her with pleasure, her body singing in delight, weeping with need. After a series of conquering plunges, he slowed to clinging plucks that had her almost keeling over him again. He finally relinquished her lips with a last groan of regret.

Feeling her legs had turned to jelly, she barely reached the facing armchair before collapsing on it.

"I hope you've had your fun."

At her rasp, his eyes simmered like some supernatural

beast's. "You know I didn't. You know exactly how I have fun. Hard, protracted, borderline-fatal-with-pleasure fun."

She managed not to shudder. Yeah. She knew. Every cell in her body seemed to know nothing else. They'd had mega doses of "fun" in the five months they'd been intimate. Whenever she'd thought it couldn't get better, it had, like a force picking up momentum. Familiarity had only kept shifting the addiction to higher gears. It had been so intense, had felt so pure, it had been a devastating blow when she'd learned the truth.

Exhaling the remembered misery, she made her decision. Letting your enemy find out how much you knew wasn't wise, but maybe getting it all out would help purge it—and him—from her system once and for all.

"Let's start with when Najeeb left New York. Or shall we say when you set up the emergencies he'd been called back to Saraya to handle, with his father allegedly sick and unable to deal with them."

His eyes lost that languid sensuality, but there was no other sign of response.

She went on. "For months everything seemed to thwart him, and he grew suspicious, decided to go to the source of all info—his mother. After making him swear he'd never confront his father, Queen Safaa admitted that King Hassan believed Najeeb would end up marrying me, a daughter of the hated Aal Masoods, and it would cost him his position as his heir, as Saraya's tribes wouldn't abide the introduction of Aal Masood blood into the royal family. He even feared the Aal Ghaanems might lose the throne altogether to an uprising."

Mohab still had no reaction. But then again, why should he react? He already knew all this.

She exhaled. "To stop this calamity, King Hassan had one hope of breaking up our relationship. You. The kingdom's most lethal secret weapon. I was a homeland security threat of the highest order after all. As someone who was raised to despise the Aal Masoods, the idea that your crown prince might sully your line with the blood of your hated enemies was probably as unthinkable to you.

"Najeeb's mother related how you shared your king's opinion of me—the then-minor princess who flaunted her region's values and disgraced her brothers by living a degenerate life in the West. You agreed that I was manipulating the honorable Najeeb, using our shared ordeal to ride him to the status of a future queen. When the king authorized you to get rid of me, he knew how you'd do it. The same way you rid the kingdom of every black widow who tried to compromise the royal family or the integrity of the kingdom."

His gaze remained unchanged, betraying nothing.

Figured. He'd betrayed nothing through their five-month relationship. Not one action or glance or word had given her a clue that it had all been an act. The reverse had been true. Everything from him had been fierce, consistent, unequivocal, had felt more real than anything she'd ever experienced. Discovering the truth had hit so out of the blue, it had crushed her.

Her world had warped, every emotion and passion she'd felt for him becoming shame, humiliation.

She went on, emptying her voice of any remembered anguish. "You seduced me only to make me ineligible for Najeeb, then asked me to marry you to perfect your act, no doubt to drop me like a used napkin the moment you were sure your crown prince was safe."

Najeeb had been livid at his father, but more at Mohab, if only for the interference, the duplicity. His outrage had been mitigated by his belief that he'd saved her in time. She had never exposed the depths of her fall and folly to her friend. Only wanting the mess over with, she'd made Najeeb promise he'd never confront Mohab. She'd just wanted to walk away.

Numb and feeling used, she'd stumbled home, had stood in that shower for what might have been hours. Then Mohab had come. His urgency and passion, which her senses still hadn't been able to recognize as fake, had had her body detonating with a fireball of lust and her mind spiraling in blankness.

Afterward everything had spilled over, razing her with the devastation of fury and mortification.

After Mohab had finally gone, she'd collapsed. Not in any dramatic way, just a gradual descent into depression, her misery deepening with time and repercussions. It had taken her years to climb out.

Now, just as she was finally over her ordeal and firmly on stable footing, the man responsible for it all had come back to destroy the peace she'd struggled so long and hard for.

"So that's why you decided you didn't want to marry me after all, and so abruptly."

His deep statement roused her from her musings.

She gave him the only answer he'd get from her. "It just gave me the reason to bail, as I'd been wanting to, without caring how I did it."

"That's why you didn't confront me, no matter how much I pushed? You weren't interested in hearing my defense, since you'd already decided to walk out on me?"

At her nod, he shook his head, as if deprecating himself for wanting to hear her discoveries *had* been the only reason behind her rejection. No doubt out of pride, as that would make her the only woman who had walked away from him. Buying her claim didn't make things better, but it *was* something, since she'd rather crawl back to the airport in today's heat wave rather than give him the triumph of knowing how fully he'd taken her in.

"So craving me was one thing, marrying me was another."

"Who said I craved you?"

His mock reproving look sent blood surging to her loins. "Let's not dispute the indisputable, *ya jameelati*. You did, and I just proved you still do."

Her insides clenched at his taunt, his calling her his beauty. "I'm just a hot-blooded woman."

"That's why you were a virgin when I first took you?"

The way he said *took you* reverberated in her being.

For there was no other way to describe what he'd done to her that first night. Or any other time after that. He'd shown her what her body and being had always been capable of, but would have lain untapped if not for his unlocking their potential. Her wildest dreams before him hadn't known to venture into the realms where he'd taken her.

But she'd still woken up in his arms that first time feeling anxious. Though she'd believed him to be progressive, Saraya was even more ultraconservative than Judar, and she'd feared he might despise her for surrendering to him outside the marriage bed. She feared that because it would have meant he wasn't the man she'd fallen in love with. And if he did, she would have considered him worth nothing but good riddance, but it would still have wounded her terribly.

But he'd assuaged her fears as soon as he'd opened his eyes. He'd seamlessly played his part, had been euphoric, indulgent, even poetic about how proud he'd been that she'd bestowed her innocence on him, given him the honor of initiating her into intimacy. Then he'd asked her to marry him.

Even though she'd never thought of marriage, except to reject it, she'd found herself saying yes....

"Well?"

His challenge reminded her she hadn't answered his taunt. "Oh, you're harping on my being a virgin at the advanced age of twenty-one? A young woman still struggling to leave her stiflingly conservative upbringing behind? You expected me to go to the States and hop into bed with every man I fancied?"

"You'd been there for three years. Enough time to change your outlook and behavior, especially at that age, if you'd wanted to. But you fancied no one. I was your first. In every way. I know."

"You mean as the infallible intelligence god you are?"

"No. As the man who awakened you."

Damn him. He saw too much, knew everything.

"And once I *awakened,* thanks to your expert...rousing..."

"Nothing happened. You didn't replace me in your bed."

She gaped at him. How did he...? Did that mean...?

Before she could blow a valve, he went on calmly, "*This* I know as the incomparable intelligence god that I am."

IF PEOPLE COULD EXPLODE, Jala would have, Mohab thought.

He'd tripped the one wire that could set her off. One of *two* wires. The first was passion, which he was gratified he could still trigger with a touch. The second was privacy.

It had always been her biggest hang-up. She'd been near obsessive about it. Her insistence on never meeting him where anyone might recognize her had at first made him think it was a cunning effort to have his cake and eat Najeeb's, too. But as his preconceptions had melted, and she'd opened up with details of her life in Judar, he'd understood how hard-won her autonomy had been. After a lifetime of having her breaths counted and steps monitored, she'd sworn…*no more.*

He watched her rise, every inch aching to have her in his arms again. But that wouldn't move anything forward. And he was afraid that if she surrendered again, he wouldn't be able to stop.

"You had me under surveillance?" she seethed.

He sighed. Not his favorite topic, discussing his obsession with her. "I'm not good at letting go."

"Sure. Do you have a bridge to sell me with that? So what was it, really? You forgot to call off my surveillance detail and reports kept hitting your desk?"

At his raised eyebrow, she took a furious step toward him. "We're in full-disclosure mode, aren't we? So how about you not pretend you didn't have my every move documented before you approached me? It's evident you formulated a plan to entrap me in the most time-efficient manner based on my character analysis. But after you ended my supposed threat to your crown prince, what purpose did keeping tabs on me serve? Was it to make sure I didn't go after another of your kingdom's princes after you made sure Najeeb found me 'ineligible' to be his future queen?"

Wincing at the words that had haunted him with shame, he shook his head. "I didn't tell Najeeb anything."

"I don't believe you."

Her instantaneous rejection was what he deserved. Not only had he threatened to do just that, Najeeb *had* cut off all relations with her, proving to her that Mohab had carried out his threat.

But he hadn't. He'd lived dreading news of her impending marriage to Najeeb. When that had never come to pass, he'd found out why. His uncle had told Najeeb that Mohab *had* fulfilled his mission in proving that Jala was dissolute, but if Najeeb desired her, he could enjoy her, as Mohab once had.

Even though he'd been hurt and jealous, believed she'd chosen Najeeb over him, he'd also come to admit that she'd had every right to change her mind about marrying him. And he'd been *furious* that Najeeb had ended what he'd professed to be a strong friendship based on hearsay, or even the truth of their relationship. If that made her dissolute in Najeeb's eyes, when the man hadn't staked a prior claim, it made him despicable.

He'd been unable to abide his uncle's defamation and his cousin's desertion of her. In a gesture of ultimate contempt, he'd resigned his job and left their and Saraya's service.

He exhaled. "Ask Najeeb. He'll tell you I haven't talked to him since that night. You had every right to leave me, and I'll be forever ashamed I threatened to slander you for it."

Her glare wavered only to harden again. "Even if I believe that, you have other transgressions waiting in line. How dare you have me followed?"

Savoring the bewitching sight she made in her fury, he said, "As long as I'm already damned, and I have no hope of having the extenuating circumstances sanctioned, I might as well tell you that I've been keeping tabs on you far longer than you think. I started right after I first saw you attending a conference with your oldest brother Farooq in Washington."

Her eyes rounded. "That was ten years ago!"

"*Aih.* You were only eighteen and the most incredible thing I'd ever seen. I felt the chemistry that sizzles between us singe me even then, even when you didn't see me."

Her disbelief was almost palpable. "It's not *possible* I didn't see you."

"You do remember what I do for a living, don't you? If I want to stay out of sight, that's where I remain."

But he'd been unable to stop following her after that first sighting. He'd known he'd never approach her, but she'd become his fantasy when he'd never had one before.

Then that hostage crisis had happened. Her name had been the only thing he'd seen on that hostage list before he'd stormed in, and he'd made the decision to save her first right then. Facing that had made him more enraged at himself, his anger mounting the more he found himself struggling not to go after her, and to hell with all the reasons to stay away.

"And you expect me to believe you were enthralled at first sight? A sight I didn't even reciprocate?"

"Seems you never looked in the mirror."

"C'mon…you have tons of gorgeous women littering your path, and I'm not even that. I'm too…androgynous."

An incredulous laugh burst out of him. "Then I don't know what that says about me, since you define femininity to me." Before she ricocheted with another rebuttal, he cut her off. "Aren't you going to hear my version of what happened?"

"Will you tell me Najeeb or I jumped to conclusions, or some other lameness like that? Don't bother. I already told you I don't care. It was just a welcome bit of news that made breaking up with you much easier."

He had to accept that. It seemed he hadn't realized how controlling his kind of life had made him, how severely allergic she had been, and still was, to any infringement on her free will. Her distress *had* been acute every time he'd pushed to announce their engagement. She'd kept saying she wanted more private time before their families and their feud infringed on their relationship. It seemed the more he tried to push for moving forward, the more she'd resented his attempts to herd her toward his objective. She would probably have ended it on that account alone. Her discoveries about his subterfuge had just rushed everything to its conclusion.

He patted the space beside him again. "You still need to know my side, just so you know 'everything' for real."

She only flung a dismissing hand at him. "Suit yourself."

"Thank you, Your Ungraciousness." He bowed his head mockingly. "So…when my uncle assigned me the mission of sabotaging you and Najeeb, I pounced on it, but only as a pretext to finally approaching you. That alone made me wonder if you might be as dangerous as my uncle believed. After all, how could you be the sweet innocent I thought you to be if you affected *me* this way, when the world's most lethal seductresses didn't turn a hair in me? If I was so enthralled from afar, what chance did Najeeb have?"

He *had* approached her, hoping she'd turn out to be nothing like his fantasies and he could end her hold over him. Saving Najeeb would have been incidental.

But from that first night, he'd lost sight of the whole world in her company, then of his own reality in her arms. He'd forgotten who he was and what kind of life he led to the point he'd asked her to marry him.

"But you changed your mind once you were with me, right?"

"When I was with you I *had* no mind. But if anyone gets your reservations back then, it's me. You had your reasons for shunning marriage, and I had mine."

Not that his dread had stopped him from wanting to go through with it, from becoming progressively more impatient with her postponements, even when he hadn't realized they'd been signs of trouble. This obliviousness had been why he'd been so shocked when she'd ended it.

Then, after he'd found out why she hadn't hooked up with Najeeb, she'd disappeared.

He'd turned the world upside down searching for her, to no avail. He'd only found her when she'd resurfaced on her own, following a yearlong humanitarian trek in uncharted areas in South America. He hadn't let her out of his sight since.

And all the while, he'd been seeking a pretext to go after her again. Now that he'd finally found it, he would get her. She just didn't know it yet.

He swept her in an aching glance. "But my proposal, as ill-advised as it was, *was* real." At her disbelieving huff, his lips twisted. "Whatever you think I thought or felt, not even I can feign that much hunger, for that long or at all."

"But men don't have to feign anything. Put a willing woman in their bed and that's all she wrote."

"Your inexperience with anyone else but me is showing." He rose, savoring every nuance of her chagrin at being unable to contest his exclusive ownership of her body. "Those indiscriminate men you describe are aroused by the novelty, the challenge. They are notorious for losing…steam quickly when with a familiar body, no matter how tempting. But the more I had you, the more my hunger for you raged. I craved you enough that I would have jumped into an inferno—or even into marriage—to keep you."

"Then it's fortunate Najeeb's revelations pushed me to make the decision I'd been circling for a while, saving us both from a fate worse than hell."

"I'm just telling you my side. And now that you've told me yours, I understand why you walked away. A combination of commitment phobia, resentment and outrage is pretty potent. You were doing what you believed was right for yourself. But that's your mind. What about your body? How long did it ache in demand for mine? How severe were the withdrawal pangs?"

Something dark and enormous expanded in her eyes. His heart hammered. *Ya Ullah,* was that…anguish?

The disturbing expression was gone before he could be sure he'd seen it. "I can tell you for a fact that for the next year there was no aching or withdrawal."

That didn't sound like a spiteful denial. She meant this.

Could it be she'd walked away at no cost to herself? There'd been no emptiness in her gut and loins, no burning in her senses and skin, needing his assuagement, his completion? Could the love she'd sobbed out loud in pleasure-drenched nights have evaporated so absolutely that not even a remnant of the physical yearning remained?

No. He wouldn't buy that. She'd melted again at his touch. Her body still proclaimed him its mate and master.

As if to contradict his conviction, she said, "I haven't had other men since because I was too busy with work, and I'm not the kind for one-night stands. It wasn't because I was pining for you."

"If you'd found the intensity of attraction and totality of arousal you had with me, you would have made time. But you wanted that or nothing at all. Sometimes hunger is so vast, nothing but what you crave would fulfill it." Giving her no chance to back away, he took her in his arms. "I know, because nothing could fulfill my craving but you."

"Yeah, sure." She squirmed, only inflaming him more.

He hauled her tighter against him. "Fact is sometimes stranger than fiction. It was as unreal to me as it sounds to you now. This chemistry we share wasn't only an aphrodisiac, but a mind-altering substance."

"Sounds like something you wouldn't want to abuse. So why are you doing this? Or are you just making the best of your 'mission' this time, too?"

"This time, it's all me. How much has Kamal told you?"

Sullenly, she told him. Kamal had only told her the general situation, hadn't even mentioned him by name. So he now filled in his part of the story, leaving out only that he could abort the hostilities without her marrying him.

She digested everything, inert in his arms, eyes somber. "So you're going to be king. That's unexpected. But it also enables you to resolve this without little Aal Masood me."

Her analytical powers were unerring. As he well knew.

But he couldn't corroborate her analysis or this was over before it began. "The peace through marriage is what my uncle would agree to."

"How ironic. I was the only woman he couldn't abide for his heir, now I'm the only one to serve his purposes." She pushed away, hard. "He can go to hell, right along with you."

He hated to play this card, but he'd run out of options. "You once said you would repay me one day."

That made her go rock still, a world of reproach filling her cognac eyes. "I also said I won't do that with my life."

"I'm not asking for your life. Just your hand in marriage. Just your body in my bed."

A scoff burst from her. "My choice, my future and my body. That just about wraps up what makes up my life."

He shrugged. "Not really."

"Oh? What else is there that you're not laying claim to?"

"Plenty. Your heart, your mind, your soul." At her immovable glare, he found no recourse but to push. "I *am* collecting my debt now, Jala. It is that imperative." For him.

Apprehension gradually replaced ire on her exquisite face.

Then she finally exclaimed, "You're all really going to do something insane if we don't get married?"

And he seized that first wavering in her resolve, drove his advantage home. "We have to get married. Nobody said we have to *stay* married."

CHAPTER FIVE

Jala couldn't believe it.

That gargantuan weasel had made her say yes.

He'd used his every weapon, from seduction to logic to cajoling, playing havoc with her vulnerabilities and convictions, making her revoke her edict consigning him to hell.

But then, the situation *was* dire.

From her work in regions festering with conflict, she was too familiar with how wars ignited over much less than the current stakes. In places like their region, where pride and tribalism and other inherited, obsolete conventions still ruled to a great degree beneath the modernized veneer, once blood was spilled, enmities could—and did—rage for centuries.

Kamal and Mohab, damn them both to hell, had pegged her accurately. They'd both counted on her inability to stand by and let something like this happen if she could help it. They'd known that after her first shock and outrage, once she realized it was true only she could help, she would.

But she drew the line at marrying Mohab to do it. The best she'd do was agree to a fake engagement.

Yeah, another one. But one she *knew* was fake. She'd go through the motions for the sake of peace.

And that was *huge* of her. Engagements around here

were excruciating, rife with maddening customs and ob-
scene intrusions. Wedding preparations made some of the
war zones she'd been to look peaceful.

But she'd use those torturous rituals to draw out this
charade until treaties were signed. Then she'd bail out.

One thing still had her red-alert sensors clanging,
though. The ease with which Mohab had agreed to her
terms.

At first, he'd insisted only an actual marriage would appease King Hassan, that they'd have to dispense with an
engagement to give him the quick union that would force
him from his warpath. He'd suggested a six-month period
before separating. According to him, that was enough time
to settle all treaties and resolve all disputes.

But when she'd countered with the most she'd agree to,
and that he'd have to convince King Hassan to sign the
treaties *during* their pseudoengagement, he'd consented
with disturbing equanimity.

Suddenly she felt as though a rocket had gone off inside
her head. She knew *why* his acquiescence had disturbed
her. Because it must have been what that insidious rat had
been after all the time!

He must have anticipated her first point-blank refusal.
So he'd let her get this out of her system. Being ruth-
lessly results oriented, he must have known an agreement
wouldn't be a possibility. The best he could expect from
this first encounter was to stall her, stop her from leaving
Judar and secure any level of cooperation.

So he'd kept applying pressure here so she'd sidestep
there, pushed and pulled, kissed and caressed, laid bare secrets, exhumed heartaches, appealed to her ego and seared
her senses in a steady barrage. When he'd felt her waver,
he'd hit her with a solution that had too high a cost. At this
point, he must have projected two outcomes. Since she'd

already entered the cooperative zone, either she'd buckle and accept outright, or she'd counter with her own offer, bargaining a lower price. Either way, he'd achieve his objective. Her, here, playing along.

That it was only for now and not for real didn't bother him. This was only round one to him. Being Machiavellian and a long-term thinker, he most certainly wouldn't abide by the limits of what she'd granted. And as a master strategist, he had every reason to expect he wouldn't have to. If he'd gotten her to concede that much in under two hours, he'd probably estimated he'd have her dancing to his tune in two days.

She was now certain he would keep on giving her as much rope as she asked for…and use it to lasso and truss her up.

Consternation bubbled on a stifled shriek. She even stomped her foot. It landed with a damp thud on the sand, not the satisfying bang she'd needed.

Groaning in frustration, her gaze jerked around the four-mile shore. Still alone. At least, apparently so.

But of course she wasn't alone. Kamal must have given his guards orders to keep out of her sight. He wouldn't want to infringe on her personal space, aggravating her more than he'd already had.

But there was no doubt dozens of eyes were watching *the* princess of Judar taking a stroll along the shore surrounding the royal palace. She wondered why they'd even bother. No one came within ten miles of the palace or its extensive grounds, by land or by sea. It wasn't even one of those days when the palace and satellite buildings were open for tourists. The only way someone could target her would be by satellite or long-range missile.

Oh, well. She had known what kind of intrusions she'd signed on for the moment she'd agreed to stay in Judar and

play Mohab's game. The kind that had once had her running to the States and hiding in blessed anonymity and
heavenly aloneness.

The first eighteen years of her life here had surely taken
their toll. Though she loved her brothers fiercely, her experience in Judar had been the opposite of theirs in every
respect. Even if, at the time, they'd just been three of the
former king's multitude of nephews, they'd been everything the region and the royal family valued. Male, magnificent, with personal assets running out of their ears. They'd
had every freedom, along with privilege and power, to
counter all the responsibilities, expectations and pressures.

While she, the unplanned child her parents had had
twelve years after they thought they were done having
children, had been a mistake—and a female one at that.
To compound her problems, when she'd been only three
her mother had been diagnosed with cancer. After a long
struggle, when she'd been forced to relinquish Jala's upbringing to others, she'd died when Jala was ten. Less than
a year later, her father, totally destroyed by his wife's long
illness and death, had died, too, leaving Jala to the care of
her older brothers, relatives and hired help.

The next years had been a nightmare. Her brothers,
while they'd doted on her, had been too busy forging their
success to have much time for her. As one who hated to
ask for help or attention, she'd never let them know of her
dismal state of mind. She'd felt isolated from the royal family, and from her culture, where she'd never felt she fit in.

But as she'd grown older, she'd been progressively more
besieged by the restrictions that being female in Judar entailed, compounded by the fact that she had no mother to
fend for her. And while she had enough royal status to suffer its downsides, she had enjoyed none of its advantages.
Her situation had been further complicated when she'd re-

fused the privileges offered women here, which she considered condescending and sexist, making her an outcast among her peers. By the time she was finished high school, she'd felt she'd do something drastic if she didn't get away.

Then her maternal aunt's husband was appointed the ambassador of Judar to the United States. Frantic to make use of this possible ticket out, she'd hounded her brothers until they'd agreed to let her go with their aunt to continue her education there. She'd arrived in the States four months before her eighteenth birthday and had left her aunt's custody the day after her birthday party.

Seizing on her freedom of choice at once, she'd started fulfilling her lifelong ambition to follow Farooq in his humanitarian relief efforts.

It had been while attending that ill-fated conference in Bidalya that she'd first set eyes on Mohab. And it had been during the ceremony where she'd received her first work-related award that he'd effectively entered her life.

Now he'd reentered it. And she was back in Judar.

And it was all because of him.

Mohab. Even his name aggravated her right now. His parents had to give him such a lofty one, didn't they? And he had to be an exasperating bastard and live up to it, didn't he? Awe-inspiring. Feared. Even frightening. And he'd gone on to be far more. Spellbinding. Overwhelming. Devastating.

Okay. It wasn't all because of him. This impending war wasn't of his orchestration. And the cruel twist of fate that made her the king of Judar's sister, and Mohab the imminent king of Jareer, was also beyond him.

But now she thought of it, another thing was his fault. Their whole confrontation last evening.

After that preemptive opening seduction scene, he'd proceeded to scramble her entrenched belief that she'd just been another body and mission to him, asserting that he'd wanted her for far longer than she'd even thought. He'd claimed he'd monitored her for years, compromised his duty and disregarded his orders for her, craved her so much that he'd proposed for real. And all along, he'd kept pulling her back into mindlessness, as if he'd been unable to keep his passion in check.

Then she'd agreed to play her part and he'd just… stopped. He'd stood by calmly and just let her leave.

Did that mean everything he'd told her had been more manipulation designed to shove her into the slot where he needed her? Then, once he had, he'd just retracted his tentacles and settled back into neutral mode?

That made the most sense. She *had* long ago become reconciled to the fact that a man who'd chosen Mohab's line of work must be made of a different material than other human beings. To deal with the atrocities he was required to face head-on, he must have long since shut down his basic human emotions. And to fulfill his stealth missions, he must have become an expert at simulating those emotions at will.

But even knowing that, he'd managed to fool her again. He'd anesthetized her judgment and nullified her instincts. She'd actually begun believing his claims and had all but drowned in his passion. His nonexistent passion.

And that was the worst of it all. That after everything that had happened, her senses and responses would forever remain dependent on a mirage. Like Tantalus, she was destined to shrivel up with thirst for an illusion.

What kind of fate was it that always made her his target, his chess piece? Why had fate infected her with this unremitting hunger that nothing had ever eradicated, when he felt none for her, for real, in return? Why, after she'd suppressed it for years until she'd thought she'd been cured, had it taken only his reappearance to drag it out of her depths? And now that the fever had spiked again, how could she subdue it, at least enough to keep on functioning?

A wave of too-familiar dejection crashed over her as she slit her eyes against the brilliant setting sun, suddenly cold to her marrow in the balmy March breeze.

Legs heavy and numb, she started back to the palace. And, in spite of everything, it took her breath all over again.

Anyone looking at it would think it was a historical monument, but she'd attended its inauguration as the new seat of power in Judar just eleven years ago during her late uncle's rule. It had since become a monument as important as the Taj Mahal, and sure gave that legendary edifice a run for its money. It was still as mind-boggling to her as it had been the first time she'd seen it.

Nestled in an extensively landscaped park and surrounded by silver beaches and emerald waters, it crouched in the middle of the peninsula, its grounds almost covered like a massive starship from beyond the stars. Now in the golden drape of a breathtaking sunset, it felt as if it had been conjured by magic from another realm.

That wasn't too far from the truth. Thousands of unique talents, all masters of art and architecture, had put this place together. And from what she'd seen of its interior, modern magicians of technology had imbued it with the ultimate in luxury and functionality, too.

Approaching the palace from its shore-facing side took her through street-wide paths paved in earth-colored cobblestones and lined by soaring palm trees and flower beds. She strode through gates, courtyards, pavilions, everything bearing the intricacies and influences of the cultures that had melded together to form Judar. If she'd been in anything approaching a normal frame of mind, she would have savored the magnificence of this place. But now the majesty that surrounded her—and what it signified of her royal connections and their current implications for her life—oppressed her.

Scaling the convex stone steps that converged like a fan from a hundred feet at the bottom to thirty at the top, she gazed up at the massive palace that soared on four levels, echoing every hue of the desert, topped by a complex system of domes covered in mosaics and gold finials.

As she approached the entrance, two footmen in ornate uniforms seemed to materialize out of nowhere to open the twenty-foot mahogany double doors inlaid with gold and silver.

Smiling at them or offering thanks was useless, since they looked firmly ahead, avoiding eye contact. She crossed into the circular columned hall that had to be at least two hundred feet in diameter with a ceiling dome at least half that.

Her gaze swam around the superbly lit sweeping spaces, getting only impressions of neutral color schemes and sumptuous decor and furnishings. Again it felt deserted. Or everyone was giving her space. Which was very welcome. She didn't want to meet anyone right now, even in passing.

At the end of the hall, she entered an elevator that transported her in seconds to her fourth-floor quarters.

As she entered the expansive three-chambered wing and crossed to the bedroom, the sensory overload of sweet incense and opulence hit her. Yearning for her simple, cozy, two-room American abode twisted inside her like a tornado.

"Oh, you're here!"

The bright exclamation had her swinging around, almost severing her already compromised balance.

Aliyah. Kamal's wife and her queen. And a more fitting queen she'd never seen. As a former model, Aliyah was even taller than Jala, but now boasted the lush curves of a woman who'd ripened with the passion of a virile man, and with bearing his son and daughter. Her mahogany hair was in a thick braid over her shoulder, and she was swathed in a floor-length dress the color of her chocolate eyes.

She had Carmen with her. As Farooq's wife, Carmen was the crown prince's consort and yet another specimen of feminine gorgeousness, looking like a statuesque Rita Hayworth in her garnet-haired period but with turquoise eyes. Farah, the wife of her second-oldest brother, Shehab, was the only one missing. Shehab called her his Emerald Fairy for her eyes, and in Jala's opinion he was right all around, and Farah was the most ethereally stunning of the three.

If she'd cared about her looks, Jala would have suffered serious insecurity in the presence of those three visions. As it was, she was delighted her brothers had found women who were as beautiful on the outside as they were on the inside and who adored them. It was always such a pleasure to see them. Even though their relationship consisted mostly of video chatting, since the three couples seldom left Judar due to their growing families and responsibilities.

"We did knock." Carmen grinned at her apologetically as she beckoned the four women who accompanied her and Aliyah, no doubt their ladies-in-waiting. All were laden with packages. "We assumed you weren't here when you didn't answer, and thought to leave you the stuff with a note."

"We brought you everything we could think of to see what you need and what fits," Aliyah explained.

Carmen smiled at the women who'd piled the "stuff" in

the sitting area, then gestured for them to leave. "Kamal said you need everything since you left New York without packing a thing."

"Yeah, because he told me your husband was lying in hospital battling the grim reaper."

Carmen blanched, the very idea of that evidently making her sick to her stomach. "He *what?*"

"*Exactly* what I said to him when he revealed that it was only a ruse to get me here."

"*Ya Ullah!*" Aliyah groaned, looking mortified. "I'll brain him for you. If you haven't already."

"I only let him live for you and the kids," Jala mumbled.

Aliyah hugged her, contrite on her husband's behalf. "I'm *so* sorry. He's a colossal pain but…" She sighed, eyes becoming dreamy. "I let him live because he's so utterly irresistible."

Jala knew exactly what she meant. *She* was caught, again, in the web of such an inexorable force. Just not happily so.

"You're talking to the world's second foremost expert on Kamal, regrettably my so-called twin and now horrifically my king, too. I am thinking of surrendering my Judarian nationality so I'd deprive him of wielding that kind of power over me."

"As if anyone can make you do anything you don't want." Carmen's scoff was certainty itself.

Farooq's wife had once told Jala she thought her the strongest, most courageous and independent person she knew. If only Carmen knew that there was someone who'd always made Jala do whatever *he* wanted. Was still making her do it.…

"Listen, we know you must be dying for an early night, so we won't keep you." Carmen linked her arm in Jala's.

"Let's open everything, and we'll see what suits you, what you need changed and what we forgot."

Aliyah followed them. "When Kamal said we should leave you alone all day, since you had a big day yesterday, I had no idea how big it was. No thanks to him. Giving you the scare, then the surprise of your life in succession."

"He told you, huh?" Jala huffed. "What am I *saying?* I think he tells you stuff before he tells it to himself."

Aliyah's exquisite face lit up with that expression of a woman secure in her power over her man, of his total love, which she reciprocated to her last breath. "He does think aloud with me. But not this time. I was told after the fact."

"After he settled the pact to sign me over in marriage to the future king of Jareer, you mean? To stop a war that old goat king of Saraya wouldn't think twice about instigating?"

Aliyah whooped. "Kamal calls him 'old goat,' too. You two really are twins!"

Carmen chuckled. "We heard you met said future king of Jareer last night. With how things are between Judar and Saraya, we never had the pleasure, but we've been hearing all sorts of things about him…like he's materialized right out of *Arabian Nights*. I've even heard women here make blasphemous comments about him—that he's even more impressive than *our* men."

Even loving her brothers as she did, Jala had to agree. Regretfully. She didn't know if it was better or worse to get more confirmation that he affected all women the same way.

Suddenly she jumped.

Carmen started. "What is it?"

Groaning, Jala got her phone out of her pocket. "Just my phone. It never vibrated that hard." Or she had surplus electricity coursing through her system. "Just a sec."

She cast a look at the number as she answered. A blocked one. Probably one of her colleagues that the service provider here was unable to show on caller ID due to the international number.

"I am here."

She lurched harder this time. *Mohab.*

Here? Where? In her wing? Outside in the sitting room…?

"In the palace."

Oh.

"Are you in your quarters?"

She snatched a look at Carmen and Aliyah, who'd turned their backs, giving her privacy. "Yes."

"Where is it?"

"Why?"

"I plan on visiting you."

"And I plan on not receiving you."

"*Zain.* Turn on your laptop."

"Huh?"

"I'll have to improvise. Making love to you across cyberspace isn't ideal, but it might be a good idea to keep my distance until I take the edge off…the first few times."

Her knees almost buckled. "Why don't you go ahead on your own? Cyberspace is full of…material you can help yourself to."

She saw Carmen's back stiffen. It was imperceptible, but she'd heard her. And no doubt understood.

And that royal bastard continued to pour more dark magic into her inflamed brain. "I'm very fastidious about the…material… I help myself to. I have a specific movie that I have…helped myself to, times beyond count. I've long memorized every frame, had remastered it for better image and sound quality so I can help myself to it… into infinity."

A movie. Of her. As he'd massaged her, pampered her, owned her every inch, brought her to ecstasy over and over again before he'd mounted her and thrust her to oblivion.

It had been one of her deepest scars, knowing that she'd trusted him so much she'd allowed this, that he had that evidence of her stupidity and self-destructiveness, a weapon to wield against her to serve his purposes.

"I would do anything for new material." His voice dropped an octave into the darkest reaches of temptation. "*Anything,* Jala." He let out a ragged breath that all but fried her synapses. "Turn on your laptop and we'll proceed."

She ground her teeth, refusing to press her legs together. He wasn't doing this to her, and over the phone, too, with her sisters-in-law feet away. "So I turn my laptop on and you magically see me from yours?"

"You keep forgetting who I am."

"You can tap into my computer?" she snapped.

"Of course. But I don't need to now. I just need to know your chat login. Which I do. Now hurry. The longer you make me wait, the longer before I'm appeased. I'm already half out of my mind with keeping my hands off you last night."

"You did no such thing!"

Her exclamation made both Aliyah and Carmen fidget. They must now be formulating a very good idea of what was going on.

*Ya Ullah...*she hated him!

"You know I did." He did that thing again with his voice that strummed the chords in the core of her being. "You know what I do with my hands when I don't keep them off you. But I kept something on. Your clothes. I almost had a heart attack needing to peel them off you. Take them off for me now, Jala. I want to see you now, want to imagine my hands on you. Show me yourself, *ya jameelati.*"

Ya Ullah—even now, he had her spontaneously combusting from a distance. Her body was readying itself, the clothes he'd asked her to remove were suddenly suffocating shackles, abrading aching flesh.

"I have company."

"Get rid of them." His command was terse, tense, uncompromising.

"I can't," she choked, smiling wanly at the two ladies who'd finished unpacking and were fidgeting, not knowing what to do. "I'm hanging up now."

"Do that, and I'll come over."

"You don't know where I am!"

"I can pinpoint your location via GPS. I was only asking as a courtesy, so you'd volunteer it willingly."

"What do you think I can do now, huh?"

"Would you have done what I asked had you been alone?"

Carmen strode by her to usher in the ladies, who brought in more packages, looking relieved to stop pretending to be talking to Aliyah and not hearing everything Jala said.

Jala cast her a brittle smile, trying to sound neutral as she almost choked on her answer. "I would have considered it."

"Liar." This was crooned in the darkest, deepest tone he'd ever hit her with. "You would have made a protracted feast of tormenting me."

That coming from the master of torment. Oh, the irony.

"*Zain*. If you can't open your laptop, we'll use the phone. I'll show you myself, instead."

Her legs gave out. She groped for the nearest chair, gesturing weakly at the ladies that she was okay, hoping they'd just leave. They didn't. They continued to work until she almost screamed she wanted to be alone to deal with this nerve-racking man without having them witness her being seduced out of her mind by him.

Mohab droned on until she felt her brain sizzling. "Remember how you used to revel in exposing me? Taking each shred of clothes off me with fingers that shook with urgency, with teeth that chattered with arousal?"

"Mohab..."

As soon as his name moaned out of her, begging mercy, she could almost see Aliyah's and Carmen's ears pricking up. Now they knew for sure who'd been tormenting her all this time.

"But I'll leave you to your visitors on one condition."

"What?" she croaked.

"The moment they're gone, you'll come to me."

To THEIR CREDIT, after Mohab released her from his long-distance torture, Aliyah and Carmen behaved as if they'd heard nothing as they concluded their business, which it turned out they *had* needed to stay to conclude. Before they disappeared, she thought she saw them exchanging furtive smiles.

Yeah. They were probably putting two and two together. And coming up with a thousand.

She took her time, showering, drying her hair, dressing in fresh clothes. Then she headed to the wing Mohab had been given. Aliyah had backhandedly provided its location.

At his door, she knocked, then stood back.

The door opened almost instantaneously. Across the threshold, there he was, looking fall-to-your-knees gorgeous—*Mohab*.

In a black-on-black suit and shirt, his skin simmered and his eyes glowed in the soft ambient light. Only the top section of his hair was held back now; the rest flowed like thick sheets of silk to sigh over his collar.

A wave of fierce hunger rolled over her. She bore its impact without any outward sign, looking up at him across the threshold. He only stepped aside. Knowing there'd be eyes documenting her entry into his chambers, she walked inside.

The wing looked much like the one she occupied, but it smelled different. His scent had already permeated the place. It coated her lungs, tingled on her tongue. His unique brand of virility and vigor, of scorching desert sun and flaying wind, of ruthless terrain and cleansing rain. Of cold-blooded termination and boiling-over passion.

His appreciation sizzled over her as his eyes swept her white-cotton-clad body, sensuality playing on his sculpted lips, humming from him like electricity from a high-voltage cable.

She bore the brunt of his silent, sensual onslaught, then, in utmost tranquillity and premeditation, she swung her arm and socked him in the jaw.

CHAPTER SIX

Pain exploded in Jala's hand.

She'd thrown punches before, but nothing had ever hurt that bad. Figured. Mortal beings' jaws weren't made of some indestructible amalgam like *Arabian Nights* refugee here.

She might have broken her hand. And wrist. And elbow.

But she wouldn't obey the need to shake the agony out and howl. The unmovable bastard hadn't even rocked under what she'd thought a very good punch. Only his smile had vanished, his expression becoming that of a predator who'd just encountered an unexpected opponent, exhilarated by the discovery, raring for an all-out tumble.

Then, oh, so slowly, he raised his hand and rubbed his jaw, softly scratching against his beard. It sent a frisson of stimulation through her, as if those fingers had scraped against her most sensitive spots. She managed not to shudder.

"Was that so hard?"

Huh? What?

"Giving me that first voluntary touch." He rubbed his jaw again, this time moving it from side to side, as if making sure everything was still slotted in place and functioning. "Not bad at all, as first voluntary touches go."

Wishing she could generate heat vision, she glared at

him. "If only you'd told me you expected a first voluntary *punch,* I would have obliged you much faster."

His grin turned into a wince and back to a grin. "Good thing I'm sporting a beard. I would have had a hard time explaining the bruise. That *was* a perfect jab. Or should I say, sucker punch?"

"*Please.* You saw it coming a light-year away. You could have blocked it if you wanted."

"If you think I saw anything but you glowing like a golden goddess in that torture device of a dress, you give me too much credit. You reduce me to my basic beast and the most simpleminded and oblivious of men."

Why was he *doing* this? Reengaging his seduction program? Was there something he still needed from her? Was he making sure she was hot enough for the required malleability?

"At least believe that if I'd seen this punch coming, I would have ducked so you wouldn't hurt your hand."

"Oh, sure. You care about the hand that just socked you."

"I care about nothing *but* your every bone and pore and inch. All I want is to show you how much… I care. But wait…"

He suddenly turned and strode away, disappeared into the kitchenette. In moments, he came back with a bag of ice. Stopping before her, he took her hand, ran gentle fingers over the knuckles that throbbed with a dull ache, his eyebrows knotting as he examined the forming bruise. Placing the ice on her knuckles, he gritted his teeth, as if her gasp hurt him.

"Next time, use a heavy, blunt object."

A shudder rattled through her, at his dark mutter more than at the icy numbing. She'd known she'd pay the price for her recklessness in pain and limited mobility for a while. But she'd thought it a small price for venting her frustration in the one way she hadn't tried yet. Physically.

She only felt worse now—stupid on top of out-of-control and futile. And his solicitude had turned the tables on her. She'd known he wouldn't retaliate, but she'd hoped it would surprise him into baring his fangs, or at least dropping his mask. He'd done that once, that night six years ago.

She'd always conjured those moments when he'd snarled at her like a wounded beast, when unstoppable longing for him had almost snuffed her will to go on. But even then, he'd exposed her to the full range of his faces. Passionate, anxious, shocked, angry, possessive, bewildered and betrayed. Thinking none of those had been real had only made her unable to trust her judgment again. Just as she couldn't now.

Carefully removing the ice, he lifted her hand to his lips. Holding her eyes as if he wanted her to let him into her soul, he feathered each knuckle with a kiss that was tender, almost reverent. And something in the center of her being buckled.

For him to be kissing the hand that had just inflicted an act of aggression and affront on him was too much. Unsteadily, she withdrew her hand.

He exhaled, flexed his hand as if it hurt, too, before it went up to the side of his neck.

Then he suddenly grinned at her. "What do you know… you fixed my neck!"

The spontaneity of his grin, the ease, the *warmth,* how real this all felt—her longing for the man she'd once loved with every fiber of her being—suddenly overwhelmed her. The yearning that had writhed inside her like a burning serpent lurched so hard that her nails dug into her good hand's palm until they almost broke her skin.

"Okay. You achieved your purpose, made sure my sisters-in-law heard the kind of conversation you forced on me...."

His hand rose in protest. "How could I have known they were with you?"

"Because you apparently keep me under surveillance every second I'm awake, maybe even when I'm asleep."

"I told you I didn't know where you were."

"Even if I believe this, I told you I had company. In fact, having anyone else present would have been even more damaging. But you established what you wanted. That our relationship goes far beyond last night, and its past nature is also implicit if you could talk to me with such... audacity."

"How could they have known I was being...audacious?"

"Because your phone seduction session made my responses clear to anyone who knows anything about sexual innuendo. So—you've established my 'impurity' and your role in it. Now, even if I want to back down, it will be at the cost of disgracing my family, now that my 'shame' is out. While you will keep the high moral ground, even if you're the once defiler of my honor, since you're here now doing the honorable thing."

He coughed an incredulous laugh. "Where are you getting all this? If you believe your sisters-in-law suspect anything, and it disturbs you, I'll take care of it. I started my 'phone seduction' before I knew you weren't alone, and I didn't continue it because of any of the motives you assign me. You're crediting me with a premeditation I already told you I'm incapable of around you."

Feeling her head would burst with frustration, she began to turn away when a cabled arm slipped around her waist, clasping her to his formidable length. "I was up all night, Jala, every inch of me *roaring* for you. I let you go last night because I thought I must give you some breathing room. But my resolutions vanished the moment I got here. All I could think was that you were near, and all I planned was having you, and this time not letting you walk away. As you did last night. As you did six years ago."

She pushed out of his arms. "You can stop doing this."

"I can't. I can never stop wanting you."

"I mean it, Mohab. Stop it. I already told you I'm going through with this charade. Now drop the seduction act."

The arms reaching for her stopped in midmotion, dropping to his sides. "What reason do you assign me for acting this time, if, according to you, I've already fulfilled my purpose?"

She shrugged, shoulders knotted, throat closing. "I never know anything where you're concerned."

"Didn't you say you know everything about my motivations and methods?" He shook his head. "Does this mean you didn't believe anything I said last night?"

She didn't know anymore. The dejection in his eyes, the intensity she felt from him, all added to the verdict of her senses. Even if she couldn't trust those, she couldn't disregard her observations.

His reaction to her punch had been seamless. If he'd been acting, he would have been resenting it—and her. It would have manifested in even momentary fury, in an instinctive spark of retaliation, before he curbed it. He'd only been astonished, and the instant hue of his surprise had been acceptance, indulgence, even elation. As if he'd meant it when he'd said he'd take anything from her, as if he welcomed any punishment she inflicted if it would vent her anger toward him.

She *could* be seeing what she wanted to see all over again, but she...

All her hairs stood on end. Something had slithered in the background, at ground level....

Her tension deflated on a squeaked exclamation. "A cat!"

She blinked at the magnificent creature. A robust white Turkish Angora, clearly just woken up from a sound catnap with the way it stopped to stretch and arch. Then it slunk toward them, languidly weaving its way around furniture.

"I wonder whose it is!" She turned incredulous eyes to Mohab. "Did you know it was here?"

Her eyes almost popped at the change that came over Mohab's expression as he looked at the cat. It was the tender delight she'd only seen on people's faces when they beheld their babies.

"I should hope so, since she's mine. Or should I say, I'm hers?" He bent as the cat approached him, tail straight up and trembling in the cat-tail-language equivalent of "I'm crazy about you," before rearing up on her hind legs like a baby asking to be picked up. Mohab obliged at once, scooping her up, cradling her expertly against his massive chest...and getting white fur all over his pristine black clothes.

Purring so loudly the sound vibrated in Jala's ears, the cat surrendered to Mohab's pampering as he cooed to her. "Who's awake? Who's had a good nap?"

She gaped at the incongruent scene. Mohab, that lethal juggernaut, all but melting over a cat.

Mohab had a cat.

As the knowledge hit bottom in her mind, another movement made her snap her gaze to the same direction where Whitey had come from, only to find more felines advancing.

He had *cats. Four* of them.

Or maybe there were more still napping in there. At this point, she would believe just about anything.

One of the cats, a miniature glossy-black panther, broke into a lope and threw himself at Mohab's feet. Then, butting his head against Mohab's legs, he made him widen his stance so he could weave between them in excited figure eights. The other two cats, a tabby Scottish Fold and a Russian Blue, soon joined in, purring the place down.

Mohab looked over at her when he had two cats in his arms, his expression that of a proud dad.

The tightness in her throat grew thorns. "Is this your... pride?"

"They are my pride and joy. They're my family."

The word *family* penetrated her heart, a shard that had never stopped driving deep.

He'd once told her his life story. He was an only child and, like her, both his parents were dead. But he hadn't lost them to illness or to heartbreak. He'd lost them—twelve years ago, now—in a terrorist attack. One meant for him.

Whenever she remembered that she'd used that knowledge to take a stab at him, she still choked with shame. It hadn't mattered that she'd been mad with agony—it had still been unforgivable. Some things should never be used as a weapon, no matter what. Should never be used at all. It had been dishonorable of her to use such an intimate and painful injury against him.

It never ceased to torment her that she owed him that much. Her life, and an apology for that cruel transgression. But since she'd thought she'd never settle those debts with him, she'd added them to her forward payment to the world.

But he'd invoked her debt last night. Then there'd been everything else. And just when she thought she was confused enough about him, she discovered he had cats!

She found herself asking, "You travel with them?"

He bent down, gently letting both cats jump lithely from his embrace. "People travel with their kids, don't they?"

The way he said that tightened her throat more. "You never told me you liked cats. Or that you had any."

Straightening, he approached her with a stealthy grace, like a huge version of the felines, his eyes radiating this new warmth that seeped to her core. "I didn't then. I've always loved cats, all animals for that matter, but my lifestyle made me unable to adopt any. In my previous post, I had no control over my schedule. After I resigned—and after I settled a…personal project that took me all over the world five years ago—I set up my own business. Then I got my beauties, here—all rescue kitties, each with a story of her or his own." Suddenly his expression changed, as if something disturbing had just occurred to him. "You don't like cats?"

Her heart thudded at the alarm in his eyes. "I'm *crazy* about them. I had three cats when I lived in Judar, but I lost them all before I left. I fostered only in the States, since my globe-trotting lifestyle wouldn't accommodate a cat. Unlike you, I don't have my own private jet to haul them along with me."

His smile broke out again. "Let's test this claim, shall we? My darlings are cat-lover detectors. We'll let them scan you, but be advised…their verdict is final and incontestable."

He might be joking, but she was anxious they might snub her. Why, she didn't know. She was doing her best to alienate him, so why did she wish to appeal to his "kids"?

She swallowed the contrary lump of nervousness. "How will you know they approve of me?"

"How do cats show approval?"

"Each cat has his or her own way of showing it."

"Exactly." He flashed her a sizzling smile as he prowled to the sitting area, took off his jacket, dropped it to the ground and let his cats walk over it. "I should have changed into something light colored as soon as I let them out of the carriers. Only Rigel goes with this outfit."

His shoulders seemed to widen as he slowly started to unbutton his black shirt. Her heart stuttered. He was stripping.

She could swear the silk slithered off his skin with an aching sigh, as if it hated to separate from his flesh. She knew just how it felt, remembered how her hands used to ache for the time when they could glide all over him.

As his formidable back was exposed, symmetry and perfection made into a symphony of muscle and sinew, her salivary glands gushed. She was literally drooling over him.

At the damask burgundy couch in the center of the sitting area he turned to her, giving her a full frontal assault.

He was even more magnificent than she remembered. His chest had broadened, his abdomen had become more defined, every bulge and slope harder, packing more power, every line chiseled by endless stamina and determination. Her breasts swelled, reliving nights of abandon writhing beneath that chest, her stomach clenched with the memory of that ridged abdomen bearing down on her, working her into a frenzy. Her core throbbed with the moist heat that had been simmering since he'd walked into that stateroom.

Then in one of those movements that made her want to devour every glorious inch of him, he sank down on the couch.

Spreading his bulk over the cushions, he braced his legs wide apart and caressed the couch on both sides. The invitation was for his cats this time, who zoomed to obey, climbing all over him, butting their heads against every part of him, jumping on the back of the couch so they could reach his face and rub and kiss and lick him all over it. He surrendered to their love with a look of bliss, his eyes fixing her in a steady barrage of seduction.

Before this, he was the most overwhelming man to her, just by existing. Now this was…cruel. This had to be the most mind-bending thing he'd ever exposed her to. The sight of him, surrounded by cats, letting them plumb the depths of his love, roaming all over him in total trust and affection.

Did that man want to blow her ovaries?

He caught the ginger Scottish Fold who was crossing his lap and deposited a kiss on his head. "This is Mizar… as you can see why." She certainly could. The tomcat was a magnificent tabby with the cutest white apron in history. Mohab put him down to answer the impatience of the Russian Blue as she asked for her turn. "And this is Nihal. She is addicted to water taps, so I have to leave her a trickle on all the time. Always a challenge on flights." Nihal meant thirst quenching, so very appropriate, too. After she took her turn in her "daddy's" embrace she moved on and Mohab turned to the little panther. "And this is Rigel. I bet you know why I called him that."

She sure did. *Rigel* meant foot, and Rigel was definitely a foot cat, the one who'd hurled himself at Mohab's feet. Actually Rigel, the star, meant The Foot of the Great One, which was very apt for both cat and owner.…

Hey…wait! "These are all star names, ones discovered by ancient astronomers from the region."

Surprise flared in his eyes. "They *are* my little stars. Very observant…and knowledgeable of you."

Pleasure revved inside her stomach. She'd once craved his praise, praise he'd lavished on her, that had made her feel like the most special person in the world. So even in that regard, nothing had changed.

"And this is Sette—my mistress and queen of my household." The white cat jumped on his lap, curled up and rested her head on his thigh, eyes focused in the distance. Mohab swept her in strokes, making Jala feel his hand running down *her* back. "But *you* can be my human mistress and queen."

Queen. She still couldn't get her head around the fact that Mohab wasn't just a prince anymore. Or just a major force in the world of extragovernmental crisis management. He would have his own throne. And if she married him, she'd be his queen.

Which couldn't happen. He would have to look for someone else to...

The thought lodged into her brain like a red-hot ax.

How dog in the manger was that? She wouldn't be his, and she couldn't bear completing a thought where another woman was?

But that wasn't new. She'd spent years shying away from any thoughts along these lines, always keeping her mind in a fever of preoccupation so she'd never focus on images of Mohab with other women, when he must have had scores....

"Won't you proceed with our test?"

His soft question severed her oppressive musings. Feeling any sudden movement would collapse her to the ground, she started toward him. The moment she moved, all four cats seemed to suddenly take notice of her, ears pricking, bodies in attention mode, eyes fixing her with the same intensity as their daddy's.

She came down on the far end of the couch, taking care not to touch any of the cats. Mizar was the first one who approached, sniffing her tentatively. She'd missed having a cat so much, all she wanted was to grab his robust body and bury her face in his thick fur.

Reeling back the urge, she gave Mizar her hand to sniff, cooing to him, "*Ma ajmalak ya sugheeri*...do you know how beautiful you are, my little one?" Mizar answered by bonking her hand with his head. Her heart trembled with this affection it only reserved for animals. "Oh, you do know exactly how delightful you are, you compact package of joy, you!"

The cat made his decision and climbed onto her lap, reaching up to bump his head into her chin.

She giggled, everything emptying from her mind but the delight cats always engendered in her. "*Ya Ullah*...you magical creature. I had a ginger boy like you once, but without your apron. He was as sweet as you and I miss him so very much…."

Hot needles pricked behind her eyes, dissolved in moist pain that she'd thought she'd expended so many years ago.

Needing to hide it from Mohab, she picked up Mizar and buried her face in his nape. A prod on her shoulder came from her side. It was Nihal, asking to be introduced. She turned to the cat, offering her hand. But Nihal, having seen Mizar already on her, dispensed with preliminaries and climbed down Jala's arm to arch and rub against her side and then settle down against her thigh, a front leg draped over it. Rigel jumped from the couch, sniffed her feet first, then jumped up and joined the lap-warming party. At last, Sette rose regally from Mohab's lap and sashayed over, pushing Mizar out of the way in the center of Jala's lap and making the spot hers.

Distributing strokes, delighting in their softness and trust, heart dancing to the frequency of their purrs, Jala looked at Mohab, her smile unfettered for the first time since…her days with him. "This is the best way to die, drowning in cats!"

He didn't smile back. Before her smile faltered, Mohab rose quietly, came to stand before her, his legs brushing hers as she sat covered in his cats. Then he came down on his knees before her.

Her breath left her in a choking gasp as he leaned forward, his hands brushing her heavy, aching breasts as his arms slid behind her. "You didn't only pass, *ya jameelati,* you broke my cat's fastidiousness and suspiciousness barrier in record time. They didn't even take to me that fast. It's official, they have marked you as a bona fide cat slave."

Her smile broke out again, wavering this time. He bore down on her, this time making his cats vacate her lap and rearrange themselves around her. He pressed himself between her legs, making her open them for him, bringing him fully against her, the hard flesh of his bare chest burning through her dress, his harder arousal pressing into the junction of her thighs. She watched his face approaching hers with the same fatalism one would give an approaching train.

"How about *living* drowning in cats?" His lips landed on her jaw, nuzzled its way up to her ear. "I and my family are all yours for the taking, *ya jameelati.* So take us."

This was so…incredible an offer it would have been everything she'd want from life if it had been real and only for her. If it had been in another life where the past and its losses hadn't taken place. This way, it was just more pain.

Her useless arms pushed against him. "I said I will *say* I'll marry you, not that I will."

He gathered her closer again. "And I will take anything you're willing to give. If you won't marry me, even temporarily, you can still be with me. You can still have me."

"You expect me to sweep everything under the rug and just fall into your arms again?"

"Under the rug is where all the irrelevant crap of the past belongs. And in my arms is where you do."

Her senses leaped so hard she felt as if they'd tear out of the confines of her body. All they'd ever wanted was to smother themselves in his nearness, his pleasures. Damn them. And damn him. Pulling her strings, dangling himself, reminding her how it had felt to be mingled with his flesh, riding his need, drenched in pleasure, inundated with satisfaction.

"You and *Al Shaitaan* are closely related, aren't you?" She exhaled. "Forget that. The devil must come to you for conniving lessons." And temptation and seduction ones. "You must be his chief consultant."

He just smiled. And why not? He felt her buckling.

She'd be damned if she did again, when he'd already condemned her to six years of misery. She wasn't letting hormones run amok again, wouldn't let them suppress her self-preservation.

"Why are you *doing* this?"

"Because it's the only thing I *can* do, *ya ameerati al ja-meelah*. I've starved for you and I'll do anything so I can sate myself with you again."

She stared into his eyes and again could only *feel* his sincerity. As if whatever else hadn't been right, this was the one thing that had always been real...his desire for her.

Years of damaged self-worth and disbelief in her judgment trembled one last time...then everything shattered.

As if feeling the second it did, his arms tightened, bringing her colliding with his steely mass, his lips taking hers and swallowing her moan of surrender.

Then she found herself being plucked up by his momentum as he pitched backward on the lush Persian carpet, sprawled over it and stretched her on top of him. She vaguely felt the cats jumping after them, felt them prodding, as if to make sure they were okay.

Cradling her head in his large palms, Mohab turned his to his cats. "I'm going to make love to Jala now, so go eat or bathe or something. We won't have time for you for a while."

As if they understood him, the cats slunk away.

Turning his attention back to her, he pulled her down, had her lips sinking into his and her core on his erection. He rocked against her, promising her, deluging her in readiness. Coherence dissolved on his invading tongue, drowned in his taste, her senses igniting like firecrackers with every plunge, sweep and groan....

Remember what he cost you. The havoc he'd still wreak if you surrender. And you still *didn't contest your main gripe.*

Feeling as if she'd left a layer of skin stuck to his hot lips and hands, she scrambled off him, getting to her feet clumsily before plopping on the couch again.

Brooding with hunger, radiating it, he rose to his elbows, stretching before her half-naked like a god of abandon.

Before she crawled back over him, she bit her tingling lips. "So I got this part. You want me. Fine. How about we discuss another concern? Your transgressions?"

He was on his feet in what should have been an impossible movement. She was in good shape herself, but this was a level of fitness and strength that was almost scary.

His lips twisted. *"Ma gatalnahom bahthann baad?"*

Haven't we already killed them with investigation? The regional expression for draining a topic of life.

She nodded, still shaky. "The old ones. But with you,

there's always new ones." She sucked in a burning stream of aggravation. "You spied on me. You evidently still do."

"I tried to stop. I couldn't."

So simple. So stymieing. Why couldn't she do herself the life-saving favor of not wanting him anymore?

He threw himself down beside her, grimacing. "That's not true. I *didn't* try. I knew I couldn't stop watching over you." Head resting on the couch, he turned his face toward her, inches from her own. "Jala, we both try to save the world in our own ways. But I'm the one who's versed in its dangers, who can take measures to eradicate them. I won't apologize for keeping tabs on you. You lead a very dangerous life."

"I do social and humanitarian work!"

"In the world's most dangerous places. Apart from the damages that could befall anyone just being there, you're a temptation to even the most harmless of men."

She gaped at him.

"It's bigger than me, Jala, the need to know you're safe. And since I'm the one best equipped to keep you safe, I do."

Incredulity burst out of her. "*I* keep me safe."

For a split second, his eyes said she knew nothing.

This brought her sitting up. "Are you telling me you saved me from a danger I was unaware of?"

Another blip said he'd saved her from far more than *a* danger. But he just shook his head. "Just leave it. I wasn't 'spying' on you. I was reassuring myself of your safety and making sure you were safe. There's a big difference."

The lump that now inhabited her throat again grew harder.

Believing this would change so much. Mean too much. And she couldn't handle more changes of perspective right now. The foundations of her existence, as miserable as they'd been, had constituted her stability. Losing them all, having to erect so many new ones so suddenly, was too... overwhelming. And he was already enough on his own.

In defense, she groped for one of her established suspicions. "Or you were afraid I'd go after Najeeb again?"

He huffed a mirthless laugh. "And what would I have done if you did? I believed you'd gone to him when you left me, and there was nothing I could do about it." At her glower, he ground out, "I *didn't* tell him anything."

She had no idea why, but this time, she believed him.

Yet another pillar knocked over.

After a moment in which he seemed to debate the wisdom of divulging another piece of the puzzle, he said, "I only found out later why Najeeb cut all ties with you."

And he told her why. At least what he believed to be true. *She* knew the real reason why Najeeb hadn't contacted her again. Because she wouldn't let him. But Mohab believed King Hassan's slandering had ended her relationship with Najeeb.

After discovering King Hassan had been behind her ordeal in the past, and knowing he was now the reason behind this current crisis, she didn't feel bad about not exonerating him from *that* specific crime. It hadn't been for lack of trying that he wasn't guilty of it after all.

Mohab was continuing, "Then you disappeared, and I couldn't find you for months. When you resurfaced, there was no way I was going to let you out of my sight again."

She let out her bated breath. "If I say I believe you, you have to promise to stop."

He must have gauged they'd entered the negotiation zone as he bore down on her again, deluging her in a fresh wave of temptation. "Why? Who wouldn't want a guardian angel like me? I'm very handy, you know. People pay me tens of millions to keep them safe. I am offering you a free ride for life."

His arms were halfway around her when she pushed out of them again and stood up, teetering with the urge to throw herself back into them, come what may. But this was just too soon, too fast…too much. She needed to slow down, take a look at where she was jumping, before she plunged into the deep end…again.

Groaning, he stood up as well, his eyes suddenly totally serious for the first time since she'd seen him again. "I've told you the truth about everything so far. All but one thing."

Her breath deserted her as she turned fully toward him.

Looking as if he was dragging shrapnel from his own flesh, he rasped, "You don't have to marry me…or even say you would. You can leave right now, and there'd be no war."

CHAPTER SEVEN

Mohab met his own eyes in the steamed-up mirror and reached a conclusion. He was insane.

He'd gotten Jala to agree to a fake engagement, then progressed to alleviate her every doubt about the sincerity of his desire. Her surrender to his lovemaking, her mind-blowing response, had admitted her equal need. Her capitulation had only been a matter of time. If he'd just kept his mouth shut, he might have had her in his bed again by now.

But he hadn't kept his mouth shut.

Mizar and Sette rubbed against his legs, distracting him from wanting to bash himself over the head.

Sighing, he picked them up and headed out of the bathroom with Nihal and Rigel weaving between his legs. Even they couldn't make him feel better now. They actually made him feel worse. All they did was remind him of his pleasure at Jala's delight in them, of how it had felt to share them with her.

Topping up their treats in the kitchenette, he told them he needed to be alone. As usual, they understood him and gave him space, not following him to the wing's reception chamber.

He stood in the middle of the magnificent space Kamal had bestowed on him and could still barely believe he was actually here. An Aal Ghaanem treated as an honored guest in the Aal Masood stronghold. A week ago, that would have been the material of a ridiculous joke. But Kamal had been given a second chance with his queen and was making a real effort to pay it forward.

And what had *he* done with all of Kamal's support and all the ground he'd managed to gain with Jala? He'd voluntarily blown it all to hell.

He could still see Jala standing across from him, her face a frozen mask after he'd divulged that last bit of truth. Then she'd said one word.

"Explain."

He had. He'd told her everything, hadn't left out one single detail this time. After he'd finished, she'd just turned and walked out of his quarters.

That had been three days ago. She'd left the palace that same night. He'd thought she'd head straight to the airport and fly out of Judar, never to return. But her security detail had called to report that she'd checked into a hotel on the other side of Durgham. Moving all the way across the capital had been a clear message that she'd wanted to distance herself from the palace. And him. Trying to call her had yielded no results. She wasn't answering anyone's phone calls. Then she'd turned her phone off. And it was all his fault.

Exhaling forcibly, he moved to the French doors, stared sightlessly at the palace grounds. He had to face the fact that he couldn't have done anything else.

He'd lied to her too much during their relationship, hidden too much. At first believing he had to, then fearing the consequences of exposure. Then he'd seen her again, and she'd given him the full disclosure he'd long craved. And he'd realized that, apart from her own hang-ups about intimacy and commitment, the real reason he'd lost her all those years ago was because he hadn't been honest with her. After realizing that, he could hide nothing anymore. He'd wanted her to want him based on full disclosure, too, needed to have her this time in total honesty.

But after he'd confessed everything about the past, about his feelings, only one thing had remained. Her total freedom of choice about whether to be with him or not. So he'd given it to her.

And she'd chosen not to be with him.

The only reason he'd stayed in Judar till now was because she had. According to Farooq and Shehab, the ones she'd let near, having ostracized Kamal as well, she'd stayed only to see their kids a few times before she left. But she wouldn't remain in the palace where both the perpetrators of this latest deception resided. It was probably a matter of a couple days before she left. It would be over then.

Who was he kidding? It was *already* over. It had been over the minute she'd realized she didn't have to put up with seeing him again. And it didn't matter if she still wanted him. To Jala, freedom and autonomy and honesty had always mattered far more than her desires, no matter how ferocious those were.

A growl of exasperation burst from his depths. Enough. He'd set up an elaborate gamble to resolve this need for her that continued to eat at him, and he'd lost. Everything had depended on being able to win her, and he'd done so fleetingly, before he'd lost her again...big-time.

But he hadn't lost her because he'd told her the full truth—it was because he'd started this whole thing with another charade. He'd catastrophically miscalculated all over again. Seemed it was hopeless. Whenever it involved her, he, the master strategist, had once more been reduced to a bumbling idiot.

Growling again, unable to stay where she wasn't, he strode out of the wing.

He had to see Kamal before he left, tell him they'd have to plan another way to contain his uncle's wrath. As for Jala, he'd have to get her out of his system some other way....

"You're better than I gave you credit for. *Way* better."

Mohab squeezed his eyes shut as the deep, amused voice hit him between the shoulder blades.

His condition was much worse than he'd thought. He hadn't even felt Kamal approach.

What the hell. Get this over with.

He turned to Kamal...and almost winced. That was it. He no longer considered Kamal his new favorite person. This guy was just too happy. And it swamped Mohab with such...futility. A hopelessness that he'd ever feel anything like that.

"I was coming to see you...." he began.

Kamal took his arm. "I could have just called you, but I had to see you again and picture you in your future capacity, now that it has emerged from the realm of speculation to fact."

Mohab's frown deepened. He didn't get one word of what Kamal had just said.

Kamal went on, spouting more gibberish. "I really thought the next I heard from Jala would be with a proposal on how to avert the war without her involvement. And the worst part? Even if we'd been dealing with the original, critical situation, I had no doubt she'd present me with a real solution."

Kamal huffed a laugh at the word *solution,* which had evidently become an inside joke between them. However, Mohab wasn't in any laughing mood over it, or over anything else, anymore.

Kamal continued, "She's been known to formulate workable solutions for some seemingly impossible situations to the satisfaction of all sides in some of the world's most volatile regions."

Mohab knew that. He'd followed her work closely, with the utmost interest and admiration. And more than a little humility and self-deprecation. For she'd been able, with far fewer resources and powers, to peacefully do what he'd thought could only be resolved through his extreme measures. And while he'd discreetly helped her wherever he could, he'd been honing his methods on her example.

But why was Kamal telling him all this now? Or was he the one who couldn't make sense of anything anymore?

Kamal, who'd taken him back to his quarters, was going on as they entered. "Then she leaves, and I think the next time I want to see her I'll have to chase after her on one of her jaunts around the world. But I should have known better than to predict Jala the Unpredictable. She left the palace only to go stay in a three-star hotel."

"I know that."

Kamal's fond expression deepened. "She was never one for luxury, but her work seems to have made her allergic to it. Not to mention her chronic independence issues. The eyes around here must have had her climbing walls. *Ya Ullah!*" His exclamation made Mohab blink. "I was told you brought cats, but I thought they mistook some other containers for carriers."

His cats were scurrying to welcome him back, slowing down to a curious, cautious prowl when they found he had company.

Grinning widely, Kamal bent to offer them his hands to sniff. "Four cats! There's no end to your surprises, Mohab, is there? Wait till my kids find out you have these beauties. You'll be their favorite uncle."

The word *uncle* stabbed him. He was destined not to be

anyone's uncle. Anyone's anything. Seemed Kamal was still under the misapprehension that he might marry Jala.

Gritting his teeth, he watched his cats show Kamal the same level of instant trust and acceptance they'd shown Jala. Kamal probably *felt* the same as her to them, too.

Which was another reason he couldn't be around her brother any longer. "Listen, Kamal…"

Kamal straightened with Mizar in his arms, grinning. "I *do* want to listen—to just how you did it. I knew you were effective, but this borders on magic."

And Mohab had enough of all the ambiguity. "What the hell are you talking about?"

"I'm talking about Jala, of course. She just called me and told me to start the wedding preparations."

FOR THE FIRST time in his life, Mohab was totally in the dark.

Jala had told Kamal she would marry him.

Then, after Kamal had left, she'd called, making him certain he hadn't been hallucinating. She'd informed him that their "engagement" would be celebrated tomorrow over a family dinner.

He'd demanded to see her before said dinner, but she'd hung up without even a goodbye. He still wondered if he'd only listened to a prerecorded announcement.

Yet he couldn't care. This was his third, and probably final, chance—and he was not going to squander it this time.

To that end, he'd better get that wild-eyed look under control. Though the tuxedo-clad man who was reflected back at him in the ornate full-length mirror looked suave and polished, his expression was that of a starving wolf.

"I see why you didn't hear me knock. You're lost in admiring your own grandeur."

The soft mockery lashed him, had him swinging around. *Jala*.

She'd always been his ideal of femininity, the sum total of his fantasies, but tonight, she'd taken her sorcery to a new level. In an old-gold dress made of ethereal materials that wrapped her every curve to distressing advantage, she was overpowering…even otherworldly.

She headed for the open French doors and stopped with her back to him, contemplating the gardens at night. He approached her as if afraid she'd disappear if he made any sudden moves, and she looked at him over her shoulder with eyes as mysterious as Judar's night. Her hair sifted in the jasmine-laden night breeze with swishes that strummed his every nerve.

"You said you wanted to talk."

"Since you hung up on me, I didn't think you registered my request, or thought it not worth consideration."

"I reconsidered. We need to touch base before we face the combined forces of our families for the first time together."

He slid his arms around her, crisscrossed them beneath her breasts and pulled her back against his body. This was probably a damaging move right now. But he was beyond holding back. These past three days had been three days beyond the limits of his endurance.

Even though he felt her tense as he bent to breathe her in, she didn't resist. He went dizzy as the feel and scent and heat of her vitality and femininity eddied in his arteries.

"I thought I'd never see you again. Jala, *habibati*…"

He turned her in his arms and captured her lips with all his pent-up hunger and frustration.

Feeling her luscious mouth open beneath his, having his lungs fill with intoxication as she gasped a scorching gust of passion, tore aside any semblance of moderation.

Bypassing all preliminaries, he plunged into her depths, his tongue dueling with hers as he squeezed her against him, his hands kneading down her body to bunch up the chiffon layers of her skirt and seek the sizzling velvet of her flesh. He dipped beneath the lace, cupping the perfection of her buttocks.

She tore her lips from his. "This isn't why I'm here…"

Gritting his teeth, he reluctantly let her go. If their engagement dinner wasn't less than half an hour away, he would have convinced her otherwise.

It was still with utmost satisfaction that he watched her hands tremble as she smoothed out the disarray created by his passion. "I'm here to explain why I'm doing this."

"As long as you've reconsidered, I don't care why."

"You should, because I think you miscalculated."

Hah. Tell him about it. But she was probably referring to some other miscalculation he was as yet unaware of.

"You think you can curb your uncle and dictate your terms, resolving the crisis without my…participation. And though I commend you for deciding to be forthright at last, even when it was counterproductive to your other purposes, I believe you're wrong in thinking I'm not necessary to achieve your goal. You'd be right if we were talking about someone other than your uncle. But with his track record of paranoia and volatile pride he could still escalate the situation if Saraya's percentage doesn't appeal to him, or if he feels slighted, even if it means going to war against you, too."

"So what are you saying, exactly?" he asked carefully.

"That the marriage solution remains what he'd be most likely to accept, the one that would save him face. If you give him the added deference of being the one who puts his hand in Kamal's, with both acting as our proxies, his pride would bind him to peace from then on."

Kamal had been right. She was totally unpredictable. This was the last thing he'd expected her to do.

But there she was, doing exactly what Kamal had said she would. Coming up with a levelheaded and thorough analysis of the situation, based on her knowledge of all the players, and formulating the most workable solution. It again showed him he shouldn't have tried to manipulate her to seal the deal, should have come clean and hoped she'd make this offer on her own.

He inhaled. "That's extremely astute. And exceptionally thoughtful of you, to go to the effort of thinking this through so thoroughly and then agree to help, even after I tried to maneuver you into doing so under false pretenses."

Her strong shoulders jerked dismissively, causing her breasts to jiggle slightly and sending another rush of hormones roaring through him.

"Seems the first time is the worst. Then you get used to it." Before he could swear there'd be no more manipulation, she went on, "So anyway, I am your best bet, as you've already figured out, so I've decided to pitch in."

He pulled her back into his arms, meshing their gazes. *"Ashkorek, ya jameelati."*

She again pushed out of the circle of his arms. Story of his life from now on, it seemed.

"Don't thank me yet. I said this is what's most likely to get your uncle to cooperate, not that it's certain it will."

He shoved his hands into his pockets. "I don't care about the outcome. I only care about your intention."

She slanted him an unfathomable glance. "You seem to be in an uncaring mood today. Or is this your usual state? Probably." Another shoulder jerk. Another surge of lust. "You should start practicing caring. Being a king is quite a bit different from being a terminator."

"If anyone can teach me to care, it's you. As my queen."

Her gaze wavered. Was that…vulnerability?

Next split second it was gone, making him wonder if he'd even seen it.

"So about tonight…" she began.

No comment? Since she didn't intend to be his queen? "What about it?"

"My sisters-in-law must have told my brothers their deductions about our relationship, based on your famous phone striptease session. Or, if by some miracle they managed some discretion, everyone must know by now that we're not strangers to each other. So how do you intend to play this in front of my family and yours?"

He raised her hands to his lips. "I intend to show everyone how proud I am to be your intended, that this was a hope I had harbored since I first saw you."

She withdrew her hands. "No need to go overboard, or you'll only make them suspicious."

She didn't believe him. Maybe because his statement was untrue. He *hadn't* thought of marriage in the years he'd craved her from afar, since he'd never thought marriage was in the cards for him at all. Even when he'd proposed, he had no picture of how marriage would fit into his existence.

But now, with the turn his life had taken, everything was different. Although he'd initially come here unclear about what he wanted, beyond the fact that he wanted her with a hunger that continued to consume him, he now wanted everything he could possibly have with her.

Her own stance seemed to be unchanged, though.

He had to hear her spell it out. "So your original agreement stands, as is?"

He held his breath. Hoping against hope…

Then she breathed, "Yes."

CHAPTER EIGHT

As soon as Mohab entered the expansive dining room in the king's quarters with Jala, the nine people seated at one end of the gigantic table stood up and clapped.

Mohab saw only one person. *Najeeb.*

Heat shot to his head. What was *he* doing here?

As per Jala's mandate, only the people necessary to the peace efforts should have been present. That had meant Kamal and his queen, Mohab's uncle and his queen and him and Jala.

He'd wholeheartedly welcomed that, had been enormously relieved when his uncle had begged off attending on account of illness. But to support Mohab's bid for the "incomparable Jala's" hand, King Hassan had promised to send her a priceless set of jewelry from Saraya's royal treasury.

It had been the ultimate irony to hear his uncle speaking in such glowing terms of the woman he'd once gone to dishonorable lengths to ensure didn't sully his royal family. Now that she was *the* princess of Judar, Hassan was embarrassingly eager to have her blood mingle with that of his family.

But Mohab had relaxed prematurely about tonight. King Hassan had sent Najeeb in his stead. Najeeb had also brought Jawad and Haroon, his second-oldest brothers among nine full and half siblings. But it was Najeeb's presence alone that disturbed Mohab. He'd avoided Najeeb for years, for every reason there was. A face-to-face with him, now of all times, topped the list of his least-favorite surprises ever. And he'd had some doozies in his time.

"Fi seh'hut al aroosain." Kamal raised a crystal glass filled with burgundy liquid, no doubt Judar's famous date wine, toasting the health of the bride-and groom-to-be.

Everybody raised their glasses and voices in salute, smiles of pleasure coating all faces. All faces but Najeeb's.

He didn't approve of this.

"So I had to do something as drastic as get engaged to end the Aal Masoods' and Aal Ghaanems' centuries-old theatrics, you testosterone-overdosed cavemen?"

General laughter rose in answer to Jala's humorous admonition as she smoothly unspooled from his loose embrace and entered the circle of welcome that opened for her. She was at once enfolded into the love and delight of her brothers and their wives. He envied them her readiness to go into their arms, to receive and return their kisses, to exchange smiles with them that were unmarred by the past.

Then she turned to his cousins, and his envy became resentment. Watching her bestow ease and humor on them actually hurt when he'd gotten nothing that approached either from her. When it brought back how it had felt to be inundated in both. It didn't help that those two hulking buffoons were totally enthralled as this magical creature welcomed them as friends and future family members.

Then it was Najeeb's turn.

He watched them approach each other with all the trepidation of someone watching a collision, one that would pulverize him. The hesitation of the long absence and the uncertainty of the other's reception evaporated with every step until they met halfway. Then she reached out both

hands to him and he clasped them in his with just as much
eagerness. But it was the tenderness on both their faces as
their tentative smiles blossomed that had jealousy surging through him like a geyser. He felt that if he opened his
mouth right now, he'd scorch the whole room.

He had no idea what he said to Jala's family as they
gathered around to congratulate him. All he could see was
Najeeb's head bent close to Jala's, making his blood boil.

"Take it easy, Mohab, or the guy might drop dead."

That was Shehab. Mohab curbed an imprecation as he
tore his gaze away from Najeeb to look at Shehab. The
man's black eyes were dancing with mischief, having evidently documented Mohab's reaction to Najeeb and Jala's reunion.

Another surge of savagery coursed in his blood. "Right
now, I'm not sure that would be a bad thing."

Shehab chuckled, looking very pleased with Mohab's
response. "If Najeeb drops dead, Jawad won't be far behind. He'd jump out of his fighter jet without a parachute
if he found himself the crown prince of Saraya. Only Najeeb, in his endless wisdom and stamina, can deal with
your uncle."

Mohab almost bared his teeth at Shehab. Hearing about
Najeeb's endless wisdom—and stamina—was more fuel
to his fire.

"And don't be too hard on Najeeb. It's only expected that
any man would turn into a slobbering fool around Jala."

Mohab forced a smile to his taut face. "You trying to
make me go rearrange my little cousin's face, and spend
the rest of my engagement night in *your* little brother's
dungeon?"

Shehab guffawed this time, definitely delighted with
Mohab's vehemence, which he no doubt considered revealed the depth of his involvement with his sister.

"Wouldn't *that* be a far more memorable engagement night than this inane dinner you and your fiancée imposed on us?"

Farah, Shehab's wife, turned to her husband, emerald eyes gleaming with curiosity. "What am I missing?"

Shehab scooped her to his side, his smile so bedeviling Mohab considered manually wiping it off his face. "Mohab here is so head over heels with Jala, he's having a male aggression crisis just watching her greet an old friend."

Farah waved her hand dismissingly. "Najeeb is a *really* old friend." Then she started recounting the story of Jala's and Najeeb's friendship.

Mohab suffered all he could before interjecting, "I already know all that. I was there the first time they met." When she looked confused, he explained further. "I was the one who led the extraction team and ended the hostage crisis."

Delight surged on Farah's face. "Oh, you're her knight in black-ops armor! How unbelievably romantic that after saving her life all these years ago, you'd reenter it as her prince charming!"

"That even tops the way we met, *ya rohi*." Shehab gazed down at her with such indulgence, Mohab made a mental note to check his blood sugar as soon as he left their company.

Farah poked Shehab in equal adoration. "You mean when you set me up?" Mohab wanted to scoff "you, too?" as Farah turned to him with a mock-stern expression. "This perfect husband you see now first approached me swathed in Tuareg garb and masqueraded as someone else to seduce me into marrying him, thinking I was the former king of Zohayd's illegitimate daughter, all in the name of keeping Judar's peace."

Mohab couldn't hold back his scoff this time. It seemed

seducing a woman for their kingdom's sake, then falling for her was an epidemic among the princes in this region.

"Let's get this engagement party under way, people," Kamal called out. "We're all experts at talking while eating."

As voices rose in approval and everyone moved back to the splendidly laid-out table, Mohab found himself surrounded by Jala's family while she was assimilated into his.

For the next hour a superb dinner was served, but he could taste none of it. Being separated from Jala and watching her with his cousins, with Najeeb, killed any appetite and any ability to enjoy her family's company.

At one point, as he stared at the grinning faces of the loving couples around the table, he reached a final conclusion. The Aal Masood family all suffered from toxic levels of happiness, and exposure to them was detrimental to his health. And sanity.

But he could see something besides sickening bliss on their faces. It was the shrewd realization that all was not as it should be with him and Jala. He waited with bated breath for someone to allude to this, but as if to stop their suspicion from becoming conviction, Jala left his cousins and came to stand behind Farooq.

Leaning over her oldest brother, she draped supple arms over his shoulders and kissed his cheek. "Can I have my fiancé back now? Cross-examined him to your heart's content?"

Her arm brushed against him and her hair swished forward, deluging him in her scent. Everything inside him clamored, almost drowning Farooq's guffaw.

"As if. You've got yourself one tight-lipped groom-to-be here. Figures, though, with what he does for a living. But the poor guy barely touched his dinner since he was busy eating you up. I don't think he even heard most of what we said to him."

Kamal chuckled. "I bet Mohab's ideal engagement dinner would have been having you alone somewhere secluded by the sea. I think we only managed to torture him with this dinner."

"Which is as it should be," Shehab said, winking at her. "In another age, we would have made him roam the desert in search of mythical treasures, then return to jump through hoops of fire for the privilege of your hand."

Mohab twisted his lips at her brothers. "Braving the desert unarmed and on foot, and then ending my trek by battling hungry hyenas over a fire pit *would* have been preferable to sitting across this ridiculously wide table from Jala throughout our so-called engagement party." He swept the three men a challenging look. "You *should* test me. The honor and privilege of her hand demands every proof that I actually deserve it. So prepare your trials. The more impossible, the better."

And he meant every word. He'd do anything for Jala. For this wasn't a matter of wanting to get her out of his system anymore. This was about winning her. Properly this time. And forever. He finally faced what he'd avoided acknowledging for years: what she was to him. This woman he'd wanted from the first moment, who he had pined for through the years of alienation, who he had watched over and learned from.

He'd never stopped loving her. And with everything she'd done and still did, every breath she took, she kept proving to him that he'd always been destined to love her.

He loved her now more than he ever had or even believed possible.

Feeling her eyes on him after his impassioned pledge,

he turned the force of his conviction on her, told her, wordlessly, but with everything in him, what he felt.

Meeting her eyes, he felt her spirit touch his, as it had from the very beginning. Now, even through the barrier she'd erected between them since that fateful night, it jolted through him again, how kindred it felt, how deep her hold over him was, how absolute. And he no longer wanted to sever it. He only wanted to cherish and revel in it. He only wanted to convince her to let him in again, to let him love her with everything he had, as he'd failed to in the past.

But something in her eyes sent his heart hammering. That vulnerability. And something else. Pain. Bottomless pain.

It disturbed him so much it had him on his feet, just as Farooq stood to vacate his place for her.

Heart ramming his rib cage, he held her seat as she sat, trying to catch her gaze again, to confirm what he'd seen. But there was nothing but a bright, neutral smile as she murmured thanks and looked away as her brothers continued poking and prodding him.

"No surprises here, Mission Impossible Man," Shehab said. "Wrestling impossible odds and facing lethal dangers must be easier for you than sitting still through a social function."

Kamal sighed. "Wait till you're king. You'll suffer through those till you want to *cause* mayhem to escape them."

Taking Jala's place between his cousins, Farooq chimed in, "Hmm, I can make use of your willingness to do anything for Jala. I have some chronic...problems I need taken care of."

Reaching for the hand Jala rested on the table, he enveloped it, a thrill going through him when she relinquished it to him. "Make me a list and consider them resolved."

Farooq grinned at Jala. "I'm sold. I like your fiancé. It's very handy to have a cleanup expert in the family."

"How about you ask him for a thousand red camels in the bargain?" Carmen ribbed her husband.

Everyone laughed at Carmen's allusion to one of the most famous folklore stories in the region, the immortal love story of Antarah and Ablah. Antarah, a slave who won his freedom through heroic feats, asked for his beloved's hand, only for her father to get rid of his nuisance by sending Antarah on an impossible mission to acquire rare camels from far-flung enemy territory, alone, unarmed and having nothing to bargain with. Antarah, of course, accomplished all this, and in the end won his Ablah.

If only everyone knew *his* mission impossible—winning back what he'd lost of Jala's heart and then reaching the parts he'd never been able to touch—was far harder than any overwhelming odds they could throw at him.

After an interval of gaiety as they exchanged anecdotes and tales from the past about more men in his situation, dessert was served.

Jawad, who'd been the most outspoken of his cousins during the evening, grinned at him so widely he wanted to hurl a plate between his perfect teeth. "When Najeeb told us Mohab was getting hitched, we just had to see the impossibility of who'd made him consider this suicidal move."

"Then we see Jala…and the rest of you ladies—" Haroon made a theatrical gesture around the table "—and now we know. Judar is the ultimate babe producer…and magnet."

Najeeb glared at his younger brothers. "I knew it was the biggest mistake I've made in recent memory letting you two tag along. Now I know how the enmity between our families started. It must have been instigated by men with big mouths and bigger eyes, like you."

"Chill, bro." Jawad grinned unrepentantly. "Those guys know for a fact they have rare jewels that anyone with a heartbeat would admire." He flashed the ladies another killer smile. "I bet they'd be offended if we pretended we didn't notice."

"Yeah." Haroon smirked at Najeeb. "So maybe it was a tight ass like you, one who couldn't take a joke or wholesome admiration, who started the enmities."

Najeeb looked heavenward, then over at the Aal Masoods, focusing on Kamal. "See what I have to put up with? Now that you've seen my spare heirs, I hope you really appreciate yours."

"Oh, our baby brother, Kamal, appreciates the hell out of us." Farooq chuckled, eliciting an exasperated growl from Kamal. "You on the other hand, Najeeb, are to be pitied…"

Having had enough and still holding Jala's hand, Mohab rose. "And here I want to thank you all for celebrating this momentous occasion with me and Jala." He panned his gaze among Jala's family. "But though I truly appreciate the welcome you've shown me, and *forood walaa'ee wa ta'ahtee,* my pledge of allegiance and obedience stands. Kamal was right. There's nothing I want more than to have Jala to myself, at least for part of the evening, to make its memory a perfect one. So please, continue to celebrate, and excuse us as we go have our own personal celebration."

As he pulled back the chair for Jala and she stood up lithely, his heart again convulsed when he noticed the glance she exchanged with Najeeb. Shehab and Farooq ribbed him some more, while Kamal said nothing, the gaze encompassing him and Jala still…unconvinced.

Kamal must realize Jala's lack of interaction with him wasn't a matter of shyness in front of her brothers, or on account of the suddenness of their resumed relationship and its rapid development. After all, Kamal was a man versed in both his sister's nature and in matters of the heart. He must realize something was wrong.

But still giving him all the support he could, Kamal waved his hand in mock imperiousness. "You may be excused, but only because we now have said pledge of allegiance and obedience, and can do anything at all with you."

As everyone laughed again, Jala said, "It's only fair to warn you that while you'll have the allegiance, you'll be out of luck where the obedience is concerned. From personal experience you know where *that* will be expended." She turned and winked at her sisters-in-law. "Right, ladies?"

As her family all laughed, and Jawad and Haroon begged to hear some obedience examples—to fortify their resolve *never* to marry—she waved a final goodbye. Then she turned and headed out of the dining room, with him a step behind her.

Once they were away from the royal quarters, he opened the first door he found and pulled her into the chamber's darkness, lifting her off the ground, already kissing her.

Her gasp filled him as her lips opened beneath his. Tasting the tart sweetness of berry sauce on her tongue, he groaned, plunging deeper, seeking more of her taste, demanding her surrender. For long minutes, she gave it to him as he pressed her against the door, opening her thighs around his hips and grinding at her core through their clothes, simulating the possession he was going insane for.

"Jala, *habibati*..."

She suddenly lurched and pushed at him.

Putting her back on her feet, he twisted a hand in the luxury of her hair, able to see her now that his sight had adapted to the faint lights coming from the windows. "Let me love you, *ya jalati*. Stop pushing me away. Let me close again. I know you want me as much as I want you."

Her breasts still heaved against his chest, her body arched involuntarily into his even when her words rejected him. "I don't care what I want. This isn't what I agreed to."

"Then agree to this now. To giving us another chance."

"*No.* I don't want another chance. I want to play my part until we're sure your uncle will sign the treaties, then I want to leave. This is what I want to do. What I *need* to do."

The desperation in her voice struck him in his vitals, made him stagger away.

And because he had admitted to himself that he loved her, only wanted her to be happy whatever the cost to him, he couldn't pursue his seduction anymore. Not if, for some reason he couldn't fathom, it distressed her that much. It might kill him to let her go, but he'd rather die than hurt her.

His shoulders slumped with defeat. "My uncle is sending you a set from the royal treasury. It's his way of saying the peace treaty is as good as signed."

After a long moment of staring at him, she whispered, "That's great. I mean, that you think he'd sign, not about the jewels."

He waved her qualification away. He knew she cared nothing about material things, and not because she had plenty of them. She made no use of her status in any way, not for herself. She used all her privileges to serve the world.

"I have the drafts of the treaties ready, and after Kamal approves them, I'll present my uncle with them. My package for Saraya is very generous, but as you believe, he wouldn't have felt secure enough or irreversibly connected to Judar without a union of blood. Which he now believes he'll have, thanks to your cooperation. I don't expect he'll pose any further threat to peace."

Her eyes wavered. This had clearly come out of left

field for her. She'd expected him to continue his pursuit, his seduction. And here he was telling her there was no longer any reason for her to play along at all.

He exhaled roughly. "I had my chance with you, and I blew it. Or maybe there was never a chance to be had with you, then or now. I will take part in all the wedding preparations, so both my uncle and Kamal believe everything is in order and on schedule. I'll push for an early signing of the treaties, which, now that my uncle is so amenable, I expect will be soon. Once he signs, I'll reveal the truth and absorb whatever fallout ensues, away from you. Until then, I'll give Kamal some convincing reason for leaving the palace. I'll go in the morning, so you don't have to put up with seeing me again."

CHAPTER NINE

Something tore Mohab from the tentacles of fitful sleep.

The heart that no exertion or danger managed to send thundering, thundered now, past the comfort zone and into distress.

It only ever beat that way for Jala.

Jala. Had something happened to…?

He shot up in bed, alarm swamping him.

"Sorry I startled you."

Mohab felt as if he'd been hit by lightning.

Jala. Here. On his bed.

Leaning across him, body draped in white silk, silvered by the moon's cool illumination, hair raining in sheets of solid darkness across the thighs twisted in his sheets, she looked like a night goddess, his every fantasy made flesh.

This had been the dream he'd been having. That she'd come to him. He'd felt her entering his room and…

He was still asleep!

But he felt awake. She felt real. But she couldn't be real. She'd said no. Such an impassioned, desperate no.

So had he gone over the deep end? He'd been building up to a breakdown for years now. Was this it? He'd start wish-fulfilling wide-awake? Having delusions?

"I couldn't stay away anymore. I couldn't let you leave without telling you I still want you. Now more than ever."

He *was* hearing those words. She was saying them. He knew because even he couldn't imagine the way she made them sound, wouldn't be that ambitious, that delusional as to make them such a throb of passion, such a scald of longing.

She was here. And she had said those words. Not the ones he needed, but still far more than he deserved.

I still want you. Now more than ever.

On their thousandth rotation inside of a single second, he reached out a hand to her face, still half expecting to find nothing but emptiness, for her image to dissipate.

His fingers touched the hot velvet of her cheek.

Groaning at the confirmation, he swung around to his bedside lamp. He had to see her better than the crescent moon through his open windows allowed.

With the chamber flooded in golden light, he turned to her and saw that the lace and satin nightgown and matching robe were cream, not white, the color offsetting the rich gold of her polished flesh.

Then he saw her eyes. Unlocked for him at last, letting him see inside her, see the full measure of her hunger.

Already hard beyond pain, heart trembling with disbelief still, he reached back to her, careful not to make any sudden moves, still afraid this dream might come to an end as every tortured one had in the past six years.

When he was an inch from touching her again, she did something that stopped his heart. What she'd done that night he'd first taken her to his penthouse.

She melted back on the bed, as if she couldn't support herself anymore, threw her arms above her head, arched in surrender, a sultry moan spilling from deep rose lips.

"I *want* you, Mohab."

Surging with her demand, he came over her, straddled her hips, cupping her face in trembling hands. "*Aih,* want me, *ya habibati, atawassal elaiki*—I beg you. I'm yours to want."

"Mohab…kiss my lips, give me yours…"

She reached up and grabbed his hair. This was why he'd let it grow, because she'd once told him she wanted it longer to pull him by, to tether him closer to her on their wild rides. Now she dragged his head with it, surging up to crash her mouth against his. Her tongue delved inside him, tangling in abandon with his.

He let her storm him, let her show him the measure of her pent-up craving and impatience. Then he took over.

He'd show her six years' worth of hunger. Then he'd give her satiation well worth the wait.

He bit into her lower lip, showing her the power of his own craving, before he suckled it inside his mouth in long, smooth pulls, drawing more plumpness into her succulent flesh, then plunging his tongue inside her.

Her whimpers became incessant, her hands clenched in his hair as she wrestled with him for deeper surrender, the pain of her urgency excruciating pleasure. She crushed her breasts into his chest, cushioning him, one leg escaping his prison to wind around his hip in abandon. She was showing him she wanted anything he'd do to her. Anything at all.

Then she moaned into his mouth, "Touch me, Mohab, all over. Do everything to me, don't be gentle… I can't bear for you to be gentle…. I want your full force. I want you inside me, hard and long and now…*now,* Mohab. I can't wait anymore… I can't wait…."

Elation sizzled in his blood. She'd never been this vocal, never told him what she wanted or how she wanted it.

"*Aih, gulili aish betridi*—tell me what you want, *ya galbi.*" His voice shook as he pushed the robe off her shoulders, then raised her arms over her head once more and, in a luxurious upward sweep, freed her from her nightgown.

She only had bikini panties beneath, which he took off, as well. Then he pulled back to fill his eyes with her. *"Ma ajmalek, ya habibati, ajmal men zekrayati, men ahlami."*

"You are." She pressed kisses onto any part of him she reached, his chest, arms, hands. "So much more beautiful than my memories and my dreams."

Arousal hammering in his blood, pounding in his loins, he sculpted her in a frenzy of memory and rediscovery, owned each remembered inch of her silken skin, kneading new curves, digging into strength and soft femininity. Her flesh hummed beneath his fingers, electrifying him.

Her teeth sank into his hand. "Touch my breasts...."

A chuckle revved in his chest, resonating his delight that she was so aggressively demanding his pleasuring. He loved it.

"Amrek ya hayati, command me." He took their weight in his palms and stared at their ripened perfection, stroking their turgid flesh in wonder, squeezing their incredible resilience, circling the buds he'd tasted during so many rides to ecstasy. They were thicker now, darker, more mouth-watering.

With a long whimper, she attacked his pajama bottoms. He let her push them down his hips, growling as she released an erection that had long hardened to steel. Rising to release himself fully, he watched her fling herself up at him, then rumbled as she bunched her hands in his back muscles and latched her teeth into the muscles of his abdomen and torso, writhing against him as if she'd mingle their flesh.

He subdued her back to the bed and she wound herself around him, her voice a thread about to snap. "Come inside me, Mohab...don't make me wait anymore...please... *please...*"

He devoured her pleas, unleashed now that he knew only the savagery of his need would satisfy her.

His lips relinquishing hers, he sowed a path of kisses and suckles lower, until he possessed her breasts, raining bites over their engorged beauty until she crushed his head to her, mashing her flesh into his mouth. He latched on to one nipple, then the other, alternating heavy pulls and sharp nips, each rewarded by a lurch and a shriek.

When he felt her stimulation becoming distress, his hands dragged over her soft, satiny flesh to her core. Spreading her, he slid between her feminine lips, growling with the extent of her readiness. He was coming apart needing to be inside her, but he had to prepare her. For he *wouldn't* be gentle when he took her. As she'd commanded. Clamping his lips on hers, he probed her, plunged two, then three fingers inside her hot channel.

Her thighs clamped his hand, her fingers dug into his scalp as her body convulsed, sharp, spasmodic squeals gusting into his lungs. She was climaxing. With but a touch. He'd aroused her that much.

He allowed himself a moment to watch her in the throes of satisfaction, the sight he'd starved for for six bleak years. Then he took her mouth again, doing to it what his fingers still did to her core, feeding her frenzy, loving every jerk, drinking every last whimper until she slumped in his arms, all precious, satisfied woman.

Or so he thought. In a minute, her lips found his chest again, her leg rubbing against his hardness. Imprisoning it in both of his, he clamped the hand that greedily caressed his shaft.

"I want to touch you, Mohab, taste you…."

The memory alone of her head bowed at his loins, her hair spread on his thighs, the sweep of her back, the flare of her hips as she rubbed herself against his legs like a feline in heat, moaning her pleasure as she worshipped him with trembling hands and swollen lips, almost made him come.

"Later, Jala. Own me later. *Areed aklek, akhullusek*—I want to devour you, finish you."

"No…just come inside me…." She wrapped her legs around his hips, ground her moist heat over his erection.

He savored the torture for a moment, absorbing her need, then opened her folds with the head of his erection, and she mewled and spread herself wider for him, the sound and sight almost making his skull burst. He circled the engorged bud of her arousal, drawing more keens, more prodding twists in his hair. Then he slid from her grasp and moved between her thighs.

Before she could protest again, he took her feminine lips in a voracious kiss, his tongue lapping her in long sweeps. Her protests fractured only when he suckled her bud until he had her thrashing, begging. When he knew she couldn't stand anymore, he bit down on her.

The force of her release razed through his body, almost triggering his. He again pushed three fingers inside her, sharpening her pleasure, lapping up its flood until her voice broke and her body slumped.

Still lapping at her, soothing now, he rested his head over her trembling thigh, tenderness a rising tide through the sustained agony. How he'd missed pleasuring her.

Her shaking hands wound in his hair again, dragging him up by it as he'd dreamed she'd do for so long. He obeyed her, swept up over her, sank languorously into her kiss. Reveling in her hands roaming his body, he could feel her extracting his soul, reclaiming him with her raging need.

She suckled his earlobe, bit it, sending a million arrows lodging into his erection, whispered in a voice rough-ened by abandon and satisfaction, "*Now* will you come inside me?"

"*Enti to'morini*...you only have to command me."

"I did nothing but command you...to no avail."

A guffaw ripped out of him. The fact that she was teasing him now was so unexpected, so delightful.

His hands dug into the buttocks undulating against him. "You call this 'no avail'?"

In answer, she pressed her body and lips to his. "I call anything that doesn't end with you inside me that."

"I spent six years planning all the ways I'd pleasure you when I finally got my hands and lips on you again, *ya rohi*."

She pulled him back over her, eyes feverish. "I only want one way. You. Inside me. *Now,* Mohab."

His heart boomed with gratitude and pride. She didn't want just any pleasure, no matter how fierce. She wanted the pleasure of union, with him.

It was humbling that she desired him as much as before and more. But his passion had intensified through the forging of denial and disappointment, frustration and separation, though mostly by total, unconditional love. Why had hers strengthened? He couldn't tell, could only give thanks.

For one last moment before he joined them, he held her eyes as he loomed over her, and they swallowed him whole.

"Take me."

Obeying her desperate demand, he thrust into her in one savage plunge, sheathing himself inside her tight heat to the hilt, hurtling home, his only home. Her scream felt as if it tore from her lungs, pure, excruciating pleasure, as his bellow had been. She arched up in a steep bow, seeking his possession, needing his urgency and ferocity, and he gave it to her. He withdrew all the way, then forged back even deeper, harder, the near impossible fit driving him out of his mind, until he'd built to a jackhammering rhythm with his full force behind it.

Too soon, her screams merged as she bucked beneath him…then shattered in convulsions that clamped her around him, wrenching at his length in a fit of release. He rode the breakers of her orgasm, withdrawing and plunging in a fury, feeding her frenzy until her screeches stifled and her heart accelerated beyond the danger zone, her tears pouring thickly.

"Come with me…."

Her sob broke him. He let go, buried himself to her womb, wished he could bury all of himself inside her, and surrendered to the most ferocious orgasm he'd ever known, jetting his essence into her depths in gush after agonizing gush, roaring his love, his worship.

"Ahebbek ya hayati, ya rohi… Jala, aabodek…"

Pleasure stormed through him, held him in a merciless vice for long minutes, then it suddenly unleashed its grip, let him breathe, unlocked his muscles. He collapsed over her, driving deeper into their merging.

When he had control over his body again, he withdrew to look down at her, and his heart swelled at the sight of the goddess she'd become. A soundly slumbering one right now. His lips shook on a smile of satisfaction. So he could still pleasure her into oblivion.

Gratitude swamped him again as he made his pledge to the fates. If he couldn't have her love, he'd wallow in her desire, fulfill her every need, lavish all his love and trust and honor on her. He'd keep her hungrier for more still, do anything to keep her beside him.

Until he made her love him. For real. And forever.

JALA JERKED OUT of a place of total darkness and bliss to the sight of Mohab over her, the feel of him inside her.

His weight felt like the gravity holding her universe together. The universe that had spun out of control when he'd told her he'd leave and she wouldn't be seeing him again.

The eruption of despair had overwhelmed her. She'd pushed him away, thinking she'd been defending herself, saving her sanity. But the idea of losing him again and forever had torn aside inhibitions, rationality, even survival. She'd had to have him again, even if the cost was eternal misery. Nothing had changed, or would ever change. She would always need him beyond self-preservation. And she'd thrown herself into the heaven and hell of his arms again.

The conflagration that had followed, what he'd done to her, proved she'd only forgotten how it had felt to be with him. Or that this ecstasy was new.

It *was* new. And far more potentially destructive for it.

"Jala, *habibati*..." Mohab's voice cascaded like warm midnight waters over her as he turned them around, draping her over him, maintaining their union. "Are you all right?"

No. You exist and I'll never be all right.

Forcing herself to keep it light, she rubbed her face into his pectorals, response gushing again in the core he occupied as the glistening sprinkle of his chest hair tickled her lips. "You really need to ask?"

He smoothed large, calloused hands over her back. "You were moaning. I thought I was too heavy so I took most of my weight off you, changed positions, but you're still tense. You're uncomfortable with me inside you?"

He *was* too big, too thick, and it seemed as if he hadn't subsided at all. He did stretch her into an edge of pain that was addictive, overwhelming, and as he'd driven all that power inside her, it had been beyond exhilarating. The idea of all that he was, focused in one act of sheer desperation, as much at her mercy as she was at his, filled her, body and soul. She'd thought her younger self had experienced the height of shattering emotions, and that was why she'd felt so empty and bereft when she'd lost him. Turned out, she'd known nothing.

When her answer was delayed, he started raising her off him. She panicked, squeezed him with all her strength, kept him inside her.

He threw his head back on a bass groan, his mane fanning on the rumpled sheets, his hands digging into her buttocks, thrusting his own buttocks up to grind himself farther inside her.

She collapsed on him, a cry of shocked pleasure opening her lips on his corded neck as he nudged her womb. *"Mohab..."*

Rising to a sitting position with her straddling his hips, he leaned against the headboard, held her hips in his palms and raised her until the head of his erection emerged from her entrance, then he let her sink over the girth slicked in their pleasure.

"Ride me, *ya rohi*. Take me and take your pleasure of me."

Feeling faint with sensation, she braced herself against the worked wood, thighs trembling as she tried to scale his length. She'd managed only half when his mouth engulfed one nipple, his fingers twisting the other.

She crashed down on him, felt him push into her cervix. *"Mohab...please..."*

He took her arms from their slump, placed them on his shoulders, then held her hips and moved her up and down, traveling the length of his erection in leisurely journeys to the rhythm of his long, deep suckles of her nipples until the pressure in her core threatened to implode. "Before you, I never dreamed pleasure like that existed. I never want to stop pleasuring you, *ya hayat galbi.*"

Life of my heart. One of the extravagant endearments that he'd lavished on her in the past.

Hearing it now nearly tipped her over into the abyss, made her wail, "Mohab… I can't… Too much…"

Again he understood. Easing her onto her back, he rose above her, spreading her wider around his bulk as he lunged forward, letting her feel the rawness of the strength that could and had pulverized men twice her size, now leashed to become carnality and cherishing instead. He stretched her around his invasion and stilled, throbbing in her depths, his fiery eyes holding her streaming ones, until she was one exposed nerve ending.

"*You* are too much. Everything you are. Take me, Jala, all of me." He withdrew as he talked, then rammed back into her.

As if this was his first thrust all over again, she shredded her larynx on a shriek. She dug her fingernails into his buttocks, wanting him to stab her to the heart, destroy her once and for all.

And he did.

She convulsed, stilled into a whiteout before everything detonated, wave after wave radiating from his driving manhood to raze her, reform her for the next sweep.

Then it shot beyond her ability to withstand. He'd joined her in this darkest ecstasy, roaring his completion, his orgasm boosting hers as surge after surge of his seed splashed into her womb, finishing her with delight…and desolation.

FROM THE DEPTHS of satiation, Jala opened eyes that felt glued shut. Her breath hitched, and her body heated instantaneously as she found herself enveloped in him.

Mohab. As in all her dreams, as in those five months they'd been lovers. Curved around her, his legs encompassing her, his head propped on one hand, the other sweeping her in caresses, his eyes and lips radiating pure male satisfaction.

She reached out, ran numb fingertips down his beard. It was amazingly soft, just the right length to lose any stubbly feel. Just remembering how it had felt against her lips, against every inch of her, was enough to have her squirming with arousal again. Not to mention the feel of his hair as she'd binged on the freedom of twisting her hands in it and pulling on it.

"How long have I been out?" Her voice was thick and raspy. The voice of a woman who'd been savagely pleasured. She did feel gloriously sore, every cell shrieking with life.

"An hour or so," he teased. "Watching you tumble into unconsciousness in the aftermath of my possession, then documenting your abandon to slumber, every inch flushed and drained with satiation..." He sighed deeply, rubbed his beard against her shoulder as he plastered her more securely to his length. "It remains the most fantastic sight I've ever seen. It *is* the most gratifying thing in the world, knowing that I can still knock you out with pleasure."

"Anything I can do for your male ego," she croaked.

He hugged her exuberantly before pulling back, his eyes turning serious. "Mine is all tied up in my ability to satisfy you, Jala. And now that I know for certain that this is something only I can do, I won't let you fight our need anymore. We must and will be together."

She closed her eyes, warding off the intensity in his.

It did nothing to reduce the brutality of temptation. She couldn't resist him or her need for him. But she had to lay down limits before he swallowed her whole.

She opened her eyes. "As I just proved, I want you beyond my ability to resist. So I will be with you."

He sat up, his eyes intent. "What do you mean…with me?"

"I'll marry you. For those six months you proposed."

CHAPTER TEN

It had been a torturous whirlwind since that night she'd surrendered to her need for Mohab and told him she'd take his original offer of a six-month marriage.

When she had, he'd brooded down at her for a long moment…then he'd proceeded to plunder her throughout the rest of the night…and morning.

That had been three weeks ago. Time had never passed so slowly. Or so fast.

And tonight was their wedding night.

Once Mohab had secured her agreement, he'd pushed for cutting short the intended three-month engagement. Now he knew he'd have a sure response from his uncle after their wedding, he wanted it as soon as possible. Especially since it was clear, after their one night together, that they'd have no more until they were officially married.

After their explosive reunion, they'd suddenly found themselves surrounded at all times. She suspected Kamal's eyes in the palace had reported her nocturnal visit to Mohab, and to curtail the scandal that would surely ensue if it became known the princess of Judar was entering her intended's bed prematurely, he'd conspired to keep them apart. Since Kamal *had* alluded to the fact that the anticipation before the ceremony invariably made the wedding night all the more…special, she was positive that her constant state of deprivation was her dastardly brother's doing.

But maybe she shouldn't be so impatient to start the marriage that would have her in Mohab's bed again. Because once it did start, she'd start counting down the minutes to its end.

But knowing there would be nothing permanent between them, she'd already decided to take what she could of him, with him, hoard memories for the future. A future she'd always known would be empty, but would now be bleak.

Emptying a chest tight with futility, she forced burning eyes to take in the vista from her window. She wouldn't let heartache dissolve into tears and face tonight with eyes that told its story. She had to play her part tonight, had to honor Mohab in front of his people, fill her temporary position as his bride and queen as best she could.

But even the land that felt untouched by time, being exposed to its ambiance of purity and the serenity that permeated it, failed to imbue her with any measure of calm.

Though this land had touched her on her most fundamental level from the moment she'd laid eyes on it, just like its most influential son had, she still regretted that she'd agreed when Mohab had insisted their wedding take place here.

Jareer. His ancestral land. Where he would become king tonight. And she'd become his queen. Temporarily.

Once she'd lost the right to be here, the memory of experiencing this place with him would be one more injury and loss to live with.

At Mohab's insistence, Kamal had relinquished the right to have his sister's wedding in Judar. He'd thoroughly approved of Mohab wanting to make her his—and Jareer's—

queen on the same night of his *joloos,* when he claimed the newly forged throne.

Since being this accommodating was so unlike Kamal, she'd teasingly accused him of letting Mohab walk all over him just so he'd end her long-lamented spinsterhood. Kamal had only teased back, "Of course, why else?"

And here she was, in Zahara, what passed for Jareer's capital.

They'd come two weeks ago to prepare for the dual celebration. By *they,* she meant *everyone.* Her getting hitched was such a big deal that her family had left Judar unattended to make sure her wedding went, well, without a hitch.

Not that Mohab was letting anyone do anything. Apart from Carmen, who was a master event planner, and Aliyah, a world-renowned artist who had eagerly taken charge of dressing everyone, he had adamantly refused to let anyone lift a finger in anything but recreation. As such, he spent his every waking hour being the perfect host to everyone.

While acting as their tour guide, he'd been a mine of information. According to him, this area had been settled since prehistoric times, and to prove it he'd taken them to see the local caves with their ancient rock paintings. He'd showed them the monuments of every culture that had left their mark on the region, with the most influential being Ottoman, Persian and Indian, but all wrapped up in an Arabian feel.

Apart from the many tourist spots the region boasted, it had surprised her how much there was to do around here. There was a vast array of outdoor activities—from hiking to dune skating to horseback riding, to swimming in and lazing around sparkling springs, to bonfire banquets at night.

It had been bittersweet watching Mohab dote on her

sisters-in-law and nephews and nieces and bond with her brothers. They had all taken to him—especially Kamal—which caused her extra delight…and dejection, when she knew that this would all end on a prearranged date.

As it had to.

But through it all, she'd done everything she could not to dwell on that inevitable end before they even began. And in those moments that she managed to forget, she'd reveled in his spoiling. For *how* he'd spoiled her.

Though nothing he did could make up for being unable to have him again. Since they'd come here, he hadn't even had a chance to kiss her. Well, he did, constantly, but only her hands, shoulders and cheeks. And then there were the scorching caresses, the devouring, brooding glances, the laden-with-promise smiles and the lavish words of praise. Everything had kept her on the verge of spontaneous combustion.

Sighing, she focused on the scene in the distance, with Zahara's houses arranged in graduated compositions of whitewashed adobe and red and yellow-ocher stone. At night, before the full moon rose, they were only shades of gray, but in the daylight they looked like an explosion of flowers atop the sandstone hills.

Mohab had insisted on coming here by land, saying the scenery on the way was worth the six-hour drive from Durgham. And it had been. She'd never seen such variations to the desert, the terrain flowing from undulating dunes to hilly pastures to mountainous heights to combinations of everything.

Then this castle had materialized in the horizon, reigning over Zahara, and it had taken her breath away.

Nestled in the containment of the craggy mountain that overlooked the vista of Zahara, against an ocean of dunes, it crouched behind soaring ancient walls shielded by battlements that summoned to mind Saladin and the Crusades. That night it had loomed against an impossibly starry night, with torchlight fluctuating from the inside and the guard posts shedding their firelight on the outside, drenching it in a deeper, supernatural tinge.

It had been the Aal Kussaimis' stronghold until the time of Sheikh Numair, Mohab's maternal great-grandfather. But after Jareer had signed the treaty with Saraya, and no one inhabited it anymore, this place had fallen into decay.

But Mohab had had it restored in order to boost Jareer's tourist business. He'd succeeded, since the citadel had become one of the region's most frequented historical sites. Like her, tourists found it a once-in-a-lifetime experience, as they wandered through its maze of passages, extensive grounds and interconnected structures, feeling as if they were taking a stroll in the past. Tonight the place would rise against a full moon, and be bathed in the lights of the extensive tent set just outside its walls for the wedding celebration.

She'd expected the guests to include world movers and shakers, but to hear that two presidents and one king from the Western world were attending had made her feel the gravity of the whole situation. This wasn't just a royal wedding, but a major political event. Mohab was claiming more than a bride tonight—he was claiming the throne of a land that would feature heavily in global power from now on.

Standing up, she looked around the chamber Mohab had assigned her till their wedding. He'd restored every inch to its original condition with painstaking authenticity, but had outfitted it with every modern luxury and amenity. She could see herself living here, going away only for work, but always coming back home here.

Home. She'd never felt she had a home. But this majestic place—which was permeated with Mohab's unique, indomitable essence—felt like home.

Not that it mattered how it felt. Her stay here was only a transient one. Now, even the hour she'd managed to negotiate alone before everyone swarmed around her to prepare her for the most momentous night of her life was almost up.

"You hour is up, sweetie."

Groaning, she turned to her sisters-in-law, who were striding through the chamber's ancient oak door. "You must have a stopwatch in your lineage, Aliyah."

The ladies laughed at her lament as Aliyah ushered in her ladies-in-waiting with everything Jala would be wearing. Jala's only input had been picking a color scheme. Living in jeans or utilitarian dresses, she hadn't been about to trust herself with an opinion beyond that. Needing to look the part of Mohab's bride and queen, she'd left it all to Aliyah's artistry and experience as a queen, and to the other two ladies who were far better versed than she was in fulfilling the demands of their titles.

Carmen clapped impatiently. "Hop to it! Your hour of meditation crunched the time to get you ready to a measly thirty minutes!"

Jala bowed. "Yes, O Mistress of Magnificent Events."

Farah chuckled as she fanned her hands in excitement. "You don't know the half of it. Everything you think you saw, or thought the preparations would amount to, is *nothing* to the end result. And I thought Carmen made *my* wedding rival a fable from *One Thousand and One Nights!*"

Carmen chuckled. "I actually didn't do much this time. Your Mohab is so ultraefficient, not to mention head over heels in love with you, he's the one who's done most of the work to give you the best wedding in modern times."

Jala was an old hand by now in maintaining a bright smile when everyone kept stating how much Mohab was

in love with her. They had no idea how it actually was between them. But how could they? To them, it must seem
like a fairy tale, and they must believe that everything
Mohab lavished on her was based on what they all defined
as love. None of them could imagine that her relationship
was nothing like theirs, that his involvement was fueled
by pure passion and garnished by convenience, and that
the whole thing had an expiration date.

Putting down a jewelry box with Saraya's royal insignia
that contained the heirloom pieces King Hassan had bestowed on Jala, insisting she wear them for her wedding,
Carmen grinned. "And this magnificent place worked on
its own. Any touch I put was multiplied tenfold by its
magic."

Jala could well believe it. Not that this diminished Carmen's and Mohab's efforts in any way.

Farah nodded. "And the people of Jareer themselves.
I've never seen a collective so ready for entertainment and
versed in preparing celebrations."

"Yeah, and I thought the people in Judar were like that
in comparison to the States," Carmen said. "But being here
showed me how modern life had taken root in Judar, too,
preoccupying everyone. Here every birth and wedding,
cultural or religious occasion is a feast *everyone* attends
and takes part in."

Farah grinned her pleasure. "And we've been the lucky
recipients of their enthusiasm and expertise through our
stay. It's going to be such a downer going back to indoor
court life and our relatively isolated family lives now."
She winked. "Good thing we have our men to keep us...
intensely entertained."

Chuckling in corroboration, Aliyah appeared from behind the screen that doubled as the dressing room. "We're
ready for you, Jala. As Carmen said, hop to it."

Jala did hop to it. She wanted this over with.

In under ten minutes, she was looking at herself in amazement in the full-length gilded mirror. It was a good thing she'd left herself in Aliyah's hands. That image reflected at her *was* a princess. And a future queen.

Still not believing how the parts she'd had fitted on her had come together, she ran her hands down the incredible deep gold Persian/Indian creation that accentuated her curves and offset her coloring. It had a deep off-shoulder décolletage, a nipped waistline and a layered skirt with a tapering trail. It was heavily embellished in breathtakingly intricate floral designs of silver and bronze thread and was worked with sequins, beads, pearls, crystals and appliqué in every shade of burnt orange, crimson and garnet. The *lehenga*-like skirt was organza over silk taffeta, embroidery sweeping down its lines in arcs. Everything was topped off by a lace and chiffon *dupatta* veil, perched on her swept-up hair, in gradations of gold and crimson with scalloped, heavily embellished edges.

She stood gazing at herself as the ladies adorned her in the priceless pieces of Sarayan treasure, which they thought were part of her *shabkah,* but in reality would only be on loan. The centerpiece of the collection was a twenty-four-karat gold necklace that spread over her collarbones and cascaded to fill most of the generous décolletage tapering just above her barely visible cleavage. It was the most amazing and delicate lacy pattern she'd ever seen in a piece of jewelry, inlaid with diamonds and citrines, with a gigantic bloodred ruby in the center of the design.

The other pieces matched the necklace's delicacy and intricacy, from the shoulder-length earrings to the *tikka* headpiece, to the armband, web ring and anklet. By the time she was adorned in everything, she looked like a walking exhibition, but had to admit—she looked *fantastic*. If no one noticed the shadows in her eyes, that was.

But even those were obscured by the makeup Aliyah applied. When Aliyah stood back and said, "Voila!" Jala could barely recognize herself.

"*Ya Ullah,* Aliyah," she groaned as she stood up. "Mohab will probably ask you what happened to his intended bride!"

Laughter rang around the chamber as Aliyah revolved around her one last time to ensure everything was in order. "You're just not used to putting any makeup on. You look exactly as you always do, but with a little emphasis."

"A little? I look like a makeup ad!"

"We women need something extra to face cameras, not like those men of ours who look fantastic in any conditions. But since you're the most beautiful woman ever, all you needed was a brush of mascara, a line of kohl and a smear of lipstick."

"The most beautiful woman ever, my foot!" Jala snorted.

Aliyah chuckled. "Being Kamal's female edition makes you incontestably that to me. But then Mohab thinks so, too, and certainly not because you look like Kamal."

"Are you ladies done making me and Mohab choke?"

Kamal. He was here to take her to her groom. And he was teasing them with the common belief that people choked when others talked about them.

He approached her, his eyes so loving, so proud, she was the one who choked and threw herself into his arms.

He hugged her off the ground, kissing her forehead. "My little, beloved sister—I am so happy you finally have someone to love you as you should be loved."

There was no stopping the tears from gushing this time. All she wanted to do was burrow into his powerful, protective arms and sob her heartache to him. If only…

Aliyah pounced to separate them before Jala smothered her face in Kamal's chest and spoiled all her efforts. "Postpone tear-inducing declarations to *el sabaheyah,* will you?"

Stepping away from Kamal, she feigned a smile. "If you think you'll ambush me and Mohab tomorrow morning, pretending to congratulate us but really checking on the satisfactoriness of the consummation, you have another think coming."

"I don't care how old you are," Kamal growled. "Or that you're getting married. You're my baby sister and I'd rather not hear about you and consummation in the same sentence."

She poked him teasingly. "So you're okay with knowing it's happening, just don't want to *hear* about it?"

Kamal shuddered. "One more word and I take you back to Judar and put you where no man can get his paws on you."

Aliyah hooted. "My husband, the hopelessly overprotective brother."

Jala smirked. "Hope he's not as hopelessly old-fashioned a lover."

Kamal mock growled and lunged at her.

Everyone continued to laugh as they left her chambers and proceeded to where both the wedding and *joloos* rituals were taking place, picking up her bridal procession on the way. Jala was relieved no one had thought her overwrought moments had been anything more than the prewedding jitters of a woman about to enter into a union that would change her life forever.

As it would. Just not the way everyone thought it would.

Then everything stalled in her mind as she entered the massive hall in the heart of the citadel. Farah had been right. She'd seen the preparations, but couldn't have imagined how it would all come together.

Wrapped in the mist of musky incense, under the fire-light of a thousand torches perched high on the stone walls in polished brass holders, the whole scene was a plunge into the most lavish eras of bygone empires, or even *One Thousand and One Nights.*

As her dazed glance swept the space, the details were almost too much to take in. Cascading satin banners with Jareer's tribal insignias. Acres of tulle and voile wrapping around columns, raining from the hundred-foot-high ceiling and spanning the elaborate Arabesque framework. And the hall that Mohab had installed exploding with flower arrangements. The hundreds of people present looked like sparkling gems themselves in all kinds of finery, from lavish modern evening gowns and tuxedos, to costumes that belonged in a masquerade.

Then everything ceased to exist. In the depths of the hall, on top of a maroon-satin covered platform, with two elaborately carved and gilded ceremonial chairs at his back, there he stood. Mohab.

His hair is loose. It was the first thing that burst into her mind. He'd never worn it down in public before. But now it brushed the top of his massive shoulders, its thick luxury and vitality gleaming with sun strands in the firelight.

The second thing that impinged on her hazy awareness was that he was dressed like he *had* stepped out of the Arabian Nights. Like everyone in her bridal procession, his clothes had the same color scheme, if in much darker tones. A burgundy *abaya* cascaded from his shoulders to his feet over a gold-beige top embroidered in his tribal motifs. Dark maroon pants clung to his muscled thighs before disappearing into darker leather boots.

He looked like the embodiment of the might of the desert, the implacability of the fates. And he glowed. She swore he did. From the inside. With power and distinction. And she loved him with everything in her. Despite the harsh lessons of the past and the permanent injuries lying in the future.

An eruption of thuds made her lurch, even though she'd known it was coming. The matrons of the tribe began her bridal procession with a boisterous percussive *zaffah* that was a variation of what she was used to in Judar.

She snatched a look behind her at the older women with their chins and temples tattooed. One of them was two feet to her side, whacking away at a *mihbaj* wooden grinder.

Then others joined on all the local percussive instruments—the tambourine-like *reg,* the bigger jangle-free *duff* and the vase-shaped hand drum called a *darabukkah*. After that rousing introduction, melody players joined in, an evocative droning emanating from the string *rababah,* and the squealing of reedlike *mizmar*. Then voices rose, from all around, singing congratulations to the bridegroom for his incomparable bride.

She found herself rushing beside Kamal, powered by Mohab's hunger that demanded her at his side. Once they were on top of the platform, her eyes clung to her most beloved people, Kamal and Mohab, locked in a firm embrace that exchanged pledge and trust, before withdrawing to grip each other by one hand, while their other exchanged her from brother to husband.

Then she was clasped tight to Mohab's side, drowning in him, in the hyperreality of it all.

Putting his lips to her ears as the song continued, he whispered, "Do you know I play the *darabukkah?*"

The totally unexpected comment had her gasping, "Can I have a demonstration later?"

"Only if you promise to dance for me."

She lurched as if he'd scalded her. And he had. He'd injected a whole scene of abandoned sensuality into her imagination. Of her, in an explicitly revealing belly-dancing costume, undulating in a fever to the carnal rhythm, getting hotter with every move before he pulled her on top of him, thrust up into her and rode her into oblivion....

The music stopped, bringing her runaway imaginings to a grinding halt. Then the *ma'zoon* came forward to begin the marriage ritual. *It was really happening.*

Mohab took her hand in his and the cleric covered their clasped fingers in a pristine white cloth, placing his palm atop them and intoning the marriage declarations. They repeated only the last parts after him, each accepting the other as a spouse. As the cleric stepped away, she thought that was it and she'd managed to survive the ritual without further upheavals. But before she could move, Mohab took her other hand in his.

Looking soulfully into her eyes, his voice rang out to fill the hall, deep and reverent. "That was what any man pledges to any woman he marries. But *my* pledge to you is that you have all of me, have always had all of me and will always have all of me. All that I own, all that I do and all that I am."

She stared up at him, nothing in her bursting heart and chaotic mind translating into words, let alone anything as evocative as what he'd just said. It was all she could do to remain on her feet as the crowd roared with applause again.

In a tumult over what he'd just said, wondering if it had been for show or if it could possibly be true, she watched the Aal Kussaimi tribe elder climb up onto the platform.

He announced that by the unanimous vote of all tribes of Jareer, Mohab was appointed as king of their land, with his heirs after him inheriting the title.

After that, she could barely register anything as the cacophony rose to deafening levels while every tribe elder came up to kiss Mohab's shoulder and offer him the symbol of their tribe, pledging their allegiance and obedience.

Then only she and Mohab remained, and he was talking.

"By the responsibility you granted me, and the privilege you bestowed on me, as your king, I pledge I will rule with justice and mercy, doing everything in my power to fulfill your aspirations and achieve your prosperity." He led her to the edge of the platform. "As my first decree as king of Jareer, I give you my one treasure to rule beside me, in her wisdom and compassion, your queen... Jala Aal Masood."

Cheers rocked the hall, rising to thundering levels as Mohab smashed the region's every ban on displays of public affection and devoured her in a deeply explicit kiss.

Without hesitation, she sank into the rough demand, the ecstasy of his taste and feel. She *would* take it all with him, every second, every breath, every spark of his desire, and make a reservoir of memories for the life ahead devoid of all of that, of him.

Amid a storm of cheering led by her family, he finally relinquished her lips. Then, grinning down at her, eyes blazing with exhilaration, he shouted to her over the din, "Shall we give them the *joloos* they're after?"

Nodding, his enthusiasm infecting her, she rushed after him to their thrones. After he'd seated her in hers, he came down before her on one knee, his eyes roiling with hunger as he kissed her hand. Then he whispered something she couldn't hear. But she read it on his lips. *"Maleekati."*

My queen.

Somehow she didn't burst into tears. But she knew the memory of this moment would fuel weeping jags far into her future, probably till the day she died.

With one last kiss on her hand, he rose to his feet and a hush descended, as if everyone held their breath. She knew just how they felt. Her breath clogged in her lungs as she watched him glide to his throne with the regality of a king born. Then, sweeping his *abaya* aside, he sat down.

Still holding his *abaya* back with a hand at his hip, he leaned forward to prop his right hand over his knee and struck a pose, a display of grandeur and entitlement that would be the standard for every king who came after him.

After he was satisfied everyone had enough photo and video documentation, he turned to her, his smile flaring again. "How about we feed all these enthusiastic people? They've yelled enough for their dinners, don't you think?"

Suddenly she was spluttering with laughter, then with surprise as she found herself plucked from her seat and up into his arms. He descended the steps, with her cradled against him as if she weighed nothing, and waded through the growing din of approval as people parted to let him pass.

The world spun with every thud of his powerful steps, with his feel and scent. Hoping she didn't mess her face or his clothes too much, she clung around his neck, burying her face in his chest, letting him take her wherever he wished.

Excitement swelled as he whisked her outside the citadel walls, where the gigantic wedding tent had been erected in the clearing overlooking Zahara, which was celebrating their new king and his wedding in the most delightful way.

Under a rising full moon, every dwelling in town had its windows open, and in each room blazed a light with a different color, turning the hills they were built over into a spread of glowing gemstones as far as the eye could see.

Then they came to the tent that looked like a fairy castle made of malleable materials, its whiteness silvered by moonbeams and gilded by the flickering flames of the thousand torches surrounding it at a safe distance. It was so big it would accommodate the three thousand people who were attending from the three kingdoms and the world.

The inside was adorned in the same color scheme of her bridal clothes, the rich tones giving everything a deep luxury bordering on decadence. Mohab carried her past hundreds of tables spread with satin tablecloths, lanterns, flowers, the finest local pottery and blown glass, all in vibrant, complementing colors. Then he was setting her down in their *kousha,* a gilded arabesque "marital cage," open on one side so they'd preside over the celebrations. Right in front of them was the biggest dance floor she'd ever seen covered in hundreds of hand-woven *keleems.*

As soon as everyone took their places around the semi-circular tables, affording everyone the best view of the action, Mohab gestured for dinner to be served, and hundreds of waiters poured from every opening of the tent holding huge serving plates under brass domed covers. Her family and his were in the first row of tables across the dance floor. Her family looked so elated, it twisted the shard in her heart deeper. She brought it under control as she contemplated *his* family. Everyone, including that old goat King Hassan, looked happy with the whole thing. Everyone except Najeeb.

He hadn't talked to her again since the engagement, but his disapproval grated on her every nerve. Najeeb had long come to terms with what his father had done, yet another of his parent's ongoing transgressions that he'd had to put up with all his life. It was *Mohab* he couldn't forgive. Najeeb also couldn't understand why Jala was giving Mohab a second chance after everything that had happened.

As every hurt she'd ever suffered began rushing to her eyes, Mohab tugged at her. The music started to an overpowering rhythm and dozens of young men in flowing beige robes and red headdresses rushed in to form lines.

Many women followed to face them, wearing beige-and-garnet dresses and head covers embroidered in cross-stitch designs. Then one of the most energetic folk dances she'd ever seen commenced, one she hadn't witnessed during all the entertainment they'd had in the past two weeks. It must be one reserved for big occasions.

As if reading her mind, Mohab shouted over the music. "That's a special dance for weddings. You haven't seen one before because they postponed all weddings to focus on ours."

As he talked he started clapping, urging her to clap, too. She did and was soon swept up in the unbridled energy of the performance. Then her family and all of his, except Najeeb, were rushing to the middle of the dance floor, uninhibitedly imitating the steps and soon becoming one with the choreography.

Suddenly the dancers streamed toward her and Mohab, the women converging on her and the men on Mohab.

"You put them up to this!" she accused laughingly, as she was carried on their wave away from him.

He gestured to her, feigning innocence. Then the two waves of dancers rushed toward each other with them in the middle, met then receded, leaving only her and Mohab together, with their families forming a circle around them. Guffawing, he caught her by the waist and swung her round and round, then put her back on the ground and prodded her to dance with him. Recalling long-unpracticed dance steps from Judar, she was soon moving with him to the primal, blood-pounding beat, her heart booming exuberantly in her chest. Finding herself transported into another realm where nothing existed but him, she felt his eyes dominating her, luring her, inflaming her, as he moved *with* her. It felt as if he was connected to her on fundamental levels, as if it was his will that powered her body.

The dances went on and on, interspersed with brief pauses to snatch refreshments and bites of food, then resuming. At one point, the singers handed mikes to each of the celebrity dancers to sing part of the songs. Mohab, of course, sang his motherland's songs perfectly, but when she warbled through her own effort, the kind crowd still roared in approval.

At some point the music came to an end, and she couldn't tell how much time had passed, minutes or hours. It felt as though she was wading in a dream. Then hundreds of people were shaking her hands or kissing her, insisting they'd never enjoyed themselves like this before. Even her family said this rivaled the delight of their own weddings.

Then Mohab disappeared from her side.

CHAPTER ELEVEN

Before alarm could descend on Jala, her brothers swept her into a 4x4 and drove with her into the desert.

As Farooq drove and Shehab sat beside him, Kamal accompanied her in the back. She nestled into him, still stunned by everything that had happened, endorphins and adrenaline fogging her brain. She didn't even ask where they were taking her. It had to be to Mohab.

Then the car stopped and Kamal pulled her out, and there he was. Mohab. A dozen feet away, at the top of three-foot-wide stone steps leading to a columned patio that wrapped around a one-level adobe lodge. Fiery light glowed behind its closed windows.

His hair rustled around his head like silk, and his *abaya* billowed around his body like the wings of a preternatural bird of prey, with him in the middle of the enchantment, her every fantasy come to life.

Then he spoke, his voice as deep as the desert night enveloping them. "*Skokrunn ya asdeka'ee* for delivering your most valued treasure into my safekeeping. In return for this privilege and trust, I owe you everything."

"Oh, you certainly do," Farooq said, chuckling.

Shehab nodded. "And we have a lifetime to collect."

Kamal rounded it all up. "And don't think we won't."

Mohab bowed his head, his palm spread over his heart in pledge. "I'm counting on it."

With senses fixed on him, she barely registered her brothers kissing her one last time, then driving away.

As their vehicle receded, she forced wobbling legs to move toward Mohab. He wasn't smiling. Or moving. He stood there, his gaze roasting her alive, making her feel he was memorizing her down to her last cell.

"Is this another tradition in Jareer?" she whispered, her voice loud in her ears in the desert's pervasive silence. "Grooms here don't go to the trouble of sweeping their brides away but have their families provide delivery services?"

He smiled then. She didn't know how she remained on her feet with the eruption of arousal.

Ya Ullah...how was it possible to want that much?

He came down a step, then another, his movements tranquil, as if he was afraid she'd bolt if he moved too fast. He reached out a hand to her with the same care.

"Welcome to my sanctuary, *ya ajaml aroos fel kone*."

The way he said *the most beautiful bride in the universe* had her stumbling into his embrace. "One of your lairs?"

"Back to the predator motif?"

"I do feel I'm walking into a starving wolf's den," she confessed.

"That's perfectly true. I *will* gobble you up."

"I'm counting on it."

At her giving him back his words, a chuckle rumbled deep in his chest. "Everything you say or do rouses unprecedented reactions from me." His eyes suddenly sobered. "And after all these years, after I first laid eyes on you and wanted you—but thought I could never have you—here you are, my bride, in my sanctuary where I have never let another."

Shying away from dwelling on his declarations, she focused on his statement about this place. It was that vital and exclusive to him. That had to be why she felt as if her essence was flowing through the ground beneath her feet to forever mingle with this place. Why she felt she'd never belong anywhere else again but in this land, with this man.

She stared up at him, towering above her, swathed in moonlight, as one with the desert and the night, unattainable as the stars. But the universe was giving him to her for now. Sort of on loan. Not having him forever meant she only had to wring every minute with him of all it had of pleasure and intimacy.

Surging against him, she buried her face where his top was open, teeth pulling gently at the muscled power beneath, catching in the perfect cover of silky hair. "Here I am."

"And what you do to me…." Groaning, he swept her up in his arms, made her feel weightless.

She clung to him, burying her lips in any part of him she reached. "Show me, Mohab. Everything I do to you. Everything you need from me. Show me everything, do it all to me."

His growl was savage this time as he took her lips, making her nerves fire in unison.

He relinquished her lips only to stride into the lodge. Kicking the door closed behind them, he swept through a dimly lit corridor that made her feel as if he was taking her deeper into a wizard's den. Which he was. He'd always practiced magic on her. And for the next six months, she'd revel in surrendering to his spell—until the enchantment expired.

She now surrendered to the experience, every foot deeper making her realize for the first time what it meant to *have* a sanctuary. This place. Where he was.

It was as far as could be from the opulence of the palace of Judar or the ancient majesty of his citadel in Jareer. It was composed of elements of the desert, unpolished and unpretentious, and more evocative and atmospheric than those mind-boggling edifices for its starkness and simplicity.

He took her into a great room that seemed to comprise the whole place, apart from a kitchen and bathroom. It had stone walls and adobe floors, and was strewn with thick, hand-woven *keleems*. On one side was a settee with a long table in front of it spread with serving dishes on gentle flames. A fireplace presided over the area, its fires leaping in a hypnotic dance, with the other sources of illumination, brass lamps, on every surface. A mosaic incense burner emitting musk and amber was hanging by thick copper chains from the beamed ceiling.

On the other side of the room was the bed. A ten-by-ten-foot, two-foot-high concrete platform with a thick mattress on top of it was draped in the only luxurious touch around—solid dark gold satin sheets, pillows and covers.

He lowered her down on top of it, then mounted it and brooded down at her as he removed his *abaya* and top, muscles rippling beneath his polished skin, his face all noble planes and harsh slashes and grim hunger, all of him painfully male and beautiful. And hers. For now.

She scrambled to her knees, needing to be rid of her own shackles. She'd removed only the veil when he knelt in front of her, stopping her, his sure, deft hands replacing her clumsy ones. She moaned in protest. "You took *your* clothes off when I spent the whole night promising myself I'd do it."

"You can dress and undress me from now on. But I spent the whole night having minor coronaries every time

I looked at you in this getup, betting myself I'd get it off you in ten seconds flat."

And he did. He got the dress off as if by magic, his eyes on every part he exposed, making her feel purely feminine and utterly desirable. Then he moved around her so he was enveloping her from the back, his hard flesh plastered to her flaming back, his harder erection digging into her buttocks through his pants, making her feel contained...dominated.

His breath steamed down her neck as he whispered, "You want me to show you what I wanted to do to you during those three weeks of torture?"

Her nod was shamelessly frantic. "Yes, yes, show me. Do it all."

"I wanted to catch you, wherever I found you, and do this...." His hand cupped her breast, squeezing until she moaned and arched back, thrusting against his erection, making him growl and snap his teeth over her shoulder. "And this...." The other hand slid down over her abdomen to cup her mound, his fingers delving between her molten feminine lips, finding her entrance, slipping up her flowing readiness.

Her cry rang around the lodge.

His chuckle into her neck was unadulterated sensual devilry. His fingers twisted inside her, making her grind into him, desperate for assuagement. "I take only verbal requests. Graphic ones."

She'd give him graphic. "I want you buried all the way to my womb. I want you to ride me until you shatter me, until I wring your life essence from you."

He snatched his hand from her insides, the withdrawal as exquisite as the plunge. "I changed my mind. Be graphic later. Right now I might have a major coronary."

The sound of his zipper sliding down screeched through

her nerves. Moistness gushed from her eyes and core when his erection thudded against her back, hot and hard and heavy. Mohab. Here. With her. Her husband. For now.

He thrust against her, up and down, burning a furrow in her buttocks and back. "Here I am, everything you need. Take all of it inside you, take me whole, as I take you."

With what felt like the last heartbeat left in her, she turned, rose and sank on him. A cry of welcome rose from her center outward. His erection felt as big as a fist forging inside her. Filled beyond capacity, she writhed against him, pain and pleasure amalgamating into an indecipherable mass. She'd never get used to how he felt inside her, to the sensations his invasion wrung from her every nerve.

Delirious with the feeling of reclamation, she sobbed it all out to him. How he felt inside her, what he did to her, how he inundated her with exquisite pleasure. He only gave her more, thrusting up, harder, faster, forging new depths inside her, panting his own confessions.

The pressure built in her loins with each word, each abrading slide and thrust, spread from that elusive focus of madness he hit over and over. She rode him harder, each thrust layering sensation until she was buried, incoherent, insane for her release from the aching spiral of urgency.

Then it started, like shock waves heralding a detonation too far to be felt yet. Ripples spread from the outside in, pushing everything to her center, compacting it into a pinpoint of desperation. He plunged into her, taking her into one more perfect fusion…and it came. The spike of shearing pleasure, followed by slam after slam of satisfaction.

He pitched her forward, crammed a pillow beneath her stomach, angling her hips upward, then pounded into her wracking convulsions, pouring over her gushing pleasure with the long, hard bursts of his own release.

The next moments or hours, as pleasure raged, they

strained against each other, shuddering all over, driving him deeper inside her than he'd ever been, until she felt they'd dissolved into each other.

Then the intensity broke, eased and everything receded, left her replete, complete, spiraling into oblivion....

IT WAS MORNING when she came to. He had knocked her out for hours this time. And he was again propped beside her, watching her with a smile of supreme gratification.

She stretched luxuriously against him, rubbing her legs against his, delighting in finding him fully aroused. "Sorry I zonked out on you. Not what I planned at all."

"That was the best wedding night gift you could have given me. Lovemaking so explosive it pleasures us both into oblivion. *Aih,* I was knocked out right after you were."

Her lips spread, bliss humming in her bones. "You mean *I* knocked you out."

His indulgence deepened until she drowned in it. "That you surely did. I just woke up. I've never slept that well in...probably ever."

Her hands roamed his face, his head, shoulders, arms and back, reveling in every inch of him. "Anytime. And I want you to take that literally. I want you *any*time, all the time."

"Habibati." His growl went down her throat as he took her lips, pressed her under him and came fully over her.

And he took her up on her offer, plunging into her without preliminaries, knowing she'd be molten with need for him, would love his urgency, his ferocity. She more than loved it, she was mad for it, the fullness and the power and the domination of him. Just a few unbridled thrusts hurled her into ecstasy all over again. And he joined her in the abyss of pleasure, roaring his completion, jetting his seed inside her until he filled her.

He spoke as soon as she opened her eyes. "All these years, all I wanted was to have you again, have what we had, what kept me starving for you. Now I have you again, and it's not the same." Her heart thudded. Did he mean…? "It's way better. When I never thought there could be better."

Her heart filled with so much she couldn't reveal. But she could tell him at least one thing. "It *is* way better."

She didn't go on to say that she believed it would be that way only at first, with six years of frustration behind the initial explosiveness, before everything leveled then tapered off.

Needing to take them away from such disturbing discussions, she asked one thing that had been worrying her since she'd arrived here. "Why didn't you bring the kitties?"

His laugh revved beneath her ear. "Not even I would bring cats to my wedding night." He laughed again. "Though I might have considered it if the place had another room. They're good about staying in another room if I want to be alone…or with you, like that first night back in Judar. But they're in their favorite new place back in the citadel with all those places to explore."

Another worry struck her. "What if someone leaves a door to their quarters open? Or a window? Or if one zooms out when someone goes in to feed them or…"

Mohab swept her in a soothing caress from shoulder to buttock. "I've left as many paranoid instructions about keeping them safe as your heart can desire."

Still not satisfied, she said, "Can we check on them?"

"We certainly can. Mizar would even come to the phone. *Then* I will devour you again, and this time longer and harder, just for being so protective of my kitties."

She gasped as he turned her onto her back and reached

over her for his pants on the ground. "Aren't they mine, too, now?"

"Oh, yes, they are. They are part of me, and I've already given you carte blanche to me and mine."

And as he called his people to fulfill her wish, she threaded her aching fingers through his silky hair, and wondered.

Did he mean everything he said to her the way it sounded? Did he really feel this way about her? The way she felt about him? Did she even want him to feel that way?

No. She didn't. She wanted to have this with him, let them enjoy each other as much as they wanted, as much as they could and nothing else. For six long—and way too short—months.

CHAPTER TWELVE

"Can you believe six months have passed so fast?"

Jala felt the smile beginning to sink its claws into her flesh as she handed Sette to Ala'a, Kamal and Aliyah's five-year-old son. It gave her something to do so she wouldn't answer Aliyah's exclamation.

For what could she say? That there was nothing else she'd thought about every minute of these six months. That the days were passing so *horribly* fast? And now that the six months were up, she felt as if her very life was, too?

Aliyah threw herself beside Jala on the couch, grinning at her son's retreating back as he rushed to his sister in the other room with the last piece in his treasure, the tolerant Sette, having now collected all four cats.

"I thought once I got the kids four cats, too, they'd stop demanding to visit you to see yours every week, but no… your foursome are their first loves."

"One more thing to thank the cats for, then, making me see you all much more frequently than I would have without them."

Aliyah laughed. "We all thought we loved cats, but you and Mohab put us to shame. Last time I saw Mohab he said you'll adopt dozens more as soon as you settle your schedules and make the citadel your base, because cats hate traveling."

Every word fell on her like a blow so that she almost
gasped in relief when Aliyah's phone rang.

Thankful for the respite, she contemplated her sister-in-
law. Aliyah was her very antithesis, glowing with health
and happiness, her world built on the unshakable founda-
tion of Kamal's love and of her certain future with him.
While she… She'd been counting down the days she had
left with Mohab and was withering inside. She'd taken to
putting on makeup to prevent outward signs from showing.

Watching Aliyah melt with love as she talked to Kamal,
she couldn't be happier for them, but at the same time, it
made her own despondence deepen until it suffocated her.

With a last intimate whisper, Aliyah ended the call.
"Kamal sends hugs and kisses. But insisted I tell you that
your husband conned him."

Alarm burst inside her chest.

Aliyah went on. "He says Mohab said he doesn't know
the first thing about dealing with the executive realities
of running a kingdom, especially one that is growing and
changing as much and as fast as Jareer. He now believes
Mohab's protestations were just total pretense so he'd get
him involved—not because he needs his help, but to get
on his good side, so he'd help him have you, and now con-
tinues to rely on his input for your sake, too."

"I don't believe this is true…."

Aliyah waved her hand, her smile widening. "Kamal
said you'd think that, but he knows a man who'd do anything for his woman when he sees one. And take it from
me, that 'twin' of yours has…extensive experience and
insight in that arena."

Any other woman would have considered this everything worth living for. Knowing the man she loved with
all her being felt the same. But having someone corroborate the depth of Mohab's involvement, which she'd been

becoming more certain of with each passing minute, only sank her deeper into despair.

"Kamal would have respected the hell out of Mohab for achieving what no one believed could be done around here, let alone in this time frame. But the fact that he has you at the top of his priorities makes Kamal feel progressively more smug that he pegged Mohab right from the first meeting, when he came proposing peace between our kingdoms…and offering it all as your *mahr*."

Time did keep proving that she and Kamal were identical. For it had substantiated that she'd pegged Mohab right, too, from that first second she'd laid eyes on him. That he was everything she would ever want in a man, everything she could—and did—love, respect and admire. And that everything that happened to make her believe otherwise had been just tragic mistakes and misunderstandings.

Contrary to what she'd tried to convince herself of in the years of alienation, that Mohab was unfeeling by necessity, he actually turned off his feelings on demand only in his work. In his personal life, with her, she'd never known anyone who was more in touch with his emotions and so generous with demonstrating them. And it had been killing her to realize how she'd misjudged him, what she'd done to him. What she'd have to do still.

Time had also proved she was a superlative actress. Not even Mohab, Kamal and now Aliyah, the people who loved her most, suspected there was a thing wrong with her.

Demonstrating her obliviousness, Aliyah went on, "I think you're making one hell of a queen, too. It's like you're made to rule this specific place beside your man, your every skill and quality just what it needs. I'm so impressed by the originality of your social and educational projects and the effects they're already having. I need you to teach me how to translate that to Judar."

And she could take no more. "Please, Aliyah, stop."

The pain in her voice had her sister-in-law sitting up in alarm. "What's wrong, Jala?"

Everything, she wanted to scream.

Up until Aliyah's visit today, she'd been escaping making a decision, thinking she could go on for a while more, maybe another month, maybe another six.

But after what Aliyah had told her earlier, so offhandedly, believing it would be nothing to concern her, she'd been feeling her world had already ended.

She swallowed past the burning coal that used to be her larynx. "I want to tell you something, Aliyah. And I need you to make Kamal understand that it is in no way Mohab's fault...."

"HOW ARE MY darlings today?"

Mohab walked into their bedroom, taking off the band that held his hair in that severe ponytail, his smile flooding the soothingly lit chamber.

By the time he reached the bed where Jala was sitting with the four cats arranged all around her, he'd stripped off his jacket and shirt. Then he threw himself down beside her, grinning, spreading himself for his cats to climb all over him, stroking and kissing them. After a purring storm interlude, he turned his focus to her.

Before she succumbed and attacked him in her desperation for his feel and passion, he preempted her, dragged her down to him, surging up to take her lips as she tumbled across him.

Knowing, now that the kissing had started, neither Mohab nor Jala would want them around, the cats jumped off the bed and prowled out to the quarters' farthest sitting room.

"Habibati, wahashteeni..." Mohab groaned into her lips as he swept her around and bore down on her.

I missed you, too, my love almost burst onto her lips. But as she'd done for the past six months, she swallowed back the endearments and the confessions until they'd scarred her forever with the intensity of their need for release, with the necessity of withholding them.

Mohab had them both naked in seconds, and she groped for him, opened herself for his possession as he cupped her buttocks and thrust inside her. This fever was a continuation of last night's conflagration, no need for buildup, just an instantaneous and ferocious plunge into delirium. He was soon pounding inside her, his force and momentum building along with her cries of abandon until it all exploded into a blaze of intensity. She remained conscious this time as he collapsed on top of her, his weight completing the magic and delivering the final injury.

When she couldn't take it anymore, she fidgeted beneath him. He rose off her, separating their bodies. For the last time. As she had to make it.

She took the plunge. "The six months are up tomorrow."

A slow smile spread on his heartbreakingly beautiful face. "So they are. How about extending for another six months?" He plucked her lips. "Then another?" Another pull, harder, deeper. "And so on and on?" His teeth sank into her trembling flesh, sending shards of pleasure and heartache splintering through her. Then he pulled back, grinning. "These constant extensions might be a great idea to renew the novelty and keep the fire raging...*if* we needed help in those departments. Which we don't. None what...so...ever."

"That won't be necessary."

"So you're going for the permanent version straight away. I approve."

"I am actually reinforcing the terms of our marriage. I agreed to six months, then it's over. As it is."

He stilled, the smile faltering on his lips, draining from his eyes. "What do you mean?"

And she smashed her own heart. "I mean I want a divorce."

THE SENSE OF suffocating déjà vu closed in on Mohab.

This couldn't be happening again. Not this time. This time he was certain of what she felt for him. Of what they had.

Numb, he sat up. "Joke about anything but that, Jala." When she made no response as she, too, sat up, he tried to find a sign of mischief in her eyes. There was none. "You can't be serious!"

"I am. *Ermi alai yameen al talaag.*"

The oath of divorce. She was asking him to "throw" it at her, ending their marriage.

Ya Ullah...she wasn't joking.

A bewildered groan escaped him. "Why? Why are you doing this? Again?"

"I'm only doing what we agreed on."

"But you can't want the same thing you did six months ago. Just last night, just *now*.... *Ya Ullah*...you've never been more incendiary in my arms."

"You know I could never resist my desire for you. But I have to now. It has to end."

"It wasn't only desire. You *love* me."

"I never said I did."

He opened his mouth to roar a contradiction, then it hit him. Skewered him right through the heart. She'd *never* said it. He'd only assumed she did. From her actions and desire.

He couldn't accept it. Wouldn't. "Even if you don't feel

for me what I feel for you, if you want me that much, why leave me?" She only averted her eyes, and the expanding shock shredded his insides. "And if you'd already decided to leave me all along, what was last night and just now all about? Were you giving me one last ride before you walked away?"

She rose from the bed, so slowly, as if she was afraid she'd come apart if she moved any faster. "Let's not make this any worse than it has to be, Mohab."

Again. Just as she'd said almost seven years ago when she was leaving him the first time.

Paralyzed, he watched her reach for the dress he'd yanked off her half an hour ago. When she'd been his. She put it on now, no longer his, had said she'd never really been.

Then she was walking away.

At the door she turned. "I'll go to Judar until you conclude the procedures. Please, don't make any further personal contact. Goodbye, Mohab."

"Did you put her up to this?

Najeeb rose as Mohab burst into his office, placed both palms flat on his desk, his pose confrontational. "I assume you're talking about Jala."

"It won't take much to snap the last tethers of my sanity, Najeeb. Then I won't be responsible for what I do."

"King of Jareer or not, you're on my turf. Even if you weren't, you don't threaten me and walk away in one piece."

"I'm not threatening you, I'm promising you. If you're the reason why Jala left me…"

Najeeb straightened, a vicious smile of satisfaction spreading on his face. "So she finally did. Good for her. She should have never been with you in the first place."

"I swear, Najeeb…" Mohab's apoplectic surge drained. "You mean you had no idea she did, or *would*?"

"Do you have such a low opinion of the woman you married, you think someone can put her up to anything, let alone something like this?"

"*No.* But…" Anger deserted him, leaving him enervated with desperation and confusion, and he sank onto the nearest armchair and dropped his head in his hands, darkness closing in on him. "I don't know. I can't think anymore. I can't find a reason why she left me and I was groping for anything, even if it was insane or impossible. I just want to understand, so I can do something about it." He raised his eyes to Najeeb, who came to stand over him, his gaze pitiless. "I have to stop her, Najeeb. I can't live without her."

"*Ya Ullah,* if I didn't know better, I would have believed you without question, would have run out right now and tried everything I could to bring her back to you. But I *know,* Mohab. So stop your act right now. Now that Jala will no longer be your wife, it releases me from my promise to her."

"What promise?"

"Not to be your enemy. But now I will be, Mohab. I knew you were manipulating her when you announced your engagement out of the blue, but I couldn't object since I realized she was making a decision knowing full well that you were. Then it seemed as if your marriage was real, and happy, and I no longer knew what to think." He narrowed his eyes to dangerous slits. "But if she left you, then you must have dealt her another unspeakable injury. And for that alone, Mohab, no matter what it takes, I will destroy you."

"*B'Ellahi*…what are you talking about?"

"About how you set her up in the past. She made me

promise never to confront you, wanted the ugly page turned
and forgotten. I honored her request till this moment."

Mohab shook his head. "I know you found out and told
her, and that was one of the reasons she left me then. She
told me everything the very first night I saw her again. It's
why I thought it might have been something you said to her
that made her end it this time, too." He exhaled roughly.
"This...and the dread that never went away—that I did
come between you in the past, that your feelings for each
other went beyond friendship...."

Najeeb wrenched his shoulder, his face contemptuous.
"You think Jala could have had emotions for me and still
came to your bed? Betraying us both?"

"I said it was a dread, not a suspicion. She's the most
upstanding person I know, the most forthright."

"She is. I share a bond with her that was forged in the
fire of our lives' worst experience and later nurtured by
our kindred natures. There was never the least romantic
involvement on either of our sides, as I told my foolish father. You should have both believed in *my* forthrightness
and that if my emotions for her had been of that nature, I
would never have denied them."

"That's why I'm going insane. Because I believe in *her*.
And everything she did, said...indicated she'd forgiven
me, proved she loved me now, even if she never truly did
in the past."

"She did love you in the past. So completely your deception destroyed her."

He shook his head. "She told me what she felt for me
wasn't strong enough to counterbalance her aversion to
commitment and her fear that I was a threat to her independence. Her discovery of my deception was just the
last straw."

"Then she told you a lie, so you wouldn't know the

depth of her past involvement and what your betrayal cost her."

Mohab gaped at Najeeb, a vice squeezing around his heart. If this was true, then he *had* hurt her more than he'd ever realized. Which made her being with him again at all a miracle. Was that her revenge? To make him fall as fully in love with her as she'd fallen for him once, then give him a taste of his own poison?

But…no. She *wouldn't* do that.

Najeeb went on, ending his confusion…and delivering a crippling blow. "When I told her the truth, she pretended that you hadn't succeeded in seducing her, that I saved her in time to salvage her dignity. But then I discovered the depth of your exploitation of her when I stumbled on her in a relief mission in Colombia…and found her pregnant."

By the time he arrived in Judar, Mohab felt he'd lost whatever remained of his sanity. On receiving him, Kamal had said he didn't care how this had happened, only that Mohab resolve it or have him as an enemy for life.

Mohab had told him to stand in line.

Now he entered Jala's quarters and found her standing at the French windows. She spoke as soon as he closed the door.

"I told you not to do this, Mohab, not to force another confrontation on me. I have nothing more to say to you."

And all his shock and anguish bled out of him. "I almost went insane all those months I couldn't find you after you left me. Now I know I couldn't because you did everything to disappear. So I wouldn't find out you were pregnant."

"You went to Najeeb." A ragged breath left her. "But you're wrong. I disappeared so I wouldn't cause my family a scandal. I didn't think you would bother with me again."

Every word made him realize he had dealt her an indelible injury.

But right now, there was one injury in particular that he needed to heal. "I want you to tell me what happened to our baby."

"What do you think happened? That I gave him away?"

Him. It had been a boy. The knife hacking his vitals twisted. "I think you lost him. I want you to tell me how."

"It was a landslide while driving up a mountain in Colombia. The jeep rolled over into the valley. One passenger died…and I lost the baby. I was seven months pregnant."

Her telegraphic account, condensing her horrific experience, felt like bullets. "And you hated me that much, you didn't think to tell me you were carrying my baby? Distrusted me so totally, you didn't even think it a possibility I'd want to be there for you after your ordeal?"

Another ragged exhalation. "I believed I didn't matter to you either way, so I assumed you wouldn't have cared if I carried your baby. And that you would have probably been relieved I lost it."

He squeezed his eyes. He'd hurt her even worse than his worst projections. "Is this why you're leaving me? Because you still don't believe I care?"

"I left because we had a deal."

And he stormed toward her, his every nerve firing as he grasped her shoulders, felt her again. "To hell with that deal. I never really meant it when I first proposed it, and I faced the truth of what I always wanted right before our engagement. *Ahwaaki, ya hayati, aashagek wa abghaki bekolli jawarehi.* I love you, and I worship and crave you with every spark of my being. You're not in my heart, you *are* my heart. And I can't live without my heart."

She wrenched herself free from his grasp, her features suddenly contorting out of control, her voice strangled with tears. "That's what you say now, what you think you mean. But you're not only a man, not only a prince, you're a king now. You will need an heir. An heir I *can't* give you."

He gaped at her, a cascade of mutilating suspicions crashing in his mind. Her next words ended them, solidifying them into terrible reality.

"My miscarriage was so traumatic, at such an advanced stage, the doctors told me I'd never have children again."

This was it. The dark secret that explained it all. All the pain he'd felt from her and could never account for.

When he'd learned she'd been pregnant, he'd thought losing their baby explained it. But it wasn't only the loss, the injury, but the permanent scar. She'd lost their baby, and any hope of having another.

He stared at her as her tears began to flow, as her shoulders began to shake, at a total loss.

What could he do to mitigate her anguish?

He heard his voice, choking on his own agony. "I don't *want* an heir, *ya hayati*. I didn't inherit my title, I was chosen for it based on merit, and when the time comes for me to step down, I will pass the throne to whomever deserves it."

A shaking hand wiped at her tears. "You do need an heir. Aliyah told me King Hassan is withholding signing any treaties until he knows the reason he blessed our marriage, the blood-mixing heir, is a reality. She wasn't worried, but only because she thinks we're postponing having children voluntarily."

And then he exploded. "To hell with my uncle and Saraya and the peace treaty. To hell with Judar and Jareer and everyone in them. I only care about you."

"You can't say that. Now that you're king, you owe it to your subjects to keep the peace in their kingdom. I'll be what stands in the way of your achieving it."

"I *will* keep the peace, and it won't be by bowing to any backward tribal demands. I only pretended to so it would give me a chance to approach you again."

She shook her head as she escaped his grasp, tears falling faster. "Even if you do, you *will* want a family...."

"We *already* have a family—me and you and our furry babies, and we'll have as many more as you want. And if you long for the human kind of kid, we'll try. The doctors' verdict doesn't have to be final...."

"It is. I didn't use protection, hoping they were wrong. They weren't. There is no hope."

"Maybe there will be with minimum intervention. If there isn't, or you don't want even that, I don't care."

"I can't, Mohab... I can't let you give up your right to have a child. I can't let you give *anything* up."

"But *I* want to give up *everything* for you, *ya habibat hayati.*" She shook so hard, her tears splashed over his hands, burning him through to his marrow. He clamped her shaking head in trembling hands, tilted her face up toward his. He had to convince her, stop her from leaving him, destroying them both. "You carried my baby inside you, nourished and nurtured him in your body and with your essence. You wanted him and loved him, even when you thought I never wanted or loved you. And I wasn't there for you...."

A hiccup tore out of her. "I was the one who pushed you away, who made it impossible for you to find me. You looked for me, even thinking I never really loved you...."

"I should have looked more efficiently, not let my anxiety mess up my methods. You can't imagine how much it hacks at me to know you were pregnant, without me, and then had to go through the pain and desolation and loss... *Ya Ullah, ya rohi*...if I can't give you all my life in recompense, I would end it in penance."

"Don't say this…. *Ya Ullah*…don't…feel this way."

"I do feel this way. And as far as I am concerned, you *have* given me a son, and *we* lost him. And now I grieve with you as I should have at the time, and we cling to each other even more, and forever."

"No." Her shriek of agony pierced him as she stumbled around and staggered away.

He hurtled after her, caught her back and crushed her to him, out of his mind now with dread, begging her over and over. *"La tseebeeni tani, la tseebeeni tani abaddan."*

DON'T LEAVE ME again, don't leave me ever again.

Mohab's litany sheared through her, and his tears—his *tears*—rained over her face, mingling with hers, singeing her soul. She never thought she'd ever see them. And now that she did, felt their agony rain down her flesh, she couldn't bear them, would do anything to never see them again.

But she had to do this for him. He would come to regret his emotional outburst when his head cleared and his passion cooled. He'd sooner or later long for a child of his flesh and blood. And she'd be what deprived him of fulfilling this need. He'd come to resent her for it. It was better for her to die, to leave him now than to live with him till this came to pass.

She pushed out of his arms, shaking apart, tears a stream draining her life force. "I never suspected you loved me as much as I love you, Mohab. That was why I agreed to marry you. I wanted to have some more time with you, give you the closure you said you needed, then disappear from your life again. If I suspected you felt the same, I wouldn't have done this to you." A sob tore out of her depths. "Please, believe me, I never thought I'd hurt you. But once I realized you had become emotionally involved, I knew it was better to hurt you temporarily than hurt you for the rest of your life. When I'm gone, in time, you will forget me."

He groaned as if she'd just stabbed him. "If I never forgot you when I thought you didn't love me, when you weren't my wife, you think I'd ever forget you now?"

"You *have* to."

"Would *you* have left me? If you discovered I couldn't give you a child? Especially if you knew I couldn't on account of an injury you caused me?"

"You had nothing to do with my accident. I won't have you feeling guilty over this."

"I *am* guilty. Of injuring your belief in me and in your own self-worth. Anything that happened from that moment forward is my responsibility, my guilt."

She wiped furiously at her streaming eyes. "I once held you responsible, too, but I was wrong. If there was guilt, then I share it in full. I didn't give you a chance to defend yourself, intended to deprive you of your child. I deserve what happened to me…."

"*B'Ellahi*…you were a victim in all this, *my* victim."

At his desperate shout, her sobs ratcheted until they drove her down to the ground.

Jala gazed up at him as he stood over her, looking as if his heart had spilled on the ground, and she wailed, "If you love me, Mohab, let me set you free. I'm not leaving you. This time I'm begging you to let me go."

He let Jala go.

But only to set the plan to get her back in motion. Now that he knew she loved him, too, he was never letting her go.

He had called a summit of all the people who were players in this mess. His uncle, Najeeb and her family. They were all convened in Kamal's stateroom. Jala was there, too. This had been the last favor Kamal had said he'd ever do for him.

He walked in, swept them all in a careless gaze, before he focused on Jala. She looked pinched and drained, her beloved eyes extinguished. It nearly drove him to his knees, how much she suffered, how injured and scarred she was. He wanted to lay down his life so she'd be whole again, so she'd stop feeling any deficiency. But since he couldn't undo the damage, he could only move heaven and earth, dedicate his very life to making it up to her.

He started talking at once. He told them the truth about the past, what he'd done, what he'd cost Jala.

Feeling her brothers' rage boiling over, he went on, "I want you to know that I will accept, even encourage, any punishment you exact from me. But that isn't why I called you here. I did so to inform you that no matter what you do, no matter what happens, I'll part from Jala only when I die."

His uncle heaved up to his feet. "But you have to. I only agreed to the treaty, *and* the marriage…"

"Shut *up,* uncle." His roar made King Hassan sag back to his chair. "*You* didn't agree to anything, I was just humoring you, trying to save your face and avoid your folly. But if you make any more trouble, or if you don't sign the treaty, I will be the one to declare war on you."

"You don't even have an army," his uncle spluttered.

"I'll make one. Or I'll borrow one if it's faster. Jareer is far more important to so many powers today than Saraya, and they would do anything for me if I ask. I bet they'd help me depose you just to be rid of your nuisance. So *enough,* uncle. You've already cost us what your very life doesn't begin to make up for. Take my clemency and never let us hear from you again except as a voice corroborating peace."

His uncle looked shocked to his core. Najeeb, while looking at his father pityingly, seemed to wholly approve.

And he couldn't care less about either of them right now.

He turned to Jala's family. "My happiness, honor and all my hopes lie in whatever will make Jala happy, will honor her and fulfill her hopes. If she wants to try to have children, this is what we'll do. If she wants to adopt..."

"You can't adopt!" That was his uncle again. "It's prohibited by law in our region!"

"Uncle, you are now tampering with the gauge of your life. I won't warn you again. We will adopt as many children as she wishes, if she wishes it. I will give up my throne and two nationalities, and acquire one that will allow me to fulfill her every need." He walked up to Jala, knelt before her. Her whole frame was shaking, her tears like acid in his veins.

"Jala, you *are* my life. I want nothing but you, need nothing but your love. I would only have wanted a child as one more bond with you. I lost our baby, too, but my pain is over your loss. And the only loss that would finish me is if I lose you. Nothing is of any importance to me—not my throne, not my homelands, not my very life—if I don't have you."

Kamal suddenly heaved up to his feet. "This is not for our eyes or ears. Everybody, *out*."

Kamal's barked order had everyone rushing out, everyone except his bewildered uncle giving Mohab bolstering, approving glances. Kamal was the only one who stopped as he passed him, bent to squeeze his shoulder.

Then, dropping a kiss on Jala's shuddering cheek, he whispered to her, "I know when a man would die without his woman, *ya sugheerati*. You got yourself a prime

specimen of that rare species. As only you deserve. So just
take him back and keep him for life, if you don't want to
kill him." He straightened, winked. "If you *do* want to kill
him, then by all means, walk away."

EVERYTHING THAT HAD happened in the past years, everything Jala had suffered, everything she'd shared with
Mohab in the past months, everything he'd just said and
offered, built inside her until she felt herself overload-
ing. Then Kamal winked teasingly at her, and everything
snapped inside her.

And she howled. With laughter.

Mohab's jaw dropped. Kamal only bowed, as if he was
taking applause for a job perfectly done, then with another
wink, he walked out, too.

Recovering from the shock of her sudden transforma-
tion into a hyena, Mohab's smile broke out as he surged
up, enveloping her in his arms.

"Ah, *ya habibati*...how I missed your laughter, feared
I'd never hear it again."

A snort interrupted her howls. "You're that desperate
for me...you call *this*...laughter?"

This drew a chuckle from him before her raucous glee
escalated it into laughter, then guffawing.

It was only when she sagged in his arms, still gur-
gling and sobbing at once, that he stopped, too, storming
kisses all over her face, murmuring extravagant endearments and professions of worship before stilling her gasping lips beneath his.

Breathing life and certainty into her once more, he
managed to quiet her down. Then, holding her face in his
palms, he withdrew, his heart in his still-beseeching eyes.

"I am that desperate and more. I'm also desperate in
case you will keep thinking you'd be doing me a favor

by walking away, that I can forget you 'in time.' When I wanted you for over ten years, had you only for just over ten months out of those, and couldn't forget you in between, that I never even thought of having anyone but you."

Everything stilled, inside and out. "You mean…?"

"I mean just as you never had anyone else but me, I never had anyone else but you. I'm yours, whether you take me…or leave me. So will you have mercy on both of us and take me, and this time never leave me?"

This was just too…enormous. He'd always been hers, just the way she'd always been his.

Everything inside her crumbling, she threw herself at him, hugged him with all her might, until her arms and heart ached. "I—I never wanted to leave you. I just want you to have everything you need and deserve."

He kissed one eye, then the other. "That's you, and you."

"Ah, *ya habibi*… I've loved you for so long."

He suddenly bombarded her with kisses. "And she says it at last."

Spluttering with laughter again, she gasped, "I made you wade in 'I love yous' in the past."

"Then forced a years-long drought on me in compensation."

"When I thought I would have to leave you, I didn't want to compound the mess with revealing my emotions. And then 'I love you' was no longer adequate to describe what I felt for you since I became your wife. *Ahwak wa abghak wa aashagak, ya roh galbi.*"

His eyes filled again as he heard her confess more than love and adoration and worship, *everything* anyone could feel with the whole of their hearts and minds and souls.

She surged to kiss his eyes, tasting his precious tears, which she swore she'd never cause again.

Withdrawing, she voiced her last lingering fear. "I'm just so scared...."

He wouldn't let her continue, enveloping her again. "That I don't know what I'm talking about? That I'd change my mind? If ten years don't prove to you that I was made to love you, that you are the one thing I need to be happy, I demand another test to prove that to you. The next fifty years."

And she surrendered. To his overwhelming love, to the unimaginable happiness of an inseparable life together... come what may. "If I have those, they're all yours. As I am. Always have been. Always will be."

* * * * *

Carrying A King's Child
Katherine Garbera

MILLS & BOON

Katherine Garbera is a *USA TODAY* bestselling author of more than fifty books and has always believed in happy endings. She lives in England with her husband, children and their pampered pet, Godiva. Visit Katherine on the web at katherinegarbera.com, or catch up with her on Facebook and Twitter.

Books by Katherine Garbera

HARLEQUIN DESIRE

Texas Cattleman's Club: The Showdown

The Rebel Tycoon Returns

Miami Nights

Taming the VIP Playboy
Seducing His Opposition
Reunited...With Child

Matchmakers, Inc.

Ready for Her Close-up
A Case of Kiss and Tell
Calling All the Shots

Baby Business

His Instant Heir
Bound by a Child
For Her Son's Sake

Dynasties: The Montoros

Carrying a King's Child

Visit the Author Profile page at millsandboon.com.au or katherinegarbera.com, for more titles.

Dear Reader,

There is nothing I love better than a sexy alpha hero, a feisty heroine and some juicy scandal. *Carrying a King's Child* has all of that plus a lot more! When Emily and Rafe meet, he is running away from a decision he knows has to be made. He needs a weekend to forget and just enjoy being young and carefree. They have that and more. So when Emily shows up on his doorstep six weeks later and tells him she's pregnant...well, it's more than either of them bargained for.

Emily doesn't need a man to raise her child. A single mother raised her and she's strong and independent. The only thing is, she never knew her father and that left questions inside of her that can never be answered. She doesn't want her child to have that same experience.

I was born not too far from where this story is set in Miami, Florida, and could swim before I could walk. I shared a little bit of myself with Emily and her past. I know what it's like to grow up with the sand between my toes and the sun always on my shoulders.

I had a great time writing their story and working with the other authors in this series. I hope you enjoy reading it!

Happy reading,

Katherine

DEDICATION

This book is for my Facebook posse who are always willing to chat about hot guys, good reads and the general craziness of life.

CHAPTER ONE

Emily Fielding was shaking as she stepped off the elevator into the foyer of Rafael Montoro IV's penthouse in South Beach. The Montoros had settled in Miami, Florida, decades ago, when as the royal family of Alma, they had to flee their European island homeland because of a coup. Now the dictator who'd replaced them was dead and the parliament of Alma wanted the Montoros back.

With Rafe as king.

Great. Happy ending for everyone. Well, everyone except for Emily, the bartender who was pregnant with the soon-to-be-king's baby. Or at least that was what her gut told her. Her gut and three home pregnancy tests. She wasn't easy to convince.

She had debated not telling Rafe about the baby, but having grown up without knowing who her father was, she just couldn't do that to her own child. Sure, she'd had to lie to get up here to his very posh penthouse apartment, and she knew her timing sucked because Rafe had a lot of royal duties to attend to before his coronation, but she was still here.

Getting past security hadn't been that easy, but she'd made a few calls to friends and found that one of them had a connection to Rafe via a maid service. So she'd used

Maria's pass to get into the gated community and her key to get into his building.

Sneaking around wasn't her style. Normally. But nothing about this situation was normal.

She was shaking as she stood on the Italian marble floor and let the air-conditioning dry the sweat at the small of her back. Luxurious and well appointed, the apartment was exactly the sort of place where she expected to find Rafe. His family might have fled Alma in the middle of the night, but they'd brought their dignity and their determination with them to the United States and this generation of Montoros had truly flourished.

Rafe was the CEO of Montoro Enterprises. He had been featured in *Forbes* long before the recent developments in Alma. He'd earned the wealth she saw around him, and the fact that he played as hard as he worked was something she could respect. She played hard, too.

She forced herself not to touch her stomach. Not to draw attention to the one thing that changed everything. Since she'd looked at that stick in the bathroom and realized she was going to have a baby, everything had changed.

Pretending that there was more to her visit than ensuring that her child would know who its father was would be stupid. A wealthy businessman she could have had a shot with, she thought. But not a king.

Still…

She'd seen photos of Alma. With its white sand beaches and castle that looked like something out of a dream, it was a beautiful place. The kind of place that she might have dreamed about as a little girl. A fairy-tale kingdom with a returning prince. Sounded perfect, right?

Except that Rafael Montoro IV was a playboy and they'd had a fling. She wrinkled her nose as she tried to come up with something else to call it, but a two-night stand didn't cover it, either. One weekend spent in each other's arms. She could lose herself in the memories if she wasn't careful.

Hell, she hadn't been careful. Which was precisely why she was here. Pregnant and determined. She walked down the hallway toward the sounds of Jay-Z playing in the distance. She paused in the doorway of his bedroom.

She'd had to charm her way upstairs, but no way could this wait another moment. Rafe needed to know before he left. She needed to tell him.

She felt queasy and swallowed hard.

There were right and wrong ways to deliver this news, and as appealing to her sense of outrage as it would be to throw up on his carpet, she was hoping for a little sophistication. Just a tiny bit.

After all, she'd seen pictures of his sister and jet-setting mother, though his mother wasn't really in the picture since her divorce from Rafe III. Still she was an elegant woman.

She cleared her throat.

She listened to Jay-Z and Kanye West singing about how there's no church in the wild. She almost laughed out loud as she watched Rafe stop packing his suitcase and start to rap along. She leaned against the doorjamb and admitted her anger was really fear. She wasn't mad at him. She just wanted him to be a different kind of guy so that she could have the fairy tale she wanted.

Not a castle and a title, but a man who loved her. A man who wanted to share his life with her and raise children by her side.

And no matter how fun Rafe was, his path lay somewhere else. He was duty-bound to become the constitutional monarch of Alma. She was determined to return to Key West and live out her life. She wasn't interested in being involved with a royal; besides, she'd read in the pa-

pers that the heirs would have to marry people with spot-
less reputations.

He was really getting into dancing around the room
and rapping.

She applauded when he finished and he turned to look
at her.

"What are you doing here?" he asked, shock apparent
on his face.

His body was tense. She suspected he was a tiny bit embarrassed to be caught rapping. Nerves made her mouthy.
She knew that. So she should just say she was sorry for
using her friend's key to get into his penthouse.

But that wasn't her way.

"Hello to you, too, Your Majesty. Should I curtsy or
something? I'm not sure of the rules."

"Neither am I," he admitted. "Juan Carlos doesn't like
it when I am seen doing something...well, so American
but also undignified."

"Your secret is safe with me," she said. "Who is Juan
Carlos?"

"Juan Carlos Salazar II, my cousin, head of the Montoro Family Trust and advocate of decorum at all times."

"He sounds like a stuffed shirt," she said. "I doubt I'd
meet with his approval."

"Emily, what are you doing here? And how did you get
up here? Security is usually very hard to get past."

"I have my ways."

"And they are?" he asked.

"My charm," she said.

He shook his head. "I'm going to have to warn them
about feisty redheads."

"I actually used a key that I procured from your maid
service."

"You've been reduced to criminal behavior. Curiouser

and curiouser. Why are you here? Did you decide that you wanted to give me a proper send-off?" he asked. He strode over to her, his big body moving with an economy of motion that captivated her. The same way it had when she'd first glimpsed him in the crowded Key West bar where she worked as a bartender.

He was tall—well over six feet—and muscly, but he moved with grace and she could honestly watch him all day long.

"Why are you here, Red? You said goodbye was forever."

Goodbye.

She'd meant it when he'd left. He was a rich guy from Miami and experience had shown her they were only in Key West for one thing. Having given it to him she'd wanted to ensure she didn't give into temptation a second time.

"I did mean it."

"Help me, Red. I don't want to jump to conclusions," he said.

She chewed her lower lip. Up close she could see the flecks of green in his hazel eyes.

He was easily one of the most attractive men she'd ever seen. He'd make a killing in Hollywood with those thick eyelashes and those cheekbones. It wouldn't matter if he could act, just putting him on screen would draw the masses in.

She wished she were immune.

"I'm pregnant."

He stumbled backward and looked at her as if she'd just started speaking in tongues.

PREGNANT!

He stepped back and walked over to the Bose speaker

on the dresser to turn off the music. A baby. From what he knew of the tough-as-nails-bartender, he could guess she wouldn't be standing in his penthouse apartment if he wasn't the father. His first reaction was joy.

A child.

It wasn't something he'd ever thought he wanted. He hardly knew Emily so had no idea if she was here for money or something else. But knowing his child was growing inside of her stirred something primal. Something very powerful. The baby was his.

Maybe that was just because it gave him something to think about other than the recent decision that had been made for him.

He'd been dreading his trip to Alma. He was flattered that the country that had once driven his family out had come back to them and asked him to be the next king, but he had grown up here in Florida. He didn't want to be a stuffy royal.

He didn't want European paparazzi following him around and trying to catch him doing anything that would bring shame to his family. God, knew he worked and played hard.

"Rafe?"

"Yeah?"

"Did you hear what I said?" Emily asked.

He had. A baby. Lord knew his father hadn't been the best and as a result, Rafe had thought he'd never have kids. It wasn't as if either of his parents had set a great example. And he was still young, but damn if he wasn't feeling much older every day.

"Yeah, I did. Are you sure?" he asked at last.

She gave him a fiery look from those aqua-blue eyes of hers. He'd seen the passionate side of her nature, and he guessed he was about to witness her temper. "Would I be here if I wasn't?"

He held his hand up.

"Slow down, Red. I didn't mean are you sure it's mine. I meant…are you sure you're pregnant?"

"Damned straight."

"I get it. I had to take three at-home pregnancy tests and visit the doctor before I believed it myself. But trust me, Rafe. I'm positive I'm pregnant and that the baby is yours."

"This is a little surreal," he said.

"I know," she said, with just a hint of softening on in her tone. "Listen, I know you can't turn your back on your family and marry me and frankly, we only had one weekend together so I'd have to say no. But… I don't want this kid to grow up without any knowledge of you."

"Me either."

She glanced up, surprised.

To be honest, he sort of surprised himself. But he knew all the things not to do as a dad thanks to his own father. It didn't seem right for a kid of his to grow up without him. He wanted that. If he had a child, he wanted a chance to share the Montoro legacy…not the one newly sprung on him that came with a throne, but the one he'd carved out for himself in business. "Don't look shocked."

"You've kind of got a lot going on right now. And having a kid with me isn't going to go over well."

"Tough," he said. He still wasn't sure he wanted to be king of Alma. He and his siblings hadn't grown up with the attitude that they were royalty. They were regular American kids who'd never expected to go back to Alma. "I still make my own decisions."

"I know that," she said. She tucked a strand of hair behind her ear. "I've just been so crazy since I realized I was pregnant and alone. I didn't know what to do. You know my mom raised me by herself…"

He closed the gap between them again and pulled her into his arms. He hadn't realized she'd been raised by a single parent. To be honest, a weekend of hot sex didn't really lend itself to sharing each other's past like that. "You're not by yourself."

She looked up at him. That little pointed nose of hers was the tiniest bit red and her lip quivered as if she were struggling to keep from crying. That's when he realized how out of character it was for Emily to be unsure. The baby—his baby—had thrown her for a loop as well.

"Thanks. I just need… I have no idea. I mean, a kid. I never expected this. But we used protection."

"I didn't the third time, remember? I was out and we…"

She blushed and rested her forehead against the middle of his chest, wrapped her arms around his waist and held him. He'd thought he hated being trapped, but in Emily's arms this didn't feel constricting.

"Ugh. My mom was right."

"About what?" he asked. He looked over her head at the man in the mirror and remembered how many times he'd wanted to see some substance reflected back. Was this it? Of course it was. The baby would change things. He had no idea how or why, but he knew this moment was going to be the one that helped forge his future and the man he'd become.

"She said all it takes is a sweet-talking man and one time to get pregnant."

"I'm a sweet-talking man?" He tipped her head up with his finger under her chin.

"You can be."

"What are we going to do?" he asked at last. It was clear she'd run out of steam as soon as she entered the room.

Marriage was the noble thing to do. He knew that's what Juan Carlos would suggest, but he and Emily were strangers, and tying their lives together didn't seem smart until they knew each other better.

She pushed away from him and walked over to the window. He knew the view she was afforded. This place had been hard-earned. He'd worked just as his siblings had to make Montoro Enterprises into the success it was today.

"I just wanted you to know. Beyond that I don't need anything. Someday the kid is going to ask about you—"

"Someday? I'm going to be a part of this," Rafe said.

"I don't see how. You're going to be jetting off to Alma to take the throne. My life is here. The baby's life will be here."

He rubbed the back of his neck. The timing on this sucked. But he didn't blame Emily. He'd been running when he went to Key West, afraid to admit that he was in over his head. He'd just gotten word that his family was definitely interested in returning to Alma and as the oldest son he was expected to take the throne.

He was the oldest son. He was Rafael the Fourth. He should have been in command all the time. But the truth was, he was lost.

He wanted his own life. Not one that was dictated by rules and the demands of running a country. If he'd made the decision to return to Alma on his own he might feel differently but right now he felt strong-armed into it.

But somehow in Emily's arms he'd found something.

EMILY DIDN'T REALLY feel any better about her next steps, but now that she'd told Rafe her news she could at least start making plans. She didn't know what she expected… Well, the fairy-tale answer was that he'd profess his undying love—hey, their weekend together was pretty spectacular—then sweep her off her feet to his jet, and they'd go to Paris to celebrate their engagement.

But back in the real world, she was staring at him and wondering if this was the last time she'd be alone with him. It didn't matter what the fantasy was or that she knew how he looked naked. They were still strangers.

Intimate strangers.

"You are looking at me in an odd way," he said.

She struggled with her blunt nature. Saying that she knew what he looked like naked but not how he'd react to their child would reveal too much insecurity. So she searched for something light. Keeping things light was the key to this.

"Well, I never heard you rap along with Jay-Z and Kanye before. Sort of changed my opinion of you."

"I'm a man of many talents," he said.

"I'd already guessed that."

"Did you?"

"Yes."

He walked over to her, all sex on a stick with that slow confident stride of his. His hazel eyes were intense, but then everything about him was. Last time they were together, she'd sensed his need to just forget who he was, but this time was different. This time he seemed to want to show her more of the man he was.

The real man.

"What else have you guessed?" he asked in a silky tone that sent shivers down her spine.

He had a great voice. She knew he had flaws, but as far as the physical, she couldn't find any. Even that tiny scar on the back of his hand didn't detract from his appeal. "That you are used to getting your own way."

"Aw, that's so easy it's almost like cheating."

"Have you figured out that I'm used to getting my own

way, too?" she asked. Suddenly she didn't feel as if things were just happening to her. She was in control. Of Rafe, the baby and this entire afternoon. The pregnancy had thrown her. Brought up junk from her childhood she'd thought she'd moved on from, but now she was getting her groove back.

"Oh, I knew that from the moment I entered Shady Harry's and saw you standing behind the bar."

"Did you?" she asked. "I thought it was my Shady Harry's T-shirt that caught your attention."

The spicy scent of his aftershave brought an onslaught of memories of him moving over her. She'd buried her face in his neck. Damn, he'd smelled good. Then and now.

"Well, that and your legs. Red, you've got killer legs."

She looked down at them. Seemed kind of average to her. But she wasn't about to argue with a compliment like that.

"I like your ass," she admitted.

He winked at her, and then turned so that she could see it. He wore a slim-fitting suit that looked tailor-made. Given who he was, it probably was.

He was going to be king.

She had no business flirting with him. Or even staying here a moment longer.

"Sorry."

"What?" he asked. "Why? What happened?"

She shrugged. No way was she admitting she was intimidated by his title. But that was the truth. She wasn't in control of that. No matter how much she wanted to be.

"This suit doesn't do anything for me, does it? I asked Gabe if these pants made me look fat but he said no."

She had seen pictures of his entire family in the newspaper and knew that the Gabe he referred to was Gabriel Montoro, his younger brother.

She laughed, as she knew he wanted her to. But inside something had changed. She no longer owned this afternoon. "I should go."

"Why? What happened just now?"

"I remembered that you aren't just a rich guy from Miami who came to Key West for the weekend. That your life isn't your own and I really don't have a place in it."

His expression tightened and he turned away from her. She studied him as he paced over to his bed and looked down at the expensive leather suitcase lying there. She'd interrupted his packing. He probably didn't really have time for her this afternoon.

"You said you never knew your father." With an almost aristocratic expression, he glanced over his shoulder at her. She had the feeling she was seeing the man who would be king. And she had to admit he made her a little bit nervous. Maybe it was simply the fact that she knew he was going to be a king now. But it seemed as if he was different. More regal in his bearing than he had been during their weekend together.

"Yes. I don't see what that has to do with anything."

"I did know my father and my grandfather and great-grandfather. From my birth I was named to follow in their footsteps. I've never deviated from that expectation, and to be honest, I took a certain pride in carrying on our family name and trying to set an example for my brother and sister."

"I'm getting a poor little rich boy feeling here. You have been given a lot of opportunities in your lifetime and now you have the chance to lead a nation," she said, but inside she sort of understood what he was getting at. His entire life had been scripted since birth. She understood from what she'd read in the newspapers that the Montoros may have left Alma in the middle of the night, but they hadn't left their pride behind.

"All my life I've done what is expected of me. I haven't shirked a single duty. I'm the CEO of Montoro Enterprises and now I will be king of Alma, but for this one afternoon, Red, can I be Rafe? Not a man with his future planned but your lover? Father of your baby?" he asked.

He came back over and dropped to his knees in front of her, wrapping his arms around her hips. Then he drew her closer to him and kissed her belly. "I want you to be able to speak to our baby about me with joy instead of regret."

She looked down at him as he rested his head against her body. Tunneling her fingers into his thick black hair, she understood that from this point on, when she left this penthouse they couldn't be this couple again.

She sighed, and the woman she'd always been, the one who lived by the motto Never Say Never, took over. Rafe and she might not have more than this time together. And she wanted this one last time with him.

She hadn't expected to be a mom this soon. She had made all these plans for her life and then when she'd taken those pregnancy tests it had all gone out the window.

But for this moment she could forget about tomorrow. She hoped this would be enough, but feared one more afternoon in his arms would never be enough to satisfy her.

CHAPTER TWO

Rafe pushed aside all of his thoughts and just focused on Emily. It was amazing that she'd come to find him. She was strong enough, independent enough to keep the baby from him if she'd wanted. It embarrassed him a little, humbled him, too, that he would never have known about the baby if she hadn't shown up.

He'd been focusing on the royal legacy and managing everyone's expectations. Especially people he didn't even know and hadn't cared existed until last month. Funny how he'd gone from worrying about financial targets and managing a multinational company to worrying about a little thing like protocol.

But as long as Emily was here he could forget all that. Concentrate on being the man and not the king.

He held her tightly as he stood up, lifting her off her feet and letting her slide back down his body. She was curvy and light, his woman, and he wanted to be just her man. He carried her to the big brass bed and stood next to it, just waiting for a signal from her.

She owed him nothing.

She sighed and then lowered her head and brushed her lips over his, and something tight and frozen inside him started to melt. She kissed him not like the bold bartender she was when they'd met, but like a woman who wanted to relish her time with her lover.

They both knew without saying it that this was the last time they'd be together like this. Maybe if they'd met two years from now after he'd been on the throne and had time to figure out what being king meant, their path would have been different. But they hadn't.

They had this afternoon and nothing more.

He wanted these memories of the two of them to keep for himself as he moved into a life that was no longer his own.

He pushed his hands into her thick red hair, cradling her head as he took control of the kiss. He thrust his tongue deep into her mouth, tasted peppermint and woman. Her arms slipped lower and she stroked her hand down his back as he deepened the kiss.

Though he knew this long, wet kiss was just the beginning, he wanted to savor it. Dueling desires warred inside him as he wanted to make every touch last as long as possible. The intensity of his lust for her was almost unbearable; he needed to be hilt-deep inside her right now.

He lifted his head, rubbed his thumb along the column of her neck. Her pulse was racing and her eyes were half closed. Her creamy skin was dotted with freckles and the faint flush of desire.

He dropped nibbling kisses down her neck. She smelled of orange blossoms and sea breeze. She was like the wildest parts of Florida, and he felt as if he could hold her for only a fleeing moment and then she'd be gone. Tearing through his life like a hurricane.

He slid his hands down her back, tightening them around her waist, and lifted her off her feet again. She wrapped her legs around his waist and put her hands on his shoulders. Then she looked down into his eyes with that bright southern-Atlantic-blue gaze of hers. He felt lost. As if he were drowning in her eyes.

She nipped at his lower lip and then sucked it into her mouth and he hardened. He was going to explode if he didn't get his damned tailored pants off and bury himself in her body.

He reached for his fly but she shifted on him, rubbing her center over his erection. He shook, and the strength left his legs as he stumbled and fell back on the bed. She laughed and then thrust her tongue into his mouth again. And he gave up thinking.

She was like the wildest hurricane and all he could do was ride this storm out. She moved over him and made him remember what it felt like to be alive. The same way she had four weeks ago in Key West. She made the rest of the world pale, and everything narrowed to the two of them.

The heat flared between them and his clothes felt too constricting. He needed to be naked. Wanted her naked. Then she could climb back on his lap. He tore his mouth from hers, his breath heavy as he drew her T-shirt up and over her head and tossed it aside.

She wore the same beige lace bra she'd had on the last time they'd had sex. He traced his finger over the seam where the fabric met skin, saw the goose bumps spread from her breast over her chest and down her arms. Her nipple tightened and he leaned forward to rub his lips over it as he reached behind her back and undid the bra.

The cups loosened, but he didn't lift his head from her nipple. He continued teasing her with light brushes of his tongue over it until she reached between them and undid his tie, leaving it dangling around his neck as she went to work on his shirt buttons.

He shifted back, taking the edge of her bra between his teeth and pulling it away. She laughed, a deep, husky sound he remembered so well. And he got even harder. He had thought there was no way he could want her more, but he'd been wrong.

She pushed the fabric of his shirt open and peeled it down his arms, but she hadn't undone his cuffs so his own shirt bound him. His hands were trapped.

"Undo my hands."

"Not yet, Rafe. Right now, I'm in charge," she said. She scraped her fingernail down the side of his jaw to his neck and then over his pectorals. He sat there craving more of her touch, but damned if he was going to ask her for it. Control and power were two things he always maintained. But with Emily it was as if they'd flown out the window.

She took what she wanted, and though he'd never admit it out loud, he didn't want to stop her. It felt good to just let go.

Flexing her fingers, she dug her nails into his chest and then shifted forward so that the long strands of her hair brushed against him. He shuddered with need, turning his head to try to catch her mouth with his, but she just laughed again and shifted back on his thighs, looking down at him with those eyes that were full of mysteries he knew he'd never really understand.

She drew one finger down the center of his chest, following the path of the light dusting of hair. She swirled her finger around his belly button in tiny circles that made everything inside him contract.

She stroked his erection through the fabric of his pants, and he canted his hips.

She rocked against him and smiled when he moaned her name. Wrapping her arms around his shoulders, she caught the lobe of his ear between her teeth and bit it lightly before whispering all the things she was going to do him. He felt his control slipping with each thrust of her tongue as she flicked it into his ear and then shifted backward on his thighs to reach between them, stroking his length through his pants again.

Cursing, he tried to reach for her but his bound arms wouldn't let him. She rotated her shoulders and rubbed her nipples against his chest. She closed her eyes as she undulated against him, and this time he pulled his arms forward with all of his strength and heard the tear of fabric. She opened her eyes and then started laughing.

He grabbed her waist and rolled to his side, pulling her with him. He rolled over top of her, carefully keeping his weight on his elbows and knees so she wasn't crushed under him. He took both of her hands in his and stretched them high over her head and then rubbed his chest over hers and heard her moan.

Damn, she felt good. Better than he'd remembered her feeling, and that said a lot because he still had erotic dreams of their weekend together.

He lowered his head and sucked her nipple into his mouth, holding both of her wrists above her head with one of his hands. He reached lower between their bodies and undid her jeans, pushing them down so that he could cup her in his hand. He rubbed her mound, and then traced the seam of her panties. Her legs scissored underneath his and he shifted until he lay between them. He let go of her wrists as he slowly kissed his way down her body.

She was covered in freckles; up close he could see that they were all different sizes. He flicked his tongue over each of them as he moved lower and lower until he found her belly button ring. The small loop had a starfish dangling from it. He tongued it and traced the circumference of her belly button.

He moved lower, catching the top of her bikini panties with the tip of his finger and drawing them slowly down.

She shifted her hips and he pushed her jeans and panties down to her knees. She kicked them the rest of the way off.

He traced the pattern of freckles from her thigh to her knee, circling her kneecap and the small scar there before caressing his way back up the inside of her thighs. He felt the humid warmth of her body and traced her feminine core with his fingertip. She shifted on the bed, her hands reaching for him, but it was his turn to tease her. Plus if she touched him, he feared his control would splinter into a million pieces and this would be over too quickly.

He parted her folds and then leaned down to taste her. He closed his eyes as he sucked her intimate flesh, causing her to draw her legs closer around him and her hands to fall to the back of his head. She gripped his hair as her hips lifted upward toward his mouth and his tongue.

She was addicting. He couldn't get enough of her. He pushed one finger into her body and heard her call his name. She was wet and ready for him. He fumbled, trying to free himself from his trousers. He lifted his head, looked up at her and saw that she was watching him. Her eyes were filled with passion and desire.

He stood up, shoved his pants and underwear off in a move that definitely couldn't be called graceful, and then he lowered himself on top of her. He slowly used his chest and body to caress hers as he moved over her. She shifted her legs so that her thighs were on either side of his and he moved his hips forward, felt the tip of his erection at the opening of her body. He hesitated. This time was different from their weekend in Key West, but the passion in her eyes was the same.

Slowly he entered her, trying to make it last because she felt so damned good. She gripped his rock-hard flesh as he entered her and drove himself all the way home and then forced himself to stay still once he was fully seated in her body.

Her hands were on his shoulders, running up and down his back and then reaching lower to cup his butt and try to get him to move. But he needed a moment before he did that. A moment to make sure that she was with him. He lowered his head to her neck, and then bit her lightly before moving lower, kissing the full globes of her breasts.

She tightened as she arched underneath him. She looked up at him and whispered dark, sexual words that made his control disappear along with his willpower, and he found himself thrusting deeper into her body. Driving toward his climax and carrying her along with him.

He pushed her legs higher, putting her feet on his shoulders so he could go deeper, and pounded into her faster and faster until he heard her calling out his name and he spilled himself inside her. He thrust into her three more times before he let go of her legs and fell forward, bracing himself on his arms. He kissed the pert pink nipple on her left breast as he rested his head on her shoulder and tried to catch his breath.

He got up and left her for a few moments to wash up and then came back and lay down next to her on the bed. He was aware of the time and knew he should already be at the private airport and getting on his family's jet so he could travel with them to Alma, but he couldn't make himself leave.

He knew that this wasn't love. He wasn't going to lie to her or himself. But she was pregnant with his child and this fired him with an enthusiasm he just couldn't muster when he thought of being king. He didn't want the throne, but his father, who couldn't inherit it because he'd never had his marriage annulled after divorcing Rafe's mother, had been very clear that he thought Rafe needed to do his duty.

He stroked his hand down Emily's arm. She had turned on her side and had her head on his shoulder.

"What are you thinking?"

"That I'm glad you came here today. Did you ever think of not telling me?" he asked.

He suspected he knew the answer, but wanted to hear it from her.

"No. It wasn't easy to track you down—you're pretty secretive about this penthouse bachelor pad, aren't you? But Harry has lots of friends who have connections. It only took him six hours to find you."

"Harry scares me," Rafe admitted. The owner of Shady Harry's bar had been fun and gregarious when Rafe had been partying and buying rounds for the entire place. But the next morning when he'd spotted the older man as he'd left Emily's cottage, Harry had given him a look that said to watch his back. "What's he to you?"

"He and my mom dated for a while," Emily said. "He's sort of like my stepdad. Why?"

"I have a feeling if I show up in Key West he's going to be waiting with a shotgun."

"You're not going to Key West, you're going to Alma. I've seen pictures. It's really beautiful," she said.

Not as beautiful as she was, Rafe thought. He leaned up on his elbow, put his hand flat on her stomach and realized he couldn't control this any more than he could say no to the people in Alma who'd asked his family to come back and rule the country.

"It is. They've had a rough time since the revolution and I guess… I have to go," he said.

"I know. I told you I wasn't here to ask you to stay. I just needed you to know."

"Why?"

"I didn't know my dad. My mom has never mentioned

his name to me. I asked her one time about him and she started crying. I want more than that for our baby. It's not that I had a deprived childhood, but I always wonder. I have this emptiness inside me that nothing can fill. It's that empty spot where everyone else has a dad."

He was humbled by her explanation. He knew he wanted to be more than a name and a face to their kid, though. "We need to figure this out."

There was a knock on the bedroom door.

"Rafael? Are you in here? Your father is in a car waiting downstairs and if you're not down in ten minutes he's coming up here and getting you." It was his personal assistant, Jose.

Jose was his right-hand man at Montoro Enterprises and at home. He took care of all the details.

"I have company," Rafe said. But Emily was more than just company. She was his lover. The mother of his unborn child.

"I am aware of that," Jose said.

"Tell Father I'll be down when I'm down," Rafe said.

But the mood was broken and Emily was getting up and putting her clothes on. She had her jeans on and buttoned, but he stopped her before she put her T-shirt on. He pulled her into his arms. It seemed the sort of gesture that would reassure her, but since he was already thinking of everything he had to do, it felt hollow. He knew she noticed it, too, when she pulled back and shook her head.

The mantle of being a Montoro was tightening around him. "I—"

"Don't. No excuses and definitely no lies," she said. She reached into her back pocket and pulled out a business card for Shady Harry's; he turned it over and saw she'd written her name and number on the back. "If you want to know about our child, contact me."

"I do. I will," he said.

She smiled up at him. "I know that the next few weeks are going to be crazy for you, so no pressure."

She pulled her shirt on and then tucked her underwear into her purse and started for the door. He watched her walk out. Part of him wanted to run after her and make her stay so he could talk her into trying a relationship or maybe even marriage. Another part wanted to scoop her up and run away with her to some Pacific island where no one would know their names, far enough away from his family and everyone they knew.

But Emily was a brave sort of woman, and running had never been his style, either, so he had no choice but to get dressed and head down to the car.

His father didn't speak to him the entire way to the airport. Rafael III had wanted the throne enough to try to convince his ex-wife to come back, but Rafe's mother wasn't interested in doing anything to help out her former husband. To say the two of them had a strained relationship was putting it mildly.

They were a prime example of how getting married to the wrong person didn't make for a happy family. Rafe had the childhood to prove it.

During the ride, his cousin Juan Carlos spoke too much. Telling him what was expected of the next king of Alma.

Juan Carlos had been orphaned and seemed to be fixated on the monarchy as a way of proving to himself and the rest of the family that he could carry on his parents' legacy. Perhaps if Rafe's parents hadn't divorced and been horrible to each other, he'd have felt the same way about the family honor.

Rafe freely admitted to himself that if Emily's pregnancy became public knowledge it would create a scandal

that would make protecting that legacy even more difficult. But Rafe tuned Juan Carlos out and tried to figure
out what he expected of himself as a man.

CHAPTER THREE

Key West was a tourist town and there was no getting around that. The atmosphere was laid back and everyone had a sort of hungover look. There was something about being on the edge of the ocean that inspired indulgence in sun, sand and drinks.

Emily sat on the front porch of her flamingo-pink and white cottage with her feet propped on the railing, desperately needing to absorb that laid-back attitude. She'd left Miami and Rafe behind. She'd done what she'd set out to do, namely tell him he was going to be a father. That had gone well—differently than she'd expected, but the end result was the same. She was back here.

Alone.

"Em. Your mom asked me stop by," Harry said as he walked around the side of the house.

He was tall, at least six five, and wore middle age well. His reddish-blond hair had thinned a little but was still thick enough, and he wore it cut short in a military style. His beard was equal parts red, blond and gray, and he had an easy smile. He was the closest thing she had to a dad. So she was glad to see him.

"Why?" Emily asked. Though she knew why her mom had sent Harry. If anyone could make her forget her troubles it was the jovial bar owner.

"She thought you might need some company. She's on her way back to port but won't be here until tonight."

Emily sighed. "I don't really want any company."

"Figured you might say that, so I brought you a cup of decaf and a blueberry bagel. We can both sit here and eat and pretend we're alone."

Decaf.

Seemed like a little thing, but she always drank full-on caffeine. Now she knew that her mom had spilled the beans about her being preggers. Harry handed her a bakery bag from Key Koffee with the bagel and the coffee.

"You know?"

"I know. It was that slick guy from South Beach, right?"

She tipped her head back and closed her eyes. "He's not that slick."

Harry laughed. "They never are. Talk to me, kiddo. Do I need to take my .45 and head to Miami?"

She opened her eyes and lifted her head. "You would have made a really good dad," she said, smiling at him.

"I think I have been to you," he reminded her.

"You have. But no to the .45. Besides, you'd have to fly to Europe to find him."

Harry took a bite out of his everything bagel and settled down on the top step, turning sideways with his back against the railing to face her.

"Europe? He seemed American to me," Harry said.

"He's Rafael Montoro IV. Part of… I'm not sure what to call him. But his family was royalty in a tiny Mediterranean country called Alma. They were kicked out decades ago but now they want them back. He's the oldest son and heir apparent to the newly restored monarchy."

"Complicates things, doesn't it?" Harry said.

"You have no idea," she said. "But I didn't expect him to do anything when I gave him the news. You know?"

Harry took a sip of his coffee and then gave her one of those wise looks of his that she hated. He knew when she was lying, especially to herself.

"Okay, fine, I wanted him to be, like, we'll do this together. Instead, I got...he was sweet but clearly torn. He can't let his family down. And he and I only had one weekend together, Harry."

"Sometimes that's all it takes," he said.

"It wasn't enough for the guy who fathered me," she said. "Please don't tell Mom I said that. But really, that complicates everything. I've always thought I was okay with the fact that I don't know who he was, but this baby..." She put her hands on her stomach. "It's making me realize I'm not."

Harry didn't say anything. And after a few minutes Emily looked away from him and back to the foot traffic on the street near her house. What could he say? He was her substitute dad who'd stepped up when he didn't have to. Harry must have thought that she was making a mess where there didn't need to be one.

"I get it, kiddo. It's hard to not want the best for your baby. We all do that," he said. "Try to fix the problems in our past so that our kids don't have to experience them."

"Did you do that for Rita and Danny?" she asked. Harry had two kids who were both more than fifteen years older than her and lived in Chicago. They came down for two weeks each spring to visit Harry.

"I tried. But I ended up making my own mistakes and they have done the same. It's all a part of being human," he said.

"I'm getting Zen Harry this morning," she said. But his positive attitude helped take her mind off Rafe and the sadness she'd been feeling.

It wasn't that she'd expected anything else from him,

but that she'd wanted something more. She shook her head as she realized that what she'd wanted was to be wanted.

For him to want to stay with her.

It was unrealistic, but a girl could dream.

"Well, I do have all this wonderful advice and no one to share it with," Harry said with a wink. "You'll be okay, kiddo. You'll make decisions and choices and some of them are going to be fabulous and others you're going to regret. But I do know one thing."

"What's that?" she asked.

"You're going to love that baby of yours, and in the end that's all that really matters."

"You think so?"

"I do. Your own mom did that for you. Look how you turned out," he said.

"Not bad," she admitted. She liked her life. She could have followed her mom into a similar career—she was a marine biologist—but Emily liked being on the land and not out at sea. She had a degree in hotel and restaurant management and one day hoped to open her own place. She knew she had a good life, but a part of her still missed Rafe.

Another part of her knew she just missed the idea of Rafe. So far every time they'd been together they'd ended up in bed. It wasn't as if he was even a friend.

She wanted that picture-perfect family that she kept in her head. She wanted that for this baby she was carrying. She didn't want her child to have the piecemeal family that she did. No matter that she loved her mom and Harry fiercely. For her child she wanted more.

And being the bastard of a European king probably wasn't what her child would want. She was going to have to be very protective. Raise the baby to know its own strength and place in the world.

She noticed Harry watching her, realized she wasn't alone and that made the loneliness she felt when she thought of Rafe a little less painful.

ALMA WAS BREATHTAKINGLY BEAUTIFUL. The island was surrounded by sparkling blue seas and old world charm seemed to imbue every building. They'd landed at a private air field and were driving to the royal palace in the urban capital of Del Sol.

Rafe had heard there was a lively nightclub scene and before Emily's visit had sort of thought of checking it out. But now that he had the dual mantle of monarchy and fatherhood hanging over him, he figured he should rethink that.

Del Sol was even more striking than the black and white photos he'd seen in the albums his *tia* Isabella kept. While there were modern buildings dotted throughout the city many of the old buildings remained. Tia Isabella had been a young woman when she'd been forced to flee Alma with the rest of their family. When Rafe and his siblings and cousin had been growing up they'd been entertained by her stories. Tia Isabella had spent a lot of time talking about the old days and what it had been like to grow up on Alma. But Rafe thought he understood why his grandfather hadn't talked that much about it. Rafe would have been sad to leave this homeland, too.

As the royal motorcade made its way into Del Sol, Alma's capital, people on the streets craned their necks to get a glimpse of the Montoros. Rafe was used to a certain level of fame and notoriety in Miami, but not this. There he was one of the jet-set Montoros. The young generation who worked hard and played harder.

Here he was the future monarch. He'd be the face of

Alma to the world. And while his ego was sort of jazzed about that, another part of him wasn't.

"Maybe you should put the window down and do that princess wave," his sister Bella said with a sparkle in her blue eyes. Their father and the rest of their party were in a separate vehicle.

"Princess wave? That's more your cup of tea," he said. "Maybe I'll throw up the peace sign."

She giggled. He'd always been close to his little sister, and making her laugh helped him to relax.

Bella looked like a fairy-tale princess with her pretty blond hair. Not anything like Emily. He wondered what Emily would think of Alma. It was an island not that unlike her hometown of Key West, but the laid-back attitude in the Keys was a world away from this charming European nation.

For a country that had been ruled by a dictator for decades, the people in the streets seemed happy and prosperous and the buildings were clean and well-maintained. Rafe didn't see any signs of financial ruin. But economic danger lurked whenever there was a change of regime. And if there was one thing he was good at, it was making money.

But would the government here listen to him?

To be honest he wasn't the kind of person to negotiate for what he wanted. That was one of the reasons Montoro Enterprises had thrived under his leadership. He made bold decisions. Sometimes they didn't pay off, but most of the time they did.

"You okay?" Bella asked.

He started to shrug it off. There was no way he was going to mention Emily or the fact that she was pregnant to his sister. Not until he had a chance to figure it out for himself. But the family stuff was also getting to him, especially how Juan Carlos was going really crazy about protocol and proper image and all that.

"This return to Alma is throwing me," he admitted to her.

"How?" she asked. "You've always handled whatever the family has dished out. This will be no different. Pretend you're the CEO of the country."

As if. Being the king was a "name only" position. No power. Maybe that was why he hesitated to fully embrace it. He was a man of action. Not a figurehead.

"Good suggestion," he said, glancing out the window as they approached the castle. Surrounded by glittering blue water on three sides, it rose from the land like a sand castle at the beach. He groaned.

"What?"

"I was hoping the castle would be in disrepair."

"Why?"

"So I could hate it."

Bella laughed again. "I love it. It's everything I thought it would be," she said.

"What if there's not a hopping club scene? Will you still love it then?" he asked. Bella liked to party. Hell, they all did. They hadn't been raised to assume the throne. They were all more likely to show up in the tabloids in a compromising position than on the society pages at a formal tea. The closer he got to the throne the less sure he was that he wanted to be there.

He felt Bella's hand on his shoulder. "You're going to be fine. I think you'll make a great king."

"Why? I'm not sure at all."

"You've been a great big brother and always ensured our family's place in business and in society."

"Business is easy. I understand that world," Rafe countered.

"I never thought the day would come when you'd admit

that you aren't sure of yourself," she said, taking her phone from her handbag.

"What are you doing?"

"Texting Gabe that you have feet of clay."

"He already knows that."

"We all do," Bella said. "Why are you acting like you are just figuring it out?"

"I'm going to be a king, Bella. It's making me nutty," he said.

"You weren't as thrown by it a week ago," she said. "What happened yesterday to make you delay your flight?"

Nothing.

Everything.

Something that could change the man he was. If he let it.

"Business. Running Montoro Enterprises does take a lot of time," he said.

The car pulled to a stop and an attendant in full livery came to open the door for them. Bella climbed out first but looked back at Rafe.

"Lying to me is one thing. You can keep your secrets if you want to," she said. "But I hope you aren't lying to yourself."

He followed her out of the car, and the warm Mediterranean air swept around him. She had a point. He knew in his gut that this didn't feel right. He should be in Miami with Emily. He missed her.

The porte-cochere led to an inner brick-lined courtyard. There was a fountain underneath a statue of Rafe's great-grandfather Rafael I. He was surprised it hadn't been torn down when the dictator had taken over. Bella stopped walking and spun around on her heel, taking in the beauty of the palace.

For the first time he felt a sense of his royal lineage settling over him. If their family hadn't been forced to flee he would have grown up in this palace. His memories would be of this place that smelled wonderfully of jasmine and lavender. Where was the scent coming from?

His father came up beside him and put his hand on his shoulder not saying a word. Something passed between them. An emotion that Rafe didn't want to define. But Alma became real to him. In a way that it hadn't been before. In Miami it had been easy to say he wasn't sure if he wanted to be king but seeing this palace—he felt the history. And he sort of understood Juan Carlos's perspective for once. Rafe didn't want to let down their family line.

If Alma wanted the Montoros back on the throne than Rafe would have to put aside the feelings he felt stirring for Emily and figure out how to be their king.

That surprised him. He hadn't expected to feel this torn. He was isolated from the rest of his family who seemed to think this return to royalty was just the thing they needed. They were all caught up in being back in the homeland. But as much as he felt swept up in the majesty of their return to Alma he knew he was still trying to figure out where home really was.

EMILY WORKED THE closing shift at Harry's and walked home at 2:00 a.m. Key West wasn't like the mean streets of Miami, but she moved quickly and kept her eyes open for danger. It was something she'd teach her kid.

She was starting to find her bearings with this pregnancy more and more as each day passed. Being a mom was going to take some getting used to, but as her own mom had said, she had nine months to make the adjustment.

Her cell phone vibrated in the pocket of her jeans and she reached back to pull it out. Glancing at the screen, she saw it was an international call. She only knew one person who was traveling internationally right now. She did some quick math and figured out that it was early morning in Alma.

"Hello?"

"Hey, Red. Figured you'd be getting off work. Please tell me I didn't wake you." Sure enough, it was Rafe.

"You'd think you'd be more careful about disturbing a pregnant woman's rest," she teased. She didn't want to admit it but she'd missed him. Three days. That was all it had been since she'd seen him, but it had felt like a lifetime. His voice was deep and resonated in her ear, making her feel warm all over.

"Well, maybe I did call the bar earlier to determine if you were working tonight," he admitted.

That sounded like Rafe. He was a man who left little to chance. "What can I do for you?"

"How are you feeling?" he asked. "How's Florida?"

"I'm feeling fine," she said. "I have had a little bit of morning sickness, and it's not just limited to mornings. I've been getting sick midafternoon."

She saw her house at the end of the lane and got her keys out. She'd left the porch lights on and it looked so welcoming. The only thing that would be better was if Rafe was waiting for her. And to be honest, as he talked to her on the phone, it was almost as if he was there with her.

"Makes sense since that's when you wake up," he said. "Is there anything you can do to help that?"

"No," she said. "It's not too bad. How's Alma?"

"Nice. You'd like it. It's all sand and sea for as far as the eye can see and quaint little villages. Not as laid back as Key West but still nice."

"Any places to go paddleboarding?"

"Not yet. Why, do you think you'd move here and start a business?" he asked.

It was the closest he'd come to suggesting that she be near him in the future, and she felt numb even contemplating it. She had her own plans to open a restaurant around the corner from Harry's. Not to be Rafe's hidden mistress in some far-off European country.

"Not at all. I've got a place picked out for my future restaurant," she said.

"Is that what you want to do?"

Once again she realized how little they actually knew of each other's lives.

"Well, I can't be a bartender forever."

"I guess not. Tell me about your dreams," he said.

She thought she heard the sound of footsteps on a tiled floor on his end. "Where are you?"

"Not ready to share that much with me?" he asked, countering her evasion.

In a way she wished they were playing a game. It would make everything easier. She could concentrate on winning and not really have to think about the emotions. But the truth was she was tired and still a little unsure of what she was doing. Sure, just hearing Rafe's voice made her feel not so alone. But she didn't want to allow herself to become dependent on him.

Not to turn her life into one big sob story, but usually when she started to feel comfortable with someone they left. It wasn't that they abandoned her, just moved on and left her to her independent self. Even her mom and Harry. And she didn't want that with Rafe.

"Nope. I want to hear about Alma. I read a little online yesterday. Seems like the change of regime is going to have a big impact on the economy. I know you are good at making money. Is that why they chose you and your family to come back and lead the country?" she asked.

"Our family ruled the country before the coup that installed the late dictator, Tantaberra. That's why we were chosen. But my parents are divorced so Dad, who would be next in line, can't assume the throne. They want someone with the right pedigree and the right reputation."

"Um… I'm guessing if they found out about me that could put a wrench in things."

"Possibly. I'm not going to deny you exist, Emily."

"Really?"

"Yes. Would I be on the phone with you if I didn't care?" he asked.

"I don't know," she said honestly. "We're strangers."

"Who are about to be parents to a baby," he said. "Let's get to know each other. And while we have half the world between us maybe I can talk to you without being distracted by your body and that sexy way you tilt your head to the side. You always make me forget everything except wanting to get you naked."

Her breath caught as she sank down into the big armchair where Rafe had sat the one time he'd been to her place. They'd made love in the chair and she felt closer to him now. She tucked her leg up underneath her and let those memories wash over her.

"Red? You still there?"

"Yes. Dammit, now you've got me thinking about you naked."

"Good. My evil plan worked," he said. "Tell me something about yourself."

"What?"

"Anything. I want to know the woman who's going to be the mother of my child."

She thought about her life. It was ordinary: nothing too tragic, nothing too exciting. But it was hers. "When I was six I thought if I spent enough time in the ocean I'd turn into a mermaid. My mom's a marine biologist and we were living on her research vessel, *The Sea Spirit*. She made me a bikini top out of shells and sent me off every day to swim."

"I'm glad you didn't turn into a mermaid," he said with a quiet laugh.

They talked on the phone until Emily started drifting to sleep. She knew she should hang up, but she didn't want to break the connection. Didn't want to wake up without Rafe.

"Red?"

"Yes?"

"I wish I was there to tuck you into bed," he said.

"Me, too," she admitted. Then she opened her eyes as she realized that she was starting to need him.

"Good night, Rafe," she said, hanging up the phone before she could do anything stupid like ask him what he'd wanted to be as a boy. Or to come back to Key West.

CHAPTER FOUR

Rafe secluded himself from the rest of the family in the office area of the suite of rooms he'd been given. The deal he'd struck for Montoro Enterprises to ship Alma's oil was taking a lot of his time.

Alma was a major oil producing country to the north of Spain. Montoro Enterprises would be shipping the oil to its customers in North and South America where the bulk of their business interests were. It made good business sense but he also wanted it because he'd get a chance to explore the country of his ancestors. When he'd first done the deal he'd anticipated his father becoming King not himself.

Plus truth be told, he'd been so focused on work because he was avoiding his family and the coterie of diplomats who seemed to be lurking whenever he stepped out of his suite. He didn't want to talk about his coronation or about the business of running the government. Yet.

But sitting around and hiding out went against the grain, so he'd been working nonstop. He hadn't shaved in the three days, and Mozart had replaced Jay-Z and Kanye on the stereo because no one would ever be tempted to stop working and rap to Mozart. He hadn't even contacted Emily, though he'd thought of her night and day.

She was an obsession. He knew that. He had the feeling

that if he were in Miami maybe it wouldn't be as fierce, but he was far away from her and thinking of her was nice and comforting in the midst of this storm that was brewing around him.

He banged his head on the desk.

"I can see I'm interrupting," Gabe said as he entered without knocking.

"I'm working."

"Yeah, I noticed," Gabe said, nodding toward the empty cans of Red Bull that littered the desk and the floor. He walked to the window and pulled back the drapes.

Rafe blinked against the glare of the sunlight. "What time is it?"

"Four in the afternoon. You're expected for dinner tonight and if you don't show up Juan Carlos is going to have a stroke. I know he's been a pain lately with all this royal protocol, but we don't want our cousin to have a stroke, do we?"

Rafe shook his head. "No." He scrubbed his hands over his face. His eyes felt gritty and the stubble on his jaw felt rough. He was a mess. Truly. "This sucks."

Gabe laughed that wicked, low laugh that Rafe had heard women found irresistible. He just found it annoying.

"Yeah, it does. Not so cool being the older brother now, is it?"

Not at all. "I should walk away…that would leave you holding the bag."

A fleeting glimpse of panic ran across his brother's face. "Dad would disown you. I'm pretty sure the board would fire you from Montoro Enterprises. Then what would you do?"

Run away to Key West.

Seemed simple enough, but to be fair he wasn't sure

what type of reception he'd receive if he just showed up on Emily's doorstep.

"I think I'm too American to want to be a royal, you know? Maybe Dad still wants it, but it feels weird to me. I don't want to be called 'Your Majesty' or 'Your Highness.'"

Rafe watched his younger brother. If there were the slightest sign that Gabe was interested in being king, Rafe would just walk away and let his brother have it. But Gabe rubbed the back of his neck as he paced over to the window. "Me neither."

"Then I guess I'd better stop acting like a jerk and get out there," Rafe said. "What's the plan?"

"Dinner with some supporters. And a family who'd love for you to meet their daughter," Gabe said with a wry smile.

Rafe shook his head. He'd do his duty to his family, but he was already involved with a redhead who wouldn't take kindly to him catting around. He was getting to know her, starting a relationship with the woman who was going to be the mother of his child. What if she didn't feel possessive toward him the way he did toward her? And he did feel possessive. Emily was his. "I'm not interested."

"Are you interested in someone else?"

"It's complicated, Gabe."

"I never thought I'd see the day when you said that. Is she special?"

"She could be," Rafe said. Or at least that was what his gut was saying. The rest of him wasn't too sure.

Once his brother left and Rafe had wrapped up what he was working on for the day, he started getting ready for the state dinner. When he got out of the shower, he saw that he had a text message from Emily.

It's official. Just got word back from the doctor's office. I'm due in January.

Would he be able to get back to the States in January?

Being with Emily would mean giving up the monarchy… and possibly his job, depending on how much it pissed off his family. Montoro Enterprises and Alma were now all linked together. Could he walk away from one without walking away from them all?

But what kind of man walked away from his own child?

Not one that Rafe wanted to be. He knew that but as he'd said to Gabe earlier, it was complicated.

He braced his hands on the bathroom counter and looked into his own hazel eyes searching for answers or a solution. But there was nothing there.

And that really pissed him off. He needed to take control of his personal life the way he did the boardroom. No more doing what everyone else wanted unless it fit with his own inner moral compass.

Except that he'd been a playboy for so long he wasn't too sure he had one. Everyone had one, right? Then shouldn't the answer be clearer than this?

When he was finished shaving, he took the towel off his hips and tossed it at his image in the mirror before he walked into the bedroom to dress.

He hit the remote for his sound system and switched from Mozart to "The Man" by Aloe Blacc . He stopped in his tracks. Right now it seemed as if everyone had a piece of him and the man Rafe had always wanted to be had been lost.

He knew what he had to do. No use pretending he was going to do anything else. It wasn't that he thought the path would be easy, but then when had he ever taken the easy path? It was simply that spending time with his siblings made him realize that family was important to him.

His mind made up, he grabbed his phone and began typing, hitting Send before he could have second thoughts.

I'll be there. When is your next appointment? I'd like to go with you if I can.

He owed it to himself and to his child to at least see if he could be a real partner to Emily. And be a real part of the baby's life.

Really? Okay. If you do this then I don't want you making promises you can't keep.

That right there showed him how little she knew of him. Hell, what did he know about her? He knew how she looked in his arms. He knew that she had wanted to be a mermaid when she was little. He smiled at that one. He knew she was having his baby.

I'm a man of my word, Red. I'll be there.

TWO DAYS LATER Emily woke up to a beautiful sunny morning. Since it was her day off, she decided to take her paddleboard and head to a quiet cove on Geiger Key where there weren't many tourists. She'd been too much in her head since she'd found out she was pregnant and needed to forget for a few hours.

After she'd had her daily bout of morning sickness, she took the prenatal vitamins the doctor had prescribed and then got dressed in her usual bikini. She stood in front of the full-length mirror mounted on the back of her walk-in closet door and looked at her body. No signs of her pregnancy were visible. In fact, she looked a little bit thinner than she had before. Her boobs were getting a little larger, though.

She'd always sort of been...well, smallish, but now she was actually filling out the top. Not bad, she thought. She patted her stomach and shook her head. She definitely needed today for herself.

Someone knocked on her front door. She grabbed her board shorts, putting them as she went to answer it.

There was a man in a suit waiting there.

"Hello, Ms. Fielding. I have a package for you from Rafael Montoro. He asked me to deliver it to you personally."

She took the package from him. "You look a little fancy for a deliveryman."

"I'm Jose, his assistant at Montoro Enterprises," Jose said.

"That explains the suit," she said.

She wanted to ask more questions, debated it for a moment, and then decided to heck with looking cool. "So when will he be back in the US?"

"I'm not at liberty to say."

"Really? He sent you here but you can't tell me that?" she asked. "I know it's your job to protect his privacy, it's just that he said...never mind. Thank you for getting up early to deliver this. Are you driving back to Miami?"

"Nah. I took the company chopper."

Of course he did. Men like Rafe—and his assistant, for that matter—didn't drive almost four hours to Key West like other mere mortals.

"Safe travels," she said, turning around to go back inside.

What had he sent her?

"Ms. Fielding?"

She glanced over her shoulder at Jose. "He's hoping

to be back next week but that all depends on the people in Alma."

She smiled at him. "Thank you."

"Don't rat me out," he said with a wink, and then left.

His assistant was nice. She wondered if that was a reflection of Rafe as a boss, but she knew no matter who worked for him he might still be a jerk at work. "Jose!"

"Yes."

"What kind of man is Rafe to work for?"

"Demanding. He won't settle for a job half done. But he's also very generous when a project is over. He's a good man," he said.

"Thanks," she said.

He walked away and she thought about it. A good man. Was she a good woman? Hell, yes, she was. She sat down on what she was now calling the Rafe chair and opened the package. When she pulled back the sides of the cardboard box there was a pretty paper inside with the words *Handcrafted in Alma* printed on it in scrolling letters.

She carefully pulled the sides of the paper back to reveal something in Bubble Wrap. Lifting it from the box, she carefully removed the Bubble Wrap and caught her breath as she saw that it contained a stained glass mermaid that looked a lot like her.

She traced her finger over the details and tried to downplay the importance of the gift. But she couldn't avoid the fact that he'd taken her childhood dream and given it to her.

She took a picture and then attached it to the text message.

She's even prettier than I imagined a mermaid could be. Thank you for this wonderful gift.

The response was almost instantaneous.

I'm glad you like it. I'm just coming out of a meeting. Do you have time to chat with me?

She thought about the paddleboarding she'd planned for the day, but as her mom always said, the ocean wasn't going anywhere. Plus a part of her realized she'd been running away from her house and her situation so she didn't have to deal with it on her own. Talking to Rafe was a solution. She didn't want it to be, because she'd always prided herself on being independent and handling anything life threw at her. But she knew she wanted him by her side.

Yes. I can talk.

Good. I'll call in a few minutes.

She paced around her living room and ended up back in the kitchen. She took the stained glass mermaid and held her up to the back window, where she got the light from the morning sun, and realized she'd fit perfectly there.

She jotted down the supplies she'd need and then made herself a mango and passion fruit smoothie. By the time she was finished with it, he still hadn't called.

He was a man who would be king, she thought. Obviously his time wasn't his own. She waited another thirty minutes before she turned the ringer off on her phone, got into her car and drove to Geiger Key.

She tried to shake it off. She'd known that the only one she could count on was herself, but it stung just the tiniest bit that he hadn't messaged her back to say he'd been delayed.

RAFE WAS IN a bad mood by the time he escaped the royal palace in Del Sol and drove down the winding coastal road to his family's beach compound in Playa del Onda. He'd spent the entire day either in meetings or being cornered by Dita Gomez.

Dita was the oldest daughter of one of the best families in Alma. Her parents were part of the newly forming royal court and they were hoping for a royal match. Dita was a lovely lady, no doubt, but as his man Kanye might say, she was a gold digger. Rafe wasn't entirely sure how she had access to his schedule but everywhere he went, she was there.

He'd been so busy dealing with getting rid of Dita that he hadn't been able to call Emily. And he knew her well enough to know that giving the excuse that he'd been dodging the advances of a beautiful blonde wasn't going to go over well.

Wanting to punch something, he shoved his hands in his hair. This was too restricting. He hadn't felt a connection to Alma or to the people the way that Bella seemed to. While he was busy plotting ways to get back to Miami early, she was happy to stay for a little while longer.

He wondered if something had happened to make Bella so happy with the land that time forgot. He made a mental note to talk to her, but he had no idea when he'd get a chance. His schedule was grueling.

He glanced at his watch; it had been seven hours since he said he'd call Emily. That meant it was probably midafternoon in Key West. He dialed her number and waited. It rang twice before he got a text message that had obviously been tailored for him saying she didn't want to talk to His Majesty.

First he was angry. Screw her. He was doing his best

to keep all the balls in the air. Family, business, kingdom. He'd expect her to understand.

Then he remembered what she'd said to him a few days ago. *Don't make promises he couldn't keep.*

So he dialed her number again and this time she answered. But she didn't say anything—all he heard was the rush of wind and the faint sound of music in the background.

"Don't hang up. I'm sorry. My days over here are insane and I ended up being cornered by someone from the royal court. This is the first time I've been alone since I texted you."

After an excruciating pause, she finally spoke. "It's okay. I know you're busy. But even busy men can take a moment to text."

"Point taken. Honestly, Em, I feel like I'm running from one thing to the next and I can't catch up. I'm not used to this. And I feel like I have to play nice and by their rules. This means a lot to my family."

That was the problem. He wanted to tell them what he'd do and then say take it or leave it. But that wasn't an option. Tia Isabella was so excited to be returning home. He couldn't and wouldn't disappoint his great-aunt or any of his other relatives by ruining this for them. They'd looked to him for leadership and he was stepping up.

But he was losing himself.

"I'm trying to figure this out."

"Who says you have to do it all?" she asked. "Being the monarch and the head of a huge company is a big task for anyone. I think in most countries that isn't allowed."

"I know. But I like running the company. There I'm only answerable to the board and I have a certain degree of anonymity to deal with problems on my own. Here... I sat in a meeting today about what color napkins we should have at the coronation."

She laughed. "What color did you decide?"

"I have no idea. I tuned out," he said. "I'd never do that at a board meeting."

"Well," she said at last. "I'm no expert on that sort of thing but I think you're going to have to find what makes being king exciting to you. I bet at Montoro Enterprises there are tasks that would normally bore you but you do them because you want to be successful."

She was right. "Good advice."

"Thanks. And thank you again for the mermaid. I hung her up after I got back from paddleboarding and am looking forward to seeing my kitchen lit up when the sun sets tonight."

"I wish I was there with you," he said.

"Don't."

"Don't what?"

Don't say things like that. Let's keep this light," she said. "That way I don't start thinking something else and you don't have to worry about calling me."

Hell. "I do want to call you, Em. I like talking to you and you make me…you're the only thing that feels real right now."

"That's because I have nothing to do with Alma or the throne. And you know with me it's just about the baby and getting to know each other. But that's running away from your obligations in Alma. And I think that for a little while that might suit you, but eventually it won't."

"I'm not sure what you mean by that," he said. Afraid very much that he did know what she meant.

"That once you decide to commit to Alma and the people there, you will realize that you can't have me. I'll have been the distraction you needed to make the decision, and then I'll be left by the wayside."

Damn. He knew she was right. He didn't want to admit it to her, but then with Emily he didn't have to. "That's not my intention."

"Whether that's true or not, you can't change who you are and with you, Rafael Montoro IV, it's all about your family legacy. And we both know you aren't going to turn your back on it."

She was right. She'd taken the debate he'd been having with himself and boiled it down to its essence. He was a man who was all about family; it was the compass he used in every decision he'd ever made. Now he just had to decide if he could shift away from the Montoro legacy to pursue his own future with Emily and their child. And the decision would be a tough one.

After he hung up with her he went to his office to work. He put on a little Jimmy Buffett because he needed to hear some sounds of home.

There was a knock on the door and he rubbed the back of his neck. "Come in."

"Sir, I have a few more questions for the coronation," Hector said as he entered. Hector was the head of the Coronation Committee. Since Alma hadn't had a monarch in several decades, they were anxious to make sure the coronation had all the bells and whistles.

"Please have a seat," Rafe said. This was what he'd be giving up, he thought as Hector talked about where foreign dignitaries would be seated. Alma was going to be a world player. Lots of countries were interested in doing business with them since their previous ruler had kept the country isolated. Rafe's skills in business made him uniquely suited to help Alma get the most from their entry into the global marketplace.

"Do you like that?"

Rafe had to start paying attention. As Emily said, he needed to find the things about it that excited him. "You know better than me, Hector. No offense, but I'm not at all interested in color schemes or seating arrangements."

"None taken. You're a man of action and need to be doing something," Hector said.

"True. I'm going to let you make all the choices. If something doesn't look right then I will tell you."

"Thank you, sir."

"Clearly you know what you're doing," Rafe said.

Hector stood up to leave, but turned back when he got to the door. "I mean, thank you for coming back here. It means a lot to our people."

Hector left.

Rafe felt humbled. He knew that he wasn't going to find it easy to choose between Alma and Emily. He needed her and the people needed him.

CHAPTER FIVE

"I toured the countryside today. I have to say that it is beautiful. There's a little cove that I know you would like," Rafe said.

It was 10:00 a.m. Emily sat at one of the corner tables in the coffeehouse on Duval Street talking to Rafe. It had become their date. He hadn't missed calling her one time since the day he'd sent the stained glass mermaid a week ago. She hated to admit it, but she looked forward to his calls every day.

She took a sip of her herbal tea and looked out the window, but she didn't see Key West. Instead she saw the countryside of Alma as he described the rolling hills and hedgerows. The sheep on the hillside munching on grass.

"How's the weather there?" she asked. "I've never been farther north than Georgia."

"It's nice. The island isn't that big and so the sea breezes keep it cool. I think you'd like it."

He said that almost every time they talked, but she'd read the papers and online articles and knew there was no way she could ever visit him there. There was even speculation online that he'd chosen a bride from one of Alma's aristocratic families. She knew that came with the territory of being a monarch.

"Met any nice locals?" she asked before she could stop herself.

"A few. The head of the Coronation Committee is a great guy. He's helped me find things I like to do," he said.

She noticed he didn't mention any women, even though she'd seen his picture with more than one. It still made her sad.

Not sad enough that she stopped taking his calls or looking forward to talking to him.

She suddenly understood how a woman could willingly become a man's mistress. Because she had the feeling that if he asked her to, she'd be tempted to say yes. She was falling for him and he wasn't even here with her. But the silly thing was it was more intense by not actually having him physically here. They didn't argue over the little things like what to get for dinner because they only had a few hours together each week, and then it was only by phone.

"You still there?"

"Yes," she said. "Just imagining Alma."

"What's your view like today?"

"Sunburned tourists in swimsuits and flip-flops. There was a guy last night at the bar who had a few too many and kept coming on to this group of coeds. They ignored him and so he started stripping. Can you imagine? I was laughing because he was harmless. A sunburned middle-aged man. I wanted to see how far he'd go. But Harry put an end to it."

"Sounds interesting. Did you think he'd look good naked?" Rafe asked.

"Nah. He didn't look anything like you. It was the expression on his face that had me hooked. He wasn't going to stop until those women acknowledged him."

"So he didn't look like me... Does that mean you like the way I look naked?" Rafe asked. "Because I haven't slept a single night without remembering how you felt in my arms that last time in Miami."

She took a sip of her tea and put her feet up on the chair across from her. She'd thought of little else but the way Rafe looked with his shirt off or how he'd moved when he'd been rapping to Jay-Z in his bedroom at the penthouse. She hadn't realized that she could be so lusty with this pregnancy, but she was.

"Tell me about it," she said.

"I will tonight. Why don't you call me when you get off work? I'll be waiting up for you."

She liked the sound of that. She glanced around the coffeehouse and noticed a man watching her. He looked away as she spotted him. Weird.

"Okay. I'm working an early shift because Harry is worried that late nights aren't good for me."

"They probably aren't. As a matter of fact, why don't you quit your job there?"

"Why would I do that?" she asked. She'd be bored stiff if she had nothing to do, and her savings would only last her three months. Then she'd have to look for another job. Though she knew Harry would take her back.

"I don't like the idea of you working late nights," he said. "I can support you so you don't have to work."

She put both feet on the floor and leaned forward as a wave of annoyance swept over her. "I don't need your money, Rafael. I'm not about to become your kept woman."

"Slow down, Red. I just meant that if you are tired, I'd help you out. It's nothing any man wouldn't do for the woman carrying his baby."

"That's not true," she said. Her own father had done a lot less. He'd just walked away and left her mom and her alone. "I guess you hit one of my triggers. I don't do needy."

"Hell, I know that. I don't do overprotective usually, but

with you I want to. I know that's not what you want from me, so I'm keeping my distance," he said.

"Yeah, right, you're 'keeping your distance' because of your obligation to your family. You're just as afraid of committing yourself to me as you are of committing yourself to the throne."

There was silence on the line and she wondered if she'd gone too far. A part of her almost wished she had because then he'd just break it off with her and she'd know she was on her own.

These calls, this bond that was developing between them couldn't last. She knew it and if Rafe was being honest he'd admit to it too. The way things stood, they couldn't co-parent their child. Didn't royal babies have nannies or something?

She was going to be a hands-on mom and every time she talked to Rafe she fell a little more for him, started to picture him as a hands-on dad.

"You're right," he said. "But I'm also not rushing back to your side because if I do I'm not sure what sort of reception I'll get."

"What sort do you want?" she asked. She had no idea how she'd act if he showed up on her doorstep, but frankly she imagined she'd be tempted to throw herself into his arms. And she had no idea how he'd react to that.

"You."

She caught her breath. "You don't have to keep this much distance between us, you know."

"I know. But you are unpredictable and I'm not on solid ground right now. Just know I wouldn't be calling you this often if you weren't important to me."

He didn't have to keep quite as much distance as he was for her sake. But getting to know him this way was safer. That was one of the issues she kept pushing to the back of her mind. "Okay, sorry for overreacting. It's just…a lot of things are changing in my body. You know how scary that is for a control freak like me?"

"I do. Red, that's how I feel about this entire constitutional monarchy thing in Alma."

She laughed. He was the only man she knew who'd compare being king to being pregnant. Mainly because he was the only man she knew who wasn't afraid to admit that he had doubts. That he liked to control things. That he was human. He didn't front with her and she knew that was one of the reasons she liked him.

"Okay, so about this late-night call. What do you say we use that video chat function? I miss seeing you," she admitted.

"Finally. I thought you'd never admit to missing me."

"I guess you're not as smart as everyone gives you credit for being," she said.

"Probably not," he said. "But I'm not concerned with what anyone thinks about me but you."

Those words made her heart beat a little faster and made her feel all warm and fuzzy inside. It wasn't love. Not yet. But she knew if he kept calling her every day she was going to start really falling for him, and she was starting to struggle to remember why that was a bad idea.

AFTER HANGING UP with Emily, Rafe left the royal palace in Del Sol and walked around the well-manicured gardens. As he walked, he had his iPod set to his Key West playlist, which was really his Emily playlist. But he knew better than to actually name it that—he didn't want to leave any evidence of his affair for others to observe.

He listened to Jack Johnson sing about waking up and making banana pancakes together. Pretending the world outside didn't exist. And Rafe wanted that. But then as the days went by and he met more people in Alma he started to see how much the country needed him, or at least his family, here, too. Rafe guessed they were all so relieved to have the monarchy back.

After years under a dictator he understood that. It was sort of how he'd felt when he'd turned eighteen and left his father's house. He had acted like a wild man in college for about three months before he realized that he wanted his life to be about more than tabloid headlines. So he'd gotten serious and proven to himself that he could stand outside of his father's shadow and still be a part of the family.

"Hey, big brother," Bella said, coming up behind him and linking her arm through his. He pulled his earbuds out and smiled down at his baby sister. She'd really thrived in Alma and had an affinity with the people here that bordered on mutual admiration. For the Montoros, and Juan Carlos in particular, it was as if they'd come home. They were a part of Alma and Juan Carlos was busy bringing them back into the fold. There was sincere joy in all of them at being here. Even Rafe. Though he was torn, with his love of Miami and his lover in Key West.

"Hello, Bella. What's up?"

She led him to one of the wrought iron benches nestled next to a flowering jasmine bush and sat down. He sat down next to her and looked at his sister for the first time in days. She smiled easily.

"You seem distracted lately and I'm going to do the meddling kid sister thing and ask why."

"I'm trying to figure out how to be royal after years of being so ordinary," he said. It was his pat answer, and he'd been saying it to himself for so long that when he finally heard it out loud he realized how hollow the words were.

Maybe Bella wouldn't notice.

"Yeah, right," she said. "I'd think you'd have a better excuse than that."

He wasn't in the mood to discuss this with her and started to get up. But she stopped him with her hand on his sleeve.

"I think you have someone back home," she said. "A woman who isn't from here and can't fit into this world."

"I have a lot of women back home," he said.

"Lying to me is one thing," she said with that honesty that made him feel exposed. "But lying to yourself is something else. If you have a woman, then marry her. Then take the throne."

If it were as simple as that he'd do it. But he knew from the meetings he'd been in that a smooth transition was needed. He was expected to marry someone who'd strengthen the Montoros' claim to the throne. Someone who'd make the people of Alma and its enemies believe that the restored monarchy would be around for a long time. That they were the only ones who could return Alma to its former glory.

And a bartender from Key West who didn't know who her father was wasn't going to be approved by the committee.

"Thanks, Bella, but it's not that simple," he said.

"It is if you know what you want."

He realized anew that he was lost. Hearing his little sister boil down his problems and come up with a solution was humbling. But he couldn't do what she suggested. He hadn't even seen Emily since he'd learned he was going to be a father. Their daily calls were great, but he needed to hold her in his arms again. Look into her eyes and see what, if anything, she felt for him.

Aside from lust. Sex between them had been raw and electric since the moment they'd met, and now he had to figure out if what he felt for her was more than that. Was he just using her as an escape to get away from the mantle of kingship that he didn't want? And he *really* didn't want it.

Because if he did it would be easier to make a decision about Em. Force her to take some money from him and set her and the baby up and then keep his distance. But he wanted more than that.

"I…thank you," he said.

"For what? I didn't say anything that you don't already know for yourself. Tell me what's going on."

He shook his head. "You've done enough."

"I have?"

"Yes. I just needed to hear someone else say it. I've been afraid of screwing up and embarrassing the family so I've stopped being myself. I've been trying to be regal and we both know I'm not."

She laughed and punched his shoulder. "You're not succeeding at being regal. I saw you roll your eyes when the Gomezes mentioned what beautiful babies you and Dita would have."

"I thought I showed a lot of restraint by not mentioning that the babies would probably be born with a tail and cloven hooves."

Bella laughed. "You're not that evil."

"Imp, you think it's funny having someone come after you because of your position? Wait until the princess royal or whatever title they decide on for you has to make a good marriage."

"Don't even joke about that, Rafe. I'm too young and pretty to be tied down to a man." She batted her eyelashes.

He hugged her close. "Damned straight. Besides, only one of us should be shackled by this monarchy thing. I'll do what's needed to protect you, Gabe and the rest of our family."

"Don't sacrifice yourself for us. We're stronger than you think we are."

"I know that. But I want you both to be happy."

EMILY'S SHIFT WAS LONG. Her feet hurt and she felt as if she was going to be sick until she stepped outside into the balmy June air. It was only eleven—so not that late—as she walked through the crowds toward her cottage.

She had been looking forward to chatting with Rafe all evening. But once again she'd seen him on the local news on one of the televisions at the bar. He was with a blonde woman and she hoped like hell that it was just for publicity purposes. But a part of her realized that she had no hold on the king of Alma.

But that Rafe was different from the man who she spoke on the phone with and she hadn't asked about the woman because she really didn't want to hear that his obligation to his family might force him to marry someone else.

The US press, especially the local Miami reporters, loved anything to do with royalty and since the Montoros were raised in America, the media were obsessed with them. It seemed she didn't have to try too hard to find out about Rafael, Gabriel and Bella. She learned about the private schools they'd gone to and had seen Rafe's college roommate on CNN talking about how the Montoros were all about family.

She got it. As far as the media were concerned Rafe was going to make a great king. It had been a long time since an American had claimed a foreign throne, and despite the fact that most patriots were all about democracy they did like a fairy-tale story like this now and then.

She rubbed the back of her neck as she let herself into her house. She kicked off her Vans and left the lights off as she walked to her bedroom. She'd wanted him all day.

Looked forward to the time when she could be alone and talk to him, and now she wasn't sure.

She wasn't sure how much more of Rafe she could take before he became so embedded in her soul that she wouldn't be able to survive without him.

She was sure part of it was the hormones from being pregnant with his baby. The other part was that she'd never had this kind of interaction with a guy. They talked every day. Most of her boyfriends had been busy with their own lives and had called only when they were horny or lonely.

Which had suited her.

She'd never wanted anything solid and lasting until now.

Until Rafe. And he wasn't available for her to claim.

Her phone rang. She glanced down at the Skype icon and knew that it was Rafe doing what she'd asked: calling her for a video chat this time.

She missed him. She didn't want to.

But she swiped her finger across the screen, unlocking the phone to answer the call. The image on the other end was dark with just a pool of light in the background.

Her own image popped up as a dark square in the bottom corner of the screen. She hadn't turned on the light.

"I guess you changed your mind about seeing me," he said.

"I just got home," she said. She fell backward on her bed and reached over to flick on the lamp on her nightstand. "I can't see you, either."

He turned the phone and she saw him sprawled on his back on a big bed with some sort of padded brocade headboard behind him. His shirt was unbuttoned and he had one arm stretched up over his head. He was holding the phone up above him with his other hand.

"Better?"

She sighed. She shouldn't do this late at night when her

defenses were down. And they were down. She was feeling mopey and alone. Her mom was due back tomorrow and maybe that would help. But for tonight she had Rafe.

"I miss you."

"You do?"

"I do. You look like you had a formal event tonight," she said. She'd seen him on the news entering a gala with the blonde on his arm earlier this evening.

"I did. Listen, if you saw any pictures on the news of me with a woman, it was just state business. She's nothing to me."

"Does she know that?" Emily asked. Because that woman had seemed as though she had her claws sunk into him.

"Would I be here with you if she didn't?" he asked.

She looked at him in the shadows. "Would you?"

"No. I thought you knew me better than that," he said.

She had made him angry but she needed to know if he was the kind of man who'd cheat on her. "We don't have anything official between us. I...are you a one-woman man?"

He leaned in toward the camera, so close she could see the green and dark brown flecks in his hazel eyes. "I am."

"Then stop having your picture taken with foreign blondes," she said.

He sighed. "It's not that easy. She keeps showing up everywhere I am."

Emily was tempted to go to Alma and—

Do what?

She was Rafe's baby mama, not his fiancée.

This was something she had no idea how to handle. But she wanted him to be hers. For the world to know that he belonged to her. But she didn't want to say that to him. Admit that all these late calls had made her start to fall for him.

"How was your day?" She toed off her socks and grabbed a second pillow to prop her head up.

"Interesting. My baby sister is worried about me."

"Why?"

"She said I don't seem happy," Rafe said.

"Are you?"

"Happy isn't exactly something I aspire to. I think that is a path to crazy," he said. "I'd like to be content."

"Happiness equals crazy?" she asked. "I've never thought that."

"I mean trying to be happy all the time. Life isn't about always being happy. There are quiet moments and the normal grind. That's what makes the happy times memorable."

"So is this a quiet moment?"

"It's so much more than that, Red. You're my reward for being the good son and doing what's expected of me here in Alma."

It wasn't what she wanted to hear, but it warmed her up and made the feelings that had been dogging her all night dissolve. She realized that she'd been edgy and mopey because she didn't like seeing Rafe with that blonde woman.

"I was jealous."

"Of?"

"That blonde." She made a face and put her thumb over the part of her phone that showed her end of the video chat. She didn't want to see her own face.

"Don't be."

"I want this to be light and easy, Rafe. But it's not. It hasn't been for a while."

"You want the truth, Red?" he asked, rolling to his side and propping his phone up on something so that he wasn't holding it any more.

"You know I do."

"This hasn't been light or easy since the moment I first kissed you. I'm not a one-night-stand guy and we both know you don't take guys home all the time. We've both been trying to pretend that it was nothing more than a moment, but I think it's time we stopped pretending."

She swallowed hard. Had she been pretending? Was that why she'd been jealous and lonely?

"What do you suggest?"

"That we figure out what we both want. I know I want you. Not just for sex."

"Me, too."

CHAPTER SIX

It was somehow easier to talk to her when he saw her face. She looked good, with that smattering of freckles across the bridge of her nose and the weary hope in her blue eyes. She seemed to want him to be the man he wasn't sure he could be.

He wanted to be a man of his word, but that was complicated. Making promises to her was out of the question because he had to figure out a solution that would take care of his family's future. Or did he? He was tired of walking on the tightrope between what he wanted and what he should do.

He thought of his mom, who'd divorced their father when Bella turned eighteen. It was as if his mother had served her time raising them and was ready to do something for herself. He didn't want to wait like that... Besides, assuming the throne was for life.

"What are you thinking? You got all intense all of a sudden," Emily said.

"I was thinking about my mom," he admitted quietly. "How she raised us until Bella was eighteen and then moved on with her life. What kind of mom will you be?"

"Not that kind. But I'm independent," she said. "I imagine my child will be too."

"It's our child."

"You're going to be ruling Alma, Rafe. I'm the one who will raise our child."

He didn't like her point. But he knew better than to argue it. He wasn't in a position to win. And he was tired of losing.

"You look nice. No sign of the pregnancy yet," he said.

"Thanks. A Shady Harry's T-shirt and jeans aren't exactly haute couture but they suit me."

They did suit her. He wanted to suit her as well. Be a part of that life. Yet he was torn. How could he be?

"I've got to get changed. I smell like the bar."

"Can I watch?" he asked. Seeing her brought all of his senses into sharp focus and made the life he'd been living these last few days look as if it were in black and white. He had been on autopilot doing what was expected of him and doing it well, but now he truly felt the first spark of excitement…of life.

"Is that what you want?" she asked. There was a teasing note in her voice and he caught a glimpse of the woman who'd bound him with his own shirt in South Beach.

If she only knew the power she wielded over him.

"It is."

"Well okay then," she said. "It's not going to be very exciting. I mean I've never worked in a high-end strip club or anything."

He shook his head. "I didn't think you had."

"Have you been to one?" she asked.

"Are you going to go on a feminist rant if I say yes?" he asked.

"No, I'm not. The women who work in places like that usually earn a good living. And it's their choice to make," she said. "So you have been to one."

He shrugged. Some nights that was where the crowd

he ran with back in Miami had ended up. "It's not my favorite place to hang out."

"That's good to know. You should know I've only gotten undressed in front of a few guys."

"You should know I have no interest in any of the other men in your life," he said. "I want to be the only one."

He knew he had no right to say that. That he might not even be able to claim Emily but, hell, this was the twenty-first century and he wasn't going to marry another "suitable" woman when he felt this strongly about her.

She touched her finger to the screen and he imagined he felt her light touch on his face. "As of right now you are."

She got to her feet and his screen was filled with the image of her ceiling until she got to the bathroom. She flipped on the light switch and she propped the phone up on the counter. "I need a shower, too."

"How about a bath? If I were there, I'd fill that big clawfoot tub of yours with warm water and bubbles and have it waiting for you when you got home."

He wanted to take care of her. She was the first person outside of the circle of his family he'd ever felt this way about.

"Okay. Give me a few minutes."

"Don't take your clothes off until I can see you."

"Do you have a bathtub in your big palace?" she asked. "I saw some pictures of your entire family walking around the gardens on CNN last night. Looked nice."

"I do have a very nice bathroom here. The tub is controlled by a computer," he said.

"Join me in the bath?" she asked. There was a hint of vulnerability in her words. He found it both enchanting and a little bit unnerving. Emily was a very strong woman who didn't really need anyone. But tonight he caught a glimpse behind that attitude and saw that she did need him.

That made him feel like Atlas, strong enough to carry the weight of the earth on his shoulders. And like the mythological being he couldn't simultaneously protect Emily and shoulder his burden. He had no idea where any of this was going. He was used to being the strong one. The one who knew exactly what needed to be done—

And he did this time. He needed to let her go, but for once wanted to be selfish and keep her. For tonight he was going to do just that.

"Okay," he said, getting up and going to his own opulently appointed bathroom. He selected the temperature from a computerized keypad on the wall and soon the water started flowing into the tub. He flicked on the overhead light that just illuminated the tub and then glanced back at his phone screen to see where Emily was.

She was sitting on the edge of her tub biting her lower lip as she fiddled with the taps.

Then she stood up and undid her jeans.

"Hey. Not so fast, Red. I want to see every inch of you," he said.

"Fair enough. Take your shirt off. Not that you don't look sexy with it unbuttoned and your chest showing."

He'd undone his shirt earlier because he felt uncomfortable and hadn't really known what to wear for a video call with her. He lifted his arms. "You see these buttons?"

"Yeah?"

"You're supposed to undo them first. That way I don't have to rip the shirt," he said.

"I like it when you rip your shirt," she said with a wink. "In fact the next time I see you I've got a new shirt for you to try on. One that is made of tougher material."

Arching one eyebrow at her, he tossed his shirt toward the corner and then stood there, feeling a bit ridiculous.

"Damn, you look good," she said.

The open admiration in her eyes as she looked at him made him feel ten feet tall. He rubbed his hand over his chest. And then flexed his muscles for her. He heard her intake of breath. And suddenly all those reps he did at the gym were worth it. He worked out because he lived in South Beach and owned a very successful business. He wasn't about to have a photo of himself looking like a sloth turn up anywhere. But knowing she liked his body gave him another reason to do it.

"Your turn. I want to see your...muscles."

She laughed. "I did help unload a beer delivery this afternoon, so I think my arms are looking a little buffer than usual."

He frowned. "Why are you unloading anything? Harry should know better."

"He does. He was pissed when he got there. But the delivery guys weren't our usual ones and they were piling the beer in the sun...no one else was there. Harry ripped them a new one and they apologized to me."

Good. Still, Rafe didn't like that she'd had to deal with those guys. She should be pampered while she carried his child.

She pulled the Shady Harry's T-shirt up over her head and he immediately noticed her breasts swelling around the sides of the cups of her bra. She reached behind her back and unhooked the bra and let it slid down her arms and onto the floor. Her nipples looked bigger and a darker shade of pink than he remembered. Signs of the changes his baby was having on her body. She skimmed her hand down to her stomach and he noticed just the smallest bump there.

She unhooked her jeans and pushed them down her legs with her panties. And just like that, she was standing there naked.

He touched the image on his phone and realized that seeing her like this was a double-edged sword. He wanted to be there with her.

And that's when he came to his decision. He was going home first thing in the morning. He didn't care what the parliament thought; he needed to be back in Florida with Emily. Even if it was just for a few days.

"Dammit, Red. You get more beautiful each time I see you naked."

She blushed, and he observed that the color started at the top of her breasts and swept up her neck to her cheeks. She shook her head. "I had to unbutton my jeans at work tonight. It's not like they are too tight...well, okay, they are, but it was uncomfortable for the first time."

"I can see the little bump," he said. He traced his finger over her body on the screen. The changes were small, but this was their child making itself known in their lives. Well, mostly hers as of right now. He was missing out.

"I see a little bump in your pants as well," she said with a wink.

He guessed she didn't want to talk about the pregnancy, and he let her change the subject. "Little? Woman, look again."

He undid his pants and carefully shoved them down his legs until he stood there naked. He heard her sharp intake of breath and then her wolf whistle. She was good for his ego. And she kept things light. Was he ever seeing the real woman?

"Not so little."

"Not around you," he said.

"I didn't mean for this to be phone sex," she said.

"I never mean for it to turn into sex with you, but damn, Red, you turn me on like no one else ever has."

She smiled at me. "I feel the same. But I smell like the bar."

"Not to me. To me you smell like Florida sunshine and a day at the beach."

She walked over to the tub with the phone, her heart-shaped face filling the screen. Her eyes were sparkling, and unless he missed his guess, she was happy. While he might not think happiness was a good goal for every second of his life, he was glad to see her smiling.

She propped her phone up on the ledge of the tub and then climbed in. She closed her eyes and let her head fall back against the pillow she had there. The edges of her long hair fell into the water. She looked like his mermaid.

His.

He climbed into his tub, balled a towel up behind his head. The water felt hot and luxurious against his sensitive skin.

"This is nice. But I'm always by myself," she said.

"Me, too."

"Even in that crowd that's always with you?" she asked.

"Yeah."

"If I was there, I'd climb in behind you and rub your shoulders," she said. "You seem stressed."

"I'd like that. But only because I'd feel your naked breasts against my back."

"Maybe I'd lean over you and kiss your neck. Nibble on your earlobe. I know you like that, too."

He stretched his legs to make room for his growing erection and rubbed his hand over his own chest. He wished she were here so he could touch her. But his imagination was doing a good job of filling in the gaps.

"I'd probably pull you around in my arms and kiss you. I can't resist your mouth," he said.

"That's good. I like the way you taste, Rafe. No other guy I've kissed has tasted so right."

Damned straight. He wanted to be the only guy who felt right to her. In all things. A wave of pure possessiveness overwhelmed him and he knew he wanted to claim her as his. But this damned situation with his family was keeping him from doing it.

"I'd put my hands on your waist and lift you up a bit until I could reach your breasts. Are they more sensitive now?"

She nodded.

"Show me."

"How?" she asked. She shifted up on her knees and leaned toward the phone. "I like your mouth on me."

Damn. He did, too. Her nipples felt so right in his mouth, and nothing made him harder than when he swirled his tongue around them and she gripped the back of his head.

"Touch yourself. Run your finger around your nipple and pinch it. Pretend I'm biting you," he said as she shifted back. "Just talking has made your nipples hard."

She nodded and gave him a slow smile. "I've been thinking about you touching me. Remembering how your mouth felt against my nipple."

"Show me," he said again.

She brought her hand up from the water, the droplets sparkling in the light as they fell from her arm. Then she cupped her breast and trailed her finger around her nipple. It puckered as she touched it, and he got even harder watching her as her head fell back and she let out a moan.

"Feel good?" he asked, his voice husky and low. His skin was so sensitive that each lap of the water brought him closer to the edge. He was going to come. But he didn't want to until she did. He wanted to keep watching her for as long as he could. And draw out the pleasure so he could feel as if they were together. He needed this. Needed her.

He'd been trying to deny it, but there it was. The truth that he'd been afraid to admit to himself.

She was cupping both of her breasts and he groaned as he reached for the screen of his phone and touched it. He remembered the way she felt underneath him. How her limbs felt wrapped around his.

"Not as good as when you do touch me," she said. "If I were there I'd caress your chest and then slowly tease you by working my fingers lower."

"When you do that it makes it difficult for me to think," he admitted.

"Really?"

He nodded. Words were sort of beyond him at this moment.

"Are you hard for me?" she asked.

"I am." He stroked himself, remembering how she fit him like a glove when he thrust into her.

"Show me," she said. "Let me see how hard you are."

Her words were like a velvet lash on his skin and he shuddered. This was excruciating. He wanted to come inside her and each time she said something so sexual he couldn't contain his groans.

"Red…"

"Show me, Rafe. I want to see you. See how much you want me."

He groaned, but did as she asked, shifting until he was out of the water and she could see him. He stroked his hand up and down his shaft.

"Swipe your finger over the top," she said. "Pretend it's my tongue on you."

He did as she instructed and then shuddered as he realized how close to the edge he was.

"Are you ready for me? Show me," he said.

She parted her legs and showed him. Pushed her finger up inside and moaned as she did so. "It's not the same as when you do it."

"Does it feel good?" he asked.

"It does."

"Come for me, Red."

This was too intimate and yet not intimate enough.

"I want to touch you, Rafe. If I were there I'd take you inside me. I need you," she said.

"Me, too, Red."

She moaned. "I'm so ready for it. For you."

He was, too. He remembered the way it had felt the last time they were together. How she'd gripped him as soon as he entered her body. How deep he'd gone and the way her eyes had opened and he'd met her gaze. Felt her wrapped around him all the way to his soul.

"Rafe."

Hearing her name on his lips made him come. He closed his eyes and put his head back as his orgasm washed over him. He opened them to see her doing the same. She gave him a slow, sexy smile.

"That's my kind of bath," she said, smiling.

"Mine, too," he said. "When I get home I want to do this again."

"But together in the same tub."

He hit the button to drain the tub and got to his feet. She stayed where she was, watching him, and he realized that in her eyes he was enough. He didn't have to prove anything to her. Or at least he hoped he didn't have to. Because he was coming to realize he didn't know who he was anymore. He hadn't known in a long, long time.

"Come to bed with me, Red. Let's talk until we both fall asleep."

She nodded. She got out of the tub and dried herself off and he just watched, absently toweling himself dry. He caught his breath when she padded naked back to her bed and climbed between the sheets. She'd washed the sheets but not the pillow case he'd slept on.

"This pillow smells like you," she said.

"It does?"

"Yes. I've been pretending you are here with me every night... Tomorrow I'm going to deny that. But tonight I need you here with me."

He understood. When the sun was out there were oceans between them and problems that wouldn't be easily solved. And while he wanted to do what Bella said and put himself first—maybe marry Emily so that the rest of the world would have to accept her—he knew she wouldn't go for that. She didn't want a man who could be hers only halfway.

And that was all he could offer right now. But he knew he wanted to call her his and he needed to figure out a way.

He climbed into his own bed and curled on his side. "I don't have a pillow that smells like you."

"Sorry, babe."

She smiled sleepily at him and he watched her as she started to drift off to sleep. "Thank you for being here tonight."

"You're welcome, Red."

He watched over her until he knew she was sound asleep and snoring slightly. Maybe he kept the line open for longer than he should have before disconnecting the call.

He knew he couldn't do this any longer. He was tired of making do with phone calls to Emily. He'd thought that the video call would make it easier but it hadn't. Instead it made him long to touch her. Really touch her.

He got out of his bed, pacing to the window and looking

out at the sea. The ocean was endless and as he glanced up at the moon that was almost setting he realized that in Emily's part of the world the moon was rising. He wanted to be in the same place she was. See if there was anything really between them.

Honestly he knew this wasn't real. How could it be? He was painting her the way he wanted her to be. And not to be oedipal or anything, but he was making Emily into the woman he wanted while imagining her as the mother he never had.

He got dressed and walked out of his room down the hall to Gabe's. He figured Gabe would be easier to talk to than Juan Carlos. But there was no answer when he knocked.

He rubbed the back of his neck.

Damn.

He walked to Juan Carlos's room and wasn't surprised when his cousin answered the door wearing a dressing gown with the Alma royal seal monogramed on the breast.

"What is it?"

"I… I have to return to the States."

"Why? You know that royal protocol states—"

"Screw royal protocol, J.C. I had a life before Alma came to us and I can't just walk away from it."

"You gave your word. Our family gave our word. You are the oldest."

"I wish I wasn't."

"Stop being so selfish. This country needs a leader. It needs someone who can take it from the isolated kingdom it's been into the twenty-first century. You are the man."

"I didn't choose this," Rafe said. "I'm not sure I want this."

"Too bad, Rafael, you're birthright has brought you to this. Sure, it would have been easier if we'd been brought up on the island but that doesn't make our legacy any less important."

Juan Carlos would be so much better at this than him, Rafe thought. But he wasn't from the right family line and Rafe really couldn't—

"I have to return to the States," he said again. "I'm the one who will be king so my decision is final."

"This is ridiculous."

"Why?"

"Because already I can see that your loyalty isn't to your people. And they will see it too."

"I can't take care of the people of Alma until I figure out this part of my life."

"Is there a woman?"

"Yes. Yes, there is, and I haven't had a chance to resolve anything with her."

"Is she…would the court approve a marriage to her?"

Rafe doubted it. Hell, he wasn't even sure he wanted to marry her. He had to get back to her and figure this all out.

"I have no idea if I want to marry her or not. I need some time to myself to figure this out."

"Hell. I'll go with you."

"I don't want the entire family to know," Rafe said. "Why would you come with me?"

"As you said, you can't be a good ruler until you know where you belong. I want that, Rafe. I know I seem all tied up with royal protocol, but I want what is best for all of us. You're like a brother to me."

"You are to me as well," Rafe said. Juan Carlos had grown up in their home after his parents had died. "I do need to be in Miami to take care of the details of the new shipping deal I just signed. I will let the court and the coronation committee know that's why I'm returning."

"I will back you up," Juan Carlos said. "Just be sure you make the right decision."

Rafe nodded. His impromptu decision to leave had to be delayed until he could talk to the court advisors and his family. Since it was early morning it would take time for the entire Montoro clan who were in Alma to be ready to go.

But sure enough, later that day, they were all on the plane and headed toward Miami.

CHAPTER SEVEN

Emily went to Key Koffee for a cup of decaf and sat at the corner table again. Last night with Rafe had been different. It had been fun, but also, in the safety of the darkness and with the distance between them, she felt he'd shared more of himself than he had before.

Caution, she warned herself.

Her mom was always warning her about racing headlong into action before thinking about it first. But she felt as if it was too late to change. And last night had made her fall a little more for Rafe.

Which was probably why she was up early even though she had to work later. But her mom was also due to dock at the marina at nine, and Emily wanted to be there to greet her.

"Give me a double espresso and a lemon poppy-seed muffin to go as well as my usual order," Emily said to Cara behind the bar.

"Sure thing. Feeling hungry this morning?"

"A little, but the extra stuff is for my mom. She's back in port today," she told Cara.

"How about your man?" Cara asked.

Emily shook her head. "I don't have a man."

She couldn't claim Rafe as her own until he indicated he was ready for that. And she knew despite their closeness when they were alone that he wasn't. That knowledge sort of tinged her day. She frowned a little. The smell of the espresso was strong this morning, and she felt bile rising in the back of her throat.

She swallowed hard to keep from getting sick and then realized it wasn't going to work. She ran for the bathroom but made it only as far as the hallway before she began retching. She forced herself to keep moving into the bathroom and threw up. She was heavy and aching and knew this wasn't one of the times when she could say she was enjoying her pregnancy.

Cara followed her into the bathroom with a wet towel. After Emily rinsed her mouth and splashed water on her face, Cara walked her back to her table. Emily felt as if everyone was staring at her. Cara just smiled at them.

"She's pregnant. You don't worry about our food."

Everyone nodded and went back to their papers and electronic devices.

"I sort of wasn't planning on telling anyone yet," Emily said.

"Sorry, Em. But I can't have people thinking it's my food."

"It's okay," Emily said.

"Your man should be here with you," Cara said in a kind way. "I saw you two together. He's not the kind of man who'd just walk away."

Cara tucked a strand of Emily's hair behind her ear. "Have you told him?"

She wasn't that close to Cara, but they were friends. They'd gone to the same high school and had even taken a road trip to Georgia together one time. But she didn't want to discuss Rafe with her. "Yes. It's complicated."

"Fair enough. Park yourself right there. I'm going to get your order for you."

Emily looked up and noticed a man watching her. The same guy who had been eavesdropping on her telephone conversation with Rafe the other day.

"How you feeling?" he asked, coming over with a packet of Club crackers that they kept on the tables for when Key Koffee serve conch chowder in the afternoon. "These always helped my wife when she was expecting."

She smiled her thanks and took them, weakly opening the pack and taking out a cracker. She munched on one and tipped her head back as her body stopped rioting and started to calm down.

"Are you reading this?" he asked.

She glanced down at the *Miami Herald,* which was flipped open to the society page with a picture of Rafe and his family in Alma.

"No."

"I can't believe how obsessed everyone is with that family," the guy said. "I'm Stan, by the way."

"Emily," she said. "Well, it's a fairy tale, isn't it? American royalty becomes real royalty."

"True enough. I've heard that Rafe comes down to Key West," Stan said.

It seemed to her that he was fishing for information. She didn't know if he was some obsessed royal watcher or just making conversation. "I guess he does. It's not that uncommon."

"No it's not. But surely now that he's going to be king he won't be," Stan added.

"I have no idea," Emily admitted.

"Mind if I take this paper?"

"Be my guest," she said.

"Thanks," he said, walking out.

"Here's your breakfast to go," Cara said, coming over. "What did he want?"

"The newspaper," Emily said. She started to get up but Cara pushed her back down. "Sit for a little while. I called Harry to come and get you."

"Cara."

"What? You're family, Em. We take care of our own here," she reminded her.

She felt tears burn the back of her eyes and blinked so they didn't fall. She'd always felt as if Key West was her home, ever since she was three years old and her mother moved them there. The people she knew were like family to her, but she had always figured it was a one-way street. The feelings of a girl left too many times by a mother whose job was her life, her obsession.

"Thanks, Cara. But I'm a big girl."

"Even big girls deserve to be looked after," Harry said, walking into the coffee shop and approaching their table. "We got time for me to grab a cup of coffee?"

"No need to wait, Harry," Cara said, handing him a cup and a bakery bag.

Unless Emily missed her guess, that bakery bag would have a toasted everything bagel in it. Cara was right. They were all family.

This place was as much a part of her as the baby growing inside her. And though she didn't need the reassurance, it was nice to know that she wasn't alone. That if Rafe made the choice that any sane man would and took the throne of Alma half a world away from her, she'd still have family around her. Her baby would grow up with the family she'd chosen for herself and not the one she'd been born into. The family her mother had chosen for them when she'd moved them to Key West.

"You okay, kiddo?" Harry asked.

"Just morning sickness."

"Another thing that I will bring up to Rafe Montoro the next time he shows his face here."

RAFE STRETCHED HIS long legs out in front of him as he settled in for the flight. His cousin Juan Carlos—the one in the family who was the best suited for royal life since he seemed to know so much about it—sat across from him reading a book on the history of Alma from the 1970s to today.

His father, brother and sister were all sitting in the back of the plane talking quietly amongst themselves. They were happy enough to follow his lead especially when he mentioned that the oil deal needed his attention in Miami.

Rafe had been surprised by Juan Carlos's understanding but now he realized he shouldn't have been. He knew his cousin as well as he knew Gabe…though he had to admit that he'd known both men better when they were children. But the bond among all of them was still strong. And Rafe felt less isolated that he had before. Felt a little more as if his family had his back.

Rafe read the book last week, since the government people wanted to make sure that everyone in the Montoro camp was familiar with the past. The common consensus being that maybe then they wouldn't make the same mistakes again. Rafe didn't want to have to flee the country in the middle of the night and start over with nothing.

At least his great-grandfather had his wife by his side, and his family. Something that was becoming more and more important to Rafe.

"Juan, what would you do if you were going to be king?" Rafe asked. "I'm tempted to invest Montoro Enterprises money into the manufacturing sector so that Alma isn't just reliant on oil."

"That's a start. They really need stability so that Alma's

citizens will start staying on the island instead of emigrating to countries in the EU. I think we should try to become a member of the EU as well," Juan Carlos said.

"It's one of the prime minister's top priorities. He has me scheduled to go to Brussels next month for meetings on the subject," Rafe said, rubbing the back of his neck.

"I can go with you if you like," Juan Carolos said. "I'm not as impatient as you are at the negotiating table. Of course, you are always very shrewd at getting the best deal for Montoro Enterprises."

"That would be great. I'd love to have you there with me," Rafe said. One thing about his family that had been made clear during the last few weeks as they'd traveled to Alma and gotten a handle on their new lives was how they all banded together. "When is Tia Isabella going to join us in Alma?"

"Soon, I hope," Juan Carlos said. Juan Carlos's grandmother suffered from Parkinson's and had her good days and her bad days. "We are waiting for her doctors to okay the visit."

"How is she doing?" Rafe asked. "You talk to her nurse every day, don't you?"

"Yes, I do. I think the thought of returning to Alma has rallied her spirits, and though medically I'd have to say there have been no changes, she seems healthier."

Rafe smiled to himself. The very thing that felt like a burden to him was a dream come true to Tia Isabella. She had longed to return to her home for decades and now it was possible.

That almost made his royal sacrifice worthwhile. But there was also a lot to be said for the old-world charm of Playa del Onda. And for Juan Carlos's excitement over their all being part of the royal aristocracy again as well.

It just made everything more difficult for Rafe. He

wanted to keep his family happy. He was the eldest and had the power to do it. But then he remembered Emily and he was torn.

Had been torn for too long. When he got to Miami he needed to see her and figure this entire thing out.

"Do you think that the government would accept a commoner as my wife?" Rafe asked his cousin. They were still negotiating the constitution that Alma's parliament had brought to them. Rafe had been asking for little changes because he wanted to see how far they would go to get him and his family back in the country.

"Is your woman a commoner?" Juan Carlos asked.

"Not many royals in the States, Juan Carlos." He didn't want to talk about Emily with anyone else. Not yet. Why then did he keep bringing her up? He clearly needed to talk even if he didn't want to. Not until he had her sorted out. God, she'd kill him if she knew he thought that way about her.

"I don't know. I think they want you to marry a woman who will reinforce the monarchy, and a commoner wouldn't do that," Juan Carlos said at last.

Rafe nodded at his cousin and then leaned back and closed his eyes. He'd figured as much. There was no way to have it both ways. Why was he still trying to?

Because he couldn't walk away from Emily.

There it was: the truth he'd been trying to pretend didn't exist for too long. And letting his family down, well, that wasn't something he was prepared to do, either. He wasn't even sure if he walked away from the throne that they would let him keep his job at Montoro Enterprises. Though truth be told, he was a genius at making money, so he had no doubt he could start his own company and make it a success.

But that would mean walking away from everything

and everyone. His family was so deeply rooted in his life, he truly wasn't sure what he'd do without them. When they'd lived in the Miami area, he saw them every day at their Coral Gables compound. He worked hard for all of them so that they wouldn't have to worry.

That was why he hesitated. Then there was Tia Isabella. With her deteriorating health, Rafe didn't really want to do anything to upset her. If he walked away, would he find a way to make peace with the family before her illness got the better of her? Bella would be forced into a difficult position as well. His father would more than likely try to come between her and Rafe, and that would cause her stress. She liked to keep the peace.

Gabriel would be none too pleased with him. Gabe lived a nice and easy lifestyle, enjoying the many beautiful women who flocked to Miami. No-strings relationships were his MO.

Rafe laughed to himself. Gabe always did whatever the hell he wanted. He'd be plenty pissed at Rafe if he walked away from the throne and Gabe had to take it. That would be a nightmare for all concerned. His younger brother was a player. Not the image that Alma wanted for their new king.

So Rafe was back to the exact same position he'd been in since he left Miami. Except this time he was leaning more toward Emily. Hell, last night had changed something between them.

He no longer saw her as the fun-loving bartender who had gotten pregnant, but more as Emily, the woman who was going to be the mother to their child.

Their child. If he had a son he'd be Rafael V. Or would he? Would Emily want to name him something else? There was still so much for them to discuss.

He closed his eyes, trying to picture what their child

would look like. Would the baby have his dark hair and eyes or Emily's bright blue ones? He tried to picture the little tyke, maybe with her red hair and his hazel eyes.

He wanted to be a part of that. Be a part of his child's life. He had to find a way to have it all. Perhaps he needed introduce Emily to his family so they could start to get to know her. Once that happened, they would be on his side. And marrying a commoner wouldn't be such a big issue.

At first Emily might be reluctant about this plan of action, but Rafe was confident he could change her mind and bring her around to his way of thinking.

He'd seen that look in her eyes as she'd drifted off to sleep last night. She cared for him. He was gambling that she wanted him in her life as much as he wanted to be there.

He'd never been much of a gambling man. He preferred to take risks where he could control the outcome. But there was no controlling Em. She was a force unto herself and no matter what happened, she was never going to be coerced into doing anything she wasn't comfortable with.

EMILY, HER MOM and Harry spent a pleasant day together at her house. It was nice to forget about everything and just enjoy having her mom home.

Jessica Fielding had the same blue eyes as Emily but her hair was blond and cut short in a low-maintenance bob. She'd had a look of mild concern on her face ever since she docked earlier today. "So how far along are you?" she asked.

"About eight weeks. I'm not really showing yet but have lots of morning sickness," Emily said as her mom got up and brought her a glass of homemade lemonade and a gingersnap. Emily had been ordered to sit on the padded chaise longue in the shade of a big magnolia tree in the backyard while Harry manned the grill preparing fish for their dinner and her mom bustled around doing things for Emily that she could do herself.

She'd protested at first, but then figured her mom was only in town for a few days and it was okay to let her spoil her. Well, fetching drinks and fixing dinner was probably going to be the extent of the spoiling. Her mom wasn't one of those in-your-face, hands-on parents.

"Tell me about the father," her mom said. "Is he totally out of the picture?"

Emily took a sip of her lemonade. "Not entirely. Was my dad when you were pregnant?"

"Em," Jessica said.

"Mom, I want to know more about him. I'm not going to suddenly show up on his doorstep—how could I? Is he even alive?" These were the questions she'd kept hidden away for years but the truth was, she needed to know now more than ever. She'd always wanted to know for herself but really felt as if she had to know the answers to share with your child.

"No, you can't show up on his doorstep, Emily. He's dead. He died when you were three," Jessica said at last. She rubbed her hand over her forehead and Emily almost felt bad for asking about him.

But she had a right to know. Someday her child was going to want to know about Rafe, and Emily planned to have the answers ready.

"Why didn't you ever tell me this?"

"You never asked."

"I didn't ask because you seemed sad whenever I said anything about my father," Emily said.

"Sorry, sweetie, I just thought you were too young to understand and then as you got older you never brought it up so I kept quiet."

"Is that why we moved here?" Emily asked.

"That was part of it. Also, I had the grant so I needed to live someplace where I could do my work and be home every night for you," Jessica said

She got that. Work had always been her mother's driving force. Emily had been swimming before she learned to walk and had understood boat safety by the time she was six. Her life had been on the water and as an assistant to her mother's work. The work always came first, and Em had understood that at a very early age.

Emily was beginning to think of what she would do once her baby was born, and though she hadn't talked to Harry yet, she was pretty sure she wouldn't be tending bar.

"Did he want me?" Emily asked. It was the question that had weighed on her mind for a long time.

"He did, sweetie, but he had another family. He was a married man," Jessica said at last. "He saw you from time to time before he died. But really he knew that he couldn't leave his wife."

That wasn't what she'd expected. A married man. Had her mother known he was married? It didn't fit the picture she had of her mother, of the woman she'd always thought her mother was. Then the thought struck her that she might have another family.

"Do I have siblings?" she asked, mildly alarmed by the thought of strangers who might share her DNA.

"No. His wife was infertile and they never had children. He offered to adopt you and raise you with his wife, but I couldn't let you go."

Harry left his position by the grill and went over to her mother, putting his hand on her shoulder. Emily realized now why her mom had never spoken of her father. But she was glad to finally know something about him.

She went over to her mom and hugged her tightly. Her mom hugged her back, and then kissed the top of her head.

"I love you, Mom."

"I love you too, honey. I'm sorry I never talked about him."

"It's okay," Emily said. "Thank you."

"For what?" she asked, tucking a strand of hair behind Emily's ear.

"Telling me. I hated not knowing. I always felt... Well, that doesn't matter now," Emily said. But she'd always felt an emptiness inside her where a father should be. Now she knew. Their situation had been complicated. More so than her own?

She wasn't too sure.

"Tell me about the father of your child," Jessica said.

"He's Rafael Montoro IV," Emily said. Then she realized that she always used his full name when she told people about him so they'd get why he wasn't with her. She was sort of making excuses for coming second in his life. "We had a weekend together and then I got pregnant. His family got called back to Alma to restore the monarchy before I knew I was going to have his baby."

"Harry filled me in on a few of the details via our calls on the satellite phone."

Jessica sat down on the end of the chaise longue and lifted Emily's legs, drawing them over her lap. "Well, I can see why you said it was complicated. What did he say when you told him about the baby?"

"I caught him on his way out of town, Mom. We really didn't have any time to talk. I wanted him to know he had a kid coming but I never expected anything from him."

Her mom nodded. "You're strong enough to raise the baby on your own, and you have me."

"And me," Harry said.

Emily smiled over at Harry. "I know. But I think he wants to be a part of the baby's life."

"And yours?"

She bit her lower lip. She'd been telling herself that he did, but what if she was just seeing something that wasn't there? Emotions and bonds that she wanted to see because she'd started to care about him. And not just because he was her baby's father.

"I don't know. He's been calling me every day while he's in Alma. He sent me that beautiful mermaid that's hanging in the kitchen."

Her mom smiled. "Remember when you wanted to be a mermaid?"

She nodded.

"You told him?" her mom asked. "Oh, baby, I'd hoped you wouldn't fall for a man who wasn't available."

She had, too. Of course until this afternoon she'd had no idea how much her own life might parallel her mother's, but it was clear now that the Fielding women always seemed to go for men who were already spoken for.

"I'm not sure I've fallen for him."

"You are starting to," her mom said.

"Mom." Her mom always had to push her when she wasn't ready.

"Dinner's ready, ladies," Harry said, interrupting the fight that he could sense brewing.

They went to the table and Harry served the fish her mom had caught that morning and fresh mango with grilled green onions. It was delicious and Emily forgot her ire at her mother as they finished eating.

This was turning out to be one of the best days she'd had in a while. She'd talked to Rafe this morning and felt closer to him than ever. She'd learned the details of her own parentage and felt closer to her mom than ever before.

Her mom picked up the dishes and went into the kitchen to watch the evening weather forecast, something she did every night so she'd know what to expect on the water the next day.

"You better come in here and see this," her mom said as she leaned out the window.

Emily got to her feet, looking up at the evening summer sky and wondering if it looked similar in Alma.

She stepped inside and noticed that that instead of the local fishing report the television was tuned to E! News. She'd been watching *Keeping up with the Kardashians* earlier. Now the words *Montoro Baby Mama!* were on the screen and Emily felt as if she was going to be sick.

CHAPTER EIGHT

Rafe turned his phone to flight-safe mode once they were getting ready to land. There was a tingle of excitement in the pit of his stomach as he made plans to bring Emily to his family. She was stubborn, so he knew it wouldn't be easy to convince her to leave Key West, but he was fairly confident that he had his ways of persuading her.

They landed at the private airfield the Montoros always used. As Rafe got off the plane and started walking across the tarmac, he noticed there seemed to be a swarm of reporters waiting. Had something happened in Alma in the last ten hours while he'd been on the plane? He slowed down, as did the rest of the party, all looking at one another as they flicked on their phones and scanned headlines.

Gabe was the first one to spot it and cursed under his breath.

"Your baby mama is headline news," Gabe said.

His baby mama.

Damn.

"It's not like that," he said.

Juan Carlos looked pissed but he was quiet as he simply turned away from Rafe and walked toward the hangar. He couldn't have known that the press would find out about Emily while they were in the air. Rafe shoved his hands into his pockets and rocked back on his heels.

Gabe clapped a sympathetic hand on his shoulders before following the rest of their party into the hangar. Rafe's phone finally connected and he saw he had a dozen missed calls from Emily along with seven text messages that all said the same thing. Call me.

She'd already seen the news.

Of course she had. For a brief moment he wondered if she'd leaked the news, but then he remembered how fierce she was about keeping to herself. It was doubtful that she'd rat herself out.

When Rafe got into the hangar, Gabe immediately introduced him to a tall, dapper man in a white linen suit. Geoff Standings was a British press agent who'd once worked for the British royal family. Apparently he'd been sent by the royal advisers back in Alma to meet Rafe's plane and start doing damage control.

Gabe didn't look as amused as he had a few minutes ago.

"We need to fix this," Gabe said.

"Duh."

"No, I mean if the people of Alma decide that you are too hot to touch, then I'm going to have to take your place as king. We need to fix this. Now."

"Fine. Geoff, what do you recommend? I have been planning to introduce Emily to the family, and was even thinking of having a dinner next week where she could meet the members of my family who came with me on the trip. Do you think we should get engaged? Should I marry her?"

"Well, marriage usually is the right step for an illegitimate baby. But in your case I'm going to have to figure this out. I have already sent my assistant to start researching her lineage. Maybe we can find a relation—however distant—to a royal somewhere."

"If that doesn't work?" Rafe asked.

"I think we can make a case for you as a love match. Prince William married a commoner and perhaps Alma won't mind so much if we can make her into a style icon the way Kate is."

Style icon? Rafe doubted Emily would go for that. He loved her style but it was bohemian and beachy. Not exactly what Geoff was talking about.

Geoff was frantically typing away on his smartphone. "Either way, I'm going to book you some shows so you can get out there. Yes, you need to be engaged to her. I'd like to send a press release out that says she's your fiancée, not just your 'baby mama.' Who do you think leaked this?"

Good question.

"I have to ask her before you say she's my fiancée. She might get stubborn if she sees that online or in a paper before I ask," Rafe said.

"Fair enough. Any ideas on the leak?"

"None," Rafe said. "I think she's told her mom and her boss and that's it. Neither of them would tell a reporter."

"Let me look into it and see if I can find out where the information came from. Where will you be?"

"Key West. You've got my cell number, and here is Jose's as well. He's my assistant based at Montoro Enterprises headquarters in Miami and he's at your service."

Juan Carlos returned. "I'll take the family out the front of the airport. I've had your car brought around. Resolve this, Rafe. This needs to be made right."

"I know," he said. "I'll be back in the office in a couple of days to take care of the details of the Alma shipping deal, but I need to go to Key West."

He didn't like answering to his cousin and normally wouldn't have but if Juan Carlos was upset Rafe knew the court advisors in Alma would be as well.

"I was trying to keep this under control," Rafe said.

"I realize that. That's why I'm going to help you as much as I can. Alma needs the Montoros back on the throne."

Juan Carlos gathered the rest of their family. Bella gave Rafe a hug and Gabe shook his head but clapped him on the shoulder before they headed toward the main airport area and the waiting reporters.

No one said another word as Rafe strode out of the airport to his waiting Audi. His phone rang as soon as he was inside. He synched it to Bluetooth and hit the button to answer it.

"Jose here. Have you seen the news? I'm getting calls from morning news shows asking you to come on and tell your story. What should I do?" Jose asked.

"Coordinate with Geoff. He's the PR expert that the Alma court hired to make the scandal go away. I need some media prepared and he's the expert. They are all going nuts over this. Any idea where the leak came from?"

"No, sir. She wasn't visibly pregnant when I delivered your gift and I didn't see any reporters hanging around her place."

"Thanks, Jose. I'm going to leave the phone off while I drive to Key West.

"Why don't you take the chopper? I already have it ready and waiting at the Coral Gables compound."

"I'm trying to decide if I need more time alone to clear my head," he said.

"It's up to you, sir."

If he took the chopper he'd cut his travel time in half and be at Emily's side that much sooner. But he was still not sure what he was going to say when he got there. The plans he'd been hatching as he flew back from Alma were all moot now. He was in damage control, and so was the rest of the family.

"I'll take the chopper."

"I'm turning around and will be in Coral Gables with your bag in a few minutes."

"Where were you headed?"

"Key West," Jose said. "I also have procured two jewelers to meet you. They are waiting in Coral Gables."

"Thanks, Jose." Rafe disconnected the call.

Jose had thought of everything, which was why Rafe paid him the big bucks. Still, Rafe was uncertain. Having the chopper and his bag and even a ring might make going to Key West easier for him, but he had no idea what kind of reception he was going to get when he saw Emily. How was he going to tell her that they had to be engaged? He knew he needed to have that conversation in person and not over the phone. In fact, the sooner he could get to her the better. He needed to think about what he was going to do.

With Em he tended to react first and then do damage control later. This was one time when he needed to plan with his head and not his groin. He wanted her, but he needed the details to be right. There was no more choosing between the throne and Emily.

What kind of king would the people of Alma think he was if he abandoned his child? In a way it was the perfect solution to the debate he'd been having with himself. There was no more keeping Emily and the baby hidden.

EMILY GAVE UP trying to call Rafe and convinced her mom and Harry to go home around 11:00 p.m. She changed into a big T-shirt she'd gotten during the last hurricane to hit the Keys with the slogan It Takes More Than a Little Breeze to Shake Me on it.

Harry had called his buddies at the Key West Police Department and together they'd cleared the reporters from her yard and were keeping them at the end of the street.

She'd heard a chopper fly over and hadn't turned on the local news because she was afraid she'd see her home on it.

She felt as if this story about being Rafe's "baby mama" was enough to shake her though. She had an idea that the source might be that creepy guy from the coffee shop who'd watched her and made awkward conversation with her. But how had he known about Rafe?

Not that they'd done much to keep it secret. They had been flirting at the bar that weekend he'd been on Key West. Everyone had seen them together. She guessed it wouldn't take Sherlock Holmes to figure out that she and Rafe had hooked up.

But baby mama? That was insulting. She guessed it was meant to be. If it was that creep from the coffee shop, did that rat bastard have a vendetta against Rafe? She vowed to get to the bottom of it tomorrow. She rolled to her side feeling very alone as she stared out the window.

She'd done everything to pretend that it was normal. That she wasn't bothered by the fact that he hadn't called her back.

Why hadn't he?

Surely he knew she hadn't gone to the papers. Didn't he?

There was nothing in it for her if she did. Or maybe he hadn't heard about it yet. But that seemed far-fetched to her, even if she wanted it to be true.

What if he'd decided he'd had enough and the paparazzi were the last straw? It didn't seem like the man she knew to just retreat. More than likely he was coming up with some plan. Maybe he'd ask her and the baby to leave town. Disappear for a while so he could get on with his corona-tion plans.

Tired of listening to her own thoughts, she got out of bed and wandered through her empty house to the kitchen. She found the carton of frozen yogurt she'd shoved into the back of the freezer when she got home from the grocery store earlier. She'd been trying to hide it from herself because the last time she'd opened a pint of the key lime pie flavor, she'd eaten it in one sitting.

But if ever she needed the cold comfort of fro-yo, it was tonight.

She didn't want to leave Key West, to start over on her own. But she wasn't alone, was she? She had this little pod in her belly.

She dipped her spoon into the carton and took a big scoop, putting it in her mouth as she leaned against the counter. Letting the frozen dessert melt on her tongue was bliss.

She didn't care what was happening outside her little cottage. She'd just stay here with her fro-yo until she figured out how to fix this.

She'd never met a problem she couldn't solve. It was just late-night loneliness making her feel blue. That and the fact that she was getting total radio silence from Rafe. Why didn't he return her call?

She had a feeling this was going to be one of those nights when sleep evaded her. Part of it she blamed on the habits formed by spending her entire adult life working nights, but the other part was worry. She never admitted she was scared. But she was very afraid that this thing with the news might have helped Rafe decide he didn't need her or their baby in his life.

She wasn't thinking that because he was a jerk or anything. It was just that she understood that royals, especially those in a volatile newly reestablished monarchy, probably needed to be above reproach.

Her mind went to the video chat they'd had two nights ago. He hadn't exactly been staid on that call. She guessed that was what appealed to her about him.

She rubbed her stomach as she walked into the living room. Without turning on the lights, she went to her couch and turned on the television and the DVR to watch her comfort movie. But there was a knock on her door before the opening credits started to roll. She paused it and put her frozen yogurt container on the coffee table, grabbing her baseball bat from the hall closet before she went to the front door.

She pushed aside the curtain on the small, narrow window next to the door and peeked out, not sure what she'd find.

Rafe.

Illuminated by her front porch light, he stood there in faded jeans that fit in all the right places and a T-shirt that molded to his chest like a second skin. Not very regal tonight, was he. Very American and very real, though, she thought.

She unlatched the door and let it swing open, keeping her bat in one hand.

"Rafe."

Was he really here?

"Red. Planning to hit me with that bat?" he asked, pulling her into his arms and hugging her tightly. "I'm sorry I didn't return your calls."

"Why didn't you? When did you get back to the States?" she asked. She felt shell-shocked after everything that had been going on this evening. She hated to admit it but she was very glad to see him.

"No. The bat is not for you. I thought if I found that rat bastard reporter snooping around I might take it to him. I was afraid he might have slipped past the patrolmen."

"We don't need it tonight," he said. "Can I come in?"

She stood there feeling a little aggrieved now that she knew he wasn't a threat. That Rafe was here.

"How long have you been back in the States?"

"I got in this afternoon, right about the time the baby story broke," he said.

"And you came here? But not straight here," she said. "It doesn't take that long to get here and I know you've got a helicopter."

"Can we do this inside?" he asked.

She felt the need in him to get his own way but she wasn't threatened by him at all. She stepped back and he walked in, closing the door and leaning back against it. First thing he did was take the bat and drop it on the floor. Then he lifted her off her feet with his hands on her waist.

"I missed you, Red," he said, lowering his mouth to hers and taking a kiss that left no doubt that he wasn't going to walk away from her. She had no idea what he thought their future would be, but she realized as she wrapped her arms around his shoulders that she wanted him by her side.

RAFE TOOK HIS first deep breath since he'd stepped off the plane in Miami. He was with Em, and right now that was enough. His family, who had always been his stalwart supporters, weren't really there for him now. He tucked that away for further analysis later. He knew it was important, but right now he needed to figure out this threat and convince Emily that his plan to move forward was the best one.

"I thought coming home to you was going to be the first peace I've felt in a few days," he said as he lifted his head and stepped back from her.

"I didn't realize you were coming back to me," she said.

"Are you kidding me? I've been calling you every day. What else did you think that meant?"

She bit her lower lip, reaching behind him to bolt the

door before picking up her baseball bat and leaning it against the wall. "I didn't know."

She walked down the hallway lit only by little night-lights plugged into the wall sockets, and he followed her.

All this time he'd thought he was courting her…wait a minute. Was that what he'd been doing?

Yes.

No matter how he'd tried to rationalize it, that was exactly what he'd been doing.

"That's my bad. I was trying to be cool and see if you liked me," he said as he entered her living room. The television projected a soft blue glow into the room and he noted the opened container of frozen yogurt on the coffee table.

She sat in the chair that he had fond memories of making love to her in, with her legs curled under her body. With a quick economical movement she reached over and flicked on the light on the side table.

"I think we both know I *like* you," she said.

He sat down on the ottoman in front of her and put his hands on the arms of the chair. "I'm not talking about lust. I'm talking about whether you like me for the man I am. I don't think I did much but show off the last time I was in Key West. Trying to catch your eye and show you I wasn't like all the other men in the bar."

"You did that," she said softly. "If that was you showing off, you did it very well."

He winked at her. "After all this time I do know how to present a good image."

"It worked. So is that what you were doing in Alma with the people? I saw some of the press coverage from your trip. It looks like you were falling in love with the country and the people."

"You're talking about the blonde, right?" He laughed

softly when she frowned and shook her head in denial. "Her family is nuts. They want her to marry the next king. She's not…real. It's not like when I'm with you," he said. Dita was a beautiful woman, but all the scheming with her mother made him edgy. And it was impossible to think of anything other than getting away from her.

"So what do you want from me?" Emily asked.

There it was. The million-dollar question. He had been debating it for so long and still had no answer. "Right now, I need to figure out how the media found out you were pregnant."

She nodded. "The easy stuff first."

It was interesting that she thought finding the source of the leak was going to be easy. "How is that the easy stuff? Do you know who broke the story?"

"Let's just say I have some suspicions, and if that little weasel is at the coffee shop tomorrow morning I intend to confirm them," she said. "I pretty much caught some guy eavesdropping on me when you and I were talking on the phone the other day. And yesterday… I had really bad bout of morning sickness at the coffee shop and Snoopy was right there talking to me about you. Seems odd, right?"

Rafe didn't like the idea that Emily had been targeted. How had the reporter been alerted to her presence? The community in Key West was a close-knit one and Rafe couldn't for the life of him imagine any of them talking about Emily.

It must have been someone who knew him. He remembered the way she'd sneaked into his penthouse. Maybe that was where the reporter had picked up the thread of the story. Maybe he'd followed her.

Hell, he had no idea.

He rubbed the back of his neck. He was tired.

"You're not confronting anyone," he said. "I'll go tomorrow and take care of it."

She put her hand on his chest and shoved him back so she could get up from the chair. Standing next to him, she put her hands on her hips and arched one eyebrow at him.

"One—you're not the boss of me. Sorry, I'm just not going to take orders. Two—that rat bastard played me and I want to make sure that doesn't happen again," she said. "So I'll take care of it."

It was late and he was tired of being pulled in too many directions, so perhaps that was why he let his temper slip as he stood up, towering over her. He put his hands on her shoulders and realized all he wanted to do was protect her, and that was the one thing that Emily didn't seem to want from him.

"Dammit, woman. I'm trying to keep you safe. I don't want any of this dirty press to affect you. I need to know that you aren't harmed by it."

"Why?" she asked. "Because you think I can't handle it?"

"Hell, Red. You can handle anything. I am doing this because I care about you and if anything hurt you I wouldn't be able to live with it."

CHAPTER NINE

Rafe pulled her to him and slammed his mouth down on hers, backing her up against the wall. The moment their mouths met his anger died. It felt like too long since he'd held her in his arms. She did that thing with her tongue where she twirled it around his, and he instantly got hard.

He cupped her butt and flexed his fingers, lifting her up until he could rub his erection right over the center of her body. She was naked under her shirt, and he liked the feel of her cool buttocks in his hands. She moved against him and he feathered his finger in a circle around the small of her back. She moaned and arched against him before tunneling her fingers into his hair and holding him to her while she plundered his mouth.

There was too much pent-up emotion between them. They'd been in the same room together three times and each time it hadn't been enough. He wanted her. The way she got to him was unlike anything else he'd ever experienced, and his gut was starting to say he wouldn't find it with anyone else.

He sank to the floor when she sucked his bottom lip between her teeth and bit him lightly. Once he was on the floor, he pushed his hands up her back, felt the way her body arched over his. He rubbed his hand up her delicate spine, finding the sensitive nerves at the back of her neck, tracing a pattern over the skin of her nape.

She pulled back and looked up at him. Her lips were swollen, her face slightly flushed pink, making her freckles more prominent. Her eyes were brilliant in the dim light and he realized he'd never seen anything more beautiful.

He wanted her so much at this moment he couldn't think of anything but getting inside her.

"The other night was a pale imitation of this," she said, her husky voice turning him on.

"Damned straight," he said. He pulled her shirt up over her body and tossed it aside.

He set her back on his thighs as he stretched his legs out and held her there so he could look at her. He took in her breasts, which were slightly larger since her pregnancy, and those darker, fuller nipples. He lightly caressed them, running his finger over first one, then the other. She reached between them and pushed his T-shirt up his body.

He let go of her to rip it off and toss it carelessly to the side. She put her fingers on his pectorals and he flexed them. She sighed and traced her finger around each of his nipples before leaning forward to nip each of them in turn.

He brought his hands back to her breasts, but she took one of them and drew it slowly down the side of her body. He reached around behind her and grabbed her ass, bringing her closer. She rocked her pelvis over the ridge of his erection where it strained against the front of his jeans.

He brought one of his arms up behind her and held her with his hand on the back of her neck as he lowered his head and kissed his way down her neck to her shoulder blade. There was a large strawberry birthmark on her left shoulder and he kissed it, laving it with his tongue before he nibbled his way lower. He dropped small kisses around the full globe of her breast and then moved lower to the underside, biting lightly at the spot where her breast rested against her chest.

She moaned his name and rocked against him as she gripped his sides, trying to bring him closer to her. But he held her where she was. He wasn't ready to let her have free rein over his body. She'd been tormenting him for days with her conversations and the little pieces of her soul that she shared with him almost as if they were an afterthought.

He had her in his arms, but she was hard to hold. So hard to keep. And he was determined that he would keep her.

He sucked at the smooth skin between her breasts and then moved on to her other breast. This one was slightly smaller than its mate. He wanted to know everything about her, to know all these details instead of just being satisfied with sex. He needed more than the physical from her this time. He wanted to lay her completely bare so that maybe he'd have the answers that he'd been seeking.

He brought one of his hands up and slowly drew his finger in circles around her areola. He felt the texture of her nipple changing as it tightened under his finger and then he rubbed his finger back and forth against it until she leaned forward, catching the lobe of his ear between her teeth and biting down hard.

He lifted his head to look into her blue eyes. He swore he could see the same desire in her eyes to get rid of all the questions and doubts that remained between them. But he knew he might just be projecting what he wanted to see. He needed something from her that he couldn't define.

She swiped her tongue around the rim of his ear and he got even harder. Uncomfortable now, he reached between their bodies, distracted by the feel of her wet sex against the back of his fingers. He turned his hand and palmed her. He liked the feel of her springy curls as he rotated his palm against her.

She arched her back and shifted against him. He teased the opening of her body with his finger and then slowly pushed it up into her. She tightened around him. And he felt as if he were going to explode. He wanted to feel her naked flesh against him.

Though he did like her naked on his lap while he was still clothed. He pulled back and looked down at her, wanting to keep this moment in his mind forever.

He used his thumb to find her clit. He tapped it lightly and then made a small circle. She responded instantly. He felt the minute tightening of her body around his finger as he continued to rub his thumb in a circle over her center.

He lowered his mouth to her breast and took her nipple between his lips, swirling his tongue over it and then sucking. Her hands were on his shoulders, nails digging into them as she rocked against his hand. She arched her shoulders and pulled her breast from his mouth.

Their eyes met and all the things he'd been afraid to say seemed to hover in the air around them. He opened his mouth and she leaned forward and kissed him.

She started to rock more quickly. She sucked his tongue deep into her mouth and plunged it back and forth to the same rhythm of his finger inside her body. Her thighs tightened around his hand and he pulled his mouth from hers.

"Come for me," he said, whispering the words against her ear.

Her hips moved more frantically and he added a second finger inside her body as she cried out his name. She thrust her hips rapidly against him and then she shuddered and fell forward, resting her head on his shoulder. Her breath was warm against his neck as she reached her hand down between them and unzipped his jeans.

Her touch through the opening of his pants almost made him come. He felt a drop leak out of him and slowly pulled his hand from her body and got to his feet, lifting her up into his arms. He didn't want this to end too quickly

He carried her down the small hallway and into her bedroom, setting her down on her feet next to the bed. She had wrapped one arm around his shoulder, holding on to him and idly toying with the hair at the back of his neck, while her other arm was awkwardly wedged between them, her hand wrapped around his length.

She stroked him up and down, her finger swirling over the top of him. His hips jerked forward and no matter how much his mind said that he was going to take this slowly, his body had different plans.

He let her body slide down his. She moaned as her hardened nipples rubbed over his chest, and he closed his eyes as he felt the dampness of her core against the front of his boxers.

He stepped back and shoved his pants and underwear down his legs and then nudged her forward until she fell back on the bed. Her legs sprawled apart slightly, her hair fanning out around her head, one brilliant dark red curl falling over her shoulder. She had her hands on the top of her thighs and she watched him with hungry eyes.

He wanted to say something profound because the emotions he felt for her welled up inside him, but instead all he could think about was touching and tasting every inch of her.

"Are you just going to stand there and stare at me?" she asked, a tinge of wry amusement visible on her face.

"I'm debating where to start. Every time we've been together I want to make it last… I haven't had the chance to taste you or to explore every one of those lovely freckles of yours."

"There's plenty of time for that later. I want you now," she said.

Her words lanced through him and his erection jumped. He shook his head. Every time he thought he had the upper hand with Emily she did something to remind him that he was putty in her hands. Now and always.

She reached for his length, circling him with her thumb and forefinger at the root. She slowly drew her hand up, closing the circle of her fingers around him as she did so. Involuntarily he thrust closer to her and she smiled up at him as a drop of precome glistened on the tip of his erection. She swiped her finger over it and then brought it to her mouth.

He groaned and crawled up over her body, and then put his hands on her hips and forced her to move back on the bed. He took her hands in his and drew them up over her head as he settled his hips between hers and the tip of his erection found the moist center of her body.

He drew his hips back and then thrust forward again, entering her slowly. She arched underneath him and yet still he resisted the urge to plunge his way all the way home. She turned her hands under his, laced their fingers together and looked up at him.

"Take me," she said.

He nodded as he drove himself hilt-deep into her body. She sighed and arched against him again and he started to thrust in and out, taking them both closer and closer to the edge. He pulled his hand free of hers and drew it down her side as he rocked back and forth. Going deeper each time and taking them higher and higher.

She ran her finger down his back and he jerked his hips forward as he came. Then he felt her legs tighten around his hips and heard her calling his name as she climaxed.

He kept driving into her until she bit him softly on the

shoulder and sighed. She turned her head to face him and he saw the completion on her face. He found her lips with his and gave her a soft, gentle kiss.

Rafe wanted to believe that everything was okay between them but he knew that sex hadn't made it so. From the beginning their bond had been strong and physical. That created its own sort of problems. He wanted to just keep making love to her and pretending that was enough, but he knew it wasn't. And there were things he had to say that she might not want to hear.

But for this moment he wanted to just hold her, look up at the moon and pretend that everything was okay.

EMILY WOKE UP in the middle of the night having to go to the bathroom. This was something that had only started in the last week. She had read in one of her prenatal books that things like this were only the beginning.

Rafe was cuddled behind her and propped himself up on an elbow as she climbed from the bed. "You okay?" he asked.

"Yes. Be right back."

He fell back down on the pillow and she knew he was tired. They'd resolved nothing except that they still wanted each other. But she felt as if this time they'd done more than just have sex. Rafe meant more to her than any other guy she'd ever dated, and she acknowledged that it had nothing to do with the fact that he was the father of her child—and yet at the same time had everything to do with that.

He made her feel more alive than anyone else ever had, and that was dangerous. She didn't want to rely on him. He could sleep in her bed and come to her bar. Hell, he could even be involved with their baby, but she didn't want to care for him.

She washed her hands and leaned forward to look at herself in the mirror.

"Don't fall for him," she warned herself. But she sort of already knew that it was too late.

That falling for Rafe was a foregone conclusion now.

He'd come to her in the middle of the night. Wanted to defend her. Everyone knew she could take care of herself, but he still wanted to protect her.

That made her feel so safe. So cherished.

Things that had never mattered to her before tonight.

She shook her head.

He had to want something. There had to be a reason he was here tonight. She wanted it to be for her, but maybe it was about the baby. Now that the world knew about their child, the decisions they'd been making together took on a different quality. Whatever he did could impact his people back in Alma.

She knew that. She wanted it to not matter, but she knew it did.

And she also was very aware that she wasn't cut out to be a queen or consort or whatever the hell they had in Alma.

Maybe that was why he was here.

She left the bathroom and stood in the doorway leading back into the bedroom, watching him as he lay sleeping, his big, strong, sexy body taking up too much of her bed, his face relaxed in sleep. He didn't seem as if he had an agenda. He didn't act as if there were some reason he was in her bed other than that he wanted to be there.

But she knew there had to be more.

She lived in the real world, and stained glass mermaid aside, Rafe had always been very real with her. . When they'd spent their one weekend together, he'd made it clear that would be it. As had she. And when she'd barged in on him in Miami and told him she was pregnant he hadn't pretended they were suddenly a couple.

"I thought you got lost, Red."

She thought she did, too. The first time she'd looked into his hazel eyes.

"I almost did. Why are you here, Rafe?" she asked.

"Come back to bed," he said.

She walked over and sat on the edge of the bed, but he lifted the sheets and gestured for her to come closer. She wanted to. She started to lie down in the curve of his body but stopped herself.

"I need some answers. So far all we've done is establish what we both already knew. We want each other. We have some kind of lust that won't be denied. But I need some answers."

"Okay."

"Okay?"

"Sure. Ask your questions," he said, sitting up and propping his back on the headboard. "I figured we'd do this in the morning."

"I don't think I can sleep until I know if you are going to take my child from me."

She hadn't meant to say it that way. But it was 3:00 a.m. and her guard was down. Her fears were all around her. Rafe was a powerful man before she even factored in the fact that he was about to become the ruler of a foreign land.

"Hell. No. I'm not going to take our child from you," he said. "Why would you think I'd do that? I'm not an asshole."

She swallowed hard. "I know you aren't. But we both know I'm not the kind of woman your family has been hoping you'll marry. And now that the world knows I'm carrying the king of Alma's child, I think the stakes have changed."

He reached for her. Took her hand in his and brought

it to his mouth. He dropped a warm kiss in the center of her palm before placing her hand on his chest right over his heart.

"I haven't changed, Red. I'm still the man you know. I'm not going to let anything change me."

She wanted to believe him. But the monarchy was bigger than Rafe, whether he wanted to admit it or not.

He tugged her off balance and into his arms. Rolling until she was tucked underneath him. He kissed her long and slow, and she felt her fears for the future disappearing slowly.

In his embrace she felt as if things would work out, but she feared that was false hope until she knew how he felt about her. Until she had some promises... But she'd never had a man make her promises. Never wanted them until now. Until Rafe. She needed something from him, but she was afraid to admit that even to herself.

How the hell was she going to tell him that she wanted him to be by her side? Not because of the baby, but because she needed him.

She tipped her head, closing her eyes and pretending that she had the answers she needed. But she knew that things were even more complicated now than they had been before.

CHAPTER TEN

Rafe woke with the sun, since he was still on European time, and left Emily sleeping quietly in her bed. Last night he'd almost lost her. He still wasn't sure he'd said the right thing or even done enough to keep her. But today he intended to change all of that.

He went out to his car and retrieved the bag that Jose had packed and brought it into the house. He scanned the street while he did so, but saw no reporters hanging around, which was reassuring. As were the two cop cars parked at each end of her street. There was no foot traffic on her block today either.

He found eggs and the fixings for an omelet in Emily's fridge and set to making breakfast for her. His hands were sweating when he put it all on the breakfast tray he'd found in her pantry. He dashed outside to pick a hibiscus from the flowering bush in her backyard and put it in a small teacup with some water. Then he patted his pocket to make sure the ring hadn't disappeared and walked back to her bedroom.

With any other woman this kind of gesture might be enough to make her swoon. But Rafe suspected it might not be enough with Red.

She was still asleep on her side with his pillow tucked up against her. She looked small and vulnerable as she slept. During the day she was a virago, constantly moving and challenging everything in her path. But like this it was easy to see she wasn't as invincible as she wanted the world to believe. Feeling like a voyeur, he put the tray on her dresser and snapped a quick photo of her with his iPhone.

Then he walked over to the bed and sat down next to her. He was tempted to slide back under the sheets with her. Make love to her again, but sex was tearing away layers that he usually used to insulate himself against women. And he couldn't afford to let Emily any closer to him than she already was.

Love was a fairy tale, one he wasn't too sure existed. He'd seen what his father had done for love and how that had torn their entire family apart.

"Em..."

"Um..."

"Wake up, sleepyhead."

She blinked up at him and shoved her hand through her thick red hair, pushing it back off her face. She sat up, ran her tongue over her teeth and then looked at him. "Aren't you chipper in the morning."

He was. He'd always been a morning person, but he sensed that she wasn't and decided silence was the better part of valor. "I'm still on a different time zone. I brought you coffee."

"I can only have decaf," she said.

"That's what I made since it was on the counter next to your machine," he said.

"Thank you," she said, reaching for the mug. Blowing on the surface of the hot liquid before taking a sip, she closed her eyes, seeming to savor it as that first swallow went down.

He felt himself stir and shook his head.

Really. Was there nothing she could do that wouldn't turn him on?

"You haven't tried the omelet yet," he said as he knelt on the bed and settled the tray over her lap.

"No. For trying to protect me. For doing this," she said. "I'm just not the kind of woman men usually do this kind of thing for."

"Yes, you are," he said.

She wrinkled her brow as she stared over at him. He took off the lid that he'd used to cover her plate so it wouldn't get cold and smiled over at her.

"Are you arguing with me?"

"Yeah, I am. I made you breakfast in bed, so clearly you are the right type. The other guys in your life haven't measured up."

She put her coffee on the tray and leaned over to kiss him. It was a little clumsy and tasted of sleepy woman and coffee. He wanted more but she pulled back.

"You're saying all the right things this morning."

"I try. How's your stomach?" he asked. "I didn't even think about your morning sickness."

"I'm not sure I can eat too much, but the coffee seems okay right now."

"That's good. I had Jose get me a bunch of books on pregnancy but haven't had a chance to read them yet," he said.

He wanted to know what was going to be happening to her so he could anticipate her needs. Make everything easier for her.

They shared the breakfast he made and then he set the tray to the side and lay next to her on the bed. "Do you have to work today?"

"No. Do you?"

"No. I'm supposed to lie low," he said. And make everything with Emily right in the eyes of the world. But that part was still better left unspoken for now.

"Good. What do you want to do?"

"Well…"

He pulled her into his arms and then rolled over, bracing his body on top of hers. He put his hand on her stomach and dropped a quick kiss there before looking up at her. He worked his free hand into the pocket of his pants and pulled out the ring box.

"I'm hoping that you'll agree to marry me, Red."

He put the ring box on her stomach and then opened it up so she could see the thin band with the pear-shaped diamond. He'd chosen the band lined with aquamarine because that stone reminded him of her eyes. He shifted to his side, knelt next to her and stared down into her heart-shaped face. "I hope you'll say yes."

She stared up at him for a long moment and he had the feeling she wasn't going to say yes. What had he done wrong? He'd made the big romantic gesture; he'd purchased a ring that reminded him of her.

He was being a good guy. Doing everything by the book of romance. He'd seen his sister reading fairy tales and *Cosmo* so he knew that he had to come across as modern and thoughtful but also deliver on all Emily's secret dreams.

It was a big ask of a man who was used to women falling for him. Especially after the time he'd spent on Alma with Dita and her ilk fawning over him.

"What did I do wrong?"

"Nothing," she said. "I like the ring and the breakfast, but I like my mermaid, too."

He processed that.

The mermaid had been a stroke of genius. Well, really it had been the gesture of a man who missed his woman.

"Doesn't matter if you wear the ring, you're mine."

"I'm yours?"

"We both know it. There isn't a wannabe debutante in all the world who can compare to you, Red."

She gave him a haughty look and then ruined it by laughing. "I know it."

"What about you?"

"Huh?"

"Is there anyone else in your life?"

"Would I be with you if there was?" she asked. "I like you way more than I should, Rafael. Your life is literally worlds away from here but I can't help letting you into my house and my bed. I'm just trying to keep us both from making a mistake."

Maybe he could convince her to say yes. This was the opening he needed. "It's not a mistake. Trust me. Together, we can take on anything."

"For now. But what happens when the newness of being lovers wears off and we have a baby who doesn't sleep through the night? And you have to run a kingdom?"

He saw where she was coming from. And realized the fears she had stemmed from the fact that she didn't know him. Didn't realize how unstoppable he was once he made his mind up.

"I said I'd give you time to get to know me, and once you do, you will know that isn't going to be an issue," he said.

FRANKLY THIS SHOCKED HER. Rafe didn't strike her as all that traditional. And she knew that he was still trying to figure out the next few months of his life. She wasn't going to be his lifesaver. His safety valve. And that's what this felt like.

"No." The little girl who never had a mom and a dad desperately wanted her to say yes. But she'd learned long ago that the things she wanted most were the ones that made her make the dumbest decisions. And marriage wasn't something to be entered into lightly. Rafe was going to be king. He should have a wife who was in it for the long haul.

He was going to have to do a lot of work to make the monarchy stick in Alma. *Alma.* She wasn't even sure where it was. Maybe she should have looked that up on the internet instead of ogling pictures of Rafe as he toured the island nation. But she hadn't.

"No?" he asked. "Red, think this through."

"I can't marry you," she said. She could, but it wasn't under these circumstances. If he'd asked her the first time she'd shown up on his doorstep pregnant she might have said yes. But too much had happened since then and she couldn't trust his motives.

They knew each other so much better now than they had a mere two weeks earlier, but still not well enough. Or from her perspective, maybe too well. She wanted that man who sent her the stained glass to fall down on his knees and beg her to marry him.

That wasn't going to happen. Rafe liked her. He wanted her but he didn't love her.

"Are you asking me because I'm pregnant?" she asked at last.

He rolled off the bed and got to his feet. He put his hands on his lean hips and stood there as if he could will her to change her mind. She wished he'd put a shirt on, because his bare chest was a tempting distraction.

But not enough of one that she'd say yes to this. She knew if she said yes she'd want him to love her. Why? She'd been fine with lust until this moment, and now she wanted professions of deep emotion from him. Emotion she wasn't prepared to admit she felt for him.

They didn't love each other. She had never thought she was one of those women who needed it, but in her heart she knew she did. She wasn't as practical as she'd expected to be when it came to Rafe. He was arguing that they'd be stronger together, and she thought if they loved each other then he might be right. But a couple who married for the sake of a child? That seemed like a steep hill to climb.

Maybe it was because her mother had never compromised and married that Emily felt so strongly about this. But she couldn't help it. She wasn't going to marry him for any reason. Unless he fell in love with her and proved it in some way that would convince her. She liked him. She cared about him and she had no intention of isolating him from his child. But marriage?

No. Definitely not.

"Partly. I'm traditional, Red. You know that. I want our baby to have my name. And to know who I am. We can do that so much better together," he said. He scrubbed one hand over his eyes and then sat down on the edge of the bed with his back toward her. "Every child needs a mom and a dad. Didn't you miss having a dad?"

"I did," she said. "But I found my way without one. And Harry's sort of filled the role for me. It's all I needed."

"I don't want our kid to have a relationship with some future boyfriend of yours," he said.

"Don't. Don't think of any of that. We are going to get to know each other. We will figure this out."

She crawled over to him and wrapped her arms around his shoulders, leaning her head on his chest to look at him. "Marriage like this isn't a solution. We'd have to be more businesslike and we aren't. The way you get to me…it's all I can do to remind myself every day that you belong on the throne of Alma and I have no place by your side."

He covered her hands with his and clasped them to his chest. "You might."

She shook her head and slid around on the bed next to him. He was so serious, this man of hers. "Is that why you are asking me?"

"Yes. I care for you, Emily," he said. "I want what's best for you and our child. And if you are my fiancée I can protect you from the media. I can bring the full force of the Montoro name and reputation to bear against these people. I can do it now, but they will just glom onto the fact that I'm not marrying you or taking you to Alma. Being my fiancée will make everything easier."

She felt the sincerity in his words. Understood that he was willing to tie his life to hers to keep her safe. But for how long? Because she knew that she didn't want to leave Key West, and there was no way he could rule from here.

"I can't."

"Don't say no. Think about it. Let's see if I can change your mind," he said.

She had no doubt that he could. If she spent time with him and fell any deeper for him then she'd say yes. She'd exchange her life for his. And she knew herself well enough to know that she'd be angry with that.

"How?"

"Let's date and get to know each other. In a few weeks I'll ask you again," he said.

"How will we do that? Do I have to fly to Alma?"

"No. I'm in Miami to wrap up a few business deals. So while I'm here let's date."

"Okay. But what if the answer is still no. What then?" she asked.

"I'm pretty determined it won't be," he said. "And I've never lost a challenge."

"Never?"

"Nope. I'm not afraid to do whatever I have to in order to win you over."

She believed him but she also knew this decision wasn't his alone. "What about your family?"

"Leave them to me. I'd like you to come to Miami Beach next week, stay at my place and meet everyone who's here with me at a dinner. Would you do that?"

She pursed her lips but then nodded. "What day? I'll have to check my schedule at the bar."

"I was hoping for Friday night. But I know that's one of your busiest nights and this relationship isn't all about me. So you tell me which day works for you," he said.

She reached for her phone on the nightstand and checked her work schedule. Harry was going to transition her to the daytime shift starting next week since her pregnancy had really started showing.

She texted Beau, the other bartender, to see if he'd fill in for her on Friday and Saturday. He was always looking for more money and immediately responded that he could.

"Friday is fine," she said.

"Great. Now what should we do today?" he asked.

"I have a few ideas," she said. "But you're going to need swim trunks."

"I packed for a couple of days. I'm good."

THE BEACH THAT Emily took him to later that afternoon was deserted and well off the beaten path. They had to carry the paddleboard from her car through a stand of mangroves to the water's edge. There were cicadas chirping and the smell of salt water mixed with ripe vegetation. It was so Florida.

The heat beat down on his back and he wore a baseball cap and large sunglasses to protect his face from the sun. Emily had surprised him by giving him a lecture about the dangers of skin cancer even to someone with his olive complexion. So he'd donned her SPF 50 sun cream and the hat even though he never burned.

Her mothering had charmed him. And it was mothering. She'd kind of ensured he had the cream on and taken her time rubbing it on his back, which had led them back to the bedroom. Hence the late start at the beach.

She'd also packed a cooler of fruit juice, sandwiches and veggies. He'd seldom—okay, never —taken a day like this. It was a Monday. He should be in Miami getting ready for the weekly management meeting where he should be discussing the new shipping deal and getting all the routes worked out for their customers, but truth be told he wouldn't trade this for anything.

The way his family had reacted when they'd landed had worried Rafe. He had the sinking feeling in his gut that they were going to make him choose between Emily and their baby and the throne. And as usual when he got his back up that meant he got stubborn. He wasn't too sure he wanted the throne, but he wasn't about to let his family force him out of it.

He had the Coleman cooler in one hand and the paddleboard under his other arm. She'd said she could help carry stuff but he'd said no. He found that he liked making gallant gestures. This morning when she'd turned down his proposal, he'd realized she hadn't had a lot of men doing that for her. And he was determined to convince her that he was the right guy for her.

On that front, he wasn't backing down.

"This spot looks good. We can leave the cooler here. Actually," she said with a blush, "we could have left it in the car. It's not that far to walk back for a snack."

"Then why did I carry it down here?"

She crossed her arms over her chest and gave him a

chagrined look. "Because you were so stubborn about me helping carry the board. I hate being bossed."

"You mentioned that. But this isn't bossing, it's pampering. Like when you insisted I wear sunscreen."

She started to argue but then stuck her tongue out at him. "You're right. But don't make a habit of it."

He threw his head back and laughed. She kept him on his toes no matter how much he didn't want to admit it. He liked the challenge of being with her.

"So you've never been on a paddleboard before?" she asked.

"Nope. Never even surfed. I am scuba certified though. Want to do that instead?"

"Yes but the water around here isn't that deep. Snorkeling would be better. We could do that tonight. I know a gorgeous place where we can go at sunset. In fact, if my mom doesn't mind, we can take her boat," she said.

"I'd like to meet your mom," he said.

She got really still. "Why?"

"Because she's your mom," Rafe said. "Why else?"

"Don't try to get her on your side with this engagement thing, okay?"

He put the board on the sand and walked over to her, putting his finger under her chin and tipping her head back so he could see her eyes under the bill of her baseball cap. "When you say yes—and I'm betting you eventually do—it will be because you've decided you want to marry me. Not because I pressured you into saying yes. Got it?"

She punched him playfully in the shoulder and ran down toward the waterline. "I've got it. Get that board and come on, Your Majesty. It's time for your first lesson."

Rafe followed her to the water and they spent the next thirty minutes with her showing him how to get his balance on the board. Finally Emily decided he could take a turn rowing and he got about two strokes in before he fell into the warm Atlantic Ocean.

He glanced at the shore to find her standing there laughing.

"I bet it wasn't easy for you at first," he said as he swam back to shore with the board.

"I don't remember. I've been on the water since before I could walk," she said.

"So you grew up here?"

"Since I was three, so I think that counts, doesn't it?"

"Pretty much. I was born in Coral Gables and grew up there," he said.

"Florida native."

"Well, just my generation," he said.

He looked at her and the future suddenly didn't seem as nebulous as it always had. The future was real and it was staring back at him with red hair and blue eyes. And that made Alma seem farther away than ever.

"Why don't you stand on the end of my board and look studly and I'll take you on a tour of this inlet?" she asked.

"Studly?"

"Yeah. Oh, is that an insult to your masculinity?" she teased. "I figured after that dunking you gave yourself you might like to play it safe."

He rushed her, scooping her up in his arms and carrying her into the water. "I never play it safe, Red. And I'm not the only one who's going to get a dunking."

He fell backward into the water, keeping her in his arms and drenching them both. She swiveled in his arms and when they both surfaced she kissed him. One kiss led to another and Rafe realized he was having the best afternoon of his life.

He told himself it was just the relief at being away from the pressures of leading Alma and Montoro Enterprises, but his heart said his future was tied to this woman.

CHAPTER ELEVEN

Emily had felt more at ease staring down a belligerent drunk at Shady Harry's than she did standing in the formal dining room of the Montoros' Coral Gables mansion holding a tonic water with lime in one hand. Rafael III had turned his back on her when she entered the room with Rafe, who had been called away by Jose. He'd seemed reluctant to leave her but she'd urged him to go. She was rethinking that opinion now.

Juan Carlos looked less than pleased to actually meet her and the PR guy Geoff had muttered under his breath that she was no style icon. Well, who was? She was a real person. She wasn't going to apologize for who she was.

Tia Isabella had been feeling well enough to be up with the family. She and her nurse were in one corner with Rafe's sister Bella. Tia Isabella was in a wheelchair and her hands and head kept shaking because of her advanced Parkinson's. When her nurse invited Emily over to join the women, she was grateful. Isabella had beautiful white hair and was the only one to smile at Emily and make her feel truly welcome.

"Hello, Emily," Bella said, coming up behind her and putting her arm around her.

"Bella right? Or should I call you Lady Bella?"

"Just Bella is fine. You look like you are about to bolt."

"I am."

"Well, don't. I've never seen Rafe like this before."

"Like what?"

"Unsettled."

"That's good. He's too sure he knows it all," Emily said.

Bella laughed and Emily noticed that her brothers smiled at the sound. "Rafe mentioned going out on your mother's boat... Is it a yacht?"

Emily realized that Bella was really in a different world. "No. She's a marine biologist. Her boat is like the station wagon of the sea."

"Did you grow up on it? Like Jacques Cousteau's family?"

"No. She had a grant that enabled her to return to Key West every night," Emily said.

"Sounds fascinating."

They were called to dinner and Rafe rejoined her. "How'd it go?"

"Most of your family hate me. If they could make me disappear they would," she said.

"They don't hate you," Rafe said.

"Don't lie to me," she retorted.

"Well, it's not you. It's the fact that I am putting our family's return to Alma and the throne in a very delicate state. No one, not even me, wants that."

Emily wanted to apologize but she couldn't. She wasn't sorry she was having his baby or that she'd gotten to know him. But she was sorry that they'd met now when his life wasn't his own. And when his family would never approve of her.

THE NEXT TWO weeks were busy and though Rafe would be happy to stop flying back and forth between Key West and Miami, he enjoyed every second he spent with Emily.

Tonight he was cruising toward the setting sun with Jessica, Harry and Emily. His first meeting with Emily's mom had been tense but ever since Emily had wrapped her arm around his waist and given her mom a stubborn look, Jessica had been sort of friendly toward him. Harry on the other hand looked as if he was going to need more than a stern look from Emily.

If he didn't know that they were going night diving, he'd have been worried.

"Beer?" Harry asked, walking up to him where he sat on a padded bench at the stern of the boat.

"Nah, I'm good."

Harry sat down next to him and took a sip of his Corona. Emily and her mom were at the helm of the boat talking and laughing as they got out of the no-wake zone. Suddenly Jessica hit the throttle and they were flying full speed across the ocean.

As the wind buffeted Rafe, Harry leaned forward, shouting a little to be heard over the noise. "What are your plans with our girl?"

"None of your business," Rafe shouted back. "No disrespect but you and I both know she'll skin us alive if we discuss it behind her back."

Harry threw his head back and gave a great shout of laughter. The other man was big and solid, but no taller than Rafe. And he'd noticed over the past couple weeks how Harry watched out for Emily as no other adult in her life had.

Her mom, though sweet and loving toward Emily, spent most of her time thinking about her research and reapplying for grants. Her entire world was the ocean and the creatures in it.

It had been startling to realize that in essence Emily had raised herself. That was probably why she was so tough, so feisty and so damned independent. She had a lifetime of doing things on her own. How the hell was he going to convince her that she needed him by her side?

But he understood why the arguments he'd been making hadn't worked. What was it that she needed? The one thing she couldn't give herself, he suspected, was the key to bringing her around.

His phone buzzed. He'd hoped they'd be out of range but no such luck. He looked down and saw he had received a text from Geoff Standings once again asking again if he could run with their release announcing Rafe's engagement to Emily.

He texted back no and then shut his phone off. His family didn't get how delicate the situation was and thought that he could order her to marry him.

As if.

"Just know if you hurt her, bud, I'm coming after you," Harry said with that slightly maniacal grin of his.

"That's the last thing I want to do," Rafe said loudly.

Jessica killed the engines and his words sort of echoed around the boat as everything went quiet.

"What's the last thing you want to do?" Emily said, coming over and sitting on his lap. She wrapped her arm around his shoulders and reached over to take Harry's beer. "No drinking and diving, Harry. That's dangerous."

"It was one beer, kiddo. And barely that," Harry said, getting up and going over to Jessica.

"What is the last thing you'd do?" she asked Rafe when they were alone. He heard the sounds of Jessica and Harry getting the scuba gear ready behind them.

"Hurt you," he said, looking down into her pretty blue eyes.

"No promises, remember?" she said, standing up.

He grabbed her wrist, keeping her by his side as he had

a sudden flash of insight into what it was she needed but was afraid to ask for. She needed promises and she needed them to be kept.

"I'm making this one, Red. And I'm keeping it," he said.

"What about Alma and your family?" she asked.

"What about them? That has nothing to do with you and me."

She snorted and shook her head. "It has everything to do with us. I'm complicating things. I think we both know that dinner with your family didn't go very well because of it. They think…heck, I have no idea what they think. But they don't like me much."

He wondered if that were true. He believed his family didn't feel one way or another about Emily. It was him they were frustrated with. They needed him to make her his fiancée or get her out of the picture. They needed him to clean up his act so they could continue with the coronation plans. But he wasn't playing their game.

"It's me they're pissed at," he said. "I'm sure they will like you once they get to know you."

She gave him an incredulous look. "I thought you were going to be a king of Alma, not fairy-tale land."

He laughed. "I am."

"You two done flirting?" Harry called, interrupting their argument. "Ready to do some diving?"

"Yes, we are, Harry," Emily said, walking over and getting her gear on.

Rafe followed her, wishing things were as simple as flirting. But nothing with her ever was.

He joined her family and went over the side of the boat after they'd put the diver down flag in the water. He noticed that everyone scattered in their own direction.

He followed close by Emily's side and reached for her hand, linking them together. She looked at him for a moment, her face not very clear behind the glass of her scuba mask, and then led him through the underwater world. She pointed out different species of fish and coral, and caught up in the natural beauty of his surroundings, he forgot his troubles. There was something very peaceful about snorkeling. But when they surfaced, he knew that nothing had changed in their world.

But he felt strongly that he and Emily had crossed a bridge into new territory.

"That was nice," she said, treading water next to him.

"Yes, it was. Exactly what I need after a day full of meetings and demands," he said as they took off their tanks and put them in the boat.

"What is?"

Time with the woman he loved.

Shock held him in place as he realized that he did love her.

VERSAILLES WAS THE most famous Cuban restaurant in Miami. Hell, probably the world. Rafe had a night away from his family planned for himself and Emily. And grabbing Cuban sandwiches at his favorite restaurant was exactly the right sort of tone he wanted to set.

He needed Emily to accept his proposal, but pressuring her wasn't the way to get the job done. So he'd been as smooth as he could be, trying not to pressure her into making a decision that he needed from her. And the sooner, the better.

Every day she waited just made his family more anxious. At first it was just the inner circle of his father, brother and cousin, but now his more distant relatives— even his ill Tia Isabella—were asking him when he was going to announce his engagement.

He suspected Tia Isabella was being egged on by his

cousin Juan Carlos, the one who wanted the family's return to the throne of Alma to be…triumphant. Not mired in scandal.

Rafe got that.

He'd even had a meeting with Montoro Enterprises' board of directors today. They had been pretty threatening; the upshot was, if he screwed up things in Alma he might not be CEO for much longer.

But the more his family pushed, the less he responded. None of that mattered tonight. The dinner with Emily hadn't gone well. And they'd called a "family" meeting to discuss the matter tomorrow.

Tonight he was going to seduce the hell out of Emily and secure her as his fiancée and then go into the meeting with his family he had scheduled for tomorrow and take control of the situation.

Waiting on Emily, waiting on his family—he felt shackled on all sides. He couldn't take action the way he needed to so that he could move forward.

He and Emily were seated against the wall in the glass-and-mirrored main room of the restaurant. All around him he heard people talking in Spanish. The Cuban dialect was different from the Castilian Spanish that many of the people of Alma used. Cuban Spanish was much more familiar to him.

"So what's on the agenda tonight?" Emily said after they had placed their order.

"Dinner, dancing and then I'll show you the harbor from my rooftop patio. I think you will be impressed."

"I'm never not impressed by you, Rafe."

"Thank you. Perhaps I should ask you that question again?"

She shook her head and her face got a little pinched.

"Please don't. Can we have tonight and just be Emily and Rafe, not the future king and his errant pregnant lover?"

He realized that she was facing a different kind of pressure. She'd agreed to come to Miami for a few days after a group of paparazzi had staked out Shady Harry's in Key West. It was either take the security offered by staying in his penthouse or go out on the boat with her mother.

He was pleased she'd chosen to come to him. He felt as if they had gotten so much closer over the last few weeks together.

"Yes, we can," he said.

"Great. So tell me why you picked this restaurant. I know it's famous and all that, but I wouldn't expect you to be a regular here."

He leaned back in the chair. "Well, the food is the best. You can't find a better Cuban sandwich anywhere in the city. But when I was younger, about ten or so, our mom used to bring Gabe, Bella and me here for dinners on the nights when our dad was in one of his moods and ranting all over the place. And later it was the first place she took us when we got Gabe back."

"Where'd he go?" Emily asked.

"In his early twenties, he was kidnapped while working for our South American division. He ultimately escaped. When we got him back, Mom packed us all up and brought us here. I always associate this place with happy times."

"Where is your mom?" she asked.

"She's remarried and pretty much enjoying her life now that she's out from under the burden of her marriage to our father."

"Do you see her at all?"

"I don't see her very often. But we text. It's enough for me," he said.

She nodded. "It's like that with my mom. I know other

people have these crazy-close relationships with their parents but that was never us. She raised me to think for myself and do things for myself."

"Same," Rafe said. "My father gave me the legacy…that sort of feeling of pride in being a Montoro, and my mom gave me the strength to stand on my own while I carry out my version of what that means."

Emily reached across the table and linked their hands together. "I wonder what we will give our baby?"

"Probably everything we never had and always wanted," Rafe said.

Their food arrived and their conversation drifted to lighter topics like bands and books and movies. Everything but the one thing Rafe wanted to discuss. But she'd asked for time, for an evening where they were like every other young couple out on a date.

And he struggled to give it to her. This felt like a game she was playing, and if he wasn't so sure of her confusion about what to do with him, he'd demand an answer. But he knew she wasn't acting maliciously. She was pregnant by a man she hadn't intended to get to know better. The fact that they liked each other as much as they did was fate.

Fate.

Was that what this was?

They weren't like everyone else. They never were going to be. And the fact that Emily wanted them to be didn't make him feel confident for their future together. It started a niggling bit of doubt in the seat of his soul where he'd been confident until now that he could have it all. The throne, his child and Emily by his side.

THE RHYTHM OF Little Havana pulsed around them as they walked up Calle Ocho. Rafe reached out and grabbed her hand, lacing their fingers together. Tonight they were pretending that nothing else existed.

But she was aware of the reporters who had followed them from Rafe's South Beach penthouse and were now probably taking photos of them. She wore a Carolina Herrera dress she'd found in a vintage shop earlier in the week. It was a cocktail number in turquoise that hugged her curves on top and had a plunging neckline that gave way to a full skirt that masked her small baby bump.

Everything had been different between her and Rafe since earlier in the week when he'd come diving with her in Key West.

She couldn't put her finger on it, but she knew a lot of it had to do with the new feelings she had for him. It was silly to call it anything but love. Except that she wasn't too sure what love was.

Her mom and she had a relationship based on mutual respect and caring. She could count on one hand the times her mom had told her she loved her. It wasn't that Emily felt unlovable before this; it was just that she struggled to believe these feelings were real.

"Have you been here before?" he asked as they approached the club.

"Little Havana?" she asked.

He nodded.

"Yes. This club—no. I'm not usually on the celebrity radar…though in this dress, I bet I could get in without you tonight."

"You might be able to," Rafe agreed. "The owner and I went to school together."

"The hottie baseball player?"

"He's married. And you're spoken for," Rafe said.

"Am I?"

"You are. We could make it official. I've been carrying your ring around in my pocket."

"Not tonight," she said. She was closer to saying yes. The more time they spent together, the more she realized that being his wife was...well, exactly what she wanted.

"Prepare to be amazed," he said. "They pulled out all the stops with this club."

Emily's breath caught as they were waved past the line of waiting guests and through the grand entrance. The Chihuly chandelier in the lobby was exquisite. But then when wasn't a Chihuly glamorous?

The club was divided into several different areas. The main floor in front of the stage was a huge dance area surrounded by high-stooled tables and cozy booths set in darkened alcoves. On the second floor, where they were headed tonight, was a mezzanine that overlooked the main club and featured a Latin-inspired dance floor. The hottest Latin groups performed there. Regular people and celebrities mingled, brought together by the sexy samba beats of the music.

"Rafael! Hey, dude," said a tall, broad-shouldered man coming over to them. "Do I have to genuflect now?"

Rafe grabbed the man's hand and did that guy hug that was part shoulder bump, part slap on the back before they stepped apart. "Only you do."

The other man shook his head. "I'm going to pass on that. Why don't you introduce me to your lovely lady?"

"Emily Fielding," Rafe said. "Eric Rubio. He owns this place."

Emily held her hand out to Eric, who took it in his, winked at Rafe and then kissed it. Emily laughed at the easy camaraderie between the two men. As they made their way upstairs to the dance club, she realized that this was the first time she'd seen Rafe so relaxed in Miami.

Emily suspected it was because he was away from the Montoros and the decisions they wanted from him. She knew that she felt the pressure, and it wasn't even directed at her.

She should just say yes to his proposal. She wanted to make everything easier for him, and her taking her time and trying to figure out what she felt for him and if he would always be there when she needed him to be was just making everything harder for Rafe.

Eric left them as the music started, and Rafe held his hand out to her and led her to the dance floor.

They spent the night dancing to salsa music, their bodies brushing against each other, fanning the flames of the desire that was always there between them.

She wished for a moment they could go back to the people they'd been when they'd first met. Just two lusty twentysomethings instead of a man and woman who knew too much about each other.

"You okay?" Rafe asked.

She nodded, but as she looked into those hazel eyes of his she realized she'd probably never be just okay again. All the debating in her mind about whether she loved him or not had been another diversion.

She went up on tiptoe and kissed him, pouring the emotions that she was too scared to admit to into that embrace. His hands skimmed down her sides to her hips and he held her pressed close to him. It felt as if everything dropped away but the two of them.

"Let's get out of here," Rafe said, taking her hand and leading her out the door.

CHAPTER TWELVE

Emily wasn't having a good morning. When Rafe's alarm went off, she sprang out of bed and ran to his bathroom to throw up. The morning sickness, which had been waning, was back with a vengeance today. But then she was still in the first trimester. It had seemed as if months had passed, but in reality it was only four weeks since she'd confronted Rafe here in his penthouse. Ten weeks since she'd gotten pregnant.

Yet her entire world had changed.

She suspected it was partially nerves, since Rafe had a big meeting with his family this morning. One that she wasn't invited to attend. He hadn't said much but it had put a damper on their evening once they'd gotten home and he'd finally read all the texts from his cousin and brother reminding him about the meeting. She thought of her little family and how her mom was never one to pressure her into making a decision. But knew she was comparing apples and oranges. Rafe was in line to become king of Alma. There was nothing in Fielding family history that even came close to that.

Both of them knew that this time of dating and getting to know each other was over. She'd overheard a very tense conversation between Rafe and his cousin Juan Carlos last night that didn't sound too promising. She rinsed her mouth out and splashed some water on her face, looking up in the mirror to see Rafe standing there. Simply watching her.

"You okay?" he asked, a gentle smile on his face. He wore only a pair of boxer briefs and she was struck again by how handsome he was. How much she loved every inch of his strong muscled body. "I didn't know what to do. I hate that you get sick in the mornings."

"Yes," she said, taking a hand towel and drying her face. "How are you?"

"I'm fine," he said. "Will you accompany me to the office? We can take the helicopter back to Key West after my meetings are over."

She nodded. "Sounds great."

"I need to shower and shave," he said.

There was an awkwardness between them this morning that hadn't been there in a long time. She wondered if he'd changed his mind about marrying her. Wondered if he wished that he'd just paid her off when she'd come here to tell him that she was pregnant. She just hoped that he didn't regret coming to Key West and Shady Harry's bar and spending that first weekend with her. But the man she'd come to know was now hidden away behind his official Montoro facade.

She knew his attitude had everything to do with his family. He seemed angry and a little bit hurt. And she was scared. For the first time she faced the very real possibility that she might be losing him.

She thought it telling that he hadn't asked her again to marry him this morning. She assumed the time for that had passed. Maybe he wasn't in the mood to pacify his family anymore.

He turned the large shower on and she watched him get

into it. For a long minute she stood there before the pain she felt radiating from him made her move.

She undressed and got into the shower cubicle with him. He was facing the wall with his face turned upward to the spray and she just wrapped her arms around him and put her face between his shoulder blades.

She held him to her, trying to give him her strength and that love she hadn't found the words to express yet. Even in her own heart and head.

He turned around, put his hands on her waist and brought his mouth down on hers. She felt the desperation in the embrace, the feeling that after this moment everything would change. He caressed her back, his palms settling on her butt as he pulled her closer to him, anchoring her body and his together.

She kissed him back, wrapped her legs around his hips and trusted that he'd hold her. And he did. He took a step forward and she felt the cold marble wall at her back. Then Rafe adjusted his hips and thrust up into her.

He filled her completely and just stayed still for a moment while her body adjusted to having him inside her. She ran her hands up and down his back, pushing her tongue deep into his mouth. She needed more and the way he was rocking into her sent sparks of sensation up her body.

He palmed her breasts and broke the kiss, lowering his head to take one of her nipples in his mouth. His strong sucking made everything inside her clench. She felt the first waves of her orgasm roll through her.

She grabbed his shoulders and arched her back to try to take him deeper and he started thrusting harder and faster into her. His mouth found hers again; he tangled his hand in her hair and pulled her head back as he thrust deeper into her.

She dug her nails into his shoulders, felt her body driv-

516 CARRYING A KING'S CHILD

ing toward climax again and moaned deep in her throat as
a second, deeper orgasm rolled through her. Rafe ripped
his mouth from hers and made a feral sound as he thrust
his hips forward and came inside her.

He turned and leaned against the wall. She rested her
head on his shoulder as her pulse slowly returned to normal. She let her legs slide down his and stood there in his
arms. He didn't let her go. Just kept stroking her back and
not saying a word.

She realized she was crying and really didn't understand why. Maybe it was because she had the answer to
the question about her love for him. It was true and deep.
And she understood that now because she was willing to
walk away from him if that was what it took for him to
have all he wanted.

JOSE WAS WAITING in Rafe's office when they got to the headquarters of Montoro Enterprises. His trusty assistant had
a cup of decaf coffee waiting for Emily and a Red Bull
for Rafe. He also had a file that needed Rafe's attention
before he went into the meeting.

"Jose, I've heard there is a sculpture garden in the building," Emily said, as Rafe skimmed his papers. She was
dressed in a scoop-neck blouse, a pair of white denim
capris and two-inch platform sandals. She'd left her hair
down to curl over her shoulders.

Rafe thought she looked beautiful, but there was a hint
of vulnerability to her. One that had been there since she'd
dashed to the bathroom from their bed this morning. Nothing he'd done had taken it away. And that was a horrible
feeling for a man to know he wasn't able to protect his
woman.

"There is the Montoro collection and exhibit. It's on

the third floor. Would you like me to show you to it?" Jose asked.

"If Rafe doesn't need you," she said.

"I'm good," Rafe said. Emily gave him a little wave and then walked out of the room with Jose.

The papers that Jose had given him to review showed him the main points of the new constitution of Alma. And he noticed that the part Jose had highlighted dealt with royal marriage. Since they were just reestablishing the monarchy, the rules were strict. Of course, existing marriages would be honored. In cases of divorce, the marriage must be annulled, which was why Rafe's father couldn't inherit the throne. The final stipulation was that the only suitable matches for a single heir to the throne were members of other royal families or the European nobility.

But since Rafe had yet to assume the throne, and this was still a new, untested document, there might still be room to maneuver. Or at least that was what Rafe hoped.

Rafe walked into the boardroom to find Gabe already there.

"I've been trying to get in touch with you all morning," Gabe said.

"Sorry. I had to turn the phone off. I needed time to think," Rafe said.

"Well, I'm the one that the family elected to talk to you. Juan Carlos has been on the phone with the prime minister and the court advisors. They are insistent that we have a scandal-free transition back to the monarchy."

Rafe shoved his hands deep into his pockets and strove for the calm he'd always had when dealing with delicate business situations. And this was the most delicate merger of his entire life. He had to keep calm and not lose his temper.

"Thanks."

"Thanks. That's it? You're losing control of the situation and that's not like you," Gabe said.

"You think I don't know that? Emily is still trying to figure out if marrying me is a good idea. She's got morning sickness and looks more vulnerable every time I see her. The entire family desperately wants me to make this right and for once, Gabe, I truly have no idea how I'm going to do it."

Gabe clapped his hand on Rafe's shoulder. "You always make things work. I've seen you pull off deals that everyone else thought were lost."

Rafe nodded. He wished it were that easy. But from the first, this entire situation had too much emotion in it. There was Tia Isabella and her emotional plea for them to consider the offer from the Alma government to return to the throne. His father's bitter disappointment that he couldn't be the next king and his determination that his eldest son and namesake would be. All of it reeked of emotion, not common sense.

His chest felt tight and for once he needed that legendary coolness he was known for.

The rest of his family trickled in. Juan Carlos led the way. His expression read loud and clear: Rafe needed to act like a monarch and not a jet-setter.

Bella gave him a sad sort of smile as she came in. And his father's glare was icy to say the least. Gabe was sort of in Rafe's corner but he knew his brother didn't want to have to give up his lifestyle if Rafe abdicated.

Right now, he knew that was the only way for them to get him out of the picture.

After his family, the Alma delegation filed in. They had

their lawyer and PR agent with them and quickly sat down on one side of the big walnut boardroom table.

His family settled in on the other side and Rafe took his customary seat at the head of the table.

"Rafael, has the girl agreed to marry you?" his father asked without preamble.

"We're not even sure he can marry her without the approval of this board," one of the members of the Alma delegation said.

"I think he should be allowed to marry. Look at the surge of popularity in the British monarchy after William and Kate tied the knot," Bella said with a wink at Rafe.

He gave his little sister a smile.

"A royal wedding would be grand. But we need to settle the subject of her being a commoner first."

"Did she say yes?" his father asked again. "If she's accepted then there is nothing more for this committee to consider. He's a Montoro and she's carrying an heir. The heir to the throne. I think that if he's engaged before the coronation that should be good enough for your council."

It was the first time Rafe could remember his father being on his side. Rafe was grateful to have his family's support for once in this situation.

"We can all appreciate that, Uncle Rafael," Juan Carlos said. "But Rafe has already let our family down and not just with the baby scandal. He's been very cavalier toward royal protocol and taking over the throne."

All of the voices at the table rose as everyone kept arguing their points until Rafe stood up and walked out of the room. He needed to come back to them when he'd made his decision and no sooner. Because they were going to keep fighting and tearing into each other, and in the end they'd tear him and Emily apart if he let them.

EMILY WANDERED THROUGH the sculpture garden, admiring the eclectic collection. Famous sculptures stood next to pieces by unknown artists that reflected the Montoro taste.

As much as she'd enjoyed the few days she'd spent in Miami with Rafe, she was ready to go back to Key West. She'd be happy to grab her baseball bat and get rid of the reporters who'd been hanging around Key West hoping for a glimpse of her and then go back to normal.

She'd heard that life changed when a woman got pregnant, but this was more than she could deal with. She wanted things to work out for her and Rafe. For his family to just let her continue to try to figure out if marriage was a good idea or not.

"Emily?"

"Over here," she said, standing up from the bench where she'd been sitting and walking up the path toward Rafe's voice.

One look at his face and the turmoil of his expression and her heart sank. There was no way she could keep doing this to herself or to him. She knew in her heart that she would always love him, but she wasn't going to move to Alma. It hadn't taken more than a night in Miami to remind her how much she loved living in Key West.

"What'd they say?"

"They are still arguing about everything."

"Like what?"

"Whether I can I marry you, whether a royal wedding would be the PR coup of the year, whether I'm an embarrassment," he said.

"You're not an embarrassment," she said, taking a deep breath.

"My cousin Juan Carlos would disagree with you on that score. But none of that matters. I know I promised you time to make a decision but I do need your answer now, Red. Will you marry me? Be my partner on the throne in Alma?"

She bit her lower lip. Hesitating as she warred between what she knew was right for Rafe and what she'd started to believe she could have for herself. But he'd nailed it when he said they weren't sure he could marry her. She wouldn't be the reason he was ostracized from his family. She wouldn't be the reason he had to give up being king.

Her stomach roiled and she was afraid she was going to be sick again, but then realized it was nerves, not morning sickness. She took another deep breath.

Rafe cursed and gave her a hard look.

"Seriously?"

"I can't marry you," she said. "While I'm sure that Alma is a lovely place, I can't imagine living there."

"It is lovely. You can have your own bar and do whatever you like once you are there."

"We both know that's not true. And I can't ask you to choose between me and the throne. I won't be the reason you aren't king, and there is a very real possibility of that happening. You'd resent me."

He shoved his hands in his hair and turned away from her.

She knew she'd made the right choice, but it hurt way more than she expected. "I know you'll support our child, but I'll be okay raising him or her on my own. I think I'll be good at that."

"I bet you do," he said, turning back around to face her. "No one there to interfere with any of your decisions."

"Don't get like that with me, Rafe. You know this is the only smart decision."

He stalked over to her and she realized he was truly mad at her. She'd done the noble thing. She was sacrificing her love and her dream of a family for him.

"I only know that you've hesitated from the moment you learned about our baby to involve me in your life. You keep pushing me away. I have given you space and tried to let you have the time you needed to see that we should be together. I know I seem angry. Hell, I am angry, but I really feel like you are making a mistake."

"And I know that you are. There is no world where you and I get to be together and raise this baby as we want to. I don't want our child to be raised with a bunch of rules on how to behave. You know that would happen. And I'm not good at conforming to them myself. It would be a constant headache."

"You're not going to change your mind, are you?"

"No."

"Fine. Go ahead and leave. You're good at being on your own. You said your mother let you be independent, but it's more likely that you pushed her away so you'd feel nice and safe with only yourself to be concerned over."

His words were mean and cut her to the core.

"You're just a spoiled man who can't handle the fact that he's not going to get his way in all things. That's what this is about. Not me or the baby, but you and your pride. They said you can't have me and the throne so you're trying to shove that down their throats. And to what end?" she demanded.

"Spoiled? You wrote the book on that, Red. I think you're describing yourself and not me. Normal couples, the ones you're always going on about, trust each other, depend on each other. And have each other's backs. They don't give themselves halfway to a relationship to try to keep from getting hurt the way you do. You don't care about anything or anyone other than yourself."

"Well, if that's how you feel I'm surprised you asked me to marry you."

"As you said, I just wanted to have it all. Make you mine for some ulterior motive. Never because I cared about you or wanted a family of my own."

She was too angry to listen as she stormed past him out of the sculpture garden and out of his life. But later she'd remember his words and cry.

Because at the end of the day, all she really wanted was to have a family with him.

CHAPTER THIRTEEN

Rafe watched Emily go and he was so angry that he didn't even contemplate going after her. Instead he thought sarcastically that at least his family would be happy. They wouldn't have to worry about him marrying a commoner any more.

But he needed time to calm down before he walked back into the boardroom, or he had the feeling he'd say something he regretted. He'd always been the one who was in control. Calm when he needed to be. Decisive. A man of action.

But then Emily stormed into his life and no matter what decisions he made he still couldn't achieve the results he needed. He remembered how he'd felt on the boat in Key West when he'd looked over at Emily and realized he loved her. He'd been so focused on everything else that the love part seemed to have gotten lost.

His mom had told him when she left to never compromise with himself, because once that happened true happiness would never be his own. As a young adult he'd taken that to mean that he should live by his moral compass and not make business deals that were underhanded. But since meeting Emily he had the feeling that his mom had meant that sometimes making the right decision in society's eyes would be the wrong choice for the person he was.

He stood up and walked slowly back to the boardroom. He opened the door to find everyone still sitting around the table, but they were no longer all talking at once. Rafe knew that they had settled something while he'd been gone and he realized as king his choices were never going to be his own. He was always going to have to compromise and go to the committee before he could do anything.

"Good, you're back," Juan Carlos said.

"I am. What have you all decided?" Rafe asked as he walked to the head of the table and took his seat. "I think you should know that Emily and I will not be marrying."

"See, this just underscores my point," one of the officials from Alma said. "He can't control his personal life. He's a PR liability."

PR liability? He'd always played by the rules. He had a double degree in business management and geology—because of Montoro Enterprises' interests in oil—and he'd always known that without a good understanding of where they got their product he wouldn't be able to lead the company.

He'd worked hard for his family to build up the company so that there was no fear that this generation or the ones that followed would ever want for anything, and this was the thanks he got.

"A liability?" he asked. "Do you all feel this way?"

Juan Carlos nodded; Bella looked down at her fingers; his father just tightened his jaw. Gabe wouldn't make eye contact with him. Screw them. But he knew he was angry in general. He'd tried to please everyone—his family, the Alma delegation, Emily—and ended up not doing a good job of it for anyone.

He stood up and walked out of the boardroom and straight to his office. Jose was waiting there as always. "What do you need, sir?"

"I need to get to Key West. I'm afraid the chopper might not be a good option," Rafe said. He didn't want to take the company helicopter in case his services were no longer needed as CEO. "Can you have my car brought around?"

"Right away."

"Jose?"

"Yes, sir?"

"You've been a great assistant," Rafe said. "I'm not sure what is going to be happening at Montoro Enterprises. Please know that I will always have room for you on my staff wherever I am."

"Yes, sir."

Jose didn't ask any further questions and Rafe was grateful. He really didn't know how to explain anything other than that.

There was a knock on the door and he looked up to see Gabriel standing there. "Damn, I've never seen a man say so much with just a look."

Rafe shook his head as he finished gathering personal effects from his desk.

"There wasn't really anything else to say. I mean when your entire family thinks you've let them down, that's a horrible place to be."

Gabriel came farther into the room and leaned his hip against the desk. "You haven't let me down. I've never seen you so…alive as you've been in the last few weeks. I think that's because of Emily. If you can have her and be happy, you should go for it. That is what you're doing, right?"

"Yes," Rafe said. It had felt wrong to just let her walk away and now that he knew there really was no pleasing everyone, he was going to take care of himself and Emily first. He loved her and he was determined to convince her of it.

"Are you abdicating?"

"I am."

Gabriel cursed.

"I can't be king of Alma when my heart is here. I guess it never felt right to me being a monarch. I'm not aristocrat material."

"I'm sure as hell not either, but I think this means I'm going to have to clean up my act."

"I probably didn't make things any easier for you," Rafe admitted. "But you are a good man, Gabriel. I think you will make a very good king."

"Truly?"

"Yes. Better than me."

"No, I know you're lying. I'm going to pretend you're not. But I'm happy you have found someone."

"Don't be happy yet. She's stubborn and ticked off. I think it's going to take me a while to make her come around."

Gabe smiled at him. "I'm confident you're just the man to do that."

Rafe was, too.

He wished Gabe luck with his royal predicament and left Miami without talking to anyone else. Traffic wasn't too heavy in the midafternoon, but the drive was a long one and left Rafe time to think.

Deciding he wanted Emily was all well and good, but he knew he had his work cut out convincing her that she still wanted him.

EMILY ARRIVED IN Key West just in time to shower and get dressed for work. It was a typical day in late June. There were too many tourists in town and she knew that she was cranky.

She started her shift with attitude. The first kid who presented her with a fake ID got it confiscated, then had a stern lecture from her before she had him escorted out of the bar.

The waitress and other bartender were all giving her a wide berth, which suited her. She didn't want to talk. She didn't want to think. She simply wanted to forget everything that happened today, get through her shift and then get home.

Harry had looked at her once or twice and made as if he was going to come over and talk to her, but she shut him down with one hand in the air that told him she wasn't ready to talk. Tonight she had no idea whether she would ever be ready to talk about Rafe and the baby or anything.

Tonight all she needed to worry about was mixing drinks and keeping the tourists happy. She didn't even have to worry about reporters sniffing around anymore. Cara had told her this afternoon that another suspicious reporter had shown his face over at the coffee shop one more time. Cara and a few other locals had explained that he wasn't welcome in Key West anymore and told him to get the hell out of town.

It made Emily feel really good to know that these people had her back. She was home. This was where she and her child would live the rest of their lives together.

They would be fine. She knew that they would. It didn't matter that her heart was breaking right now. And that someday she might have to answer uncomfortable questions about where her baby's father was.

For tonight she was doing what she was good at. Rafe had accused her of being too self-sufficient and now she knew she couldn't deny it. She did get her guard up and isolate herself when things got uncomfortable.

Even when faced with love. But there was no way she was going to be the reason Rafael Montoro IV didn't become king of Alma. His great-grandfather Rafael I had been king when the family fled. She knew how important it was to the people of Alma and to the Montoros that Rafe sit on the throne.

Another kid came up to the bar and she gave him a hard stare. He looked as though he was eighteen if he was a day. "Kid, think twice before you place your order."

"What are you talking about, honey? I need a tube of LandShark for that table over there."

"Let's see your ID," she said, ready to rip him a new one.

But he pulled out his real ID and it showed he was nineteen. Off by two years. "I can't serve you beer, Alfred."

"It's for my dad and his buddies," Alfred said. "Dad, you're going to have to come over here."

Alfred's dad came over and got the beers and the rest of the night settled into a routine. This was going to be her life.

This was what she'd chosen. She could have been with Rafe wherever he was…but she'd chosen the safety of the only home she'd ever known over him. Not because she loved Key West so much but because it was safer to love a place than a man.

Key West wasn't going to leave her.

Rafe could.

"Why don't you take a break?" Harry said. "I've got some conch fritters on my desk and a nice fruit salad."

It was really a nice gesture from Harry. His way of saying that he was there for her. She walked over to him and gave him a hug. He hugged her back.

"You okay, kiddo?"

"I screwed up."

"Want to talk about it?"

She shook her head. "I think I'll start crying and maybe never stop."

"Go eat your dinner. That will make you feel better."

She went into Harry's office and found not only dinner waiting but Rafe.

Her breath caught and her heart felt as if it skipped a beat. She wanted to believe he was here for her, but what man would give up a throne for a woman like her?

"What are you doing here?" she asked. So afraid of his answer but she had to know.

"I abdicated."

"Oh, Rafe. Are you sure?"

"Very," he said, getting up and coming over to her. "I can't rule a country when my heart is somewhere else."

"Your heart?" This was more than she'd hoped for. She had dreamed that he'd come for her but she'd never let herself believe it. She wasn't the kind of woman who a man like Rafe would give up everything for.

Yet she knew now that she was. She could see it in his hazel eyes and his wide grin. Only love made a person grin like that. She knew because she was grinning the same way.

"I love you, Red. I've never met another person who completes me the way you do. I know that sounds cheesy, but I'm new to this kind of thing."

She shook her head. "You can't abdicate. I don't want to be the reason you gave up the throne—"

"You aren't the only reason I abdicated, Em. My time in Alma was constraining. I didn't like having to follow all the rules or answer to a committee. That's not my way. I want to focus on you and our child. And I can't rule without you by my side. Plus, it wasn't really a choice when it came down to picking between you and Alma. You were miles ahead."

"Really?" she asked. "Miles?"

"Yes," he said, getting down on one knee in front of her. "Will you marry me?"

She got down on her knees in front of him and wrapped her arms around him. "I love you so much. I'm sorry for all the mean things I said today."

"Me, too," he said. "I think I knew even as you walked out that I was never going to be king of Alma. I didn't want it, especially given the way I needed you. So are you going to be Mrs. Rafael Montoro IV?"

"Yes."

He took the ring box from his pocket and put it on her finger.

"You should know that there is some question as to whether I will remain CEO of Montoro Enterprises... I might buy you that restaurant you were talking about after all."

"We can see about that. Am I dreaming this? Are you really here?"

"I am."

She still couldn't believe it. She was just so happy to have Rafe in her arms and to know that he was going to be hers. She put her hands on his jaw and kissed him with all the love she'd been afraid to admit she felt for him. He held her close and whispered softly that he was never letting her go again.

There was a knock on the door and Rafe got to his feet, lifting her up, too. "You better eat your dinner."

She went over to the desk and sat down to her meal while Rafe opened the door. It was Harry. The two men exchanged a look before Harry smiled at her.

"Everything better now?" he asked.

She nodded. "I'm engaged."

Harry let out a whoop. "Drinks on the house. And you can take the rest of the night off."

CHAPTER FOURTEEN

The moon shone brightly down, warming them as Rafe led her toward the hammock in her backyard. The grass path under her feet was soft.

He stopped, turned her around and drew her into his arms from behind. His head rested on her shoulder and his big hands spanned her waist. She stood still, feeling the heat of his body against hers.

They fit perfectly together, which was something she'd rarely experienced in real life before Rafe. There was something about him that made everything sweeter. But this was a dream. She found it hard to believe that she'd found a man she could trust with her heart and soul. But he was that man. She could just let go of everything and enjoy it. But a part of her was afraid to.

He turned her in his arms and she let him. He kept his hands at her waist and when she was facing him she was struck again by how he was quite a bit taller than she was. He gave her a half smile before he leaned in closer.

"You have a very tempting mouth," he said.

"I don't… Thank you?"

He gave a small laugh. "You are very welcome. It was one of the first things I noticed about you when you told me to wait in line at the bar. But I knew that you wanted something more from me."

"What?"

"You seemed to be begging me to kiss you," he said.

"Perhaps I was," she admitted.

His mouth was firm on hers as he took his time kissing her. He rubbed his lips back and forth over hers lightly until her mouth parted and she felt the humid warmth of his exhalation. He tasted so…delicious, she thought. She wanted more and opened her mouth wider to invite him closer.

She thrust her tongue into his mouth. He closed his teeth carefully over her tongue and sucked on her. She shivered and went up on her tiptoes to get closer to him.

His taste was addicting and she wanted more. Yes, she thought, she wanted much more of him, not just his kisses.

She put her hands on his shoulders and then higher on his close-cropped hair and rubbed her hands over his skull. He was hers now. Something that she could finally admit she'd wanted from the moment they met.

For a moment she felt a niggling doubt… There was something she should remember, but he tasted so good that she didn't want to think. She just wanted to experience him.

His hands moved over her shoulders, his fingers tracing a delicate pattern over the globes of her breasts. He moved them back and forth until the very tip of his finger dipped beneath the material of her top and reached lower, brushing over the edge of her nipple.

Exquisite shivers racked her body as his finger continued to move over her. He found the zipper at the left side of her top and slowly lowered it. Once it was fully down and the material fell away to the ground, he took her wrists in his hands and stepped back.

She was proud of her body and the changes that pregnancy had wrought in it. She could tell he was, too. His gaze started at the top of her head and moved down her neck and chest to her nipped-in waist.

He wrapped his hands around her waist and drew her to him, lifting her. "Wrap your legs around me."

She did and was immediately surrounded by him. With his hands on her butt and his mouth on her breasts, he sucked her gently, nibbling at her nipples as he massaged her backside. When he took her nipple into his mouth she felt everything inside her tighten and her center grow moist.

Then she felt as if she was falling and soon found herself lying on the hammock while he knelt over her. His mouth...she couldn't even think. She could only feel the sensations that were washing over her as he continued to focus on her breasts.

One of his heavy thighs parted her legs and then he was between them. She felt the ridge of his erection rubbing against her pleasure center and she shifted against him to increase the sensation.

She wanted to touch him, had to hold him to her as his mouth moved from her breast down her sternum and to her belly button. He looked up at her and for a moment when their eyes met there was something almost reverent in his eyes.

"My fiancée," he said. "Finally you and the baby are officially mine."

"Yes, we are."

He lowered his head and nibbled at the skin of her belly, his tongue tracing the indentation of her belly button. Each time he dipped his tongue into her it felt as if her clit tingled. She shifted her hips to rub against him and he answered her with a thrust of his own hips.

His mouth moved lower on her, his hands moving to the waistband of her jeans and undoing the button and then slowly lowering the zipper. She felt the warmth of his breath on her lower belly and then the edge of his tongue as he traced the skin revealed by the open zipper.

The feel of his five o'clock shadow against her was soft and smooth. She moaned a little, afraid to say his name and wake from this dream where he was hers. She thought she'd learned everything she needed to about Rafe, but it seemed there was still more for her to experience.

"Lift your hips," he said.

She planted her feet on the hammock and did as he asked. She felt him draw her jeans over her hips and down her thighs. She was left wearing the tiny black thong she'd put on this morning.

He palmed her through the panties and she squirmed on the hammock. She wanted more.

He gave it to her. He placed his hand on her most intimate flesh and then his mouth as he drew her underwear down by pulling with his teeth. His hands kept moving over her stomach and thighs until she was completely naked and bare underneath him. Then he leaned back on his knees and just stared down at her.

"You are exquisite," he said.

His voice was low and husky and made her blood flow heavier in her veins. Everything about this man seemed to make her hotter and hornier than she'd ever been before.

"It's you," she said in a raspy voice. "You are the one who is making me…"

"I am making you," he said. "And I'm not going to be happy until you come harder than you ever have before."

She shuddered at the impact of his words. He spoke against her skin so that she felt them all the way through her body.

"This is the one thing I should have done when you came to my penthouse in South Beach."

"Sex? Um, we did that."

"I should have taken you to bed and kept you there until you agreed to never leave me."

He parted her with the thumb and forefinger of his left hand and she felt the air against her most intimate flesh, followed by the brush of his tongue. It was so soft and wet, and she squirmed wanting—no, needing—more from him.

He scraped his teeth over her and she almost came right then, but he lifted his head and smiled up at her. By this time she knew her lover well enough to know that he liked to draw out the experience.

She gripped his shoulders as he teased her with his mouth and then tunneled her fingers through his hair, holding him closer to her as she lifted her hips. He moaned against her and the sound tickled her clit and sent chills racing through her body.

He traced the opening of her body with his other hand, those large deft fingers making her squirm against him. Her breasts felt full and her nipples were tight as he pushed just the tip of his finger inside her.

The first ripples of her orgasm started to pulse through her, but he pulled back, lifting his head and moving down her body and nibbling at the flesh of her legs. She was aching for him. Needed more of what he had been giving her.

"Rafe…"

"Yes?" he asked, lightly stroking her lower belly and then moving both hands to her breasts and cupping them.

"I need more."

"You will get it," he said.

"Now."

He shook his head. "That's not the way to get what you want."

She was shivering with the need to come. She had played these kinds of games before, but her head wasn't in it. She just wanted his big body moving over hers. She wanted him inside her. She reached between their bodies and stroked him through his pants, and then slowly lowered the tab of his zipper. But he caught her wrist and drew her hand up above her head.

"That's not what I had in mind," he said.

"But you are what I want."

"Good," he said, lowering his body over hers so the soft fabric of his shirt brushed her breasts and stomach before she felt the masculine hardness of his muscles underneath. Then his thigh was between her legs, moving slowly against her engorged flesh, and she wanted to scream as everything in her tightened just a little bit more.

But it wasn't enough. She writhed against him but he just slowed his touch so that the sensations were even more intense than before. He shifted again and she felt the warmth of his breath against her mound. She opened her eyes to look down at him and this time she knew she saw something different. But she couldn't process it because his mouth was on her.

Each sweep of his tongue against her clit drove her higher and higher as everything in her body tightened, waiting for the touch that would push her over the edge. She shifted her legs around his head, felt the brush of his silky smooth hair against her inner thighs, felt his finger at the opening of her body once again and then the delicate biting of his teeth against her pleasure bud as he plunged that finger deep inside her. She screamed his name as his mouth moved over her.

Her hips jerked forward and her nipples tightened. She felt the moisture between her legs and his finger pushing hard against her G-spot. She was shivering and her entire body was convulsing, but he didn't lift his head. He kept sucking on her and driving her harder and harder until she came again, screaming with her orgasm as stars danced behind her eyelids.

She reached down to claw at his shoulders as pleasure rolled over her. It was more than she could process and she had to close her eyes again. She reached for Rafe, needing some sort of comfort after that storm of pleasure.

He pulled her into his arms and rocked her back and forth. "Now I feel that we are engaged. That you and I are going to be okay no matter what else happens in the world."

She shivered at his words and knew that she'd found the one man she'd never realized she'd been searching for. A man who could be her partner and respect her independence. The kind of man who'd be a good father and build a family with her.

"I've been meaning to ask you something," she said.

"What is it?"

"What did you want to be as a little boy? I never got to ask you," she said. She wondered about the man he'd become. Would his dreams have been to be a sports star or business tycoon? Well, he'd become that. Surely, he hadn't wanted to be king.

"I wanted to be your man," he said.

She punched him the shoulder. "Stop making fun."

"I didn't know that you would be the woman, Emily, but I always wanted a family of my own. The chance to have someone who was always by my side."

"Well, you've got that," she said, kissing him.

* * * * *

Keep reading for an excerpt of a new title
from the Modern series,
THE BABY HIS SECRETARY CARRIES
by Dani Collins

PROLOGUE

MOLLY BROOKS WAS already hyperaware of her sale-rack blouse, cotton culottes and discount sandals when she stepped off the elevator onto an upper deck of the *Alexandra*. She hadn't had time to shop and had had to make do with what was in her closet, not that she owned clothing that belonged in this setting, anyway.

The superyacht was gliding past Cyprus as though barely touching the water, but she was thrown off balance when someone in a crisp white uniform asked sharply, "Are you supposed to be here?"

No. Definitely not.

Her immediate supervisor, Valentina, had twisted her knee while skiing yesterday. Molly had been on a plane within the hour and was strictly here as a gofer so Valentina could stay in her stateroom and keep her leg elevated.

"I'm bringing this to my employer, Georgio Casella." She nodded at the leather portfolio she held with the freshly printed document inside it. "For his review and signature."

"Why isn't he doing it electronically?" the man asked with a scowl.

Because it was a court document detailing the theft of proprietary information, not that it was any of his business.

"I'm not privy to his reasons." Molly channeled Valentina's polite smile and cool tone. "Perhaps you'd like to ask him when you show me where to find him?"

With a grumble, he led her through an opulent lounge, where emerald cushions accented ivory sofas placed to view the wall of windows overlooking the sea. A crystal chandelier sparkled and the fresh flowers on an end table perfumed the air as they passed.

They moved into a darker room with tinted windows and a curved cherrywood bar. Colorful bottles were arranged behind it and glasses dangled above. The stools were low-backed and upholstered in black leather. Highboy chairs and drink tables were arranged near the windows and the doors opened onto—

He was in the freaking *pool*.

Please don't keelhaul me, she pleaded silently as she looked into the mirrored finish of Gio's unforgiving sunglasses.

If she hadn't felt his attention zone in on her like a raptor swooping for a bunny, she would have thought he was asleep. He didn't even lift his head. He sat low with his arms splayed along the edge of the free-form pool. The water cut across his tanned, muscled chest, right in the middle of his brown nipples.

Don't look!

Molly jerked her gaze back to his sunglasses, hoping he hadn't seen her ogle him. She didn't mean to, but the man absolutely fascinated her, leaving her mouth dry every time she had to talk to him. Thankfully, that wasn't often. Valentina was his executive assistant and Molly was Valentina's support. Until this trip, she had never seen him outside the London office and he was only there on and off, as he traveled constantly, usually with Valentina by his side.

Today, he had a topless woman next to him. She lowered her sunglasses to give Molly a look that asked, *What on earth has the cat dragged in?*

Oh, God.

Gio was a guest aboard this yacht. He wouldn't like her embarrassing him or jeopardizing the deal he was working out with the yacht's owner, Rafael Zamos.

She sent a wavering, apologetic smile to the handful of people here with him: the other couple in the pool, also mostly naked, the two men at the bar, one with his shirt hanging open over his barely there swimsuit, and the two women lying topless on nearby loungers.

"I—" Her throat closed and her heart stalled as she recognized... Sasha?

She looked so different! Her burnt caramel hair was tinted a bright blond. Her face and figure were elegant and lean, not rounded by youth and pregnancy. She wore pink gloss on her lips, eyelash extensions and diamonds in her ears.

She also wore a look of horror as she yanked her filmy cover-up across her naked breasts.

"What are you doing here?" Sasha—or Mrs. Alexandra Zamos, Molly was realizing through the rushing sound filling her ears—sounded livid.

All the blood in Molly's body drained into her sandals. A plummeting sensation assaulted her gut. She genuinely thought she might faint.

"What's wrong, Alexandra? Is the help supposed to stay belowstairs?" Gio's topless paramour was laughing at Molly, though, not her friend. "You're such a snob."

"Molly is my assistant's assistant," Gio said crisply. Now his head came up. "What do you need, Molly?"

"Valentina, um..." Molly cleared her throat, trying to recover from seeing her adopted sister's mother for the first time in eleven years.

She should have done her homework! Her co-workers had been green with envy that she was leaving the blustery November streets of London to spend a week aboard the Zamos yacht, but Molly hadn't bothered looking up photos or gossip about the owners. She had used her time on the flight to Athens to study the deal the men were negotiating. It had been made clear to her that she was expected to stay on the crew level. If anyone would rub elbows with Gio's vaunted peers, it would be Valentina, exactly as it always was.

And how could Molly ever imagine she would bump into Sasha like this? She had known Sasha's family was wealthy, but not *this* wealthy.

"Valentina finished the, um…" She waved the portfolio, mind splintered, voice still jammed. "She said you wanted to sign it as soon as it was ready."

She hoped Gio attributed her raging blush to the mortification of finding them all like this, rather than the anguish that she was dragging Alexandra's painful past into what seemed to be the happily-ever-after she very much deserved. Would she tell Gio to fire her? No. She wouldn't do that to her. Would she?

"Your executive assistant has an assistant?" the man behind the bar drawled as he poured from a silver shaker into martini glasses. "No wonder it was so difficult to get hold of you to extend this invitation."

He must be Rafael Zamos, the yacht's owner

and Sasha's husband. Molly couldn't make that detail work in her head, but she pushed aside her utter astonishment, even though she was highly curious about him. He was very easy on the eyes, with dark hair and a tanned, powerful chest, but she made herself look away.

She glanced once at the ashen face that Alexandra was smothering with big sunglasses and a floppy hat, and pulled herself together. Betray *nothing*.

"I'm very sorry I've interrupted your..." Orgy? "Shall I leave this?"

She forced herself to meet the glint in Gio's sunglasses again when she actually wanted to sprint to the bowels of the ship.

"No. Valentina is right. I want to keep that moving." He turned and set his hands on the ledge, propelling himself upward, seemingly without effort. One foot touched the ledge and he was standing before the water had fully sluiced off him.

How dare he? Now he was nothing but swarthy skin, sculpted muscle and neatly trimmed body hair. He had the lean physique of a swimmer with broad shoulders and long limbs. His narrow hips wore a slash of black that barely contained whatever cockatiel he was smuggling. Not that she was looking!

"Sir." The purser hurried forward with a towel.

Gio—he was always Gio in her head, even

though she'd never called him anything but Mr. Casella—took the towel in a laconic reach of his arm and wrapped it around his hips. He rolled his wrist to invite Molly closer.

With her heart pounding, she picked her way past Sasha's painted toenails and opened the leather portfolio.

She felt everyone's gaze pinned on them as he read the top page, then swiped his fingertips on the towel before he lifted the second page.

Rafael began dishing out martinis, briefly distracting everyone's attention.

"Thank you, my love," Sasha said, then took a hefty gulp of hers. Her hand seemed unsteady. Did Rafael's gaze linger on his wife an extra second, noticing that?

The yearning to talk to her old friend was so strong, it was like a scream trapped in Molly's throat. Her hands felt sweaty and all her muscles were threatening to twitch violently, purely to discharge the tension trapped within her.

"Pen?"

Gio had finished reading. She stared at her own reflection in his sunglasses, wishing she could see his eyes, but also glad that she couldn't. His mother's Icelandic blood was crystal-clear in his blue eyes and they often felt as though they pierced into her soul. His eyes always mesmerized her, being such a contrast to the rest of him, which was a reflection of his father's Italian heritage.

She shakily fished into the pocket of her culottes.

"Calm down," Gio said in an undertone that only she could hear. "I'm not angry that you're here."

He had noticed how rattled she was. As much as she loved her job, however, getting fired right now was the least of her worries. She was terrified of exposing Sasha when she had promised so sincerely and solemnly that she would never, ever reveal her secret.

Gio took the pen she offered and grasped the edge of the portfolio. His cool fingertips grazed the overheated skin of her own hand.

What fresh hell was this?

She stayed very still while he applied the weight of his signature, holding her breath until she could bolt.

"You can get this to the mainland for me?" he asked Rafael as he returned the pen to her. "I'd like it in London by morning."

"Of course." Rafael nodded at the man in the white uniform, who continued to stand by, waiting to escort the riffraff back where she belonged.

"Again, I'm very sorry," Molly said to the gathering, closing the folder and doing her best to hide behind it. "I'll stay below from now on."

"I was just surprised," Sasha said in a defensive tone. She adjusted the fall of her bathing suit cover so it was level across the top of her thigh. "I like to know who is on board, including any staff our guests bring along."

"You thought we had a stowaway?" Rafael was sipping his martini, once again watching his wife with a narrow-eyed, inscrutable expression.

"What exactly do you do for Gio?" Sasha asked without answering her husband.

"As Mr. Casella said, I report to his executive assistant, Valentina. I help her with emails and correspondence, assist with reporting and presentations. I also run personal errands to free her time, so she can be more accessible to Mr. Casella. She suffered an injury so I came along at the last minute to be her legs. That's probably why you didn't see my name on the passenger list."

"I didn't see 'Legs,' either," Sasha said, prompting a few dry chuckles. She turned a pout upward to her husband. "Much as it pains me to admit it, I think you may be right, darling. I need my own assistant. Either that or you should hire an assistant for Tino, so little things like sending me an updated passenger list doesn't fall through the cracks."

"Happy wife, happy life. I'll have Tino call an agency today."

"I'll reach out to him myself once I know exactly what I want. Tell me a little more… Molly, is it?" Sasha didn't give her a chance to reply. "Never mind." She flicked her hand. "We don't need to discuss that here. Come by my stateroom tomorrow. Have breakfast with me," she offered with a pleasant smile. "You can tell me about your duties so I can hire exactly the right person. Would you mind, Gio?"

"If you're planning to poach her, then yes. I mind very much." He threw off his towel and levered himself back into the pool. "I'm sure Valentina would, too." He took little notice of the woman who drifted closer, bare breasts practically grazing his rib cage as he stretched out his arms again. "Molly may make her own choice, of course."

Was that a threat? She shot a look of alarm toward the water, but he didn't sound worried.

"Come by at ten," Sasha said. "The men will be in their meetings. Everyone else will still be sleeping. Won't you, dolls?"

"Oh, I expect to be up all night and needing my beauty sleep, yes," the woman in the pool purred as she slithered even closer to Gio.

Ugh. Molly did her best not to think about that and smiled weakly at Sasha. She didn't know if she should be relieved that she would be able to speak privately with her, or filled with dread.

Should she call her mother? Pack her bag and prepare to find her way back to New York?

"I'll see you tomorrow," she said and quickly made her escape.

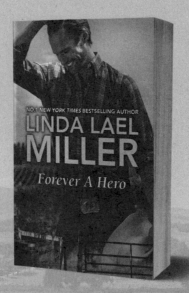

MILLS & BOON

Want to know more about your favourite series or discover a new one?

Experience the variety of romance that Mills & Boon has to offer at our website:

millsandboon.com.au

Shop all of our categories and discover the one that's right for you.

MODERN

DESIRE

MEDICAL

INTRIGUE

ROMANTIC SUSPENSE

WESTERN

HISTORICAL

FOREVER
EBOOK ONLY

HEART
EBOOK ONLY

Subscribe and fall in love with a Mills & Boon series today!

You'll be among the first to read stories delivered to your door monthly and enjoy great savings.

WE SIMPLY LOVE ROMANCE